T0195590

Beauty's No Biscuit

BOOKS BY R. H. PEAKE

From Papaw to Print: A History of Appalachian Literature,
Maplelodge Publication, 1990

Wings Across
Vision Books, 1992

Poems for Terence
Vision Books, 1992

Birds of the Virginia Cumberlands
Maplelodge Publications, 2001

Jack, Be Nimble
iUniverse, 2003

Moon's Black Gold
iUniverse, 2008

Birds and Other Beasts
iUniverse, 2007

Earth and Stars: Poems 2007–2012
Maplelodge Publications, 2012

Lovee and Death on Safari
iUniverse, 2017

Beauty's
No Biscuit

R. H. PEAKE

Galveston, Texas & Wise, Virginia

iUniverse®

BEAUTY'S NO BISCUIT

iUniverse books may be ordered through booksellers or by contacting:

iUniverse
1663 Liberty Drive
Bloomington, IN 47403
www.iuniverse.com
1-800-Authors (1-800-288-4677)

ISBN: 978-1-5320-4200-3 (sc)
ISBN: 978-1-5320-4201-0 (e)

Library of Congress Control Number: 2018901154

Print information available on the last page.

iUniverse rev. date: 02/09/2018

The voice of the Wisdom County dispatcher crackled in Sheriff Bo Mulberry"s ear. "You have visitor, Sheriff Mulberry, It's Dave Blackmun, in a hurry to see you. He isn't in a good mood. He's waiting in your office." Mulberry began to sweat profusely despite the cool temperature of his air-conditioned sheriff's car. Blackmun's visit would not be a friendly one, but he couldn't afford to keep his guest waiting. "Tell him I'm on patrol. I'll be there in less than fifteen minutes." The visit didn't bode well—*probably another criminal act to officially avoid knowing about.*

Mulberry could picture Blackmun, irritated he had to take time to remind him who was really running Wisdom County. Blackmun would want to have some fun with what he considered a poor excuse for a lawman. Lighting an expensive Cuban cigar, Blackmun would be easing his wide ass into the plush chair in front of my desk, resting his hand-made cowboy boots on the desk, making himself comfortable. He'll be looking at the list on the desk, the assignment sheet for deputies during the coming Fourth of July celebrations. After casually glancing through the list, and noting the assignment of my nephew, Mike Barton, he'll open his briefcase and begin looking through his mail.

Coming upon mowers trimming the highway right-of-way, Mulberry slowed down, proceeded slowly, then sped up after he passed the mowing machines.

Hurrying from the parking lot to his office, he hesitated before opening the door. Bo affected a friendly demeanor despite his apprehension and the smell of cigar smoke he detested. "Hi Dave, what can I do for you?"

"I hear you've got a new deputy on your staff."

Ignoring Blackmun's usurping of his chair and waving away cigar smoke, Bo walked behind his desk and extended his hand across to Blackmun. He wasn't sorry Blackmun made no effort to accept the gesture.

"Yeah, my nephew, Mike Barton, a real catch—he almost finished the FBI academy." Bo waved away the cigar smoke Dave blew at him. "His mother called him home when his father died. He was just a few weeks away from graduation. We were lucky to get him."

Blackmun stuffed his mail in his briefcase. "That may be true. He may be a fucking paragon, but he's been arresting my workers for speeding. He's been giving tickets out like candy. He searched several of 'em and arrested them for possessing pot. My men are pissed off, especially the ones who bought their pot at your jail."

Mulberry spat in his spittoon, "That doesn't seem like a big problem, Dave."

Blackmun rose and pointed his finger at Mulberry. "Well, the way I look at it, it's up to you to take care of it. I don't want to lose my workers. With the coal boom going on, they wouldn't have much trouble finding other jobs. I ain't shuttin' down. I'm aimin' to strip that rich coal seam under George Landsetter's land. It borders my Winding Fork job. I wouldn't have to move any fucking equipment when I finish the job I'm on."

Mulberry stood and leaned over his desk. "I have to give Mike honest work. My sister demands it, and I like the idea of having a highly qualified deputy. Mike projects a professional image. Besides, people like him. He'll be a real asset at next election."

Looking toward the closed door, Dave sneered and pointed at the election poster on the wall. "Your fucking professional image would suffer if those pictures of you screwing my former wife became public."

Mulberry shook his fist at Blackmun. "No wonder she left you,

you bastard. I saw the whip marks on her. You set me up, dammit, you son-of-a-bitch." He sent another stream to his spittoon.

Blowing smoke at the Sheriff's face, Blackmun smirked. "You have to admit they're good pictures. You have copies. There's no doubt who's in them. All I did was promise her not to contest a divorce, pay for her lawyer, and give her twenty thousand to get out of town. I doubt your Bible-thumping voters would believe you were just an innocent bystander and not a home wrecker."

Mulberry's face reddened, and he spat again.

Blackmun adopted a less belligerent tone. "I'm just asking you to take care of a small problem. Have a talk with your nephew. Give him something else to do. Assign him duties away from my workers."

"Okay, okay, I'll take care of it," Mulberry said. *You crooked son-of-a-bitch. I know you can ruin me or get rid of me permanently if I don't do what you want.*

Blackmun rose from his chair and blew more smoke at Mulberry's face. "Thanks, Bo, that's neighborly. I'll let you know how things go."

Mulberry stood and watched with relief as Blackmun left his office. He opened a window and turned on his desk fan to blow out the cigar smoke. He recognized the threat in his visitor's last words. Dave had been crooked even back in high school, selling his father's moonshine on the sly to fellow students. He gained a following as well as spending money. A mainstay of the high school football team, he gained more fans. Crafty, he broke the rules of legal blocking in ways officials had trouble detecting, He opened up big holes for the runners. He was rarely caught and penalized. *I should have done something to tame him then, when I was his coach, but I wanted to win—I looked the other way— too late now.*

Bo meant to keep his promise to his sister, Mike's mother. He'd make sure Mike did only honest police work. He wanted his nephew casting favorable light on the Sheriff's Office. Maybe he could shift him to a sector away from Dave's three mines. It would be difficult to arrange a territory for Mike to patrol. He'd have to think about it—maybe night duty.

Feeling deflated about giving in to Blackmun, Bo cursed, but it wasn't worth courting trouble. He didn't give a damn if that bastard never got to mine George's five hundred acres. He slipped back into his chair behind his desk. He didn't see that he had any alternative but comply with Dave's demand, unless he gave up his job and didn't stand for sheriff again in the next election. He'd have to look around for another job. He couldn't bring Blackmun to justice without implicating himself. Knowing what he did, that didn't seem like a safe way out. He could be killed as easily as another man. He knew too much, and Dave wouldn't need him any more if he weren't sheriff.

2

George Landsetter was late for his meeting with Isaiah Timmons. He had learned at the office a body had been found on Dab Whacker's mining site early that morning. He was late, but he wasn't looking forward to Isaiah's complaints or dealing with Whacker's belligerent behavior. He still remembered Isaiah's shooting out his tires when they were having trouble getting their cousin Everett Adamo Lunamin ("Moon") to reduce the size of the explosive charges he was using on Isaiah's first surface mining job. Moon had responded to coaxing and went on to make a fortune mining lawfully, but George still had had to replace the two tires that Isaiah had shot. Not much had changed in the nineteen-seventies, but fewer surface miners were breaking the law and almost all of them had learned not to ignore the IRS.

This morning George would have to hear complaints about Dab Whacker, he was sure. Isaiah must have known Dab's reputation. Why do business with someone he knew was just trouble walking? Almost half of the complaints that came across the reclamation desk now were about Dab. The only miner who garnered more complaints was Dave Blackmun.

As he entered the road into the strip job, *Crack! Vrooom! Thud!* Landsetter heard a tremendous explosion and saw a geyser of dirt and rocks ascending into the sky at least three hundred feet. *Ping. Ping.* Small rocks were raining down, hitting his truck roof. "Damn, Dab's using way too much charge. Isaiah will be boiling over." Beyond a bend, he saw a new dust-covered 1971 blue pick-up truck. Standing by it was Cousin Isaiah.

George pulled up behind Isaiah's truck, cut his engine, and slowly exited his Reclamation Bureau vehicle. The air had an acrid odor. He could taste the sour dust. Walking over to Timmons, he held out his hand. With seeming reluctance, Isaiah shook it.

"What's the matter, Cousin?" George asked.

"You must've seen for yourself. He's blowing everything to smithereens, using way more explosive than he needs. Taste that bitter smoke."

"You attract miners who like big explosions. I remember you had similar trouble with Cousin Moon." *Ping.* George felt a small rock hit his hard hat.

"Yep. But he was a junior-grade munitions man compared to Dab. At this rate Whacker's gonna kill some of us local residents. He's got rock flying all over the neighborhood."

"I'll have a talk with Dab. Is he out here now?"

"Been here for going on an hour."

"You knew his reputation. Why'd you sign with him?" asked George.

Isaiah grunted. "My greed got the better of me. He made me a mighty good offer. I'd demand damn near twice as much today. It still wouldn't be enough. He's got the whole dern neighborhood down on my back."

"A lot of Dab's jobs end up like that. I'm surprised he can get anybody to lease coal to him."

"I reckon there's a lot of us greedy fellows around. Need for money often outweighs good judgment."

"I've known a few greedy ones, but I hadn't classed you with them."

Isaiah turned his head and spit a stream of tobacco juice. "How's Cousin Moon gettin' along with his landscaping business?"

George recognized the change of subject. "Pretty well. There's a demand for his work around Asheville. Stripping's good practice for landscaping, it seems. He and Gladys have taken his son Andy over there."

"I'm glad to hear that. The boy needs a good home. His great grandparents can't raise another generation. Archie and Serafina be gettin' old."

"Okay, I'm going to talk to Dab. I don't want my tires shot out again like when you wanted me to come down hard on Moon. You hear, Isaiah?"

"Just do your job. My rifle's at home."

Getting back into his tan reclamation vehicle, George headed up the road. It should be safe now. Almost all of the smoke from the blast had blown off, and the air smelled cleaner. There shouldn't be a need for another blast today. As he approached the active strip mining, he saw Dab Whacker's heavyset body surveying his operation from atop a yellow D-12 bulldozer.

Parking his vehicle, George put his hard hat on, got out, and headed past Dab's truck on his way to meet him. He couldn't help noticing the bumper sticker on the truck: Beauty Is A Biscuit. *Put a "not" in that message, and I can agree.* George decided a friendly approach would be best.

"Howdy, Dab. You sure do make a big fuss."

"Isaiah been complaining?"

"I reckon he isn't the only one I'll hear from after that last blast. I hope none of those big rocks you threw up hurt somebody or tore a hole in a roof."

Dab pulled out some jellybeans and popped a few in his mouth. "Sam must have put a little too much charge in."

George shook his head. "I expect he had orders from you. It was way beyond the legal limit. Damn, don't you care about the danger?"

"Time's money. I'm in a hurry."

"The law's there to protect the public. Isaiah says you're causing an uproar in the community. I'm going to issue you a citation. Besides that, I learned this morning a body was found on your job. They must've hoped your blast would hide it."

"So what? I didn't kill him. My foreman found the body before setting off the charge. I don't know who planted the stiff on me. You're a typical government bureaucrat. You better not get in my way, George."

"There's no sense in using such a big charge here. There're at least four houses near here that could have damage from that last blast. I'm checking them out before I leave. If anybody has a problem, you'll be hearing from me again today."

Dab popped a few more jellybeans in his mouth. "Go screw yourself, George. I have coal to mine. I'm not like that cousin of yours, who took his coal money and ran."

"Moon learned to mine right. He made money mining. He had other reasons for getting out of the business." George moved toward his vehicle. *He knew he needed to leave before Whacker got too personal.*

Whacker yelled after him. "Yeah, like a murdered wife. Some still think he did it."

George walked back to his truck. Before getting in, he took another look at the mining. Dozers were pushing coal into piles; front-end loaders were lifting the coal into trucks, filling them to the brim. Overloading. *They'll be spilling a lot of that coal along the highway, throwing away black gold and blanketing the shoulders with wasted energy. Damn, Dab's not just careless. He doesn't have sense enough to see he's wasting money. He listens to Dave Blackmun too much.*

George drove around to places nearby that he thought might have damage. It wasn't too bad. The only person with any harm from falling debris was Deputy Mike Barton's mother. A rock had killed two of their chickens. It was a close call for Mike's mother.

Ardella Barton was still a little shaken. "A few seconds earlier and those rocks could have killed me instead of the chickens. They were eating scraps I had just thrown out from my kitchen door.

"I'm sure glad you're okay Ardella. I've put Dab on notice. He'll have to use less charge in the future."

George had planned his last call for his grandparents' house up Winding Fork. It was probably too far from the strip job to have any real damage, but he used checking on the blast as an excuse to drop in on his grandparents and his mother, Carrie, who was visiting them this week.

As he drove up the drive snaking up the hill to a white clapboard house, he could see Whacker's strip job down the valley on a distant slope and Dave Blackmun's closer. The run-in with Dab had caused him to think about why he was here in Southwest Virginia. George had been away from the coalfields a good many years before he had taken the job with the reclamation people three years earlier. Frequent visits and letters from his mother and father had kept him in touch with far southwestern Virginia.

Landsetter came to his beliefs by listening to his parents and grandparents. Archibald MacCloud, his granddad, hated to see strip miners like Whacker tearing up the land. He had approved of George's taking a reclamation job. He was happy George's father had passed on the five hundred acres of woodland to his son. For Archibald, putting the land back right was a religious duty. He disliked the strip-mining done by his other grandson—Everett Adamo Lunamin,(Moon)—and was pleased when Moon gave up surface mining, even though he lived in Asheville now.

Pulling up in front of the house, George waved to his grandfather sitting on the porch. He heard a song sparrow sing its lilting music and a crow call as he started to the porch. The red blooms of Oswego Tea and the red and white blooms of hollyhocks decorated both sides of the steps. Walking up the steps, he greeted his granddad sitting in the shade.

"Mornin', Papaw."

"Howdo, George. You been over to Isaiah's?"

"Yep. Had to check it out. Lots of complaints. There was a body found on Dab's job this morning. The foreman found it before they set off the blast. The Bartons had two chickens killed by the blast this morning. Came near hitting Ardella. Did you h ave any damage?"

"Not that I've found. One small rock hit one of my hounds, and I had a few bits of tiny rock drop around me while I was working in the garden. That was one helluva blast. With any luck, Dab might blow himself up."

"That sure would make my job easier, but I'm sure Dave Blackmun would still keep me busy. Dave wants to strip that five hundred acres of woodland you and Pa passed on to me."

"Don't listen to that devil. Pull up a chair. I've been reading in this newspaper about your Cincinnati baseball team. They're on a winning streak."

"Yeah, I've followed them a long time. I started as soon as we moved there. I was seven or eight."

"There's lots of folks here who follow Pete Rose and Johnny Bench. We used to have a lot of baseball around here. Each mining community had a team. Some of those rivalries got pretty rough."

"Dad and Mom used to talk about the old times, and I listened to stories at the reunions. I'm glad we moved back to the mountains in time for Moon and me to play together on our Winding Fork basketball team."

"You boys and Mike Barton made quite a team."

"Yeah, but we couldn't have won the state championship without your coaching, Papaw. Coach Goforth was a nice guy, but he wasn't much of a coach."

Archibald laughed. "He did his best, and he didn't mind a little help."

"Have you heard from Moon lately?"

"He and Gladys are bringing Andy over next week. He's found a good man he can leave with his landscaping business."

George sat down near his grandfather. "I miss not having him around. I feel more at home when Moon's here, but I know you're happy he's not stripping any more. After years of college, and a master's degree in geology, I don't always see eye-to-eye with all of my mountain relatives. Moon sets me straight."

"I don't blame you for being uncomfortable seeing some of your kin getting rich from digging the coal bones of the Pottsville era forests. You know I don't approve of Dave Blackmun and Dab Whacker's work. I tell myself proceeds from the stripping stays in these mountains. All of the wealth don't head to Pittsburgh, New

York, or London any more. But I'm real glad Moon got out of the business."

George gave a rueful grunt. "Just when I'd trained him to do it right. I don't begrudge anyone's earning honest money as long as that person has a care for the environment and for what few laws there are for mining black gold. I do begrudge miners like Dab Whacker and Dave Blackmun. They don't give a damn what they're destroying and cut corners to speed up the work to increase their profits."

"I'm proud you're doing your best to cut down on the harm they do."

"Thanks, Papaw—is Mom still here?"

"Carrie's out in the garden patch with Serafina, gathering truck for dinner. Go on out and say hello."

George walked around the house and out to the garden. His mother, Carrie, a tall blond woman, who still kept much of her Celtic beauty and gray eyes, was standing, holding a basket. His grandmother, an older, heavyset woman with graying hair and a twinkle in her eyes, was bending along a row of kale, cutting the large, curly green-blue leaves and placing them in the peck basket Carrie carried.

"Hi there, Ma. Hello, Mamaw.

The older gray-haired woman grunted without standing up. "That you, George?"

"Yep."

"You'll stay for dinner, then." He saw the twinkle in her eye when she looked at him.

"Glad to. I came up to check whether Dab did you any hurt." He didn't mention he had hoped to be asked to eat with them.

"None we've found so far. Clipped a few kale leaves."

George inhaled the fragrances of the flowers in the garden. Mamaw's vegetable patch was always a pretty sight with hollyhocks, marigolds, cosmos, four o'clocks, coxcombs, and zinnias adding color around the edges with the corn and beans rising up behind them. The pea vines were starting to brown on the sticks and twigs holding them off the ground. The Irish potato vines were beginning to die down, but the squash and tomatoes were still blooming, the large unripe green and ripe red fruits hanging down from the tomato vines. A few of the green cabbage plants had begun to split open, grown impatient to be harvested.

Admiring the garden's beauty, George was looking forward to eating one of Serafina's meals. He couldn't resist picking one of the smaller ripe tomatoes, wiping it on his sleeve, and starting lunch right there.

"I don't understand why Isaiah dealt with that walking disaster," Carrie said.

"He admitted it was the money Dab offered. He regrets his greed now."

"Archibald and I have never understood why Isaiah has been so dead set on stripping," Serafina said. "Surely he doesn't need the money."

"Isaiah's always wanted flat land for farming. That's why he let Moon do stripping. I guess he just wants more land to farm. But he says he needs the money."

"What would he want with it?' Carrie asked. "His children are grown and his wife Sarah still makes all of their everyday clothes. His grandchildren are in college or working. Maybe he thinks they need money."

"Some people just have to have money in the bank," Serafina said. "Remember how Moon was before the murder? He thought making money was the main thing in life. I'm sure glad Gladys changed his priorities and got him out of strip mining."

"I'd just convinced him to adopt good mining habits a few years before he quit. I miss having him around. I have to deal with too many like Dave Blackmun and Dab. Blackmun's putting on a full-court press to srip my five hundred acres."

Serafina chuckled. "I'm a-thinking a little Dab'll do you."

Chapter 3

George showered and shaved to clean up from the dust and dirt he had accumulated on strip mining jobs during the day. His telephone rang just as he was dipping his spoon in a jar of instant coffee to make a cup with the water he had heated.

A familiar female voice answered when he said hello. "George, this is Jennifer Coffee. I'm down here investigating another story, actually two stories. I thought maybe you'd help me with background again."

"Sure, Jennifer." He wanted to say something less inviting but held back. "When did you have in mind?" He wouldn't let her neglect of him ruin a pleasant interlude.

Jennifer paused for a second. "What about tonight? I know it's short notice."

"I got off work at four-thirty. Do you want to have supper with me?"

"That would be great."

"Where're you staying?"

"At the Western in Hardwood."

"I'll be right over."

On the drive from Big Stone Head to Hardwood, he watched the evening sun dipping low in the west. The sourwoods were turning red. The poplars were showing lots of yellow. He was looking forward to seeing Jennifer again. He had pleasant memories of his attempts to "educate" her about strip mining and mountain ways, but he was a little put out that he hadn't heard from her for quite a while.

Dressed in blue slacks and a white jacket, Jennifer stood outside the Western when George drove up. She had on a low-cut pink blouse revealing ample breasts. George pulled beside her and leaned over to open the passenger door.

Jennifer slid into the front seat beside him and kissed him on the cheek. "It's been awhile. I've missed you. Our schedules just don't fit well."

Looking away, George grunted. "You come here only when you need to research a story."

Jennifer tossed her hair. "The road between here and Roanoke has traffic running two ways."

"Okay, okay. Let's not fight. Let's go eat."

Possum Hunt was full of people enjoying its "down-home" fare. "I've brought a flask of gin," he told Jennifer after they were seated. "Order a drink and I'll fortify it a little with as much as you want."

Jennifer laughed. "Why, I'm a little surprised. You are thoughtful."

George ordered lemonade for himself and a soda for Jennifer. While they waited for the waitress to bring their drinks and take their orders, George questioned her.

"What caused you to make the trip to Southwest Virginia? Apparently I wasn't the sole attraction."

"I've been assigned two stories to work on, a corpse at a strip mine job and a rumor about illegal dog fighting."

"When did a death on a strip mine rate a story in the Roanoke paper? And everybody knows dog fights and cockfights take place out here. There must be something you haven't told me."

"There are suspicions about the strip-mine death being murder rather than an accident. And our information suggests the dog fighting may involve activity moving across state lines. That would involve the Feds."

When the drinks arrived, Jennifer ordered catfish, and George chose ribs. After the waitress left with their order, he pulled out his flask and poured a shot of gin in each of their drinks. Then he leaned back and gazed into Jennifer's blue eyes.

George pretended confusion. "What strip mine operation are you looking into? And why is the death suspicious? I reckon you want my take on it."

"I do. It's suspicious because whoever did the killing tried to hide the cause of death by planting the body where Dab Whacker was planning to blast. The killer miscalculated the timing of the explosion. The workers found the body before the blast. The body was intact. It revealed a bullet hole in the front of the skull. Even more suspicious, the victim was not a member of Whacker's current work force."

George wasn't surprised. "Yeah, I was at Whacker's job just the other day. He's known for using excessive amounts of explosives. I'd guess his reputation attracted somebody eager to get rid of a body. I jumped him about using too much explosive."

"The corpse hasn't been identified yet. The body's been sent to the State Crime Lab. Our sources suggest that murders-for-hire are easy to arrange here."

George grunted. "Probably arranged in Sheriff Bo Mulberry's office."

"At any rate, it's possible the murder is connected to the illegal dog-fights and other criminal activities that cross state lines. So my stories may be related."

When their food arrived along with drink refills. George added a little more gin to the refills.

"So, George, are you going to help me with my story?"

"What help could I be? What do you want to know about the geology of this area, other than we have lots of coal?"

"Don't be modest. You put me on to Rod Mashburn when I came down to do the pot story. And you introduced me to your cousin Everett Adamo Lunamin, the rags to riches strip-miner who was tried for the murder of his first wife."

"Look, Jennifer. I really like you, but I'm not going to give you any information that would harm my family. What I tell you is for background. Nobody's to know I told you anything."

15

George suspected Jennifer was trying to downplay the possibility of harm.

"Don't worry," she said. "I'm not asking you to do more than give me background. Nobody will know you told me anything."

George was sure his suspicion was correct. "For a newspaper woman, you're woefully ignorant of small town life. I'm trying to be careful."

Jennifer grinned. "You sure are up tight."

"Rod's my cousin, too, remember. He blamed Moon for the State Police arresting some of his best pot producers. Moon warned them to keep Sheriff Mulberry in the dark about their operation."

George felt he was being a little harsh with Jennifer and tried to be more tactful. "You were good about not blackening Moon's character when he was tried for murdering his wife. I appreciate that."

"Is Mashburn involved in any other illegal activities?" Jennifer asked.

George shrugged. "Rumor has it that Rod runs just about every profitable legal and illegal gambling activity in this area, but he's too clever to be caught. He manages a legitimate insurance business."

"Do you think he'd be involved in murder for hire?"

George shook his head. "That doesn't sound like Rod's line of work. Mulberry is the man to see about that. Ask him to recommend somebody for a dangerous job, and he'll give you a list of prospects. You have to take it from there."

"What's in it for him?"

"Apparently Mulberry gets a referral fee."

Jennifer agreed it was likely. "I imagine he gets a payoff for ignoring other criminal activity, like dog fights and cock fights and pot growing."

"Mulberry's deputies apprehend a lot of pot growers, but they never get around to any of Rod's operations. Those who don't pay protection get raided, and their crop's confiscated. But not much is burned. I hear that you can buy all of the pot you want from some of the Sheriff's deputies," George said.

"I came to the right guy. Will you tell me more?"

George paused before answering. "I came back to the mountains because I love the place and hate to see its reputation blackened by illegal activity."

George looked into Jennifer's blue eyes. They really set off her blond hair. He wanted to do something besides talk about murder. "Dave Blackmun's the king pen of local crime. I've already told you enough to get me and somebody else in trouble. Let's just finish our dinner. Then I'll drive you to the top of Pine Mountain. It's clear tonight. We should have a great view."

"That sounds romantic."

"Okay. No more talk about our local crime wave now. You eat your catfish and let me enjoy my ribs. Taste the sauce. He took her spoon and gave her a sample of the sauce on his ribs. These people know how to fix food."

On the drive up the mountain, Jennifer asked George how much dogfighting and other illegal activity crossed over from Virginia to Kentucky and back again.

"There's a great deal of illegal interstate traffic—lots of places to hide criminal operations and little effective law enforcement to deal with them. They go back and forth over this highway we're on."

"Has anybody asked the FBI to investigate?"

George didn't reveal his personal involvement. "Some people are working on that. It's difficult to do anything. Sheriff Mulberry is part of the problem rather than part of the solution. He has to be kept out of the loop."

At the top of the mountain, looking up at the stars, Jennifer found the constellation Orion and pointed it out to George. "We don't get to see the stars like this in the city."

George leaned over and kissed her.

After they had searched for other constellations for half an hour, an owl hooted. George was caressing Jennifer's breasts and felt her grow tense.

Jennifer shivered. "What's that sound?"

"That's a barred owl. They like the hardwood forest up on the ridges. ""You should spend more time down here if you want to see the beauty of star-filled skies and listen to the birds.'" He pulled her to him again and kissed her, savoring her minty taste. A scent of gardenias surrounded her.

"I'm getting chilly. Let's go to my motel room for a nightcap. Do you still have some gin in that flask?"

"Yes, it's still three-quarters full."

Jennifer laughed. "Great. There's tonic in the fridge at the room."

At the motel, George poured two shots of gin into each of the glasses Jennifer handed him. Jennifer put in ice and covered it with tonic. They threw their jackets over a chair and sat on the sofa as they sipped their drinks.

"Do you know if any of the members of ODSUM, the surface miners' group, are involved in the criminal activities we talked about?" Jennifer asked.

"I have my suspicions, but I don't know of any definite evidence."

"Our newspaper has been told that Dave Blackmun runs illegal operations. You seem to agree."

"I think Dave is capable of any enormity to gain money. I've been looking for evidence but haven't found any yet. I don't want to talk any more about him or crime. What about us?" He kissed Jennifer again as he slipped his hand under her panties.

Jennifer squeezed his thigh. "Let's finish these drinks." She reached over, opened her purse, and pulled out a deck of playing cards. "Let's play a few hands of strip poker. Would seven-card stud suit you?"

"I never have understood why strip poker turns you on, but go ahead and deal."

Five hands later, George was down to his underclothes. "I'm beginning to think this is a marked deck we're playing with."

Jennifer grinned. "We're even now. The nice thing about playing strip poker with a hunk like you is it doesn't matter whether I get good cards or bad. I can't lose. I'll fix us another round of drinks."

Four more hands and another round of gin and tonics and both of them were naked. "I love this card game," Jennifer said, as George nuzzled her breasts.

Chapter 4

L ess than two weeks after his meeting with Jennifer, George Landsetter's office phone rang as he entered his office, He rushed to pick it up. "Hello, Agent Landsetter here."

"It's Heidi Leaves. Could I have a moment of your time?"

He always liked to hear her sweet voice. It reminded him of her apple pie. "Sure, Heidi, what's up?"

"You may have heard about our having another Surface-Mining Symposium. This one's at the community college in Big Stone Head. I hope you'll agree to be a speaker again."

George looked at his calendar. "Can't you get somebody else? There're other people here who would like to do it. I don't want to hog all the glory." George was not looking forward to speaking at a second strip-mine gathering—surface mining as the members of ODSUM preferred to call it. The Old Dominion Surface Miners had some members who made George's job difficult. He still had unpleasant memories of the first symposium Heidi had held several years earlier

"Yes, but you're the most qualified. You really know the geology. I'll tell you what I'll do. I'll bake you a couple of pies and cook dinners if you agree to speak at the Symposium. You know I'm a good cook."

"There's no doubt about that."

"Then why don't you accept the offer?"

"I reckon I can't resist that kind of temptation. I'll do it."

"Great. I'll cook one dinner for you before the Symposium and the other afterwards. Are you free this Friday?"

"Yeah. So far." He hadn't heard from Jennifer, although he expected she'd want some more "background" soon.

"Okay, you come by my place at six on Friday. You bring the wine."

Heidi Leaves was very pretty and a very good cook. She was hard to resist. George spent the rest of the week worrying about, yet looking forward to, his evening with Heidi. He found her very attractive, but was hesitant about allowing their relationship to become a serious romance, even though he found himself tempted. Because Heidi was an outsider, all the way from Indiana, George worried about whether or not his family and friends would readily welcome her. He didn't wish to move to Asheville or some other spot a long way from the Virginia mountains as his cousin Moon had done when he married his second wife, Gladys.

Promptly at six o'clock George rang the doorbell to Heidi's apartment. He knocked to add emphasis to his arrival and heard her voice call him.

"The door's open. Come in, George."

Entering, George looked to the kitchen. Heidi, an auburn-haired, hazel-eyed beauty, adorned in a blouse and slacks beneath an apron decorated with violet designs was bending to take a turkey out of the oven.

"Something smells delicious. Is it the food or you?"

Heidi laughed so much she had trouble holding the pan of turkey. Though it tilted a little, she managed to set their dinner on the counter without spilling the turkey or any liquid. "I'm sure it's a combination of the turkey and the sweet potato casserole."

She hurried over and gave George a peck on the cheek. He handed her a bottle of wine and some flowers and watched as she opened the bottle and poured red liquid into two wine glasses. Putting the flowers in a vase and setting it in the middle of the dinner table, she reminded him of a beautiful, petite, auburn-haired whirlwind.

Heidi finished putting the meal on the table, took off her apron, and dragged George to the center of the room.

"Look up."

George did as he was told and spied a branch of mistletoe hanging from the light fixture. Heidi pulled his head down to hers and kissed him.

He grinned. "It's a little early for Christmas decorations."

"I believe in being prepared."

"That felt good, and I detect a fragrance of roses lingering about you." George responded by hugging her and kissing her. Heidi kissed him again in return, thrusting her tongue deep into his mouth.

When George released her, Heidi waved him to the table. "Sit down. I have a toast to make." Raising her wine glass, Heidi said, "To good friends and the success of our surface-mining symposium."

George lifted his glass but added a wish. "I hope there aren't any slashed tires this time."

"B. G. Hooper promised me he'd see to it that his guys behave."

Heidi carved the turkey and gave George the leg he requested. Passing the food, she beamed as he took hearty helpings and showed how much he enjoyed the meal by taking more helpings of sweet potatoes, cranberry sauce, and southern-style green beans.

"Your appetite is a compliment to the cook."

"You deserve more compliment than that. This food is delicious."

"Do you believe the old saying that the way to a man's heart is through his stomach?"

"I haven't given that much thought, but I'm sure there's some truth in it."

"I hope so. So far it hasn't proved as true as I had hoped."

George understood Heidi's meaning, but he let her remark pass without comment.

As they finished the meal and he helped her clear the table, Heidi looked up at him. "I have another favor to ask."

Sneaking another bite of turkey and sipping wine, George grinned. "Considering this wonderful meal, how could I refuse? Are we celebrating Thanksgiving two months early?"

"I plan to ask your cousin Adamo Lunamin to speak at the Symposium. I'd like you to give him a call and encourage him."

"I don't think Moon will want to come. He's started a whole new life as a landscape architect, and his company's a big success."

"But he was a model surface miner when he left the business. He was a poster boy for making money with good mining practices and reclamation. You've said so yourself. I'm sure he'll come if you ask him. He's always admired you."

George hesitated. He knew a lot of folks still thought Moon had killed his first wife even though their cousin Earl had been convicted of the murder.

Heidi looked at him intently with her hazel eyes. She grasped his hand. "Please, I want this symposium to emphasize mining and reclamation done the right way."

George melted. "Okay, I'll call Moon."

"Thanks. I really appreciate your doing it. Now to the pie."

As he ate his second piece of apple pie, George licked his lips. "This pie tastes as good as Mamaw's. That's about as high praise as I can give. I can't help being piggish."

After George helped Heidi with the dishes, she poured some more wine, put on a Ravel tape, and motioned him to sit with her on the sofa as the strains of *Bolero* filled the room. He couldn't help thinking how much he liked the aroma of roses she exuded as she snuggled closer while the romantic notes of *Daphnis and Chloe* set the mood. He was barely aware of putting his arm around her, as if his arm remembered doing this before.

She snuggled even closer. "I'm so happy you agreed to help with the Symposium."

"I couldn't help myself. It's hard to refuse you. Your hair is shining tonight. You remind me of a pixie with those piercing hazel eyes."

"The better to witch you with."

"Do you believe the old mountain tales about red-haired witch women?"

"More important, do you? I'm trying hard to bewitch you. Can't you tell? I'm very fond of you. You're committed to saving as much of this beautiful country as you can. So am I. I like being with you. I wish I could bewitch you to reciprocate."

"You don't want to talk reclamation, do you?"

"No, silly. We've done that enough. I don't cook for just anybody. I know you watch birds. Your buddy, Mike Barton, told me. My parents gave me a bird identification guide for my birthday. I didn't realize how many there are—and how beautiful. We could at least talk about the birds you see on strip jobs. Do you see many?"

"I do. The forest edges produce a lot of birds like bluebirds and phoebes coming out to hunt insects. And kestrels, the small falcons, use the bare snags as hunting perches."

"I would love to go out and look for birds with you. We could talk some more about them. Or we could talk about the two of us—our relationship. You've been avoiding me."

"I've been busy trying to rein in Dave Blackmun and Dab Whacker."

"You can't work all of the time. You could think of me as your reclamation job, but first you'd have to strip me." Heidi laughed and gently pulled his ear.

George's defenses were weakening. "I'm not a strip miner."

"I could strip for you. Then you could start reclaiming." Heidi pressed her lips against George's. She unbuttoned her blouse and unhooked her bra. Then she took George's hand and placed it on her breast.

"With a little more encouragement, I might become a stripper," he said.

"Okay, "she said as she slipped off her slacks. "How's that for incentive? Before you go further, though, I'm warning, you. I play for keeps."

George was confronted with a truth that had caused him to avoid dating Heidi for a while. "By keeps, I reckon you mean marriage."

"You bet. I think I could fall in love with you, but I'm not going to be anybody's plaything to be used and then dumped." She kissed George again. "That's something for you to think about."

As George drove back to his apartment, he had a great deal to think about. His life, both professional and personal, was becoming complicated. He had to make a choice about what course to pursue with Jennifer and how to approach Heidi. He had to contend with Dave Blackmun and Dab Whacker, and he had agreed to help Mike Barton gather information to take to the FBI.

He found both Heidi and Jennifer exciting, but he knew he could not have both. Heidi had made it clear she wanted marriage. Jennifer had made it clear her career came before anything else. So he had to decide whether he wanted a committed relationship with a woman from outside the mountains or an affair of convenience. He had to keep Dave Blackmun at bay about selling the mineral rights to his five hundred acres while he rode herd on Blackmun's and Dab's careless mining habits, and he had to be circumspect in helping Mike gather evidence to pass on to the FBI about cross-border criminal acts.

George tossed a lot in his sleep that night.

Chapter 5

On his way to inspect one of Dave Blackmun's strip jobs, George stopped in at the little store at Fox Gap to get a soft drink. The little white building needed a coat of paint and had bars on its windows. His eyes had to adjust to the dim light inside before he could see who was in front of him. Standing at the counter paying for some chips was a red-headed man an inch or two taller than George's six feet.

"How's the reclamation business, George?"

George recognized his cousin's voice and turned to see his mirror image in the dim light. They could pass for brothers though George was in his khaki reclamation uniform and Rod was wearing an expensive blue-gray suit and a striped tie.

"Howdy, Rod—okay, except for a few bad actors who put money ahead of safety."

"You must be referring to Dab Whacker and Dave Blackmun."

"I wouldn't single them out, but they're on the list." George didn't mention how happy he was that his list was getting shorter as more miners obeyed the law.

"They're big spenders, especially Dab. They need the money. I'm eager to see them get the money so that I can take some of it from them with card games."

"You do much business with those two?"

"You know I don't discuss clients."

"Do they patronize your legitimate business?"

Rod turned serious. "Sure do, insurance. They both have big policies with me. Let me write you a policy." His jovial streak resurfaced. "Considering your work, some good accident insurance might come in handy. A guy who inspects jobs run by Dab and Dave needs insurance." He made a fist with his right hand and smacked his left palm.

George ignored the black humor. "I don't expect much trouble from them. I don't object to their mining. I'm just trying to get them to follow the law."

Rod grimaced and reached in to the cooler to get a soft drink. "I play poker with them. I usually win. They're poor losers. From what they say, I don't think following the law is their strong suit. Just let me know if you decide you need some accident or life insurance."

George couldn't decide whether Rod was giving him a warning or just trying to sell a policy. "Okay, I'll think about it."

"How're the folks on Winding Fork? I haven't seen Aunt Serafina and Archibald for a while."

"He and Serafina are doing all right. They miss their great grandson Andrew since Moon and Gladys took him to live with them in Asheville."

"How's Cousin Moon doing in the landscape business?"

"Pretty well. There's a lot of building in Asheville, and he's wrangled some good contracts. Gladys is making a go of her interior decorating, too. I don't think they'll starve any time soon."

"He was a bastard to sick the State Troopers on to my pot operation. I was surprised when he gave up stripping. He was making a fortune before his first wife was murdered."

"I reckon he remembered the love of the land he learned from Archie. Papaw never has approved of the stripping."

"I thought Moon was getting away from memories of that murder charge he beat."

"I'm sure that had something to do with his moving to Asheville, but Gladys convinced him strip-mining wasn't what he should be doing. He visits here a lot. He and Gladys drive over almost every month, bringing Andy to see Archibald and Serafina."

"I'll bet Serafina's cooking has something to do with the visits."

"No doubt. I sample Mamaw's cooking as often as I can."

Rod grinned. "I wish I could get back on Serafina's good list. She disapproves of my gambling. I remember how tasty her food is. I always look for her dishes at family picnics. To change the subject, I hear that a corpse turned up at one of Dab's jobs. How much have you heard about it?

"I wish Dab and Dave would wise up the way Moon did. I've just been warning Dab about using too much explosive. I think I may have made some headway. Somebody tried to hide the murder in one of Dab's explosions. Whoever did it miscalculated. The body was still completely intact. The foreman found it in a last-minute check before they set off the explosion."

Rod grunted. "Have they figured out who it was?"

"Yeah, it was one of our MacCloud cousins from over in Kentucky. He ran a strip job of his own. He wasn't on one of Dab's crews. Just a young guy named Jameson MacCloud. I met him a few times. Like Dab Whacker, he liked the women a little too much."

"I believe I've seen him somewhere lately. He was a good-looking guy. He was our third cousin."

Landsetter wondered just how well Rod had known Jameson— probably through one of his illegal enterprises involving gambling. Rod wouldn't have had anything to do with the murder, though, George was sure. "The State crime lab has labeled it a murder. He was shot in the middle of the forehead. At close range."

"Sounds like a paid job. I wonder if Josie Roper had a hand in it. I don't like to hear of family getting killed. Third cousin is definitely kissing kin," Rod said.

"Josie's just a hired hand. Somebody else footed the bill, if she arranged it."

George picked up a pack of crackers and a soft drink and paid for them, then turned to go. "So long, Rod. I would appreciate any help you're willing to give me with Dab or Dave. Those bastards cause me a lot of headaches."

Mashburn laughed. "I'll put in a good word for law-abiding

mining, but I doubt that they'll pay much attention. I can't press too hard. They're good customers. I wouldn't want to lose my poker winnings from them either. Be careful out there, Cousin."

Driving out to Flat Gap to one of Blackmun's strip mine sites, George felt the need of an antacid pill at the prospect of confronting Dave. He reviewed his talk with Mashburn. He'd been surprised Rod didn't know more about the death of Jameson MacCloud. *Rod usually had that kind of news ahead of everyone else. Maybe he was pretending ignorance. But he did know Jameson—probably from his gambling at one of the dog fights or cock fights that Rod was rumored to promote. Jameson must have gotten in too deep with someone. He must have owed somebody more than his ability to pay.*

George's stomach churned every time he had to visit one of Blackmun's jobs. Seeing how Blackmun went about mining, George couldn't help thinking of how Dave would treat his five hundred acres of woods. He remembered what General Sheridan said after his troops looted and burned their way through the Valley of Virginia— that a crow would have to carry its own provisions when it crossed that territory. George didn't want crows to need to carry their own food to cross his five hundred acres. George called Mike Barton. "Are you in the neighborhood of Winding Fork?" he asked.

"Yeah, I just dropped by my mother's."

"Meet me at my woods in twenty minutes?"

George had been waiting only a couple of minutes when Mike's patrol car appeared and pulled up beside him. He watched as a thin man a little less than six feet tall eased out of his vehicle. He moved like the point guard George remembered from their championship basketball team. Barton was one of the few honest deputies on Sheriff Bo Mulberry's force. He owed his job to the fact that his mother was Bo's sister. Mike filled a valuable slot for the Sheriff, who tried to cover his questionable operations with a coating of honesty and community spirit. Bo saw to it that no dirt rubbed off on Mike, who had left the FBI training academy to come home to help his mother. George had promised Mike he'd help gather information on illegal interstate traffic for the FBI.

"Are we still on for the squirrel hunt this weekend?" George asked.

"Sure thing—I wouldn't want to miss a chance to hunt your five hundred acres." Mike took out some jellybeans and popped a few in his mouth. He had given up chewing tobacco for his girlfriend, Mabel Craft.

"I just talked to my cousin Rod Mashburn. Jameson's murder came up. Rod almost immediately brought up the name of Josie Roper. You've told me that gamblers often use her as an enforcer."

"Yes, we think she's linked to Dave Blackmun and murders for hire."

"Didn't you say you suspect Dave is the criminal kingpin in this area?"

"That's what the evidence says."

"He's increasing the pressure on me to sell him my mineral rights. He's worse than Dab Whacker. I hate his lust for making quick money and ignoring surface mining regulations."

"I think he's the man we're after about illegal interstate traffic in fighting cocks and pit bulls. You need to pay attention to his old strip mines, especially those out of the way of traffic."

"Maybe if we catch him breaking the law on gambling, I can get him off my back about mining my five hundred acres of woodland."

Dave had been mining the land surrounding George's holding for several years. Blackmun wanted the rich vein of metallurgical coal that lay underneath George's woodland. As Dave had pointed out, George's hunting land would eventually become an island in the sky, a bit of woodland completely surrounded by mined land denuded of forest, his wildlife completely cut off from other woodland. Dave had made it clear that he would avoid reclamation as long as possible.

"My cousin Moon will be hunting with us this weekend, and if we get enough squirrels, we'll take them to my Mamaw and hope for an invitation to one of her dinners."

"She's one great cook. I hope we can bag those bushy-tails in a hurry. It'll be good to see Moon again."

"I'm hoping he can help me deal with Blackmun."

Chapter 6

That evening, George found another call from Jennifer on his answering machine when he got in from surveying mining operations. "Hi, George. This is Jennifer. How about another dinner at Possum Hunt? Surprised to hear from me? My boss told me to stay down and look around some more. I need additional background information and companionship."

George was surprised. And a little pissed because her actions didn't jibe with what she'd told him. *Shit, she'd do anything for a story.* Jennifer had said she was going back to Roanoke the next day after the night he spent with her at the Western. She'd been avoiding him. He felt used. He cursed silently, but he pushed aside his chagrin and the thought that Heidi wouldn't appreciate his relationship with Jennifer. Despite these negatives, he remembered how much he had enjoyed his last evening with Jennifer. He wouldn't mind another date with her, so he rang the motel and asked to be connected to her room.

"This is George. Should I pick you up in front of the Western at six?"

"Fine. I'll be out there."

George cleared his desk of paperwork, answered a few other calls, and headed home to shower and change. Then he drove to Hardwood. As promised, Jennifer was out front, dressed in a pink outfit. He pulled up, opened his truck door for her, and she climbed in.

Jennifer leaned over and kissed him. "Thanks for coming on short notice."

"I'm looking forward to the evening, but I don't see how I can help you much with your news stories."

"I've been nosing around. I think my two stories really are, as I suspected, one story. The animal fighting and the murder of Cameron MacCloud are connected."

The dinner at Possum Hunt was pleasant enough. George once again fortified their drinks with gin from his flask. This night there was music supplied by a local group, so the couple danced while they waited for their food orders.

Jennifer again exuded a fragrance of gardenias. "You radiate gardenias and beauty. You're making me hungry for more than the steak I ordered," George said.

"Down, boy. Don't rush the dessert. I want to run some ideas past you when our meal comes."

As they ate, Jennifer pressed on with her story: "The murdered guy who was found at Dab's was named Cameron MacCloud. Aren't you kin to MacClouds?"

"Yeah, my grandpa's a MacCloud. He says Cameron MacCloud was my third cousin. He lived over below Pine Mountain in Kentucky,"

"I've learned he liked gambling and fast women other than his wife. Do you know anything about that?"

"Just rumors. I hear he was killed because he fell behind in paying gambling debts or blackmail or both, or that he was killed as an example of what happens to people who don't pay up. Everybody believes it was a contract killing."

"It's definitely a homicide case now. People who shoot themselves don't usually make a clean bullet hole in the middle of the forehead. Do you know anything about high-class prostitutes being brought down here from New York?"

"Again, only rumors, but the scuttlebutt also suggests blackmail of married men is part of the operation. The New York women are the bait. Cameron was married. He left a wife and two children."

George didn't want Jennifer to know how much he knew. She might connect his information to his friendship with Mike Barton.

"I questioned Sheriff Mulberry about the killing. He claims that the murder was done elsewhere, outside the county, and the body disposed of where the killer or killers thought it would be blown to shreds."

"I agree with all of that except the part about its being done outside the county. I think that's what Mulberry wants everyone to believe. He probably has a good idea who did the murder, why, and where."

"Who do you think did it? And where?"

George couldn't tell her what he thought without revealing too much about his source, Mike Barton. "Everyone who knows Bo thinks it was done here."

Dinner over, George offered to drive Jennifer back up the mountain.

"No thanks. Let's just go back to the motel and have some drinks. Do you still have plenty of gin?"

"Yeah, half a flask."

"My room has plenty of tonic. So let's go back to the motel."

George parked as close to Jennifer's room as he could, and at his request, they made their way there as quietly as possible. He didn't want anyone to know how intimate their relationship had become. Once inside, Jennifer took the ice bucket outside and filled it. When she returned from the ice machine, she pulled out the tonic water from the fridge.

"You pour the drinks while I change into something more comfortable."

George poured drinks while Jennifer went into the bathroom and changed from her pink pants suit into a pink robe and slippers. George turned on some semi-classical music on the TV console and listened to music from Aaron Copland's *Appalachian Spring* as he sampled his drink. He hoped Jennifer's love of pink meant she was on the prowl.

Jennifer had not forgotten her journalistic mission. "Where

does the dog fighting and cock fighting take place? The blackmail operation must be there too. It would have to be where cameras are set up to take pictures of men in compromising situations with women."

"I've been looking around for a place on old surface-mining sites. I haven't found one yet. I'm going to double my efforts." He didn't mention that he and Mike Barton were collecting information for the FBI.

"If what I've been hearing is true, you need to look at land in an isolated area Dave Blackmun has mined." Jennifer moved so that her robe came open, revealing her body clad only in a pink bra and pink panties. George wondered if her choice of pink in all of her wear tonight reflected a subconscious desire for him.

George's view of Jennifer's scantily clothed body distracted him, but he managed to answer. "It would be nice to catch that bastard doing something illegal, but right now I have other things on my mind." George reached his hand under Jennifer's panties with one hand while he began to unfasten her bra with his other.

Jennifer pulled away. "Whoa, you have me at a disadvantage. I think I have the solution. Fix us another round of drinks." She proffered her glass for a refill and moved to the bedside. She pulled a deck of cards out of her purse. She sat down on the bed with her back resting on pillows pushed up against the headboard.

After George poured them each another gin and tonic, he put the drinks down on the chest beside the bed. "I see you've pulled out your magic cards? What do you have in mind?"

"I think we should play a little strip poker. How about seven-card stud? That's what we usually play, but we could play five-card stud or five-card draw, if you'd like a change."

"Whatever turns you on." George didn't understand why Jennifer derived so much pleasure from playing strip poker, but it had become clear to him that for her it was a kind of foreplay. He figured she'd get more excited by seven-card stud.

He was happy when he looked at his cards. He had queens over eights. He bet two articles of clothing. His dismay was evident on his face when Jennifer showed him a heart flush.

Several hands later, George was down to his shirt and undergarments. He complained. "I know these cards are marked."

Jennifer's face was rosy. She laughed. "No way—what I've been hearing leads me to believe that Dave Blackmun has control of most of the illegal activity going on around here. Does that fit with what you've heard?"

His voice betrayed his chagrin. "It fits."

After another hand, George was down to his undershirt and drawers.

Jennifer exulted. "We're making progress. Another few hands and I'll have you where I want you."

Jennifer foretold the future. She won two of the next three hands and George was completely naked and Jennifer had on only her bra.

"You're a handsome specimen. Stand up and let me admire you."

George laughed as he stood. "You're not as comfortable as I am. I think I should do something about that since I can't seem to win many hands. We should both be naked." He leaned over and unfastened her bra. "Now we're even, don't you think?"

She smiled. "Oh, yes, I'm more comfortable now," she said as she sipped on her drink and eyed evidence of George's arousal. "We have to do something about this," she said, as she put her drink down and pulled him to her.

A fleeting image of Heidi flashed across George's mind before he succumbed to his desire for Jennifer.

Chapter 7

The weekend after his talk with Rod Mashburn, George spent Saturday morning squirrel hunting with Mike Barton and Everett Adamo (Moon) Lunamin, his first cousin, on George's land at Winding Fork. The leaves of the sourwoods and maples were already turning brilliant yellows and reds, and the hunters heard squirrels cutting nuts and chattering.

George and Mike were in their old camouflage dress, but Moon had on a brand-new camouflage outfit. Mike and George laughed. "You may scare the squirrels with that hunting garb. Has it ever been washed?" George asked.

Moon grinned. "Okay, you guys, My other hunting outfit had a lot of patched holes. Gladys said she was tired of mending it. She insisted I get something new. You know she thinks we should use money, wisely, not just have it. Don't forget. She has a graduate degree in English. She's educated me in so many ways. She says clothes are important. She's usually right."

George raised his arms in a gesture of surrender. "All right, all right—I forgot you have a graduate degree in Gladys lore."

Moon stood a good two inches above George's six feet one. He doubled up with laughter. "You could turn this woods into a fortune, Cousin. Have you given in to the serpent's temptations yet?" Moon asked, looking like a huge imp under his dark hair.

"If you mean have I sold my mineral rights to Dave Blackmun, the answer is still no. That bastard is determined to mine everything around here. His price keeps going higher," George said. "I hope Dave and his crew behave themselves at Heidi's symposium. She's really happy you agreed to speak, Moon."

"She just wants to show off a successful miner who went by the law. I'm her poster boy. You're the main speaker."

Mike Barton put his arm on George's. "You'd better be careful. The closer Dave gets to mining all of the surrounding land, the more he's going to pressure you to strip your five hundred acres."

"I promised my parents and Papaw I'd never strip this land. I don't mean to go back on my word."

Mike grunted. "Then be careful. From what I've heard, Blackmun's not above rough tactics to get his way. I'm on his black list because I arrested some of his workers. He's bugged my telephones in my office and my apartment. You're sitting on a fortune in coal he wants."

Moon put a hand on George's shoulder. "I'll tell you what, Cousin. Sell me a ten per cent share of the mineral rights to the land along with hunting rights. You know I'm through stripping. I have enough money to take care of Blackmun, if push comes to shove. You don't. I'll keep you from ever being tempted to sell. Remember how Blackmun dealt with that miner's strike. He almost set off a civil war. I don't put anything past that bastard."

"I like that idea. I'll sell you that ten per cent. We'll be on the same team again. Do you two remember our basketball team in high school? Papaw gave us better coaching than old Coach Goforth. We couldn't have won the state championship without Archibald's help."

Mike laughed. "He used to tell me that my job as point guard was to 'praise the Lord and pass the ammunition' soon to George and Moon."

Standing between the two first cousins, Mike Barton reached up and slapped George and Moon on their backs. "I'm glad we're on the same team again. That's great. There's not much hunting land as good as this, George. Do you think Moon would be interested in helping with our other project?"

"I think he might. We'll talk about it after we've shot some squirrels to take to Serafina."

. As they walked, Mike joked about the kind of "squirrel hunting" they used to do with the girls on Sunday school picnics at the swimming hole on Powers Mountain.

Mike laughed. "We didn't need guns for that kind of hunting, just a pair of sharp eyes.

Moon bent over, pretending to be looking up a girl's dress. "I see a furry red squirrel,"

George laughed. "Not nowadays, Cousin. They all wear underpants now, or swimming suits. They don't go swimming in their dresses. You can't shoot many of those squirrels these days."

"Times have really changed, all right," Moon said. "Only a few years ago I came back from Vietnam poor as a church mouse. Now I'm a modern Horatio Alger, Gladys says. All because of the black gold in this earth."

George nodded. "Dave's not the only one who's made me a good offer for my coal. I've had about ten so far. I haven't even bothered to set a price."

"You've agreed to sell me ten per cent, and my ten per cent will always be voting for hunting, not stripping. And my ten per cent will strengthen your backbone."

"With Blackmun after me, that'll be good to know."

Reveling in the fall colors, they hiked into the woods about an eighth of a mile and picked stands far enough apart to see different trees, but close enough so they could communicate with agreed-upon signals.

Soon they settled down at their stands and hunkered down to wait, George watched a big red-crested pileated woodpecker, hammering at a tree not too far from Mike. He whistled and Mike looked over. George pointed to what all of them had learned to call a wood-hen. Mike nodded and pointed at a squirrel sitting on a branch, cutting an acorn above George. Slowly George raised his rifle and shot. *Crack!* The squirrel fell at his feet. Just then, Moon's rifle rang out, and George saw a furry object fall near his cousin. Not long after, another shot brought down a squirrel at Mike's stand.

George yelled. "Hey, you guys. Bag your squirrels and come over here. I think we ought to celebrate a little. Six more and we'll have enough to take Serafina,"

When they gathered, George pulled out his flask, now filled with good Isaiah Timmons' mountain moonshine Archie had given him. He passed it around. After each of them took a swig, they moved on about two hundred yards and took up new stands. From his, George saw a flock of cedar waxwings light in a black gum tree and begin feasting on the small black berries.

While he was watching the waxwings, a doe and large fawn raced by him, and a croaking raven flew overhead.

Three shots later they had six squirrels.

"I reckon it'll soon be time to go over to see Mamaw and Papaw," said George. "Just three bushy-tails to go." We need to have more than enough for dinner."

Moon agreed. "Let's not waste too much time getting these to Serafina."

They moved on another hundred yards or so, took up new stands, and in another half an hour they had all the squirrels they needed.

After the hike back to the car and a short ride to the MacCloud place, they skinned their booty with Archibald's help, and George took the first six inside to Serafina as soon as they were ready.

"These will make a fine mess to go along with truck from the garden. "Fetch me some vinegar and put them in that big pan. I'll just soak these in a little before I fry them. I'm sure glad you boys brought them."

"Are you going to use your special recipe on those?"

"Don't I always?"

After helping Serafina, George went out to the porch to join Moon, Mike, and Archibald, who had finished preparing the other squirrels. He stood looking down the valley a long time. The contrast between the beauty of the remaining woodland and the land being stripped by Dab and Dave was stark. They were creating a wasteland with no vegetation and an old machine here and there, unpleasant to view but allowing them to delay reclamation. His eyes came back to the hollyhocks and Oswego tea, blooming in the flowerbeds at the porch.

George sighed. "It sure is peaceful here—and beautiful, when you don't look at those un-reclaimed strip jobs down the valley."

"George has been getting a lot of pressure from Dave Blackmun to strip his woods, Papaw," Moon said. "I'm buying a ten per cent interest in his mineral rights to help fight off Dave, or anybody else who puts pressure on George."

"Glad to hear that. I'd hate to see that land stripped. It's been in the family a long time—since the first white settlers. Archibald paused and pointed toward George's woods. "I've had many a good hunt there. I don't think some of these strippers will be happy until they've dug up the whole damn country."

"Have you figured out why Isaiah is so hell-bent on stripping such a big hunk of his land?" George asked. "Best I can figure is that he's got himself into some kind of bind. I hear he's got gambling debts to pay."

"From what I've heard, there's some crooked gambling going on around here," Mike said. "A lot of people are complaining they've been losing money lately."

They discussed the end of the Vietnam war, the price of coal, and the up-coming deer season. After about an hour, Serafina called them to dinner. "You all wash up and come on in to eat these fine squirrels you boys brought. Moon, you and George find Gladys and Andrew and tell them to come on. I think they're out at the old tire swing your papaw made."

The two cousins sang out in unison. "Sure thing, Mamaw."

"Just make sure Papaw doesn't eat all those squirrels before we get to the table," George said.

8

The auditorium at the local community college provided seating for about three hundred people. In a room to the side of the auditorium, the chairperson for LEAPS (Let Our Environment Alone Please, Sir) Heidi Leaves had arranged for sandwiches and other snacks and coffee, tea, and soft drinks, She was greeting people when George arrived, somewhat disheveled, carrying slides for his program, at twelve-forty-five. He made his way over to her.

"Here I am. My last inspection took longer than I expected. I'm going to try to grab something to eat before I'm needed."

Heidi grasped his arm. "Believe me, I'm glad to see you. I'll be starting promptly at one, but you won't be speaking until after intermission. You can sneak in any time."

Heidi moved on to greet other arrivals. George looked around and saw many of the people whose mines he inspected, including Dave Blackmun and Dab Whacker. There were others he knew, and many he didn't know well. As he ate, he peered through the doorway into the auditorium and could see it was already more than half full. Heidi must be pleased.

He happened to spy a handout on the table beside him. He picked it up. It was a poem entitled *The Surface Miners' Rant.* According to the name at the bottom, it was the work of Dab Whacker. George found it hard to believe that Dab was a poet, but he read the poem with interest:

The Surface Miner's Rant

The old coal miner's ballad sang of woe.
It's dark as a dungeon down in the mines.
No wonder we've turned to stripping soil
off of coal rather than digging under
the dirt and the rock to haul out black gold.
In dark tunnels methane gas deals mayhem,
death to the unwary. We've lost kin there.
If you escape gas, a roof fall will kill you.
Given the odds, why not tear up the land
to gain the dark coal that turns into gold?
You may get damn dirty and choke on dust
but you die in bed and not from black lung.
Down under it's dark as a black rat's ass
so we'll blast rock face and dig dirt fast
and yell goodbye to dark days in hell.
Who're you to tell me to put the land back
as good as I found it? Let time do that.

George had to admit Dab's poem made a good case for surface mining, but to his way of thinking it didn't justify flouting the mining regulations.

At one o'clock, Heidi opened the Second Virginia Symposium on Surface Mining with a welcome to all of the participants and the audience. George sneaked in the back of the auditorium and took a seat just as she began.

"It's good to see so many of you here representing a wide variety of views about surface mining. I'm hoping we have a frank exchange of ideas."

Her white tee shirt left no doubt about her position on coal mining or her excellent figure. Emblazoned on it in bold black and red letters were **Please Save Our Land** on the front and **Beauty's _Not_ a Biscuit** on the back.

After introducing the panel of speakers who would present before intermission, Heidi stated the purpose of this Symposium. "We hope to build upon the symposium held several years ago. It proved beneficial despite being controversial. It pointed out economically sound ways to improve mining practices without lowering profit. Many mining operators now want to discuss how to implement these practices and make them law. The Southern Mining Council and the Southern Council of Christian Churches support this symposium as they did the first.

"Our first speaker is B. G. Hooper, Executive Director of Old Dominion Surface Miners, who once again will present our surface miners' views," Heidi said. As Hooper had done at the first symposium, he began by recounting the history of the region's economic difficulties.

"The exploitation of the wealth in these mountains bypassed the descendants of the original settlers, many of whom sold their mineral rights for a pittance, and the profits fled to New York, Philadelphia, and London. Poverty beset the Appalachian South because the land and people were exploited by outside interests. The majority of the inhabitants suffered deprivation for many years. That is, until the local people discovered how surface mining could open the area's riches to them. Now all of the profit isn't going to Philadelphia, New York, and London. Surface miners keep it here."

Hooper extolled the virtues of surface mining at great length. In conclusion, he asserted that ODSUM was willing to support effective mining procedures. "Out West we have national parks whose austere beauty is undeniable. I think some of our surface mining produces equally beautiful features."

Loud laughter and a few jeers greeted this pronouncement. Unruffled, Hooper continued, "Nevertheless, we concede that better mining practices would help leave the land more productive. We see the old ways need to be altered. We are aware of that. We in the mining business will support reasonable legislation."

His final statement drew much applause. Blackmun, Whacker,

and a few other surface miners scowled, but they remained in their seats, silent.

Surface mining owner Philemon Mullins was the next speaker. "I was upset when Harry Caudill spoke at the last symposium. He read from his book *Night Comes to the Cumberlands* and described the horrors created by the broad-form deed over in Kentucky. I knew that we do *not* allow such deeds in Virginia. That's not to say there are no abuses in our state. But the majority of the members of ODSUM are willing to do things the right way. We've seen that Lunar Mining makes excellent profits doing things according to the law." Mullins went on to point out how his efforts to put good practices into effect had improved his profits.

Heidi beamed when she introduced Adamo Lunamin. Moon began by admitting that he was no longer a surface miner. "I've been asked to speak because, when I *was* surface mining, I learned to do it the way that common sense and LEAPS recommended. I made plenty of money doing things the right way." He went on to outline his methods and concluded by saying that he didn't agree with all proposed regulations.

"I don't think all mined land needs to have grass put on it. For example, the county has a successful vineyard on strip-mined land. Putting the land back to something like it originally was usually makes sense, but there should be some options in the law to allow for productive uses of land instead of putting it back to the original contour. We wouldn't have an airport here without the flat land created by surface mining."

Several others spoke before the break. They were engineers who had been hired by miners wanting to do effective reclamation. They explained how a little planning for reclamation before mining began could increase profits.

After they spoke, Heidi announced intermission. "I think everyone is ready to stretch and talk. We'll have a fifteen-minute break, and then I'll announce our main speaker."

During the intermission, Heidi spoke to George as they sampled some of the refreshments she'd supplied. "I think things are going well. I'm counting on you to provide the finishing touch." She squeezed his hand.

"I'll try to live up to your high expectations."

When his time came to speak, Landsetter emphasized his dedication to the law. "I've been sworn to uphold the current law, which I do to the best of my ability, but I think our current laws for surface mining could stand some improvement. For example, I agree with my cousin, Moon. I'm not in favor of putting all land back to approximately its original contour. I can even see some benefits from high walls, even though they are a hazard to wildlife, and I don't find them as aesthetically pleasing as Mr. Hooper does."

George was interrupted by laughter and applause. When the crowd grew quiet again, he continued.

"Rough-winged swallows nest in cavities they dig in the sides of the high walls and phoebes build nests under the tree roots overhanging their edges. But a lot of deer chased by dogs fall over these high bluffs and break their necks. I'm a deer hunter. I don't want to see deer die like that."

A voice from the audience interrupted. "Yeah, man, save 'em for deer huntin' season." Cheers and noisy laughter ensued.

George held up a hand for silence. "As I see it, the problem is complex. The main difficulty, other than the steep high walls, is the erosion that comes from un-reclaimed surface mines. This run-off fouls streams as much as any run-off from deep mines. Un-reclaimed land can remain unproductive for twenty or thirty years, yet we allow mining companies to postpone reclamation for decades merely by leaving a piece or two of machinery on the site to pretend the job is active."

George noticed that Dave Blackmun and Dab Whacker got up and left their seats. *Hit dogs holler,* he thought. "I have a few slides to show you of some of the problems I've encountered in my inspections, if someone will dim the lights."

George showed about thirty slides of what he considered the worst problems he encountered in his inspections. He followed these with some slides of effective reclamation.

After discussing best methods to be used in reclamation, George ended on a more poetic note. "'It's dark as a dungeon deep down in the mines,' that's the way the coal miner's ballad goes. It's no wonder miners turned to stripping soil from the coal seams rather than digging holes under the dirt and the rock to haul out black gold. Lots of miners die mining underground. Surface mining produces fewer fatalities. With the proper planning and engineering, surface mines can produce profitable coal without destroying the environment, or human life. There is no need for gigantic high walls and fouled streams. There's absolutely no legitimate excuse to postpone reclamation."

After George took questions, the proceedings concluded a little before five. Many of the participants lingered to discuss the ideas presented during the meeting. It was over an hour before Heidi and George could say goodbye to the last participant. They both were busy answering questions. He helped Heidi clean up.

"This symposium was a great success compared to the first one," Heidi said.

George agreed. "At least there weren't any slashed tires this time."

'I believe we're making progress. I'm glad that mining the right way is also mining the money-making way."

"I wish I could convince Dave Blackmun and Dab Whacker of that, but they're not very receptive. They think they avoid reclamation costs with rusting machinery. Besides, I think Dave is involved in serious illegal stuff beyond stripping. If I find any evidence of law-breaking, I may need somebody to check on a lead."

"Why don't you talk to Philemon Mullins. I know he's upset about Dave's actions. He thinks they reflect negatively on all the members of ODSUM," Heidi said as they walked outside.

"I'll follow you to your place." He had promised to come by her apartment after the symposium.

✦ ✦ ✦ ✦ ✦ ✦ ✦

When they arrived at Heidi's apartment, she unlocked the door and ushered George in.

"Come in. I'll cook you that dinner I owe you now. You can help me. I've already made the pies, one cherry and the other mince meat."

"Sounds good to me. What's the main course?"

"I have a beef stew cooking in a crock pot. It should be ready in less than half an hour. We can make a salad while we wait. Would you like something to drink? Maybe a gin-and-tonic, or a whiskey sour? We'll have wine with dinner."

"I'll take bourbon on the rocks, if you have it."

Heidi was pulling out salad makings. "Sure. Look in the cabinet by the bookcase. There's some bourbon there." Bourbon in hand, George asked Heidi if he could pour her something.

"Since it's handy, just pour me a little bourbon too, then some orange juice over the ice and bourbon."

Having fixed their drinks, George began helping with the salad. By the time the stew was ready, Heidi had the salad in a bowl on the table. She filled plates with the beef stew and put them on the table together with goblets she had filled with red wine.

"Bring your drink and sit down."

George could smell an aroma of beef, carrots, and Irish potatoes cooked with bay leaves and garlic. The scent of roses from Heidi mixed agreeably with the food aromas.

After he had taken a few bites, George praised the cook. "If the pies are even half as good as this beef stew, I'm afraid I'm going to eat too much."

George couldn't restrain himself. A half hour later, he had consumed two hearty helpings.

Heidi beamed. "I'll have to limit you to one piece of each pie. I don't want you to overeat. She cut the pies and gave him his two pieces. Then she put the pies away.

I'm so glad the symposium went well. Your analysis was the high point of the program," Heidi said.

"If you were serious about going to watch birds at some of the strip jobs I'm monitoring, how about coming with me one day this week."

"I'd love to. What day did you have in mind?"

"What about tomorrow? I won't go to any of Dave's or Dab's jobs then."

"Great. What time?"

"I'll pick you up at eight, if that's not too early."

"I'll be ready. Come by about seven-thirty and I'll give you breakfast. Now let's try the pies."

George ate his allotted pieces and did not object to Heidi's packing him a piece of each pie to take home with him.

"Don't pig out on these," she said. The dishes cleared away, Heidi refreshed their bourbon, put on a tape of Cole Porter music, and led George to her couch. "Let's sit and enjoy some music." Soon they were listening to *Anything Goes, Night and Day*, and *Let's Misbehave*.

After they had spent a few quiet moments and then listened to Beethoven's Pastorale, Heidi posed a question. "Have you thought about what I said last week?"

"Not much else. I'm thinking so much about you I'm finding it hard to keep my mind on my job." He leaned down and kissed her. "I've got to watch myself. I have to be careful, especially around Dave and Dab and a few other strippers who don't care to follow recommended practices."

"I want you to be careful. I don't want to lose you to some strip-mine accident."

Chapter 9

Promptly at seven-thirty the next morning, George parked his Reclamation Bureau vehicle in front of Heidi's apartment. After he knocked, Heidi called out, "Door's open, George, Come on in and have breakfast."

As he entered, Heidi was putting breakfast on the table. George could smell the aroma of pork sausage. "Sit down and help yourself to eggs, sausage, and biscuits."

"This is a better breakfast than I'm used to. I usually have toast and coffee."

"Enjoy, I'm looking forward to your showing me some birds." She pointed to her binoculars and bird book at the end of the table.

George looked as she motioned. "You seem eager. I hope I can keep my eyes off you and on the birds."

"I'm afraid I'm not very feminine in these field clothes."

"Don't worry, you'd look good in a feed sack."

"I know about feed sack dresses. My mother used to make my dresses out of the colorful cloth we got with our chicken feed."

When George finished three sausages, two helpings of scrambled eggs, and his second biscuit, Heidi asked if he was ready to leave.

George laughed. "I guess I'd better. Else I'll get fat."

"Nonsense, you don't seem to be obese."

"First we'll go to a place mined and reclaimed a number of years ago by Moon for Isaiah Timmons. It was done so as to create cropland and a surrounding area maximizing habitat variety, So there should be a good variety of birdlife. There are flat areas for crops, but these fields are surrounded by water features and shrubby areas with scattered trees. And beyond these is woodland."

"Wonderful. I hope we see a lot of wildlife."

George drove down a dirt road to one of the ponds at the site he'd picked. As they stepped out of the SUV, an indigo bunting began singing. Looking to where the song had come from, he pointed out the bird to Heidi. She found it with her binoculars.

"What a beautiful sight! It's an electric blue."

George took time to explain why the bird was so colorful. "It's a male in full sun. If the sun were behind it, there'd only be a black bird there. The color comes from refraction of light. His mate's a subdued tan."

Heidi raised her binoculars again and focused them on the bunting. "Whatever the reason, he's gorgeous."

George led her a few feet to the left. "There. Over in those cattails. What do you think of that male red-winged blackbird? Look at its yellow and red epaulettes."

"Stunning."

Moving behind her, he pointed over her shoulder to a limb above the blackbird. He breathed a scent of roses. "And in the tree above it, there's a male scarlet tanager in breeding plumage. He's red with black wings."

Heidi moved her binoculars higher. "I see him. I see him. Spectacular."

George was pleased with Heidi's response. He motioned across the pond. "Look over on the other side of the pond. There's a Green Heron standing there like a statue. This place is full of birds. Now I see a male yellow warbler in that willow tree next to the heron."

"I can see both of them. That warbler looks like an ornament on the tree. You're so good at finding all these birds." She turned her head toward his. "I'm astounded." Her breath touched his cheek. "We've seen so many in just a short time. We've hardly walked five yards from your vehicle."

"Look overhead. There's a red-tailed hawk circling, looking for a thermal to lift it higher."

"I heard a long scream. Did the hawk do that?"

"Yes, now look below. Coming down to drink. There's a six-point buck in the velvet. He'll need to be more careful this fall when hunting season comes."

By the time they had spent an hour at the site, George had compiled a list of over thirty species of birds they'd heard or seen, plus rabbits, squirrels, deer, and a groundhog. Heidi found it hard to believe they'd seen so much wildlife by walking less than halfway around the pond.

"I'm amazed at the ease with which you locate and identify all of the birds and other wildlife."

"I'm glad you're enjoying the animals. It's obvious that intelligent, effective reclamation increases the productivity of the land. Now I'm going to take you to another site. It's not so well reclaimed as this one, but it has a kind of warbler we can't find here."

A short drive brought them to a place with a steep slope of over 80 degrees known as a highwall, where the overburden of dirt above the coal seam had been cut away and left a wall of dirt almost straight up. At the top, dark roots of trees were hanging in the air like skinny, unwashed toes. Alongside the bottom of the highwall, a flat area or *bench* left from the mining had a growth of twenty-foot high black locust trees and scattered brush. "These black locusts are legumes. They create topsoil where none exists, the first stage of plant succession. That's the ecological niche of early plant succession golden-winged warblers require. If we look closely, we may be able to find one."

In a search of an hour among the locusts, avoiding the thorns on the trees as much as possible, they discovered five golden-winged warblers. When George pointed them out to Heidi, she was ecstatic. "They're as beautiful as any of the birds we saw back at the other place. I love their golden wings and black masks on their pale gray bodies."

"They are beautiful. I'm showing you something that I didn't mention at the Symposium—for a good reason. Surface mining has actually created a great deal of habitat for golden-winged warblers. They like the earliest stages of plant succession. These warblers profit from poor reclamation."

"You held this information back on purpose?"

"Yes. I believe in effective reclamation, but I delight in watching golden-winged warblers. I had to make a choice. I think restoration of the land is more important than increasing habitat for one species."

"You wonderful man, how can I thank you enough. What harm would Dave Blackmun and Dab Whacker do if they had this information?"

"I feared the worst. That's why I kept silent about these warblers."

Heidi let her binoculars dangle as she reached up to pull George's head down to kiss him with such vigor that George picked her up and returned the kiss by thrusting his tongue deeply into her mouth for several seconds.

When George put her down, she laughed. "I keep finding reasons to love you. Surely you can find some to love me."

"I *am* falling in love with you, but I've got to be careful." He looked at her intently and laughed. "I've been told you play for keeps. I've got to be sure I can measure up to your keeping standards. I might be a few inches short."

Heidi continued to laugh. "I guess we'll just have to see. Maybe I'll have to measure. You consult your schedule. If we're going to determine your keep value, you and I must see each other on a regular basis. Take me home, and I'll fix us some soup and turkey sandwiches. We'll consult my calendar. Then you and I can plan our dates. It's important we set a good schedule." George didn't like the idea of a schedule, but he wanted to please Heidi, so he didn't offer strenuous objections.

Just then a large shadow of a bird passed over them. George looked up. "An eagle, look, a bald eagle. See its white tail and white head. A good omen."

As they walked back to Moon's SUV, he pointed out a kestrel perched on a snag. "He's looking for lunch."

Before heading to Heidi's apartment, George took her to a few active strip jobs. He picked Philemon Mullins' strip job and Dab Whacker's.

"You've seen the best and worst of surface mining," he said as they turned onto the highway from looking at their last mining site. "I like woodland, but surface mining done the right way helps nature recover faster than no reclamation."

Heidi served George a rich vegetable soup she'd made the day before. As it heated, George savored its aroma. After soup and sandwiches, Heidi thanked Moon for the morning. "It was even better than I expected."

George saw an opening. "There're lots of good birding spots around. Maybe we could do another soon."

"I'd love to. Do you have to get back to work right now? I'm free until three. Could you stay with me a little while longer? We could work on our schedule."

George hesitated. The idea of being scheduled for dates didn't appeal to him, but he did enjoy Heidi's company, so he sat back down at the table Heidi had cleared. "I don't like this scheduling. I reckon I could stay until two-thirty. I have several more sites I need to look at today."

It took them almost an hour to work out a schedule Heidi considered suitable. George hated being put on a schedule. "I feel like I'm a student being put on a class schedule. That's not very romantic."

Heidi laughed. "This scheduling is serious business. I have my reasons for insisting on it. I've found out a lot about you. We're not going to be careless in our research." After another ten minutes, they'd finished agreeing on a schedule: Monday, Wednesday, and Friday nights, and all day Sunday.

Then Heidi put down her calendar and kissed George. "As the song goes, I'm looking forward to getting to know you."

George grinned. "I hope I'll prove to be a keeper."

Chapter 10

The next day, George drove to Dave Blackmun's old surface mining operation at Flat Gap. It had been mined and left to reclaim itself. Dave had leveled much of the mountain, once locally famous for the great beauty of the fall display of sourwoods, poplars, maples, and other hardwoods. No longer—no woodland remained, only a bush here and there.

Dotted about at random, old pieces of machinery stood as fraudulent evidence that mining was still active. This site was developing without any effort of Dave Blackmun, who took advantage of a loophole in the law. George's anger grew whenever he looked at the rusting machines, but he did admit that he could find birds here that are scarce in the mountains.

Flat Gap was the only place in the highlands where George could find blue grosbeaks and prairie warblers. It was also a prime location for hard-to-find yellow-breasted chats and field sparrows. For that reason, he liked to add this spot to his inspection route sometimes, but he hadn't had time to visit this area recently.

Before he visited any active mining sites today, he wanted to have a look at some territory on Blackmun's Flat Gap mining site that he had not investigated, He turned his vehicle onto a well-used but newly graveled private road. On either side of the road there was black pine scrub mixed with sumac (having learned from his grandfather, George still said *shumack*, like *sugar* and *sure*) and black locust saplings. He heard the robin-like song of a blue grosbeak and stopped. After a short search out his window, he focused his binoculars on a dark blue bird with brown wing bars singing its melodious warble in the top of a black pine. After a quick look, he drove down the road.

A little over three miles in, the scrubby growth give way to reclaimed flat grassland. A huge metal building stood in the middle of a large grassy field surrounded by a large graveled parking area.

His birding forgotten, George inspected the building. Beneath the window of what appeared to be an office, there was a flyer announcing a combined cockfight and dogfight. The date had passed, but the information on the flyer made clear that this had been a regional bout, featuring animals from Kentucky fighting contestants from Virginia. The flyer named this place as The Pit. Cockfights and dogfights were not only illegal in the state, George knew, but these birds and the fighting dogs were being transported across state lines, a federal offense. The FBI would have jurisdiction.

He didn't wish to be seen by one of Blackmun's people. After looking around and finding nobody there, he made his way out to the main highway as quickly as he could. He spent the rest of the day visiting active mining sites. He would contact Mike Barton as soon as he could safely tell him about what he'd found. It was the evidence they'd been hoping to find. George already had personal and professional trouble with Blackmun, but Dave evidently was involved in interstate gambling as well as straining at the edge of what was legal in surface mining. Illegal interstate gambling information was what George and Mike were supposed to be gathering for the FBI. *Jennifer Coffee was right. Dave's a crook. Maybe he is the local crime boss we say he is.*

Why's Blackmun hounding me about my five hundred acres? He has lhree mining sites. He must really lust for money. I've promised Pa and Papaw. I'll not strip my five hundred acres. I won't sell—whatever Blackmun offers.

When George got home from work that day, he called Mike. "I have something to hash over with you. Why don't we go hunting on my land Saturday morning? Are you off duty?"

"I'm off during the day. I'll meet you there around seven."

"Great. We'll shoot a few squirrels to take to Mamaw and hope she asks us to lunch. Then we can ask Archibald for some advice about what I'm going to propose. Not about the whole project. Just about a first move."

Next he called Heidi. He hated the scheduling she'd demanded, but he was happy he had an excuse to talk to her. The telephone rang and rang with no answer. He had more success when he tried two hours later. "I already miss you," he told her when she answered.

"That's good to hear. I'm beginning to miss you, too, but our schedule says Monday, Wednesday, and Friday nights, and all day Sundays. I'll cook a good dinner for you Friday. But I want you to know, yesterday was really special."

"Special for me, too, but I've found something disturbing. I want to talk to you about it, but I reckon it can wait. It's something I would like your advice on. We can talk about it tomorrow."

"Can't we talk about it right now?"

George paused for a few seconds, "It's not something I want to discuss over the phone. The way things have been going, I'm afraid somebody might be listening."

"That sounds ominous, cloak-and-dagger stuff."

"Not quite that bad yet, but given the people involved, it might become that bad fast."

"You certainly have piqued my curiosity, but I guess it'll wait until tomorrow night."

"I'll stick to our bargain about meeting times. I feel better having talked to you. Sweet dreams—especially if you dream about us."

"That's all I've been dreaming about lately."

George couldn't see Heidi right away, but he thought he was making progress with her. She did say she'd been dreaming of him. Good to be in her dreams, even if his time with her was still scheduled.

+ + + + + +

A few minutes after his call to Heidi ended, George had a call from Dave Blackmun. "Have you thought any more about having me strip your five hundred acres?"

"I told you that I've given my word I won't have that land stripped."

"What if I offered you a hundred thousand dollars outside of whatever we hit upon for the mining contract?"

George growled. "That sounds a lot like a bribe."

"Maybe, but since it's not related to your official duties as an inspector, there's nobody who could accuse you of taking a bribe."

"I'm not going to have the land stripped."

"That's a short-sighted view. Our nation needs energy. Mining your land would benefit our country by helping supply it."

George remembered Samuel Johnson's words, "Patriotism is the last refuge of a scoundrel," but restrained himself and remained calm, "I need a place to hunt and to relax."

"Dammit, Daniel Boone, my current job's right next to your land. I could make you a good deal, and we'd both make a lot of money."

"There are some things better than money."

"Maybe so, but I haven't found them yet." Dave hung up.

Dave's last words worried George. How far would Blackmun go to strip his five hundred acres? He knew Blackmun broke mining law. How was Rod Mashburn involved in the illegal gambling activities? Blackmun must be paying protection money to Sheriff Mulberry to overlook the Pit. George could see that he was on a collision course with Dave Blackmun.

◆◆◆◆◆

The next night, after a dinner of fried chicken, green beans, mashed potatoes, and gravy, George and Heidi sat on her sofa and discussed what he had seen at Flat Gap.

"I think this is the evidence Mike and I have been looking for. I reckon I shouldn't be surprised. Jennifer Coffee says Blackmun's the kingpin of crime in Southwest Virginia. Whether or not she's right, he has an insatiable thirst for money."

"You and Mike need to be careful how you handle this information. If Blackmun makes money from the Pit, he won't take kindly to people who upset his operation. The idea of people watching animals killing or maiming each other while gamblers place bets on the bleeding bodies is horrible. It makes me want to throw up.,"

"It's been going on a long time. Shakespeare's plays had to compete with cockfights, dogfights, and bearbaitings for audiences."

Heidi waved her hand as if trying to brush the image of fighting animals from her mind. "I still think it's horrid."

George felt obliged to defend his people. He wanted Heidi to understand. He tried to explain why people took pleasure from this bloody sport. "When I was growing up, these fights were a rite of passage for young boys around here. I admit they got pretty bloody. Not throwing up was a sign of manhood."

Heidi shivered. "I'm glad you outgrew those fights."

George wasn't sure he had outgrown them completely, so he changed the subject. "I'm going to see Mike tomorrow morning. I've arranged to go squirrel hunting with him so we can talk things over in private. Mike has contacts in the FBI. He'll get in touch with them."

"If you need a cover to pass on information to Mike, I'll be glad to include him in some of the dinners I fix for the two of us."

"Great, thanks, that would be a perfect way to get around bugged phones.'"

Chapter 11

"Without Moon, it'll take us a little longer to get a mess of squirrels for Mamaw, but there're plenty of them in these woods," George said as he and Mike Barton hiked into his five hundred acres, enjoying red sourwood and maple, and the yellow poplar, but keeping their eyes peeled for hickories and other nut bearing trees.

"I expect Dave's stripping around you is forcing wildlife into your woods. He's a negative Pied Piper. The noise of his bulldozers is chasing squirrels to you."

"Yeah, I have the best habitat around, and the last two years have been really good for squirrels and deer. The mast crops have been heavy. These woods can support a large squirrel population."

"I'm glad to have the chance to hunt here in your wildlife sanctuary. What did you want to talk about?"

"It's what I found out on Dave Blackmun's old strip job at Flat Gap. It's way back from the main road that runs over Fox Gap. It's the smoking gun."

"What did you find besides old machinery?"

"A plot of well-reclaimed ground with a big metal building sitting in it, and a big graveled parking lot surrounding the structure. I found an old flyer stuck against the window of what appeared to be an office."

"What did it say?"

"It was an ad for animal fights that took place a few weeks ago at what's known as the Pit, a match of Virginia birds and dogs against Kentucky birds and dogs."

Mike whistled and slapped George on the back. "Going across state lines for illegal cockfighting. We need to let the FBI know. They'll greet this news like bees finding a field full of flowers."

"You know they will. And Dave Blackmun must be involved. It's his land and his building. He probably gets a big part of the purse."

Mike nodded. "This is just part of a larger operation. It probably has Mulberry's protection by benign neglect, but the interstate angle brings the Feds in. I'll get in touch with Jason Brackenridge, but we'll have to have more information and evidence. We can't go through local lawmen. Eighty per cent of them are as *dirty* as dogs rolling in shit."

George stopped to look for squirrel cuttings. "We need a local source, maybe an honest strip miner. Heidi told me that Philemon Mullins is upset with Dave and Dab. Dave's been stealing Philemona's mining prospects. He might help." George picked up remains of hickory nuts. "This looks like a good spot to set up," he said.

"There must be a herd of squirrels here," Mike said.

"Would you be okay with my talking to Heidi about approaching Philemon?" George asked. "She's almost as eager to deal with Dave as we are. I've told her what I found."

"All right. She might be good help."

"Now let's get some squirrels for Serafina. Hickory nut cuttings are all over the ground, so there must be squirrels in the trees."

They picked their stands and sat down to wait. George smelled a faint aroma of skunk before the bird calls attracted his attention. A feeding flock of small birds was passing through, moving along with a pair of downy woodpeckers, whose *pik-pik* calls held the flock together. George saw and heard chickadees saying their names, white-breasted nuthatches giving their nasal *yank, yank* calls, and gray-breasted tufted titmice yelling *peter, peter, peter.* In the distance he heard blue jays harassing a hawk or owl.

Mike's whistle alerted George. Barton was pointing to a nearby limb where a squirrel was sitting, eating an acorn. George slowly raised his rifle, sighted his bushy-tailed prey, and slowly pulled the trigger. The squirrel fell close to its killer. Before George could rise to put his trophy in his game bag, Mike made a shot that brought down another squirrel.

The hunters bagged their game and moved on to a new location to repeat their harvest of acorn-eaters. They did this four times. With eight squirrels accounted for, they hiked out of the woods and drove to the MacClouds'. There they shared some of Timmons' prime moonshine with Archibald as he helped them prepare their harvest for Serafina.

While she marinated the squirrels and went to her garden to collect cabbage, chard, and beets for the rest of their dinner, George and Mike talked with Archibald about how they should proceed with their information. George began by telling his grandpa what he had seen out near Fox Gap. "We need evidence, Papaw. We've been told that Philemon Mullins might be willing to help us. Do you know Philemon well?"

"He was a private in my outfit in WWII, a good soldier. I see him at the VFW meetings. He's no fan of Dave Blackmun, so I'd say he'd help you. I could set up a meeting."

"That would be great, Papaw, but I don't want to get you into trouble," George said. "And you know, if gambling's involved, Rod probably has a hand in it."

"I know, but all I'm going to do is tell Philemon you want to meet him and that I would consider it a favor if he'd agree to do that. The rest is up to you."

—————————— ✦✦✦✦✦✦ ——————————

"Stop your jawing and come eat," Serafina called about an hour later. Carrie stuck her head out the door, "You fellows better come on before we eat all of this good food."

"Let's go, boys. Don't linger," Archibald said.

As they ate, Mike praised Serafina. "You sure do have a way with food, Mrs. MacCloud, especially squirrels."

"Thank you, Mike. I'm glad I could do justice to your hunting skill. My Archie used to be a fine hunter. He brought home lots of game then, but he doesn't do as much now."

"We have your chickens and tame turkeys," Archibald said. "I don't need to hunt as much."

After eating, they sat talking for quite awhile.

"Papaw, tell MIke about that great turkey shot you made," George said. "Five turkeys with one shot."

"Aw, Mike don't want to hear that," Archibald said.

Mike shook his head, "Sure I do, Mr. MacCloud. Everybody says you were one of a kind as a hunter. How did you get that many turkeys with one shot?"

"Why, yes, I reckon I did that once. Or leastways some folks say I done it."

"Go ahead, tell it, Pa," Carrie said. "I like to hear it though I've heard it lots of times."

George nudged Mike. "Papaw, I could tell it, but not the way you can."

"I sure would like to hear it," Mike said.

"All right, all right. Now listen. One fall day Serafina allowed that her larder was mighty nigh empty. We didn't have no turkey for Thanksgivin' dinner. 'Archibald, she says (I know she's plumb set when she calls me Archibald) we need a turkey to give thanks over when all the young'uns come to table.'

"So I says, 'I'll get old Sureshot (that's my rifle) and go turkey huntin' up over the next ridge where I'd heard turkeys a few days before. So next mornin' I got me some shells and old Sureshot and headed up the ridge and over the top to where I knew them turkeys were rootin' after acorns.

"It was a fair mornin' in the woods for certain. The leaves were all red and yellow and the air had plenty of moisture from a heavy dew. Sound was acarryin' a long way—'fore long I heared them turkeys scratchin' and talkin' low. I could taste turkey meat already. I crept up to them as quiet-like as a snake slidin' over plowed ground.

"When I could see three gobbles in front of me, I pointed old Sureshot in their direction. Then I gave my hen turkey call. All three of them gobblers raised their heads to look. I fired. Them turkeys was all in a line, you see, and my bullet went through one turkey head, and then another, and another. Three turkeys down.

"But my bullet kept agoin.' Dang if that bullet didn't keep movin' 'til it hit a big dead branch. That branch fell. It dropped on two turkeys scratchin' 'neath it and knocked 'em out cold. All I had to do was pick 'em up, tie their legs, and tote 'em home with the three I'd shot dead. Them turkeys sure was tasty."

"That was some shot, Papaw. Don't you think so, Mike?" George asked.

Mike nodded his head vigorously for emphasis. "A great shot."

"I don't recall his bringing home but one live turkey," Serafina said. "I clipped its wings and put it with my tame turkeys."

George laughed. "It still was a great shot, Mamaw."

The men sat around telling other hunting stories a while before Mike and George left. George couldn't help thinking of how the beauty of his grandparents' home place and his five hundred acres of woodland contrasted with the wasteland Dave and Dab were creating.

"I'll talk to Philemon as soon as I can," Archibald said as they stepped off the porch.

George waved. "Thanks, Papaw."

As he looked at the flowers in front of the porch and his grandparents' smiling faces, he understood why he always felt at home here in Winding Fork.

Chapter 12

G eorge called Heidi early Saturday from his office where he had gone early in the morning when it was still dark to finish some paper work. He hated filling out these reports. Almost all of them were perfunctory now, because ninety per cent of surface miners were following the law. He wished he could improve the law, but all he could do at present was apply the current rules to the letter and offer suggestions.

The phone rang for a long time. A heavily breathing Heidi answered.

"Were you outside?"

"No, I was taking a shower."

"I wish I could have been there to see you."

"You'll see me soon enough. Would you like to take a picnic lunch up to High Tom today?"

"Sounds like fun, we don't have a scheduled date? We could do that tomorrow."

Heidi teased. "Do you have another date today?"

George sensed he was being tested. He didn't hesitate. "No, a picnic with you sounds like fun."

"Great, if you come over around eight, I'll fix you breakfast."

George chuckled as he expressed his desire. "Okay, I'd be glad to stay the night after our picnic and have breakfast with you.

"Whoa. Down, boy. Come over after eight."

Later, George quit filling our reports and headed out to the town reservoir to greet the dawn listening to the chorus in the woods ringing the lake. The flute-like songs of the wood thrushes, the repetitive *three-eight vireo* of the yellow-throated vireo, and the raucous calls of the blue jays helped clear his mind from the dull work he'd been doing.

He pulled his truck up in front of Heidi's apartment at ten minutes after eight.

He could smell bacon cooking and hear it sizzling as Heidi opened the door. Her hair was pulled back in a bun and her hiking outfit was covered with a colorful pink apron emblazoned with a shovel and the words I DIG COAL SAFELY.

"Good morning, Birdman."

George whistled a bird song before he hugged her and gave her a long kiss.

"What was that whistle supposed to be? It didn't sound like a wolf-whistle."

"A white-throated sparrow. It says, *old Sam Peabody*. I heard a very early one this morning up at the reservoir. It's just come in from the north."

"Well, bring your whistler to breakfast. It's on the table. Come and eat."

"I'll be glad to. I'm hungry. That bacon smells good."

"I thought we could go up on the mountain right after breakfast and hike around the lake until time for our picnic. Then we can hike some more and come back here. I'm leaving supper cooking in my crockpot."

"Great. We'll see birds this morning, and the hike will work off this breakfast and get us ready for the picnic."

George sat down and attacked the eggs and bacon and toast with blackberry jelly. "Is this jelly homemade? It must be. It's too good to be store-bought.

Heidi bragged. "I picked the berries myself."

"You're a wonder. Amazing. And I'm crazy about you."

"Okay. I'm glad my spell is working."

"I talked to Mike about what I saw at Flat Gap. And we talked to my grandpa. He served with Philemon Mullins in the army. Philemon was a private in Papaw's company. He thinks Philemon is a good man and knows he's unhappy with Dave's mining practices."

"I like Philemon. I think he's your man."

"Papaw says he sees him at VFW meetings. He'll ask him to meet with me."

◆ ◆ ◆ ◆ ◆ ◆ ◆

The sun was shining. With the truck windows down, fresh air felt crisp and cool on George's face as they drove up into the forest on Powers Mountain. At the top of the ridge, he headed to the picnic area above High Tom Lake. He paid their fee at the self-service stand and parked. Putting two drinks in his backpack and locking their food in the truck, George led Heidi to the trail around the lake.

"We won't see as many birds now as we would in the spring and summer. Almost all of the breeding warblers have headed south, but we might run across a few late migrants," George said.

As they climbed up the path, a warbler flew across the path and lit in a low limb at eye level.

Heidi pointed at it. "What a gorgeous bird. It's all blue and black and white.

"It's a male black-throated blue warbler."

"I'm glad he stayed around for me to see him," Heidi said.

Walking up the path, they came to a stream. George showed Heidi how to hunt for stream salamanders. Pulling up stones, they found five.

'Hold out your hands in a cup," George said.

When she cupped her hands. George dropped a salamander into them. "Oh, how slippery they are." She laughed as it tried to escape. "Gosh, it's squirming…Oh, I can't hold it." The salamander slithered from her hands back to the stream.

"Shucks, I just couldn't hold the little rascal," she said.

George laughed. "A lot of people object to holding one. You're a real scout. Let's hike on some more. When we get to the other side where we'll be right at the lake edge, I'll show you another salamander. It starts in the water as a newt and ends up on land as a red eft. We may see one on the trail."

"Are there many other salamanders here?"

"Our southern mountains are hotel central for the world's salamanders.

"There're more here?"

"Nowhere else in the world has as many species. We have rare green salamanders, slimy salamanders, tiger salamanders. We have the world's mother lode of salamanders."

"You could apply for a job with the chamber of commerce."

"Okay, okay. There's no place like these mountains. It's full of coal, gas, birds and salamanders. It's a wonderful place, if you like the out of doors, and I do."

As they moved up the trail, they heard a loud *kek-kek-kek-kek*. "What's that strange noise?" Heidi asked.

"That's what I grew up calling a wood-hen. Your bird guide calls it a pileated woodpecker. The Indians called it the log-god or the great lord god." Watch and you might see it fly over. It has a big red crest and shows a lot of white in its wings when it flies. It's a stunner."

"I'd love to see something like that."

"If you get out in the woods around here enough, you're bound to see one. Some people misidentify it as the extinct Ivory-billed Woodpecker."

Further on, they flushed a small gray bird with a white belly and white outer tail feathers. "What's that?" Heidi asked.

"That's a dark-eyed junco. Another name is snowbird. They nest in the high elevations in summer and come down lower in the winter. You must have heard the song about the snowbird that Anne Murray made famous." George sang a snatch. ""So little snowbird/take me with you when you go." He broke off, laughing. "I'm no songster. When juncos first come down to lower elevations in the fall, you begin to watch for snow."

After their hike, Heidi opened the picnic lunch. She poured

lemonades and unwrapped tuna sandwiches. For dessert there was cherry pie. George had no trouble making sure they didn't have a lot of leftovers to take back, but Heidi limited him to one piece of pie. When he finished his pie, he rubbed his stomach and grinned, "Now I know how Jack Horner felt after eating his Christmas pie. I must have been a good boy today."

"You're ahead of yourself. The day's not over yet."

As they sat sipping lemonade and eating pie, Heidi asked George if he understood the danger he was courting. "You know Dave Blackmun's dangerous. He's an evil man. He'll react badly to being threatened."

"Your estimate of him is correct. He's already threatening me. I haven't told you my father left me five hundred acres in Winding Fork. It has a rich seam of metallurgical coal Dave Blackmun's eager to strip. I promised my father and grandfather I wouldn't let the land be mined, that I would keep it undisturbed, except for hunting." His lips pursed, he looked away from her.

"You've refused to break your word to your father and grandfather?"

"I could be wealthy. I've turned down Dave's offers and his bribes, and I've ignored his threats. He's turning my land into an island surrounded by completely stripped wasteland. I'm sure he'll eventually do something worse."

"I had no idea. You do have a personal problem with Blackmun."

"I wasn't hiding it from you. I didn't think the money would matter to you. It just didn't occur to me to tell you before. I hope my passing up riches doesn't make a difference in our relationship."

"Of course not. I understand. But I'll have an added reason now to tell you to be careful."

As they drove down the mountain, they enjoyed the beauty of the fall leaves turning many shades of red and yellow.

"The sourwoods are the first to turn red," George said, pointing to a large blazing red tree. "Most of the yellow trees are poplar or maple."

"I can see why you don't want to destroy your woods, even for the fortune. I don't like those Beauty Is a Biscuit bumper stickers the surface miners promote. Everyone has to eat, but that doesn't eliminate the need for beauty. Ancient people saw beauty in the natural world. They approached it with awe."

"You're pretty and tasty too." He slowed the truck, pulled her over and kissed her as if to make sure. "You taste like cherry pie."

Their vehicle edged to the wrong side of the road. "Watch your driving. Taste is very personal, but I'm glad you like my cherry pie."

George put both hands on the wheel.

"The price of being a good steward is confronting the Dave Blackmuns of our world. I have help now. I sold ten per cent of my mineral rights to my cousin Moon. He values my land as it is. He has deep enough pockets to take on Dave. Moon will be able to handle any law suit Blackmun aims our way."

The afternoon was half gone when they got back to Big Stone Head. Heidi carried her much lighter picnic basket inside, "Do you want to turn on the TV, George? I know you did your college work at Ohio University and Virginia Tech. I think one of them has a football game on TV."

George was encouraged. She'd been studying him. "Okay, if you don't need any help."

"Our dinner in the pot will be ready in an hour. I'll make a salad and we'll have some more of the cherry pie for dessert." Get a beer out of the fridge and pour some of it for me."

He did as she asked and then turned on the TV and found the Tech game. He began giving Heidi a running commentary. "Virginia Tech has the football on the Wake Forest five-yard line." Then he groaned. "The Demon Deacons stopped Tech for no gain." Then he cheered. "On third down Tech scored. That will prove to be the winning touchdown, if we're lucky."

As the outcome of the game became less in doubt, Heidi interrupted him.

"George, pour us a couple of gin and tonics, please."

He sniffed the air. "Okay, that beef stew smells really good."

"I hate to repeat so soon. But I had to hurry on short notice.:

He took up the bartending chore, while still keeping an eye on the television. He poured two shots of gin over the ice in two glasses and added tonic water.

At the table, he savored Heidi's beef stew. "This dinner's delicious. It's even better than your other beef stew we had."

"Enjoy, a cook likes compliments. I put in a few more bay leaves this time."

After dinner, when they had put the dishes away, Heidi turned off the TV, put on a Mozart tape. and listened to strains of *Cosi fan tutte*. "Come sit beside me."

George sat down as close to her as he could without sitting on top of her. "Did you enjoy the day?" Heidi asked as she ran her fingers through his hair.

"You bet I did. I'm not looking forward to working my job next week."

"But we'll be together again tomorrow."

"That's right. I'm going to take you over to Mt. Rogers. Pack us a lunch. We'll go to Enchiladas for supper, unless you'd rather do something else."

"No, that sounds like fun. I haven't been to Mt. Rogers."

"It's the highest peak in Virginia.:

She put her arms around his neck and kissed him. Their heavy petting incited George's frustration again.

"I can't wait forever. Let's get engaged."

"Are you sure? I've heard that you and that newspaper lady have a passionate affair going on."

"You mean Jennifer Coffee?"

"Yes, Jennifer. I have a friend who works at the Western in Hardwood. She says you spent most of the night with Jennifer there more than once during the last few weeks."

George guessed now why Heidi had insisted on scheduling their dates. She was making it difficult for him to carry on an affair with Jennifer, who worked out of Roanoke, a long drive away. He felt the need to defend himself. "Jennifer's dedicated to her career. She sees me as a way to get information for her newspaper assignments."

"I may not be the sharpest tack in the box, but I think it goes further than that. I want to be engaged, but I want to be sure you can be faithful before I commit to you. I'm not willing to share you."

Chapter 13

Hoping to obtain approval and advice for enlisting the help of Philemon Mullins, Mike Barton had to make contact with the FBI to pass on George's information. Mike had trained at the FBI Academy at Quantico with Jason Brackenridge.

While at the Academy, Barton had met many cadets who later became FBI field agents, but his closest friend had been Jason. Mike's training in Hogan's Alley had gone well, but he dropped out to go back to Southwest Virginia when his father died. Before Mike left, he talked to Jason about problems in Wisdom County, and Jason had told him to let him know if he could be of help.

Mike had spoken to Brackenridge after his assignment to Kentucky. "Jason, this is Mike Barton over in Virginia. I think I may be on to something that you would be interested in. If it pans out, I'll let you know."

"Great, I'm beginning to get the hang of things here. I'd be interested in any cross-border activity."

So Mike contacted Jason, who had been assigned to the field office in Louisville.

"Good to hear from you again. It was a shame you dropped out of the Academy. How're you doing with that sheriff uncle of yours?" Jason asked.

"My job with the Sheriff's office is tough. My mother's pull with the Sheriff got me the job, not my credentials from the Academy. Family ties are still important in these mountains. My uncle took me on as deputy, but he's reserved me for lawful activities Mother would approve."

"You have a hard row to hoe, then."

"Can't complain too much. I just make sure I stay honest. I have something you'll be interested in, but I'm reluctant to talk over the telephone," Mike said as he twisted his J. I. Berman class ring. You know my situation. I have to be careful."

"Could you meet me somewhere in Kentucky? Say Pikeville? That's close to you, isn't it?"

"Yeah. Pikeville would be okay."

"Are you free this coming weekend?" Jason asked

"Yes, according to my current schedule," Mike said.

Jason paused, then spoke quickly. "Then meet me in the parking lot of the Western in Pikeville Saturday at ten. I'll drive over on Friday evening.

"Thanks. See you there." Mike pulled out his handkerchief to dry the sweat on his hands and brow, relieved to know that Jason would help.

✦ ✦ ✦✦✦ ✦ ✦

Mike dropped by Heidi's office late that afternoon. She was filing her paperwork, ending her workday.

"Hi, Heidi. I see you're almost ready to leave. I won't take much of your time. I just want to pass on a message for George. Just tell him the wood-hen's made contact with the big eagle."

"That's good news, but you can tell him yourself if you'll join us at the new Mexican restaurant tonight. Just give him a ring at my place about six o'clock."

"Okay, but I was hoping for a dinner invitation. I really do need the cover. Bo has warned me that Dave Blackmun has complained about my arresting his men. If Dave has his eye on me, my phone is probably bugged."

"I'll keep that in mind in the future."

Heidi's phone rang about six as she was fixing drinks for George and herself. "Would you answer that? It may be Mike."

George picked up the receiver. "Hello."

"Mike here. I have some news. Could I meet you at Enchiladas?"

"Sure. Be there in half an hour."

"I'm already here. I'll order a draft and wait."

Mike stood to greet Heidi and George when the waitress ushered them to his table. He put his beer down as he shook hands with George as the waitress took their drink order. After she left, Mike leaned over the table. "I can't stay long. I go on duty soon."

"What's the news?" George asked.

"I contacted the FBI. Everything's going to work out. I'm meeting Jason in Pikeville Saturday. I'm being careful to avoid the phone tap. Jason will probably want to check Philemon out before we put him to work."

"Seems like the sensible thing to do. Heidi and I are ready to do our bit."

"Then I'll finish this beer and be on my way." He drained his mug, kissed Heidi on the cheek, and shook hands with George.

"Try to stay out of trouble," George said.

Mike laughed. "Don't I always? I'll probably issue warnings instead of tickets tonight, even if I catch Dave speeding."

George and Heidi surveyed the dinner crowd as they waited for their drinks.

"That's Dave Blackmun over there across the room, isn't it?" Heidi asked.

"I think Blackmun was watching us when Mike was here."

George followed her gaze and saw a handsome, black-haired, heavy-set man looking at them as the waitress arrived with their margaritas. They ordered tortilla soup and fajitas.

Heidi looked over at Blackmun while they sipped their drinks. She leaned over and said, "Dave's giving you some really hard looks."

George agreed. "We're not on the same team any more. He and I played together on the J. I. Berman football team. He opened up wide holes for me and Moon to run through. I reckon he'll stop by before he leaves. That's an interesting blonde he's with. She doesn't look like anybody local."

"I haven't seen her before. What a stunning woman."

"She's good-looking, very stylish, but she has a hard edge. I wonder where Dave found her," George said.

George signaled their waitress to come over. He ordered refills on their drinks. "Your soup and fajitas will be here in a few minutes," she said.

"Blackmun certainly looks rugged. He doesn't look like public enemy number one, though," Heidi said." He's handsome."

"Pretty is as pretty does. Ask his wife. She left him because he beat and whipped her. At least that's what she told her friends. He beat her because she objected to his peculiar sexual demands."

"What sort of demands did she find peculiar?" Heidi said.

George hesitated. He didn't feel comfortable being too explicit. "He liked to be aroused by whipping, and he didn't want to be limited in how he gained satisfaction."

As Heidi and George were beginning their soup, Blackmun and the woman with him stood and began walking toward the door. They took the long way to come by Heidi and George.

Towering over them, Dave leered. "Hello, George, Heidi. Meet Arachne Smith. She's taking care of my record keeping."

Blackmun placed his hands on his hips like a football lineman ready to take his position. "Have you thought over my last offer?" he asked.

George had anticipated Blackmun's asking about stripping his five hundred acres. He repeated what he had already told him, trying to be patient, as he added his deal with Moon.

"I've told you I vowed to my father and grandfather that I wouldn't strip my land. I've sold ten per cent of my mineral rights to Adamo Lunamin." George pointed a finger for emphasis. "Moon's as opposed to mining the land as I am. So I have to turn you down."

Dave bared his teeth in what started as a grin but became a grimace. "That's an unwise decision, but you may change your mind. You never know what will happen."

George slid a little away from Blackmun but managed a smile. "Life has many surprises."

"Be careful." Dave said, frowning and turning. He took Arachne's arm and steered her away.

Heidi tapped George's hand. "I think he just threatened you."

"Absolutely—I'll try to be careful. Dave's dangerous."

"He hides his nastiness pretty well," Heidi said.

"Poverty and a harsh father twisted him. His mother ran off with another man when he was seven. His father made a living farming, turning corn into white lightning, selling it, and raising and fighting gamecocks. Dave's life was full of chores and hard work under a nasty taskmaster."

Heidi sighed. "That doesn't sound like a pleasant childhood."

George nodded. "Dave could never satisfy his old man. The old bastard taught him number one was the only person that mattered. Dave came to school dirty and ill-dressed. The town kids made fun of him."

"Do you think some of his deeds are payback?"

"Maybe, remember how he handled the miner's strike? He acted like he was fighting a war. He's brave and ruthless. He's bad news."

"Didn't your grandpa get hurt during that strike?"

"You remember the violence. Dave drove trucks through picket lines and came close to getting killed. Papaw's a lifelong Union man, He was caught in the crossfire. He spent time in the hospital."

Back at Heidi's, she pulled out a mince pie and cut a slice for each of them while George poured bourbon on the rocks for himself and a gin and tonic for her.

"Is it possible for you to transfer the oversight of Dave's mining jobs to another reclamation agent?" Heidi asked as they sipped their drinks.

"No, he has too many active sites. There aren't but three of us mine inspectors working surface mines. I've shifted off two of Dave's jobs. I'm sure nobody else is eager to have more. They weren't enthusiastic about taking one."

"I don't want you to become just another mining accident, Sweetheart."

George laughed. "I'm glad to hear it; maybe we should get engaged before something bad happens."

"Don't joke about it."

"I'm not joking. I need you." George couldn't admit to Heidi how much he worried about Blackmun. He tried to avoid inspecting Blackmun's mine as much as he could without shirking his duty. He reached over to touch Heidi's cheek.

"For now, you have enough of me." She gave him a kiss. "When I become convinced you have a constant heart and your family approves of me, I'll agree to an engagement and you can have more. So stay away from Jennifer."

George had difficulty keeping his mind on his driving on the way home and was too troubled to fall asleep immediately after getting in bed. He knew he must avoid Jennifer if he wished to win Heidi, but he also feared Jennifer wouldn't go without encouragement. He had to summon up the will to end their sexual relationship. Knowing is easier than acting upon knowledge when old habits are at stake, George admitted. Yet he must win Heidi. His feelings for her were becoming too great to deny. He had fallen in love with her. It followed that he must end his trysts with Jennifer, no matter how unpleasant the fracture might be. As he grappled with this problem, he still could not keep Blackmun's greed for his coal out of his mind. He pulled the piece of mince pie out of the bag Heidi had given him. He ate some of it, imagining her lips, gray eyes and auburn hair as he enjoyed her baking.

Chapter 14

Mike Barton didn't sleep as late as usual this Saturday morning. He awakened before six, took a shower, and fixed coffee, toast, and a couple of eggs for breakfast—eating more than usual, delaying his start. At seven-thirty he headed his truck for the crossroads and turned right to Pikeville, hopeful but full of anxiety. Like an astronaut loading into a space vehicle, he was taking a step from which there might be no return.

The day was sunny, fall leaves were colorful, but Barton was too preoccupied with his mission to enjoy them as much as usual. They were a blur. His stomach was burning. He tried to ignore his acid reflux, popped a pill, and attempted to focus on the beauty of the scenery without much success. He did notice a kettle or two of migrant hawks riding the thermals down the ridge of Pine Mountain and made a mental note to tell George.

He arrived at the Western in Pikeville a few minutes after ten. Jason Brackenridge waved a greeting. Mike parked, and walked over to a tall, lean man who reminded him of Clint Eastwood. Despite his red hair and name taken from a not so trustworthy hero of Greek mythology, Jason had always been someone Mike could rely on.

"Hi, Jason, it's been awhile since the Academy," Mike said as Jason firmly grasped his hand.

"Yeah. It's a shame you dropped out. I know your mother needed you, but I don't see how you get along in Wisdom County. Your uncle's known for allowing his men to sell the pot they bring in.

You've always struck me as an honest man, and I've heard enough to know your sheriff's a crook."

Mike was glad that Jason still thought him honest. "It's a family thing. My mother and Bo are brother and sister. Family ties are strong here. They trump a lot of other things. Bo uses me to do lawful jobs, and I don't pry deeply into what else goes on in his department. I don't profit from the illegal sale of confiscated marijuana, for example, but it's difficult to avoid knowing the jail is the place to make a buy."

Jason gave a sympathetic nod. "You must walk a thin line."

Mike looked around to make sure nobody was listening.

"Tough work, but what can I do for you"? Jason asked.

"You asked me to keep you informed about criminal activity across state lines—I've found just what you asked me to look for. Cross border gambling activity. Betting on dog and chicken fights."

Jason looked around to confirm nobody was listening. "And you can't go to your uncle."

"No way. I've already caused him trouble with the crime kingpin, and my phones are bugged."

Jason leaned closer to Mike. "Your're out on a limb."

"Damn right, it's like a high wire act, but Ma needs me, and I need a job. Uncle Bo wants to project a veneer of law and order. That's where I fit in. I convince people the law's being enforced. It's not easy being an honest cop in a crooked outfit. And one day I hope to change things. I need your help."

"Let's go in the motel restaurant and talk this over," Jason said." We'll just be friends talking over coffee about old times."

Mike tried to look casual, even though his stomach still bothered him. They walked in and took a booth away from other customers. They ordered coffee and doughnuts., trying to look like two old buddies shooting the breeze about old times. As they put sweetener in their coffee, Jason leaned forward.

"What can I do for you? You said you'd turned up evidence of illegal activity across state lines."

"I think we've found the tip of a big operation. I'm not sure. "

"What have you found?"

"We know there have been illegal fights involving transporting fighting chickens and dogs from Kentucky to Virginia. Evidence indicates extensive gambling on the fights. Hearsay suggests prostitution for blackmail covered by the Mann Act."

"What help do you need?"

"I can't go to my uncle. I need to deal directly with the FBI."

"Do you have a reliable source for this evidence?"

"Yes, my friend George Landsetter. He's helping me. And there's been a murder I suspect is connected to the gambling, prostitution and blackmail. That wouldn't necessarily involve the FBI, but we believe the women involved have been brought in from New York."

Looking around, Jason lifted his coffee cup as if making a toast. "You need evidence."

"I know. We have evidence of one combined cockfight and dogfight, but we need more, and we need FBI cover. The Sheriff's involved, if only in turning a blind eye for a price. I think that's as far as it goes—far enough away from illegal stuff that he can claim lack of knowledge."

"How will you learn more? Do you know somebody who'll work under cover?"

"We have a man we think might do. A strip miner named Philemon Mullins. We believe another mine owner, Dave Blackmun, is the hand directing the illegal activity. Philemon dislikes Blackmun's bad mining practices, maybe enough to cooperate. We thought you could check him out."

"Right, I'll present this to my bosses. If they give the green light, I'll investigate your man."

"Great."

"What about this crime boss. What sort of guy is he?"

"He's dangerous. He acted like a loose cannon during our last miner's strike. And he's threatening a friend of mine who won't sell him mineral rights. I believe he's arranged murders for hire, but that's just a gut feeling I have."

"What causes your suspicion?"

"A body was found at a strip mine run by Blackmun's main buddy.

Whoever put it there was trying to cover a murder with a strip-mine explosion. Dab Whacker, the mine owner, has a reputation for using more explosive than the law allows. Whoever dumped the body was counting on Dab's reputation. He knew what Dab's blasting schedule was, but didn't count on Dab's foreman checking before he set off the blast."

"Sounds like a good theory."

"But I don't see any way to prove it. I think we can build a strong case to prove illegal gambling."

Jason put his hand on Mike's shoulder "I'm with you. Hang in there. I'll try to get approval to check your man. We've had a number of complaints about illegal gambling activities in eastern Kentucky. Some tips suggested interstate fighting and gambling's going on. Your information emphasizes the need for a sting. So I think I'll get the go ahead. "

Mike leaned back in his seat and grinned and sipped his coffee. His stomach received the liquid without complaint. "I'm glad to hear that. I feel less like a squirrel out on a limb being sawed off."

On Mike's drive back to Big Stone Head, he was more upbeat than he had anticipated in the morning. He felt certain that his request would be given serious attention and would probably be approved. He was eager to tell George the good news. They were not alone. He enjoyed the beauty of the fall colors much more now than he had earlier. He picked out the deep reds of the sourwoods, the yellows of the poplars, and the pale pinks of the maples.

When he stopped in Jenko to top off his gas, Mike used the store's phone to call Landsetter and leave a message.

"Mission accomplished. We should hear something soon. I'll fill you in when I see you."

◆ ◆ ◆ ◆ ◆ ◆

George called Heidi after he finished a morning in his woods. He was planning to spend the afternoon watching football on TV.

"I know it's not a scheduled day, but would you go out for a hike in my woods this evening? I'll pick you up twenty minutes after five, if that suits you. I have news from Mike."

"I'd love to. We can come back to my place later for soup and sandwiches."

Later that day, as they hiked into the woods, George exulted over Tech's football victory. "The Hokies ran through Georgia Tech like Sherman marching to the sea."

"Great. I'm happy for you. What's your news about the meeting in Pikeville?"

"Brackenridge has agreed to help. I'll find out more when I see Mike."

"I hope that means they'll accept Philemon. He's an honest, reliable person," Heidi said. "He's a good choice."

Just then George heard a pileated woodpecker giving its wild *kek-kek-kek* call. "Hey, Heidi, you said you wanted to see a wood-hen. I think one's headed our way. Keep your eyes open. "Just as he spoke a pileated woodpecker swooped by them, calling again.

George winced when Heidi pinched his arm. "Spectacular! What a beauty." Her yell was as loud as the woodpecker's call.

George laughed, grabbing Heidi and hugging her. "You're prettier than that bird, but I agree. It's a beauty."

A feeding flock of chickadees and titmice began moving past them in groups.

"It's a feeding flock, birds ganging together to find food, common after breeding is complete." Among the flock, George saw a little bird. "Look, Heidi, there's a little brown bird that flies down to the base of a tree and starts working its way up the trunk. It's called a brown creeper. It's well-named. See how it creeps up the trunk?"

"I see it. It's cute, but there's also a gray and white bird working the tree trunks upside down. What's that?"

"A white-breasted nuthatch."

"It's cute too."

George spotted a gray fox slipping through the trees ahead of them and showed it to Heidi. "I'll bet that fox is looking for a squirrel or rabbit for supper. I reckon we ought to be getting out of the woods before it gets dark."

"I promised you soup and sandwiches. Let's get back to my place."

"I hope Philemon can do what we need. If the FBI approves him and he agrees to do the job, can he do it?"

Heidi spoke with assurance. "He supported me with the symposium. He's a capable man. I'm sure he can, if you can convince him to do it. He's religious. He's serious about good works."

As he ate Heidi's pimento cheese sandwiches and sipped her vegetable soup, George drank her herbal tea and watched her with longing. He regretted his relationship with Jennifer. It was proving a huge handicap to his courtship of Heidi. It had become obvious life without Heidi would be as barren as one of Dave Blackmun's strip jobs. It followed that he must end his intimacy with Jennifer, but he had to do it in a manner convincing to Heidi. He must find a way.

"You look lost in thought. Have you forgotten me?"

"No way, I was just daydreaming about you. About our future together."

Heidi tweaked his ear. "It's up to you to make sure you're not just building castles in air."

"I'm relying on my architect. I'm trying to build to her specifications."

Smiling, Heidi reached over and patted his hand. "I hope I've found a good carpenter."

In his mind, George carried the metaphor further in mountain dialect. *I'm a-layin' the foundation, Honey. I'm gonna build for a lifetime.*

Chapter 15

George was enjoying the last minutes of an Indian summer's day when Mike drove up to the woods as dusty dark was settling.

"I thought we could choose stands for deer hunting and discuss which of us should approach Philemon Mullins while we hike through the woods and scout."

Mike stretched up his hand and tested the wind by throwing up some grass. "It's a great evening to be in the woods."

"There's an odor of skunk in the air," George said.

"Fits. Skunk hour's the right time to discuss how to do in a skunk."

George laughed. "Dave makes other skunks' odors smell sweet."

"I think you're the one who needs to make the contact," Barton said, clearing his throat. "I need to stay in the background until later. You can talk to Philemon without arousing suspicion. I can't."

"That's right. As the assigned monitor of his mining operation, it makes sense for me to approach him. I'll talk to my cousin, Isaiah Timmons, first. He and Philemon are good friends."

"Okay. It's your baby. Be careful."

George took a sip from his canteen. "You don't need to tell me. There must be a lot of gambling connected with these cockfights and dog fights. Where there's gambling, Rod Mashburn's bound to be involved."

"If we're careful, he won't know our involvement," Mike said.

"Right, no need to get stuck on a worst-case scenario."

Mike nodded. "I don't want to come down too hard on my uncle either. I have to be extra careful, so you're definitely the one to contact Philemon."

George nodded agreement.

"Then It's settled."

George brushed his hand over his brow, as if trying to wipe away the chances he would be taking as the go-between. That matter settled, they spent another hour locating their deer stands before calling it an evening.

Worried that some of their actions might get back to Blackmun, George couldn't put Dave out of his mind. He smelled skunk odor again, "I'm sure that skunk would say saving these woods from stripping is worth the risk of Dave's anger. If Blackmun had control of this woodland, it would be forty or fifty years or more before it would be anything like what it is now. You and I would be old men."

"Or dead. It's hard to put a monetary value on the pleasure this land brings. I'm biased, of course. I love hunting here," Mike said.

"That's one thing that makes me love Heidi. She dotes on nature, the out of doors. She understands how much this woodland means to me. No amount of money would bring me the happiness this woodland does." As they parted, George looked forward to an evening with Heidi.

<hr />

George visited Dab Whacker's mine on Isaiah Timmons' land the next day. He was planning to visit Isaiah but didn't need to go up to Isaiah's home place to talk about Philemon. His cousin was standing by his new truck watching Dab's operation.

"Hello, Isaiah. You live out here?"

"How do, George. Dab's men seem more careful when I'm a-watching."

"I don't understand why you're stripping more. You should have all of the cropland you need from Moon's mining. The reclamation on that site has made it a great place for crops and wildlife."

"Yeah. The deer love it. I don't need to go anywhere else to do my hunting."

"Then why strip more? Even Archie and Serafina wonder if you've gone dotty in your old age."

Isaiah looked away, adjusted his tobacco, and spit. "I need the money. I hate to admit it. I've got into debt something deep."

"Debt? Your kids both finished college a long time ago. You and Sally don't travel. You don't lead a luxurious life style."

"I've got into debt gambling like a foolish kid. Sally has just about disowned me. She lectures me almost every day. I've sworn off gambling." Isaiah shook his head and groaned,

"You into Rod Mashburn for money?"

"I was. But Rod gave me more time and a discount. No, it's Dave Blackmun. He's nasty about the money I owe. He ain't so forgiving. I've quit the gambling, but I got to pay Blackmun. He don't believe in forgiveness. Our cousin Cameron'a body on Dab's strip site was a warning; he was in debt to Dave. Dave threatened me. Dave's the one who suggested Dab do the stripping of my land. I reckon he had in mind a convenient dumping ground, if he needed to get rid of me."

"I have reason to believe Dave's behind a lot of illegal activity. Did you know about his place up at Flat Gap?"

"Yeah. That's where I run up my debt. I knowed it was wrong, but I did it anyway. Rod handles the gambling on the dogfights and cock- fights and furnishes the other gambling games. He provides the pot, too. But it's Dave's money that runs the show, and he furnishes the women."

"You been fooling around behind Sally's back?"

Isaiah paused to spit. "No—I bet too heavy on the chickens and dogs."

George grunted. "Well, there's some people who'd like to take Dave down a peg. I wouldn't mind having him out of the way, 'cause he's giving me a terrible hard time. He wants to strip my five hundred acres I promised Pa and Papaw I'd not strip."

Isaiah made a dollar sign in the dust with his boot. "I've heard Dave's hot to strip that land. You know you could make a fortune."

"Yeah, but I'm living well enough now. I don't need more money. What do you know about Philemon Mullins? How does he feel about Blackmun?"

"Hates his guts. Dave has stolen a bunch of strip jobs out from under Philemon. Dave doesn't hide it. He laughs and jokes about it, says he gets his best strip jobs just by following Philemon around."

George licked his lip in anticipation. "Do you think Philemon hates Dave enough to help do him in?"

"I've heard Philemon vow he'd slit Dave's throat if he thought he could get away with it and escape Hell's flames."

"So Philemon's a God-fearing man?"

Isaiah smacked his thigh. "You bet. He's a tithing member of Lamb o'God Flannary's congregation."

George slipped some gum in his mouth and held out the pack of gum to Isaiah. "Fred and Jauncie MacCloud are too. I've heard Moon say so. That's why he sold them Lunar Mining on an installment plan. He trusted them."

Isaiah took a piece, spit out his tobacco, and popped the gum in his mouth. "That's right. Cousin Fred's a deacon. Fred's done pretty well since he took over Moon's company. I reckon Lamb o' God's glad to have him in his congregation."

"Yeah, I reckon so. You be careful, Isaiah. Dave's a dangerous man. I'd better get over and talk to Dab now. I hear he's beginning to up his blasting charges again. What do you think?"

"Yeah, I think so," Isaiah said, a pained expression on his face. "The flying rocks are increasing. Maybe Dave has another body to hide. Maybe mine—or yours."

George nodded at this confirmation of his assessment. He always felt in danger when he visited Dab or Dave. "I'll warn him I'll give him another citation if he doesn't tell his men to lighten up on the explosives."

Isaiah chuckled as he and George shook hands. "Want to bet on whether he listens?"

"No, but I'll try anyway. So long, Cousin. Tell Sally I said hello."

George had a lot to think about. He knew now how to approach

Philemon. Besides Philemon's desire for revenge, he'd have God on his side. Philemon could fight evil and do in Dave at the same time. Still, it would take a determined man to take on Dave Blackmun.

Later that day, George visited Philemon's active surface mining site. He never had much trouble there. Philemon was a law-abiding man who reclaimed his sites so well his clients were always pleased. When George drove onto the mine, he saw Philemon surveying its progress from atop a big yellow D-12 'dozer.

George parked, got out, and waved to Philemon as he walked over to him.

"Howdy, Philemon."

"Hello, George. I hope you haven't come to fine me."

"You make my life dull. You never do anything to get fined. I have to go see Dab or Dave whenever I want excitement," George said, slapping his thigh.

"I don't see how those guys sleep at night."

"I'm with you there. My grandfather said he'd ask you to talk to me about something that needs to be kept quiet."

"Yeah, I talked to Archie at the VFW."

"There're lots of people who agree Dave Blackmun's a mean guy. Evil to boot. How would you like to see Dave in jail instead of stealing your strip job prospects?"

Philemon scratched his head. "I'd like to see Dave brought to justice, but nailing him would be dangerous."

"The FBI is looking for someone to collect evidence of illegal activity crossing state lines. I felt you're somebody who'd be willing to work undercover to gather evidence. They'd provide you with expense money and equipment."

Turning away, Philemon ran his hands through his thinning hair. "I'll have to think it over. It's true I don't like Dave, but I'm not sure I dislike him enough to take on that job. Dave is evil, so it would be like doing God's work. I want to talk to my minister about this. I won't give away anything."

"Okay, but be careful. I wouldn't mention Dave's name or anything about a sting operation."

"I'll speak in general terms."

Looking around, George lowered his voice. "All right. Be sure you do. Remember the WWII warning: *Loose lips sink ships*. I'll come around here a week from now to find out what you've decided."

George thought Philemon would come around. After all, he would be fighting for what's right. Now that he thought about his struggle with Dave, his effort to maintain his five hundred acres was doing the right thing, too. He didn't need the money as much as he needed to keep his oath and the happiness he gained from the land as nature had created it. He worked every day trying to make sure surface-mined land was restored to heal destruction of the ecosystem. He concluded he was not merely earning a salary and maintaining the environment, he was doing God's work. George wasn't a Bible thumper, but he preferred being a good steward of nature. He hoped that none of the people he was relying on let something slip.

Chapter 16

George looked down from above on the machines moving coal to a pile from which other machines were taking it to load into trucks. From above they appeared small enough to be toys when he stopped by Philemon Mullins' surface mine the next week, Driving down to the mine, George saw Philemon working on a bulldozer's engine near a large mound of coal from which front loaders were dumping black loads into haul trucks. Philemon turned and. greeted him with a smile.

Philemon looked happy. Using a cloth to wipe his hands, he reached out to shake hands. *He has made his decision,* George thought. "Are you going to do it?" he asked.

"I'll work for the FBI, "Philemon said.

George gave him a thumbs-up. "What convinced you?"

Philemon stretched his arms wide and placed his hands on his hips. "I was afraid I would be doing it for revenge. I talked it over with Lamb o'God. He's my pastor. He said I'd be fighting evil, doing the Lord's work. As long as I don't do anything extra, God will approve."

George gave silent praise for Lamb o' God Flannary. "I'm glad you decided to help. I'm as happy as a possum in a persimmon tree," he said, grinning. "But keep this to yourself."

Philemon moved closer to George. "So, what's the next move?"

"The FBI will contact you. They'll probably want to give you a little training about what to look for and how to make a record of it.

They'll give you equipment to record what you find. Mike Barton will contact the FBI to tell them you're ready to help. You pass on the information through me. Is that okay with you?"

Philemon pulled on his ear. His brows knotted. "Sure. Where would I meet my FBI contact? I don't want to do it around here."

Trying to use a soothing tone, George asked, "Would Pikeville be a convenient place for you?"

Philemon met George's gaze. "That would be all right, but I wouldn't want a very public place. Blackmun has plenty of contacts over there, I'm sure. I want to avoid being seen."

George nodded. "I'll relay your concerns. After that you'll need an introduction into Dave's gambling den. My cousin Isaiah Timmons could give you that, if you're okay with him. He's in deep to Dave."

Philemon kicked a rock. "I'm sorry to hear that. Isaiah has been a good friend to me. He helped me get a start in mining. I'm okay with having him introduce me. Does he know what I'll be doing?"

George shook his head. "That's on a need-to-know basis. I'd like to keep him in the dark about your work. Dave could put too much pressure on him. I don't want Isaiah hurt."

Philemon grinned and nodded. "All right, I'll just let him think I'm eager to gamble a little."

"Good." George shook Philemon's hand. "I'll come around for another inspection this time next week with instructions about your meeting with an FBI agent." George headed for his vehicle.

Philemon waved. "So long, George. Be careful."

George waved back as he got in his Reclamation vehicle. He thought it ironic that Philemon told him to be careful. If Philemon wasn't careful, they both might end up like Cameron MacCloud. He wished he had already convinced Heidi he could be faithful. Wished that they were married. What if this whole under-cover business came to a bad end? He hoped Philemon was as dependable as Heidi thought.

◆ ◆ ◆ ◆ ◆ ◆ ◆

George invited Mike squirrel hunting again that Saturday. In a short time, they bagged eight bushy tails. Before they took them to Serafina to be prepared for dinner, George filled in Mike about his conversation with Philemon. Then, collecting their game, they took their plunder to Winding Fork.

On the porch, they found Archibald shelling black walnuts he'd gathered. He was using a homemade crusher to crack the tough shells. As they sat with Archibald, he passed around some glasses and poured from a bottle of Timmons' liquor. "Mike, I know you're a lawman, but this liquor isn't on the market. Isaiah brews for himself and his family and close friends. No money changes hands."

"I understand. It's an art, one that should be preserved and honored."

"The Feds never should have told people how to use their corn crops," Archibald said. "Prohibition's mess proved that."

"I've been told the State's now encouraging some not-for-profit brewers to maintain the high art of the best old bootleggers as part of our cultural heritage," Mike said, laughing and sipping the gift.

"Philemon has concerns that need to be honored. He wants his meeting with the Feds to be as secret as possible," George said.

"I'll pass on Philemon's wishes to the FBI. It would probably be better for him to meet with Jason at night in his room at The Western. What do you think?" Mike asked.

George rubbed his stiff neck. "That would help. Not many people would see them there as long as Philemon's careful," George said. "Heidi thinks he'll be cautious."

Archibald poured some more brew into George's now-empty glass. "The least number of people who see him, the better. He's right to be worried about some of Dave's contacts spotting him."

"I'm sure Jason will agree." Mike took the bottle handed to him and poured another small drink. "I doubt you can buy any brew to match this. Here's to local art and our hunting success."

George lifted his glass and proposed another toast. "Here's to a successful Blackmun hunt. What do you think of having Philemon ask Isaiah to introduce him to the gambling operation? Philemon knows not to reveal why."

Archibald grunted. "Isaiah might turn him down. I think he's learned his lesson. He should have known better."

Mike nodded. "I agree that it would be good to keep Isaiah out of the loop. Best not tell anybody who doesn't need to know."

George rubbed the back of his neck again. "I thought so. I'm worried that Dave might pressure Isaiah. He's in deep debt to Blackmun."

Mike took another sip from his glass. "Yeah, I agree." He savored the taste. "This is mighty fine moonshine. You're sure Isaiah doesn't try to make money off this?"

"Isaiah's careful. He doesn't offer this to anybody but family and close friends. It's not quite as good as what his pa made, but it's pretty near."

Mike smiled. "I'm glad to be considered a close friend. I don't see how this brew could be much better. It's smooth as silk." Mike said. "Give Isaiah my compliments."

"I'll pass on your praise. But you two need to pound into Philemon to be careful. Emphasize the need for secrecy. If he's caught, Isaiah will be in trouble anyway. Best if he can plead ignorance," Archibald said.

The others nodded.

"You boys want to help shell some warnuts? I've got to pick enough meats for Serafina to make a cake. I'm almost finished. We better fix some of those bushy-tails first, though, so we can have them for dinner."

After they finished skinning and cleaning the squirrels in the back yard, Archie went back to walnut cracking.

"Tell us what to do. I'll take these squirrels to Mamaw and come back to help," George said.

"Well, Mike can man the crusher and I'll pick the meats out. When you come back, you can help me."

George took his booty to his grandmother. "Mamaw, we've

brought you some more squirrels. Is that good enough to get invited to eat?"

"You know it is. Is that Mike Barton with you?"

"Yes, Ma'am. We hunted over at my woods this morning. I hope it's not too late to have some of these for your meal."

"No problem, Honey, if they're cleaned. I'll fix four for dinner I ain't fixed meat yet. How's your papaw coming along with them warnuts?"

"He's about finished. I'm supposed to help."

"You run along, then. I'll soak these squirrels. You get back and speed up the nutcracking. The sooner I get those nut meats, the sooner I can finish this cake."

With George helping, the walnut cracking proceeded at a rapid rate. Soon they had enough nutmeats for the cake. Archibald took them to Serafina while Mike and George waited on the porch.

"I'll try to call Jason this afternoon from my home phone. We have a code worked out just in case there's a bug I've missed," Mike said.

"Okay, I'm planning to inspect Philemon's site again late next week. To go too often would raise suspicion, although in a real emergency I can pretend to be looking for a special bird. They'll think I'm nuts, but it won't be the first time. Let me know when you get instructions."

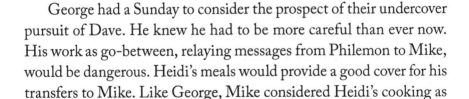

George had a Sunday to consider the prospect of their undercover pursuit of Dave. He knew he had to be more careful than ever now. His work as go-between, relaying messages from Philemon to Mike, would be dangerous. Heidi's meals would provide a good cover for his transfers to Mike. Like George, Mike considered Heidi's cooking as a sweetener that made their danger less trying.

Still, it was Sunday. George felt light-headed. He didn't even worry about Heidi's scheduling their time together. Hoping to enjoy some respite from the intrigue they'd put into motion, he had promised to take Heidi birding after they ate the breakfast she was fixing.

Heidi opened the door before he could ring. "I was looking out the window and saw you pull up. Breakfast's on the table." She raised her face for his kiss and then pulled him to the table, where she had waffles on a platter.

George could smell bacon cooking. "I'm as hungry as a bear coming out of hibernation."

"Help yourself to a waffle and butter, syrup, or jelly." She walked to the stove and came back with a tray holding a plate of bacon and a couple of glasses of cranberry juice.

George feasted his eyes on the spread. "If you weren't so pretty, I'd propose anyway just to get breakfasts like this."

Heidi smirked. "So the old saw is right, the way to a man's heart *is* through his stomach."

"I've already proposed. The cooking just sweetens the deal."

Heidi sat down. She reached over to touch his hand. "That's true. You're on probation until you can be trusted. Even a probationer deserves a good breakfast." After she ate a few bites, Heidi added, "And this *is* a good breakfast,"

After George ate more than he should have, they headed out to his truck. "We're too late for the dawn chorus, two hours and a season too late. But that's no problem. I'm taking you hawk watching. You don't have to get up early for it. You just find a good spot, then sit and wait. It's even easier if you have a tower or chairs to sit on," George said.

"Do we have a tower to sit on?"

"We do. We have an old tower up on Black Mountain. We'll drive up there, sit, and wait for the hawks. They use the mountain ridges.

Heidi gave him a quizzical look. "What's special about mountain ridges?"

"The uplift of air along the ridge—the soaring hawks circle to find the thermals, the rising air. Broad-winged Hawks and the other soaring hawks form kettles, large numbers of birds circling, rising on the thermals. Sometimes, on good days, the sky can be full of hawks.

"Is this a good day?"

"It should be. We have sunshine to create rising air, and there's a cold front moving in from the northwest. That'll give them a tail wind. Conditions are right."

The drive up the mountain amidst a kaleidoscope of fall colors entranced Heidi. "What a beautiful view. It's like a rainbow brought to earth and spread out across the land."

"The maples are at their peak up here now. It's hard to beat the southern Appalachians for fall beauty. No place in the world has more species of hardwoods making fall color. We'll be sitting in the middle of an autumn canvas, looking out and down, seeing as far as Tennessee and North Carolina."

Reaching the fire tower, George parked, and they walked to the tower. Taking the lead, he warned Heidi." This tower's old, so be careful how you step."

Up on the tower, they saw what George had promised. "It's breath-taking," Heidi said as she took in the panorama.

George peered down and looked over to Fox Gap. He could see how much of what used to be trees in prime fall color denuded by surface mining. He felt a moment of anger when he remembered the lost beauty. To the southeast, through binoculars, he spied the building he had discovered on Dave Blackmun's mining site. His eyes were attracted to it by a great deal of traffic heading toward the building where he had found the ad for an interstate cockfight. Evidently an event was being held there that day.

"Heidi, look over to Fox Gap with your binoculars and then look down in the direction of Flat Gap. Do you see the reclaimed patch? It's in the middle of un-reclaimed land?"

Heidi lifted her binoculars. "I think I see it."

"There's a large building there. It's in the reclaimed area."

"That's where all those cars are going?"

"Yeah, there'll be gambling this afternoon and tonight. It's either a dogfight or a cockfight, or both. Blood lust will prompt big wagers.

Rod Mashburn will be running the gambling, but Dave must get a big share of the entrance fees and, I'll bet, a percentage of the gambling take. We'll let Mike know what we've seen."

George looked toward the northeast. A large kettle of broad-winged hawks caught his eye.

"Look north over the ridge. Our first broad-wings are coming. And look there to your left, there's a Cooper's hawk circling."

"It made a dive at one of the broad-wings. Is it hunting another hawk?" Heidi asked.

"Just having a bit of fun. The don't fight each other in migration."

Heidi raised her arm. "George, look right, that's a different hawk."

George looked where Heidi pointed. "A merlin... A merlin. Good spotting.... See how fast it flies. It's a falcon. Look at those narrow wings. That shows it's a strong flyer. The broad-wings are buteos. They soar well, but aren't strong flyers. They depend on the uplift."

Heidi looked up. "The soaring hawks are going over."

"They're gliding, seeking another thermal to rise on."

"This is fun. Is it always like this?"

George hesitated. He felt a need to be honest. Not every day was like this. "No, when hawks don't come, it can be boring, unless there're other birds to see, but this is a good day." He put his hand on her shoulder. "You're my good luck charm."

The hawks kept coming all afternoon. They hardly had time to eat the lunch Heidi had brought. When the sun was beginning to drop to the west, hawks were settling in the trees for the night. By then, the parking area at the Pit was full, and cars were parking in the grass. George could hardly believe his eyes. He took a closer look with his spotting scope. He could see Virginia and Kentucky license plates side by side.

"This is a banner day for the Pit. Look at the crowd now, while there's still enough light. We'd better leave now. I don't want to navigate the road down the mountain in the dark." He collected his gear and headed to the steps.

Heidi took a last look at the Pit before she followed George down the tower steps. "I'm amazed that so many people find the blood-letting of dumb animals exciting."

George looked up at her as they descended the tower. "It stimulates their gambling. I reckon Dave Blackmun has a better idea of what blood-lust people are subject to than you do. You always find the best in people. He finds the worst."

Heidi scowled. "Maybe so, but I think he should be stopped."

Chapter 17

That Sunday Philemon Mullins attended The Holy Lamb Tabernacle as he regularly did. This Sunday, however, he had an additional purpose beyond his worship. He hoped to persuade Isaiah Timmons to introduce him to Dave Blackmun's den, the Pit at Flat Gap.

As usual, the service at The Tabernacle began with hymn singing led by Fred MacCloud. He lined out the hymns. Fred intoned the lines in a strong baritone. Then the congregation sang them. He always began with his favorite hymn,

> *Some have fathers gone to glory*
> *Won't you tell me if you know?*

The congregation sang the lines and Fred lined the next two.

> *Will our fathers know their children*
> *When to heaven they shall go?*

Fred lined out that hymn and several more hymns before he felt the congregation were properly prepared for Lamb o' God's message. Then Fred called on old Jeems Wright, who got up and gave a fervent prayer for the preacher, the preaching, and the reception of it by the congregation. His words lit up the bare walls of the Tabernacle, whose starkness shouted the absence of idolatry.

Lamb o' God Flannary strode to the pulpit. He bowed his head in a silent prayer, and in the hush he lifted his head and thundered: "I come to prepare you for the Lamb o' God! Sinners, hearken to the call. You've a choice to make. Will you be washed in the blood o' the Lamb or will you burn in Hell's fire?"

Several members of the congregation moaned in response.

"We have a beautiful land. God has given us beauty above ground and riches beneath. We've had these riches snatched away from us in the past by greedy locusts from outside. Now they are within our reach, but there's some among us not satisfied with getting this wealth in a way pleasing to the Lord. Not like our brethren Brother Fred MacCloud and Brother Philemon Mullins, who mine within the law and reclaim the land in a manner pleasing to God. They're men who give the Lord his fair share." Murmurs of agreement greeted these words. Philemon felt his conversation with Lamb o' God must have prompted this sermon.

"Now, there's some who rape the land and take the riches and lay them at the door of Satan. They tempt God's children to gambling and whoring and the worship of Mammon. They even engage in murder for hire." He emulated a gunshot by banging his fist on the pulpit.

Taken by surprise, some of the congregation gasped. One old lady, roused from her nap yelled, "Amen, Lord, deliver me."

"Brethren and sistren, have you been washed in the blood of the Lamb?

Have you been up that Hill of Cavalry? Aaah now, there be sinfulness in this world. Hit'll grab you when you least suspect it. Climb that hill. Don't stay on the wide valley track. It leads to Hell."

Philemon Mullins said to himself. "Lamb o'God told me to put on God's armor when I confront the Devil. I'm aiming to win."

"Take the riches God has laid out for you, but treat the land with tenderness. Put it back better than you found it. Please the Lord with the beauty you create in restitution." He raised his hand." Let the Lord smile."

The preacher lowered his hand and smiled as he lifted his eyes to Heaven. "I feel I'm being lifted up on the wings of the Great Speckled Bird. I feel the Spirit lifting me. God ain't against mining. He wants his children to be fed. Let those dozers hum, but don't forget the needy and the Lord when that black stuff turns to gold. Above all, leave the land as if it were a paradise the Lord would like to walk in of a morning, and don't sell your soul to Mammon and those that would leave our beautiful land a desert. Fight evil. Be washed in the blood o' the Lamb."

The preacher continued in the same vein for another half an hour. His sermon concluded, Lamb o'God led the congregation in reciting the Lord's prayer. Then he opened the King James Bible:

"Listen to a reading from the Holy Book: 'No man can serve two masters ... You cannot serve both God and Mammon.' Listen, and serve the Lord."

✦✦✦✦✦✦

Isaiah Timmons congratulated himself that the stripping of his land done by his cousin Moon was beautiful enough to satisfy the Lord as Philemon Mullins approached him after Lamb o' God Flannary's sermon.

"Isaiah, how're things going? That sermon breathed the Holy Spirit. I feel good about the righteousness of my mining. *And about my mission for the FBI.* You having any more trouble with Dab? Any more bodies turn up? You look depressed."

Isaiah shrugged. "Not too much trouble, George had a talk with him about his explosives the day Cameron's body was found. He's talked to him aagain."

Noting a lack of vitality in Isaiah's voice, Philemon tried to show concern. "As your dad used to say, the Devil's in the details. Dab and Dave are a real pair, but Dave's downright evil."

Isaiah waved his hand as if brushing away a bad thought. "Tell me about it. Dave ain't real forgiving. I wouldn't be stripping again if I didn't have to pay a debt to that bastard."

Philemon nodded. "He sure ain't Christian. Did you run up that debt out at Dave's place at Flat Gap?"

Isaiah grunted. "Yeah, I wish I'd never seen that hell-hole. How did you find out about it? Dave warns us to keep our mouths shut except to people who want what he's providing. And he don't fool around getting back at those who cross him."

Philemon looked around to make sure nobody was nearby. "Well, I have a favor to ask. You may not want to do it."

"What's that?"

"I'd like you to take me out to the Devil's den to get what he's offering. I'm curious about what goes on there."

Isaiah began to sweat. He wiped his brow. "Aw, no, now. You're my friend. I don't want you to get into trouble like I'm in. I lost a ton of money gambling on those fights, Honey. It's my Christian duty to warn you of the danger."

Noting his friend's concern, Philemon laughed and gave a thumbs up. "I see you're really worried about me. I'm not planning to lose much money. I just want to see the seamy side of our county for myself. I might even be able to find somebody with land to strip that hasn't signed up with Dave."

Isaiah made a fist. "I told you, I already owe too much. I hate that place. It brings out the worst in people."

Philemon persisted. He grabbed Isaiah's arm. "You just need to vouch for me this one time. I'll pay for any gambling losses you take on as long as you promise not to go in over four hundred dollars."

"That's real money. Why do you want to go into that den of iniquity? That's what Lamb o' God was preaching about just now. That was a powerful sermon."

"That's right. His sermon stirred my interest. I want to face the Devil, defy him, and quench my desire."

Isaiah growled. "I find it hard to resist that desire. That's one reason I don't want to go back there. That place has caused me nothing but trouble. Sally makes it clear she thinks I've been a fool."

"I'll drag you away if you get in over the four hundred dollars I'm fundin,' You know I'm a man of my word."

"Okay, I owe you for standing by me when I needed a helping hand. You lent me what I needed without asking questions. I'll do it as a favor, but if you see me getting the lust for gambling again, promise you'll get me out of there. Swear on the Bible you won't let me get in any deeper."

Philemon pulled his Bible from his coat pocket and put his hand on it. "I swear by the cross and this holy book. I promise I'll get you out of there before you add to your debt. I'll threaten to out you to Sally. If necessary, I'll do it."

"I know you're a man of your word, Philemon, so I'll go with you." He shook Philemon's extended hand.

"Okay, that's settled." Philemon grinned. "The next time a big gambling weekend arrives, let me know. I'll pick you up and we'll visit Blackmun's den of iniquity. I'll confront the Devil in his den."

Philemon Mullins hoped he could do his job and get Isaiah out of the Pit before he lost too much money. He wouldn't mind losing eight hundred dollars. The FBI would pay for that, but he didn't want to bear the guilt of getting Isaiah hooked on gambling again. Still, he had his marching orders from Lamb o'God. *I'm prepared to be a soldier for the Lord.*

Chapter 18

George had kept Dave Blackmun's Winding Fork site in his inspection portfolio so that he could keep an eye on Dave, who had a history of extending his stripping beyond its legal boundaries. George had postponed his regular inspection of Dave Blackmun's strip job as long as possible. This overcast morning he was on his way through fog to his unpleasant task. The one site of Dave's that George still inspected was adjacent to his five hundred acres. Seeing devastation approaching his woodland made him nauseous.

Besides having to deal with Dave, a task unpleasant enough, George had to watch as the land around his hunting grounds became gradually denuded and not reclaimed. Blackmun was working to make his hunting land a so-called "island in the sky" with nothing but un-reclaimed mined land around it. By leaving old pieces of equipment around, Dave could postpone reclamation for years while he applied pressure on George, whose acres would no longer be as productive of wildlife if they were surrounded by barren land.

As he drove up to Dave's mining site, George could see Blackmun's black truck. He would have to confront Dave, a bad way to start his day's work. Through the fog he saw Dave walk from behind his vehicle and climb on a D-12 bulldozer as George drove up. He reviewed his folder for this site and prepared a citation to give Dave. He wouldn't bother with a full inspection today. Answering the complaints people had lodged would be enough today. As he got out of his vehicle, he could smell the acrid smoke of a recent explosion.

Blackmun started the 'dozer and headed toward George, who stopped and stood when he reached Dave's truck. He felt sure Blackmun wouldn't destroy his own vehicle to hurt him, but his chest tightened as he watched the huge machine come closer. The 'dozer stopped a few feet from Landsetter, whose stomach growled.

George passed gas, spit his gum at the ground and looked Blackmun in the eye. "Morning, Dave. Still cutting things a little close, I see. I think you're working a little too loose with your explosives, too."

Dave scowled as he climbed down. "I don't see anybody around here complaining but you."

George crossed his arms. "You don't have to listen to all of the complaints we get at the reclamation office."

Dave growled, made a fist, and shook it at George. "Okay, I'll tell the men to cut back some. Anything else to complain about."

"Yeah, some of the people living below your job say that they're getting too much mud when it rains." George rubbed the back of his neck. "You know you're supposed to do something to restrain run off."

Dave pointed to George's woodland. "You haven't had any run off on your land, have you?"

"No, but all of my land is above your job. You know that."

Dave rocked back on his heels and laughed. His laugh sounded like a horse whinnying. "Yeah, now that you mention it." He pointed to George's woods again. "Have you changed your mind about selling me your mineral rights?"

Hands tightening on his belt, George spoke through taut lips. "You know I've told you they're not for sale and why. There's no law against surface mining, but there's no law saying I have to mine."

Dave frowned. "That's true, but it would make you a rich man. And not doing it could prove dangerous."

George felt his face growing hot. "You planning to blow me up on one of my inspections?"

"Be careful about giving me ideas like that, George. You know how easily that could happen. I wouldn't want to hurt the tailback I blocked for when we played football. You got the cheers for running through those big holes. Ain't that so?"

"Yeah, I guess using a dozer's not your style. I'd expect you to challenge me to a gun fight."

"That went out a long time ago. Shit, I don't like the odds. I hear you're a crack shot."

"At any rate, I've given you a warning about the run off. I don't think we need to drive over the site today. Couldn't see much in this fog. You need to take care of this citation and ease off on the explosives. Here's your warning" George handed Blackmun a slip of paper and turned to leave.

Dave laughed. "So long inspector," he yelled as George put ground between them. "Watch out for Fallen Rocks. He may get you."

Without much joy, George climbed into his vehicle. His stomach ached. He recalled the tired joke about Fallen Rocks, the young Indian chief in search of his lost love, used to explain boulders on mountain highways.

George had promised Philemon Mullins he'd stop by his surface mine that day, so he made that his next inspection. He wouldn't have much to worry about Philemon's, and he would find out what progress the new undercover agent was making. Once there, George let out a huge sigh as he got out of his truck. He could feel himself relaxing. Other than the hum of the dozers and the smell of the exhausts of the coal trucks going by, this was a peaceful, clean operation.

It was obvious from the tidy appearance of Mullins' site that this was a more carefully managed mine than Dave's. Philemon greeted George with a grin and an outstretched hand.

"Get in my truck. I'll drive you around the job. I have something to tell you, and you can see the progress I'm making with reclamation," Philemon said.

Once they were moving, Philemon filled George in on his progress. "I've made an arrangement for Isaiah to introduce me to the fight pit out at Flat Gap. He says a major bout of cockfighting and dogfighting is scheduled for this coming weekend."

George gave Philemon an intense look. "Are you ready to get some evidence?"

Philemon slowed down as he turned his vehicle. "Isaiah says we'll see handbills promoting the fights but won't be allowed to keep any. During the fights, a program will be posted on an overhead screen. The FBI has given me equipment to tape speech and a mini-camera to take pictures without being detected. We'll see how well they work." After several more minutes, Philemon pulled up beside George's truck.

"Be careful. Don't do anything to make Dave's men suspicious," George said.

"Don't worry. I'll be careful. I'll pass what I get to you next week."

That night, George and Heidi were to go out to dinner at Possum Hunt in Hardwood. Mike Barton was to meet them there. He was dating Mabel, a friend of Heidi's who worked at the restaurant, so his meeting them would not attract much attention.

Heidi wore a pale blue outfit that accentuated the beauty of her auburn hair and hazel eyes as well as her curvaceous figure. George gave a wolf whistle.

"You look ready to step out of a fashion magazine. You'll create a sensation at Possum Hunt."

Heidi whirled around, showing off her outfit. "I've already created the sensation I was aiming for."

"I won't be the last to admire you tonight. I hope I don't have to fight off any unwelcome admirers."

On the drive, Heidi glowed in the setting sun. George had trouble keeping his eyes on the road. and skidded around a particularly bad curve, "I won't enjoy my dinner if I'm a nervous wreck, Honey. Keep your eyes on the road."

Possum Hunt was full of diners who had come for music from a local band, the Pine Ridge Ramblers, as well as food. Some couples were dancing on the part of the floor cleared of tables and chairs. After they were seated at the restaurant, Mike Barton sauntered over from the bar, beer in hand. Heidi smiled at him, "Hello, Mike."

Mike grinned. "Well, look who's here. George, where did you find this gorgeous woman?"

George stood up and slapped Mike on the back. "Finders keepers. Sit down while we wait to be served."

"Thanks." Then, in a much lower voice, Barton asked, "What do you have for me?"

"Only that Philemon Mullins has convinced Timmons to introduce him to the gambling pit this weekend, "George said. "There's supposed to be a lot of activity. Philemon says he'll use the equipment the FBI gave him. I'll pick up anything he gets next week."

A waitress came to take their drink order. Mike stood. "I'll see you around, ole Buddy. Nice to see you, too, Heidi. I envy old George here."

"Sure thing," George said, as Heidi smiled and murmured a goodbye. When their drinks came, George pulled out his flask to fortify them.

Heidi leaned back in her chair. "Don't put much. These mountain roads have lots of curves," she said. "I want us to make it home. On the drive over here you spent too much time ogling my curves, and didn't pay enough attention to the highway's."

"Okay, I'll take it easy." He honored Heidi's request to keep the amount small.

When their dinner arrived and they began eating, Heidi turned the conversation to the Pit. "I've been reading about cockfighting and dogfighting. It's not a pretty picture, and the gambling that goes on at those fights is fierce enough for addicts to lose a great deal of money. It's too gory for dinner conversation. I was surprised. It was worse than I expected.

George nodded as he wiped his lips. "Well, I'm not surprised. The animals are often forced to fight to the death. Betting on those fights is what got Isaiah into such heavy debt." After they finished their meal, Heidi returned to the subject of the Pit.

The animal fights aren't all that's going on at the Pit. "I've heard rumors about prostitutes. High-priced women from New York."

107

"I'm not surprised about that either." George saw the quizzical look Heidi gave him. He rushed to add, "Not that I have first-hand knowledge, but I know of a lot of strip miners who go to New York to hire expensive women. Moon told me about special flights from the Roanoke airport. Maybe Dave Blackmun has used his contacts to bring some of the women down here. That would put him afoul of the Mann Act." Eager to change the conversation, George asked Heidi to dance and enjoyed her scent of roses as they danced to *The Tennessee Waltz.*

When the dance was over, Heidi returned to the subject of imported women. "I wonder if Arachne Smith, the woman Dave introduced to us at Enchiladas, is one of those women from New York."

"She might be. She's good-looking enough to tempt men."

Heidi raised eyebrows and stuck her finger in his chest. "I hope you're not tempted. George, you're blushing."

"I have enough temptation sitting right here. I don't need any more."

Heidi giggled as she grasped his arm. "I wish Jennifer were here to hear that."

As the evening at Possum Hunt wore on, George and Heidi's conversation turned to one of their common interests: surface mining.

"You're having success persuading mine owners to use good practices. You should be pleased."

"Sometimes I get discouraged. I spend so much time encouraging mine operators to put land back into an environmentally friendly and productive form. I try to appeal to their best instincts. I refuse to admit Dave Blackmun represents what mountain people are really like," George said.

Heidi took his hand in hers. "I have to admit that it's better to have local people rather than outside interests profiting from the mining. In the past too much of the wealth here went to Philadelphia, New York, and London."

George nodded. "Let's forget about mining, gambling, and animal fighting. Let's enjoy the rest of the evening," George said.

Heidi smiled and touched his hand. "That's a good idea. The music sounds inviting."

"How about another dance?" George asked, eager to hold her close again, taking her hand and pulling her close to enjoy the scent of roses.

Soon George and Heidi were dancing cheek to cheek to the band's rendition of *Raindrops Keep Falling on My Head* and enjoying their closeness, the Dave Blackmuns of the world forgotten.

Chapter 19

Two days later, as they watched the rain and fog outside Heidi's picture window, Heidi broached the subject of dog and cock fighting. "It turns my stomach. I don't like the idea of people screaming and betting while animals kill each other," she said as she finished setting the table. "Their owners give them drugs to reduce the bleeding so they can fight longer."

George cleared his throat. "It's an outlet for the blood lust that's part of humankind. I haven't thought about it much until lately. I went to school with guys whose families raised fighting cocks and pit bulls. My folks didn't hold with doing that, but you know how young guys like to go with the crowd."

Heidi wrinkled her nose. "The bloodier the action, the higher the betting from what I read."

Shifting in his chair, George admitted he saw problems with the fighting and gambling. "I'm sure Rod Mashburn likes the gambling. He's cynical, willing to offer what his customers want. He's in it for the money and claims the house always wins."

Heidi gave a snort. "The damn owners don't really care about the animals. I think it's ironic we use the term bestial for behavior no wild animal would engage in. People breed these animals to be vicious to please their dark human desires."

George stood up and went to look out the window. He remained silent for several minutes. He felt obliged to defend mountain people.

"Maybe it's worthwhile to let those desires out every now and then," he said.

Heidi disagreed. "You don't really mean tat. Not the way they're doing at the Pit. It just encourages bad behavior—gambling frenzy, drugs, and murder all increase as the bloodletting does—the animals are trained to kill. Owners put sharp metal spurs on their roosters to increase their ability to inflict injuries."

George didn't want Heidi to think he supported the fighting. He sat down beside her. "They don't raise pit bulls to be pets, though some dog owners pretend pit bulls are maligned—c;laim they make good pets, then act surprised when the dogs kills somebody."

"No, I'm sure they don't raise them for pets. They raise them to fight. Then they just toss them aside when they can't fight any more. Some sadistic owners torture animals no longer able to fight."

George felt uncomfortable defending behavior he didn't approve of, but he knew and respected people who bet on the fights. "That's cruel, all right, but I can't believe most people watching the fights are really bad. I know Isaiah's a good man, even if he let himself be suckered into a big debt. He says gambling's a fever. Blood-letting raises the temperature."

Heidi stopped taking food off the stove and gave George a long look. "Are you defending these fights and the gambling?"

George rose and paced across the room. "No, I'm just trying to explain why some people I know to be good folks are lured into bad behavior. Dog and cock fighting go back at least as far as Shakespeare—and beyond. They're part of the culture."

He tried to explain to Heidi how he felt as he paced. "Gambling and bear baiting are what his plays competed with. Not everybody is as evil as Dave, but we all have a dark side."

Heidi waved a finger at George for emphasis. "I'm glad that everyone isn't as depraved as Blackmun."

"That's two of us. Dave sees himself as justified. He's just providing a public service. He thinks everyone is as inhumane as he is. His dad taught him that number one is the only one that counts. I'm sure Dave derives sadistic pleasure from seeing his clientele slipping into trouble—probably sees murdering people who don't pay their debts as a moral imperative."

Heidi shook her head. "I'm getting indigestion just thinking of it. I guess we'd better drop this subject so we can enjoy the meal I've spent so much time preparing," she said as she returned to setting the table.

George poured two glasses of the red wine he'd brought. "I agree. The dinner sure smells delicious. Anyway, let's drink to the success of Philemon this weekend. We both want him to succeed and help put Dave and the Pit out of business."

Heidi smoothed her apron and took one of the glasses of wine. "I'll raise my glass to that." After they had completed the toast, Heidi waved George to the table. "I took the recipe for this meal from a cookbook. I've been looking for ways to cook healthy food. I don't want you to get fat. It's supposed to be a healthy but very tasty Brunswick stew. I have apple pie for dessert."

George chuckled as he hugged her. "That's a great combination, but I hope you didn't use any fighting chickens for the meat. They're tough."

Heidi laughed as she pushed him away. "Very funny—now pour more wine while I put the rest of the food on the table. Do you suppose Philemon will collect enough evidence this week?"

George sat down and savored the aroma of the stew. "Philemon thinks he can, based on his talks with Isaiah. I'll find out when I inspect his strip job next week."

Listening to Montovani's music after dinner, George put unpleasant things from his mind as the soothing music of the Moonlight sonata concentrated his attention on Heidi and on their attraction to one another. George was not content with the progress he was making trying to convince Heidi to marry him, but told himself she was worth the wait.

He admitted to himself Heidi's caution was justified. His stomach turned as he felt feelings of guilt as Jennifer came to mind. He was still trying to put away thoughts of Jennifer even as he enjoyed Heidi's closeness. *Jennifer's good-looking and vivacious—and a firecracker in bed. But she's set on winning a Pulitzer. I'm just another source for her pen. I can't settle anymore for the kind of casual sex Jennifer offers.*

Shaking these thoughts out of his mind, he focused his attention on Heidi. "That was a great meal," George said before he kissed Heidi and eased onto her couch.

"I'm glad you think so. I'll try some more recipes from that book." She took off her apron and sat beside him, returning his kiss. "I've been thinking of all of the beautiful scenery and birds you've been showing me. These mountains *are* beautiful. It seems a shame to tear them up."

"I've also shown you how they can be put back to be beautiful again—after the coal's been mined."

Heidi sighed. "It's a shame some miners don't want to make the effort to restore the nature they've disturbed."

George patted her shoulder. "There're less of them that way all of the time. I keep telling them that, with the correct planning, they can make more money doing things the right way."

"You're making progress," Heidi said, placing her hand on his cheek as if to comfort him.

"You said yourself my cousin Moon is our poster boy for mining within the law. I just wish we could get the laws strengthened. Most of the miners follow the law now, and a lot go beyond it to do the right kind of reclamation. Moon was making money in gobs mining the right way. It took Gladys to persuade Moon to stop and move away."

"Someone told me she's Moon's second wife, that he was tried and acquitted for the murder of his first wife."

George nodded. "That's right. One of our cousins did the murder. That's sort of reassuring. In New York or some other big city you'd probably be killed by a complete stranger."

He thought Heidi gave him an incredulous look. "You have an odd sense of humor. How did Moon meet Gladys?"

George hesitated and coughed before he spoke. "He met her in New York."

Heidi changed the subject as if she felt she'd touched upon a sensitive topic. "When are you going to show me some more birds?"

"Why don't we put up some feeders in your back yard: You have a wooded area behind you. I'll bet we can attract a lot of birds you can watch from your picture window. Fall's almost over and birds are already in feeding flocks.

"What am I likely to see?"

"It should be easy to lure chickadees and titmice with black oil sunflower seeds. Millet will bring in finches and sparrows. If we put up a suet holder, you could interest a woodpecker or two as well as Carolina wrens. Let's go buy you some feeders and food. The stores are still open. We can put the feeders up this weekend."

"That sounds great. But I want you to take me hawk watching again soon."

"Then let's go tomorrow. We can put up your feeders Sunday."

"You want an extra day with me?"

"I'd rather spend the day watching for hawks with you than scouting the woods for deer stands."

Heidi gave him a very long embrace and a kiss with her tongue deep in his mouth. "Some people would say you're spending entirely too much time with me, Mr. Landsetter,"

"What do you say?"

"I'm still thinking that over. I wonder what Jennifer would say?"

"I don't care what Jennifer would say. I'm in love with you. I'm going to do my best to convince you I'm through with. Jennifer." It occurred to George as he said this that he must first convince himself he was through with Jennifer.

Chapter 20

On a sunny Saturday afternoon in early November, Philemon Mullins picked up Isaiah Timmons and drove to Flat Gap. "How many people usually show up for one of these fights?" Philemon asked.

Thinking of the gambling temptation ahead, Philemon was feeling sick at his stomach. He'd just taken an antacid and hoped it would help. What size of crowd should we expect?"

"It varies—fifty to five hundred or more. Local fights draw less than those that draw cocks and dogs from both Virginia and Kentucky. By the way, we have to pay a fifty-dollar entrance fee at the door."

"Don't worry. I'll pay for both of us," Philemon said.

Isaiah groaned and shifted in his seat.

Seeing his friend's discomfort, Philemon voiced his concern. "Are you okay?"

"Just a little stomach pain. I ain't looking forward to this. You know I'm afraid of my gambling weakness," Isaiah said.

"No problem. Just take it easy. I'll pull you out if necessary. What's the program today?" Philemon asked.

Timmons snorted disgust. "This is a cross border double-header."

"What's that?"

"Cock fights, followed by dog fights with contestants from both states. It should draw a big crowd. There's prize money and added rewards," Isaiah said.

"What are the added rewards?"

Isaiah grunted. "Free drinks. For those so inclined who have Dave's approval, there're special ladies who will entertain them."

"Prostitutes?"

"Not local girls—Dave brings in high-class women from New York. At least that's what I was told, and I've seen six or seven good-looking women at the Pit who appeared very stylish—certainly not local girls," Isaiah said, slapping his car seat for emphasis.

"I'm not interested in dealing with them. Did you have one of those women?"

Isaiah waved away the idea. "No way, Sally's enough woman for me."

Philemon turned into the road to the Pit a few minutes after one o'clock. The dust over the road ahead indicated he and Isaiah weren't the first arrivals. Before he parked, Isaiah had him drive around the building. In the back parking area, trucks and SUV's attached to trailers loaded with fighting cocks and pit bulls from Kentucky and Virginia sat side by side.

"There're the stars of the show," Isaiah said.

Philemon stopped and took some pictures with his small camera concealed in the small binoculars the FBI had provided him. He was careful to get photos of Kentucky and Virginia license plates side by side. *No point in Isaiah's knowing; The less he knows, the better.* When he finished his camera work, he turned back to Isaiah, who still looked a little sick.

"What's the survival rate for these animals?" Philemon asked.

"Less than sixty percent, I'd say. When the betting gets high, the bettors generally demand a fight to the finish. There's a big bone yard out back, I'm told. I've seen truckloads being hauled out of here after fights."

Philemon couldn't understand how Isaiah got involved in this mess. "Bloody business—how did you get involved? Your folks never raised fighting cocks or pit bulls."

"Lord, no. My ma was dead set agin it. She thought it part of the fast road to Hell. Sally feels the same. I was drinking with some fellows one night and let them talk me into going. I had a little too much drink and got carried away with the betting. I didn't have cash on hand to cover my foolishness."

"How much did you lose?"

"It wasn't my regular bets that did me in. Rod Mashburn's my cousin. He runs the regular house gambling. He made arrangements for me. It was my side bets on the cocks and the dogs with Dave Blackmun that did me in. He made me sign an agreement to let Dab Whacker strip my land before he'd take my note. He made some threats, and I buckled," Isaiah said.

"Have you gone back?

"Like a fool—I thought I could get back some of my money. I just got in deeper."

"That's an old story," Philemon said.

"By that time, I hated the sight of blood and guts and suffering animals. I got sick just thinking about it."

"It sure went against your religion."

"Yeah, so I've quit cold turkey. That's why I didn't want to bring you. You better be careful. My cousin from over to Kentucky, Cameron MacCloud, got in over what he could pay. He fell for one of the women too. He's the one they found on Dab Whacker's job with a bullet through his head," Isaiah said.

"I'll try to be careful. I don't think the gambling will get to me— the stock market's gambling enough for me. If you begin to get the gambling fever and go over your four hundred limit, I'll haul you out. If you refuse to go, I'll threaten to tell your wife. I'll get her and bring her here if necessary."

"That's strong medicine. I hope I don't need it."

When they approached the entrance, a flyer for the event in a window touting the champion cocks and pit bulls from two states that would be competing caught Philemon's eye. He took several pictures of this advertisement with a tiny camera concealed in his shirt pocket.

At the door, past two armed guards, Isaiah vouched for Philemon, who paid their fifty-dollar entrance fees. They received ticket stubs from the man who took their money and marked their names in a ledger next to their seat numbers as another man stamped the back of their hands with the date.

Inside, an arena encircled with enough seats for perhaps a thousand people surrounded a circular pit covered with sawdust and bounded by a transparent plastic fence attached to metal posts. Isaiah pointed to these.

"This is a first-class operation. When the dogfights begin, they'll add another ring to the fence to keep the dogs in the pit. So the seats right at the pit are best for the cock fights but not as good for the dog fights."

"Are there offices and other rooms underneath the seats?" Philemon asked.

"Yeah. There's no wasted space. If you tire of the animal fights, there are gambling games underneath. You can do cards or machines. You can buy pot at any of those places. Rod handles that gambling and the pot. If you want other drugs, or women, you have to deal with Dave's people," Isaiah said.

Waiting for the fights to begin, Timmons guided Philemon Mullins through the areas where gambling was already being conducted: bingo, blackjack, poker, craps, keno, roulette, and slot machines—each had a space. All of them were becoming crowded as more and more people were arriving and seeking action before the fighting began. As the time for the cockfights drew near, the crowd started thinning.

"We'd better go up to our seats. We don't want to lose money by being late to get to our seats." Isaiah said, pulling Philemon's arm. He led the way back up to the arena and the seats numbered on their ticket stubs.

"Our seats are wired so that we can bet on a fight during the first five minutes of the bout. There's also a place where you can make later side bets directly with Dave. That's why so much emphasis attaches to seat numbers. You don't want somebody else in your seat to run up a bill for you to pay," Isaiah said.

"We've got very good seats," Philemon said. We're in the third row. *I should get some very good pictures.* He was amazed. "This place sure gives people lots of opportunities to gamble."

"Tell me about it, good buddy, tell me about it. I've taken advantage of too many of them."

A voice on the intercom announced the first chicken fight promptly at two o'clock. Philemon turned on his recorder. "Our first contest features Letcher County champion Big Jack Red against Lee County's Range Master Jeb." From an opening at each end of the oval, a man lowered a rooster into the pit and pushed it toward its adversary.

Isaiah appraised the fighters. "These are good-looking gamecocks."

"Those birds have huge metal spurs attached to their legs." Philemon said, as he quietly snapped some photos with his binocular camera. "Their combs have been cut off."

"Yeah, it's going to be a fight to the finish. The comb's removed so that the opponent can't grab hold of it. At the end of the fight, one or both will be dead or dying. There'll be a big purse and lots of wagers."

The cocks circled each other warily, lowering their heads and lifting their wings in threatening postures. Many people in the crowd soon began to cheer on the cocks they had bet on, and the amount of betting on each bird appeared on raised TV screens at each end of the seats.

"Look, Jeb drew first blood," Isaiah said, as Big Jack made a pass with his spurs and Jeb responded by raking Jack's breast with his.

Philemon bet five dollars on Range Master Jeb as he photographed the betting apparatus on his seat with his shirt camera and the screen where the betting totals were appearing with his binocular camera. It wasn't long before both birds were bloody and less active, though they continued the fight. In another five minutes, Jeb gouged out one of Big Jack's eyes. Big Jack responded by ripping the skin on Jeb's neck. The blood continued to flow.

With the mini-recorder provided by the FBI, Philemon recorded the yells and comments of the spectators as he looked around at the faces in the audience. To his surprise, some of the loudest onlookers demanding blood were women. Already fighting back disgust at the bloodiness, Philemon was appalled by the horrible faces and screams prompted by blood lust. Their ugliness was compounded by the foul odors coming from them. Fighting his nausea, Philemon used his binocular camera on the audience. The scene reminded him of a panel of an Hieronymus Bosch painting. Before long, he could not contain his nausea. He grabbed a conveniently placed barf bag and threw up.

Then, with a finishing blow, Jeb struck Big Jack's blind side, ripping his breast open to the bone. Bleeding profusely, the mortally wounded bird staggered in circles and collapsed as Philemon managed to photograph Jack's death throes though his view through the binocular camera sickened him again. Those who had bet on Jeb cheered. The owners removed their birds as employees raked the sawdust in the pit and spread new shavings where needed.

Gamecock fights and bloodletting went on for three hours. Then the voice on the intercom announced a thirty-minute intermission. The time for dogfights had arrived.

As he and Isaiah stretched, Philemon took some more pictures of the crowd. "I hope the dog fights aren't as bloody as the cock fights."

"They're worse. Pit bulls are large. They have more blood to spill."

"Then I'm not going to eat anything else. I might get sick again. How are your bets going?"

"Appears you've brought me good luck. I'm a good bit ahead."

Later, as Philemon watched the dogs' blood flowing, he was glad he hadn't eaten more. He managed to keep working during the first dogfight. He was afraid he was going to have dry heaves as he watched the dogs ripping each other. During the second fight, when one dog's entrails were ripped out, he did. As he watched the horrible fight and the equally horrible crowd, Philemon imagined this must be what Hell looks like. He had forgotten the bloody dogfight he'd witnessed as a teenager. It all came back vividly to him now. Despite finding the gory business sickening, he had continued to take pictures and record damning evidence of interstate gambling. Now he thought he had collected enough evidence; he turned his attention to Isaiah, who had been betting a great deal.

"Let's go, Isaiah."

"I've been lucky. I've won over five thousand dollars. Let's stay a little longer."

Philemon nudged his companion, who seemed to be oblivious to everything but his betting. "Come on. It's time to go—while you're ahead. I've lost most of my four hundred dollars, and my stomach is giving me trouble. I can't take much more of this. The people sicken me as much as the bloody animals."

"But I'm on a tremendous winning streak. Just give me a few more minutes."

"I don't want to tell Sally, but I will if you don't leave now."

"I don't want to leave."

"I know. The gambling lust is eating at you. I'm feeling guilty about talking you into bringing me. We leave now, or else."

A reluctant Isaiah cursed. Philemon was well known to be a man of his word. Dragging himself up, Isaiah followed his friend to cash his winnings and then walk out of the Pit. Outside, Philemon took a deep breath of the fresh air and raised his hands in thanks to God for bringing him safely through the ordeal. On the drive back to Isaiah's, Philemon watched his passenger gradually recover from his gambling lust and become the calm, reasonable man he called his friend.

As they turned into Isaiah's driveway, the recovering addict turned to Philemon. "Here's the money you gave me."

Philemon waved the money away. He figured Isaiah had earned it, and the FBI could afford it.

"Thanks for getting me out of there. I was lucky to have you pull me out while I was ahead."

"I was responsible for your relapse. I'm glad I could pull you out ahead. You can use that cash to help square you with Blackmun. I won't ask you to take me back there."

"I see that I was right to quit cold turkey. I have to stay away from gambling."

"I'm sure Sally will be glad to hear that. Don't go back."

Philemon waved goodbye and drove home, satisfied he had done all that he had agreed to do. He had bearded the Devil in his den, gathered damning evidence, and come away almost unscathed, except for his stomach, resolved not to do any more undercover work. The FBI could afford the dollars he'd lost, and the hundred dollars of entrance fees. The bloody combatants and the blood-lusting audience were still too vivid in his mind. He feared his memories of the event would haunt his sleep for a long time. He vowed to keep an eye on Isaiah to make sure he stayed away from the Pit. He'd ask Lamb o'God to have a talk with his friend.

Chapter 21

T he next Thursday, George could feel the weather changing as he stepped out of his vehicle. He reached back in his truck to pull out a jacket and get into it as he headed toward Philemon's mining activity. Moving some topsoil for reclamation, the mine owner was aboard a D-9 dozer. Philemon liked to keep a hand in his operations—unlike Dave Blackmun, who had branched out into so many other operations that he rarely worked hands-on at his mining sites. The dust lingering in the air and the acrid odor indicated Philemon's men had set off a blast that morning.

Philemon throttled down his dozer, turned it off, and leapt to the ground as George walked over from his truck. "I've been expecting you. I have some tapes and film for you." He walked over to his truck. Looking around to make sure nobody was watching them, he took out a small wrapped box and handed it to George. "I think there's enough evidence here to interest the FBI. Those were neat cameras they gave me."

"That was quick work." George took the package and hid it in the glove compartment of his truck and locked the vehicle.

Philemon shook his head. "I hope Isaiah doesn't relapse into gambling. I staked him to four hundred dollars. He had a run of good luck and made enough money to put a hole in his debts—over five thousand dollars. I had to pull him away from the fights. He truly is a gambling addict."

"I'll have a word with him—and with Sally. He's making more

than enough money on that stripping Dab's doing for him to pay off his debts to Dave and Rod. With those winnings he just made, he should have plenty to spare. Did anybody get suspicious about you? Do you want to go back?"

Philemon turned his head and spat. "No, I don't. You couldn't pay me enough to go back there. I lost a few hundred dollars of the FBI's money. It's a nasty business."

"I understand. I've been reliving some of my teenage visits to cockfights and dogfights," George said. "Did you get sick?"

"I threw up during the cockfights. If I'd eaten more, I'd have thrown up during the dogfights. As it was, I had the dry heaves. I hope I got enough evidence to satisfy the FBI. I definitely don't want to go back. I almost quit recording and photographing a couple of times, but I tried to be careful. Nobody seemed to notice what I was doing, not even Isaiah. He was too busy betting. Those cameras and the recorder the FBI provided worked fine."

"I'll be passing this information to Mike, and he'll get it to the FBI. You should be hearing something in a few weeks."

"Whatever they say, I'm finished with undercover work. That's definite. Let me take you around my job for an inspection now. I don't want any of my men getting suspicious about why we're meeting. No telling where Dave has eyes and ears."

"That's wise. I'll get in your truck." George followed Philemon to his pickup. From the acrid odor he still detected, he could tell Philemon had set off a blast to uncover coal that morning. "Let's do a quick run. It looks like a big cold front is coming in from the west."

"I'm expecting snow," Philemon said.

As they drove around Mullins' strip job, George saw some slate-colored juncos. "Look there; see those snowbirds? They've come down from the high country. They have white bills. Snowbirds from the north would have pink bills. Winter snow's not far away." He looked to the west and watched the dark clouds. The front covered the sky from horizon to horizon. He could smell the weather changing.

As George drove over to Heidi's after work that evening, he saw a few snowflakes falling on his windshield. *I knew snow was on the way when Philemon and I saw those snowbirds today. Tonight will be a good time to stay indoors. I'm glad I'm meeting Mike at Heidi's and not in some snow-covered field.*

When he rang Heidi's doorbell, she answered the door in her apron emblazoned with I Dig Coal Safely covering her blouse and slacks. He pulled her to him and kissed her as gentle snowflakes drifted down on them. "I saw snowbirds at Philemon's mining site today. Now look; they've brought the snow."

"Come on inside before we're covered."

Stepping inside, he encountered a delicious aroma created by spaghetti sauce and pumpkin pie as he took off his heavy jacket. "Something sure smells good. Have you gone all out for Mike?"

Heidi shook her head as she hung up his coat. "No, just an easy meal—spaghetti, a salad, and pumpkin pie for dessert. I didn't think I needed to do anything fancy. Why? Are you jealous? I thought Mike's your best friend."

"He is. I'm not jealous. I'm just a little worried because we haven't become engaged."

Heidi moved back to her stove. "You certainly sounded a bit put out. You know Mike has a steady girlfriend."

"Yeah, I guess I'm a little jealous at that. I don't know how I stand with you."

"We see a lot of each other."

George looked in the refrigerator and took out a beer. "I feel like my time with you is rationed. It's sure scheduled."

"I've told you that I'm the marrying kind of girl. The ball is in your court. You're on serve. I still feel like I'm in competition with Jennifer."

"She comes around only when she thinks I can help with a story she's researching."

Heidi took off her apron, "Apparently she seeks other kinds of help too. That's what I object to."

The doorbell rang. Heidi waved toward the door.

"Would you get the door? It's probably Mike. I'll put our meal on the table."

George let Deputy Barton in. As Mike took off his coat, George handed him Philemon's package. "Philemon thinks he has enough evidence in there to satisfy the FBI. When you pass it on, tell them not to rush. We'll be on the lookout for the next cross-border fights. We can tip them off when there's another big interstate contest. Philemon thinks Mann Act violations are involved, but he didn't get any evidence of that."

Mike cleared his throat as he stuffed the package in his coat pocket as he handed it to George. "Something sure smells good, and I'm hungry."

George laughed as he hung up Mike's coat. "That makes two of us."

"The FBI might be interested in what appears to be a sex and blackmail scheme," George said as they walked to the table. "Philemon thinks Blackmun is bringing down women from New York for commercial purposes and that Cameron MacCloud's murder might be connected to the prostitution."

"Hey, you guys, quit talking crime and come to eat," Heidi said.

Mike grinned. "The food sure does have a wonderful aroma. I brought a big appetite."

Heidi set a bowl of spaghetti sauce on the table beside the spaghetti noodles, the salad, and the garlic bread.

"George, would you please take the bottle of our local Strip Mine Red out of the fridge? I think some red wine will go well with the dinner."

Discussion of their undercover operation proceeded during dinner. Heidi glowed as her spaghetti disappeared. "This wine shows us that some good things come from surface mining. Who would have thought surface mines could produce a vintage that tastes smooth and fruity like this?"

"I'm glad to testify to one of the great ways to reclaim," George said as he poured some more wine in their glasses.

"Dave Blackmun will react violently if his illegal activities draw FBI action. He'll look for somebody to blame. I hope Philemon has been as careful as he claims," Mike said.

George nodded. "He says nobody noticed him. The FBI fixed him up with a couple of neat little cameras, one in a pair of small binoculars. If he didn't get enough evidence to satisfy the FBI, we'll probably have to find somebody else. Philemon quit."

Mike shook his head. "Did you try to get him to continue?"

"Philemon was very definite about not wanting to go back. He was sickened by the whole business. I've been recalling some of the fights I saw growing up. I don't want to relive those in person. It's bad enough recalling the memories I'd buried," George said.

Heidi walked over and patted his cheek. "I'm glad to hear you admit it. I wonder if that woman Dave introduced to us at Enchiladas might be one of the women he's brought down from New York."

George nodded. "Arachne Smith's a looker—and she isn't from around here."

Mike waved his hand across his brow. "I'm not going to worry about that. If we have sufficient evidence to convict him of moving animals across state lines for fighting and gambling, that should take the wind from Dave's sails. It'll be up to the FBI."

After an hour and a half, Heidi rose. "It's time for pumpkin pie." She served slices with whipped cream on top. She put some local maple syrup on the table; "If your piece isn't sweet enough, use this."

Nobody used much syrup.

"This sure is good," Mike said. George nodded but kept eating.

Later, when Mike said it was time for him to go to his night shift, Heidi packed another slice for him to take with him. "You might get hungry before your shift is over."

"Thanks, Heidi. George is a lucky fellow. Beauty, brains, and a great cook all in one package. Don't let this girl get away, Buddy."

George sighed, but grinned and adopted a mountain phrase. "I'm a-working on that."

Heidi laughed. "He's a difficult case, Mike."

After Heidi saw Mike to the door, she turned down the lights, put on some Anne Murray music and opened the drapes across the picture window. "Let's listen to the song about the junco while we watch the snow come down." She refilled their wine glasses and took them to the couch. as the music of Murray's *Snowbird* filled the room.

George took the glass she handed him, and they sat down together. Sipping the wine, they watched through the picture window as snowflakes fell gently.

Heidi ran her hand through George's hair. "I'm glad I didn't have to watch those bloody fights. Why do so many people enjoy seeing animals kill each other?"

"I reckon it's human nature."

"Yes, I know. You told me Shakespeare's plays had to compete with bear-baiting, dog fights, cock fights, and all sorts of gambling games. I suppose shedding animal blood is better than the human blood shed in the Roman arenas."

George nodded. "Now I hate such cruelty. I tired of seeing them a long time ago. It's hard to grow up around here and not see them when all of your buddies think it's part of proving your manhood." He shifted from being the focus of the subject. "Philemon says he almost quit before the dogfights started. He left as soon as he thought he had enough evidence. He found it a lot worse than he remembered from the one he saw as a teenager."

Heidi patted George's hand in sympathy. "The snow helps take my mind off those awful fights," she said.

"It won't be a heavy snow," he said as he inhaled the scent of roses surrounding Heidi.

Heidi nodded. "It's enough to turn the world white but not make a mess. An ideal snow."

"It's amazing the way a snow covers ugliness. Think how much better a surface mine looks with a covering of snow. It even covers the ugliness of Dave Blackmun's jobs."

"It's made a beautiful scene of my yard, but I'm glad to be warm and safe here with you."

"Are you ready for us to become engaged?"

"It depends on your getting free of Jennifer."

George shrugged and changed the subject. "We'll need to spend time on Black Mountain watching for the next big weekend at the

Pit, but that'll mean more weekend hawk watching." He looked forward to the duty.

"Sounds like fun for us and bad luck for Dave."

"I'm hopeful. Maybe we'll add a few birds to your life list.

Chapter 22

It was two weeks before word came back from the FBI. Jason told Mike his superiors were pleased with Philemon's work but would like to include the infractions of the Mann Act and subsequent blackmail in their crackdown. They wondered what evidence could be obtained of transportation of women across state lines for commercial sex and blackmail.

When Mike relayed this message, George was skeptical about attempting to gather that evidence. "Philemon doesn't want to continue. From what we know, Dave manages the prostitution himself. It will be very difficult to obtain the evidence without Dave's knowing who's responsible."

"Yeah, I agree. Are you sure Philemon won't attempt it?" Mike asked.

"I don't think so. He told me he definitely didn't want to go back. Watching the fights sickened him. Besides, you know it's dangerous work. Isaiah says the rumor is our cousin Cameron got shot because of involvement with one of Dave's ladies, but Cameron was in to Dave for big bucks, too."

"I reckon it's up to you to sound Philemon out about this," Mike said.

George scratched his head. "I think maybe we should think about this awhile, but I'll talk to him about it. He might have some ideas about who would do it, even if he won't. I'll wait until next week. I don't want to visit his mine so often his men get suspicious."

"Okay, I'll tell Jason he'll have to wait a few weeks," Mike said.

There probably won't be much interstate activity now anyway with winter setting in, so there wouldn't be many big fights going on at the Pit before spring."

It was a gloomy day. Every now and then a snow flurry came down on the windshield of George's reclamation truck. Some of these late November snows didn't amount to much, although big blizzards had been known to come around Thanksgiving. He had saved his visit to Philemon's surface mine until the end of the day.

The mine operations had shut down by the time he arrived. He passed a few of Philemon's crew leaving work as he headed in. George found Philemon loading some equipment into his truck.

"Something broken down?" George asked

"Yeah, I'm taking a gear shaft in for some welding."

"The FBI was impressed with your work."

Philemon hoisted the part into his pickup. "I'm glad—and glad to have it finished."

"I have to tell you. They want you to continue. They want evidence of the prostitution that can be prosecuted under the Mann Act, proof that the women have been brought across state lines for commercial sex and blackmail."

"That's something Dave handles himself. It would be really dangerous. Besides, I don't want to consort with prostitutes."

"Do you have anything to suggest?"

Philemon shrugged. "I think you should find a young guy eager for sex and bankroll him. In fact, I'd go so far as to finance it."

"Do you know anybody that fits your description?"

"There're plenty around, but you'd have to have somebody you could trust."

Taking time to think, George leaned on the fender of his truck. "It would also have to be a person Dave doesn't link to law enforcement. Is there anyone inside Dave's organization that could be bribed?

What about one of the women? The FBI would have to have evidence that Blackmun brought them here for commercial purposes."

Philemon rubbed his forehead. "I've heard stories of married men being blackmailed. Dave does it with pictures taken at the Pit showing them having sex with the women he's brought down from New York."

George had an idea. "Do you think we could find the names of some of those men? Some of them might be eager for revenge."

"I'll talk to Isaiah about this on Sunday and see if he knows anybody who's been victimized that way by Dave and wants to get even. I'll think of an excuse to ask him."

"Okay, thanks, I'll be by again next week."

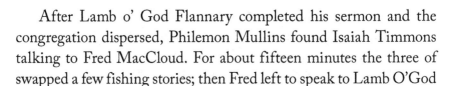

After Lamb o' God Flannary completed his sermon and the congregation dispersed, Philemon Mullins found Isaiah Timmons talking to Fred MacCloud. For about fifteen minutes the three of swapped a few fishing stories; then Fred left to speak to Lamb O'God about the next week's service.

Philemon broached the subject of Dave's illegal operation, but he pretended to be asking just because he had become curious about the extent of Dave's evil. "Isaiah, I need your help again. I'm curious. I've heard tales of married guys using Dave's prostitutes and then being blackmailed. Dave must really be evil to do that sort of thing. How much do you know about that?"

"That's a danger. I was careful to avoid Dave's women, but they're real honeys."

"Do you know the names of any of Dave's victims?"

Isaiah looked around to see if anybody could overhear them. Philemon understood his friend's caution and suggested they walk outside. Once they were out in the sunshine, Isaiah answered Philemon's question.

"I think I know some conies who've been caught in Dave's trap, but I doubt they'll be eager to admit it—don't want their wives to know. They likely live in fear of Dave's revealing the pictures he has."

"I'm looking for somebody who really hates Dave, who sees how evil Blackmun is. Somebody who'd be willing to take risks to do Dave in and would talk to me about how he feels."

"I think my cousin Cameron MacCloud was like that. I think he threatened to turn Dave in. I expect that's what got him shot."

Philemon shrugged. "I need somebody who's still alive. I can't talk to the dead."

"I remember a man who got way behind in his blackmail payments. Dave pulled the plug on him and sent pictures to his wife. She divorced the fellow and took his money and his children. I don't know of anybody who hates Dave more."

"Would you tell me his name? I wouldn't let him know you told me."

After thinking for several minutes, Isaiah sat down on a bench. A couple of minutes later, he recalled the name. "It's Wayland Stanard. He lives over in Kentucky, in Letcher County. He's made a fortune in mining, but he's come on hard times."

"He sounds like the sort of guy who'd stick his neck out to get Dave. I'll try to contact him. Just forget I asked you about it."

"He's the head of Coondog Mining," Isaiah said.

"Thanks, Isaiah."

Philemon was running a 'dozer, doing some reclamation work on the Monday a week later when George stopped by Philemon's mine in the evening after working hours. Stopping his machine and climbing down, Philemon shook hands with George "I've got a name for you. Wayland Stanard, head of Coondog Mining. You may know him."

"I know of him, but we've never met."

"I've met him a couple of times. I'll introduce you when you're ready. He may not feel kindly to reclamation officers."

"Thanks, after that you'll be done with undercover work," George said.

As George drove off Philemon climbed back on his dozer,

George headed to Heidi's He had to talk with Mike after he spoke with Philemon. He wanted to know how to proceed with enlisting Wayland Stanard. Feeling very much a special agent engaged in a secret plot, George understood that Mike would want to discuss the matter with Jason Brackenridge. He phoned the deputy to set up a meeting.

"Can you come by Heidi's to meet me sometime soon?" George asked.

"What about tonight? I'm off-duty and would jump at a chance to eat another of her meals."

"I'll check with Heidi. Honey, can you fit Mike in for dinner?"

"No problem. Tell him to come over now."

Answering her doorbell, twenty minutes later, Heidi gave Mike a friendly peck on the cheek. "Come in. I've heard you're a big fan of my cooking."

"I am. George is a lucky guy."

"That remains to be seen, but he's another fan of my culinary abilities. Do you like pork chops?"

"Sure do."

"Good, you're going to have sweet potato casserole and steamed broccoli with a cheese sauce along with your pork chop. You talk to George while I get things ready."

George called, "In here, Mike." Heidi pointed Mike to her study, which was a space shielded from the sleeping area in her bedroom by a large screen.

Standing to greet his co-conspirator, George motioned him to sit down on the spare chair. "Philemon's not eager to pursue Dave. He's suggested a Wayland Stanard in Kentucky as someone to approach. Apparently Blackmun destroyed his family."

"Who is this guy?"

"He's the head of Coondog Mining. I don't know him, but I helped out a fellow inspector by assessing one of his Virginia mines. He does good reclamation. He ran afoul the IRS. He didn't have enough money to pay Blackmun's blackmail and the IRS.

"I'll run this by Jason and have him check out Stanard. I think the FBI is ready to make a move on the animal fights and gambling whenever we give the signal. That shit is about to hit the fan."

"Okay, let's go eat," George said.

"You're one lucky s.o.b. A pretty woman who loves to cook—Heidi is a prize."

George grunted and raised his hands in prayer. "Yeah, but I haven't persuaded her to marry me."

Mike touched George's arm. "It's serious, eh?"

"I can't help myself. I need her."

"What's the problem then?"

George tapped the table in front of him. "She knows about Jennifer. I've got to convince Heidi I've quit playing the field, that my affair with Jennifer is over."

Mike grinned. "We all have to pay for our sins." George groaned as Mike patted him on the back. "Good luck, ole buddy. I sure would like to be your best man," Mike said. George sensed his friend was holding back laughter.

Heidi called. "You guys come eat this food I've fixed. Don't let it get cold."

Mike shoved George's arm. "I'll beat you to the table."

When he'd sat down where Heidi directed, Mike said, "I'm ready to do this food justice. I sure do like this fringe benefit of undercover work. The food smells delicious."

They concentrated on Heidi's meal before discussing Wayland Stanard again. As they waited for their pie, Mike beamed as he thanked Heidi for the meal. "That was a great dinner. If you decide to get rid of this guy, I'll forget Mable and ask you for a date."

Heidi grinned and patted her hair. "What if I tell Mable?" Dismay flashed across Mike's face. "But I'll keep you posted," she said as she set his pie down on the table.

After dessert, George returned to Stanard. "Philemon's willing to take me over to meet with Stanard, He said he'd introduce me because strippers aren't all that fond of reclamation officers. Then Philemon's going to drop out of this undercover business for good. He understands everything he's done is to remain secret."

"Okay, I'll contact Jason and ask him to check on Stanard."

Chapter 23

Once the FBI had approved Wayland Stanard for undercover work, George dropped by Philemon Mullins' mining site. Snow was spitting from afternoon sky and beginning to form white patches on the piles of coal still on the site when he arrived. The workers had left, and Philemon was heading to his pick-up when George arrived.

"I was wondering when you'd show up," Philemon said. "I reckon you're ready to make contact with Stanard and want my help. I'm to convince him you're a good guy even though you're an inspector."

"I've inspected one of his mining operations. I filled in for another inspector on one of his Virginia jobs a few years ago, but I don't know him. You can approach him as a fellow miner who's having troubles with Dave, then introduce him to me. Then you can drop out of the picture and nobody'll be the wiser," George said.

"Okay, I'll do that. Then it's up to you. I'll be glad to be out of the picture with my mouth shut."

The snow-covered December mountainsides hid any evidence of surface mining as George and Philemon drove over the Gap. Looking up at the three hundred foot rock wall left from highway construction, George wondered how much explosive went into the creation of this engineering marvel. Some of the blasts had rattled windows miles away.

"It's strange how well we can control rocks but still have trouble with the world's oldest profession," George said.

Philemon laughed. "Well, engineering and sex have one thing in common. They make a lot of money for some people. I uncover coal with my stripping, but some guys can't resist paying a woman to strip."

George chuckled. "Evidently Wayland Stanard was one of those strippers."

Philemon nodded. "I've had several phone conversations and two meetings with Wayland to set up your meeting today. He's okay. He sure lost a lot. He told me he truly hates Blackmun. Nothing he's said contradicts that. For him sonofabitch and Blackmun are interchangeable words."

George hoped Stanard's hatred would provide the spark needed to take down Blackmun. "You said he'd meet us at his strip job?"

"Yeah. He's let his crew off for three weeks to celebrate Christmas and the New Year—figured they wouldn't do much work then anyway."

A light snow was falling on the already snow-covered Stanard strip job as Philemon and George stepped from George's truck to meet the man exiting a tan truck.

Philemon shook hands with Stanard. "Howdy, Wayland. This here's George Landsetter. He's the guy I told you about. I'm going to get back in his truck while he talks with you."

George shook hands with Wayland, a handsome, heavy-set man with coal-black hair and aquiline, tanned features. He reminded George of Clark Gable. "Glad to see you. I've inspected one of your Virginia jobs for a colleague. You do good work. I'm told you and I have some things in common."

"What's that?" Stanard asked.

"We've both got Melungeon relatives and we've both had trouble with Dave Blackmun."

Stanard spit a stream of tobacco juice. "True. I hate that black-hearted bastard."

"He's not one of my favorites either."

'You're kin to Moon Lunamin?" Wayland asked.

"Yeah. We're first cousins. His pa was Melungeon."

"He's a legend among us surface miners. I reckon you're okay."

"Do you want revenge on Blackmun?" George asked.

"I sure would like to hurt that son of a bitch as much as he's hurt me. I wish somebody'd kill that bastard, but I want him to suffer first."

"We think Dave's involved in murder-for-hire, but what the FBI will be asking of you is to help make him suffer by putting him in jail for running a prostitution-blackmail operation."

Stanard grinned and waved toward his vehicle. "Come on and sit in my truck. No need to freeze while we talk." Stanard opened his tan vehicle and motioned for George to get in. Then he got in on the driver's side and started the engine. The noise and tobacco odor caught George's attention. Turning to face George, Wayland asked, "What did you have in mind?"

"I've heard that Dave destroyed your family, that he blackmailed you."

"Yeah, the s.o.b. liquored me up and offered me one of his whores free of charge. I fell for it, thought he was just a fellow miner being friendly. Then the threats and pictures came. What's your problem with Blackmun?"

George was convinced Stanard had a keen interest in getting even with Blackmun.

"He's threatening me. He wants to mine land I've promised my pa and grandpa I wouldn't strip. It's my hunting land. Dave suggests I wouldn't enjoy it much if I'm dead. I think a crimp in his illegal doings and jail time might get him off my back."

"What would you want me to do?" Stanard asked.

"The FBI wants evidence that he's transported women across state lines for commercial purposes. So we need you to provide that evidence. They want proof of his blackmailing in connection with one of his call girls he's brought in across state lines," George said.

Stanard lowered his window and spit a stream of tobacco. "No shit. How would I do that?"

"Do you still have the pictures he used to blackmail you?"

"Yeah. I still have them. I sit around and look at them and get drunk. I'm bitter at my wife for leaving me, but I hate Blackmun more."

The man's bitterness and despair convinced George that he would take Blackmun down.

"What about the blackmail money? Did you pay him by checks?"

"Yeah," Stanard said. "Blackmun objected, but I told him I couldn't send that much cash through the mail safely. He had me list it as payment for rented mining equipment."

"They would help, if you still have the canceled checks. Could you get in touch with the woman involved in the blackmail?

"Sure. I still see her when I can afford it. My wife deserted me and won't let me see my children. We didn't part on good terms. Wanda fills the void left by my wife. I'm not mad at her. I don't think she was in on it."

"Why?" George asked.

"Wanda Goetel's her name. She called me and asked to get together again without Dave's knowing. We did. I told her what happened. She claimed she didn't know we were being put on film. We've always met away from the Pit since the blackmail began."

"Good, then you could talk to her and record what she says. It would involve your having sex with her again, but we'd finance that," George said.

Stanard grinned. "You didn't tell me there would be benefits. She's not cheap. The times I've had sex with Wanda after that first freebee, I paid five hundred dollars each time."

George raised an eyebrow. "For that price she must be good. An FBI agent will contact you and instruct you. He'll set you up with equipment and tell you what questions to ask." George gave Stanard a phone number.

"Call me when you have the evidence. We'll arrange a time to meet and make the transfer. Here's a thousand dollars in hundred dollar bills to pay Wanda. Count them."

Wayland counted. "Great. If I don't get all I need the first time, I can arrange a second meeting."

"Good luck. Don't enjoy the work so much you get careless. We think Dave's already murdered at least one person who threatened his scheme. You need to caution Wanda to secrecy. Did you know Cameron MacCloud?"

"Yeah, we had mining jobs near each other when he was killed."

"He's another reason I want to get Dave. He was my cousin. We think Blackmun had Cameron killed because he fell behind on blackmail payments and complained—shot as a warning to others."

Stanard nodded. "I'll be happy to see that bastard Blackmun get what's coming to him."

When he returned to his office, George called Heidi. "Hello, Sweetheart."

"George, where have you been? I tried to call you."

"I've been over to Kentucky. Could you handle another dinner invitation for Mike? Or would you rather go up to Possum Hunt tonight?"

"I don't want to travel the roads tonight. I'll call Mike and invite him over. I'm working late today. We'll just have some spaghetti and pie. I have one in the fridge."

George's spirits lifted. "Thanks. When should I come by?"

"Around six-thirty. I'll tell Mike seven. That way you can tell me first."

"I'm looking forward to it. I have good news."

The snow was deeper on the road by the time George showered, changed clothes, scraped the snow off of his windshield, and headed for Heidi's. Snowflakes covered his windshield almost too fast for his wipers to remove them. *Just as well we didn't try to go to Hardwood tonight. I'd rather eat one of Heidi's meals anyway.*

Heidi was waiting at the door for him and opened it before he could ring the bell. She must have seen his surprised look. "I saw you drive up. I was watching the snowfall. What's the big news?" she asked as he came in.

"Wayland Stanard is ready to help the FBI. From what he says, he may already have a lot of the evidence they need."

Heidi shook her head. "I'm glad things are going well, but I worry about what will happen when the FBI raids the Pit."

Heidi was putting the spaghetti on the table when her doorbell rang. George opened the door for Mike, who handed him a six pack of beer.

Mike shook off snow before coming in. "We may be in for a blizzard. I'm glad I'm not driving to Hardwood tonight. What's the news?"

George told him he'd arranged things with Wayland Stanard as they made their way to the food.

Heidi greeted Mike with a smile. and a thumbs up "Help yourself. I had short notice, but what I could scrape together is on the table."

"Mike brought some beer," George said.

"I'm glad you invited me to sample your spaghetti again. Why don't you have George open some of this beer?" Mike asked.

"It should go well with the spaghetti and garlic bread," Heidi said.

After the spaghetti vanished, Heidi brought out slices of cherry pie and asked George to open more beer. The pie didn't last long.

"I swear these cherries melt in the mouth," Mike said.

While Heidi cleared the table with Mike's help, George filled Mike and her in on the details of his meeting with Stanard. "I gave him a thousand dollars to arrange meetings with Wanda Goetel. I expect the FBI will reimburse me. Moon will, if they don't, he told me."

"The FBI will repay you. Who's this Wanda Goetel?" Mike said.

"That's the name of the New York girl Dave set Stanard up with. She claims she knew nothing about the blackmail. Wayland and Wanda seem to be on very good terms. He doesn't think he'll have much trouble getting the information, but I warned him. I told him to caution her that we think Dave's already killed over this blackmail."

'Ask Jason whether the FBI will reimburse me. How soon do you think it'll be after Stanard provides the evidence before the FBI raids the Pit?" George asked.

"I think they'll want to do it whenever there's another big crowd there."

Heidi shook her head. "What will Blackmun do after the raid. You know he's going to look for somebody to punish."

Mike tried to reassure her. "We've been careful, but we'll have to keep being on guard."

George patted her hand. "Dave has no reason to go after you. And he's already after me about my coal. So I think he'll do something to me. I just have to be ready."

After Mike left, Heidi led George to her sofa, sat down and pulled him beside her. "I don't want to lose you. You know you'll have trouble with Blackmun when the FBI closes down his illegal operations."

"Don't you want to see him caught?"

"Of course I do, but I worry just the same."

George kissed her in an effort to ease her mind. The heavy petting that ensued quieted her but did not end the conversation. As George kissed her goodbye at the door, she grabbed him by the ear and twisted.

"Ouch!"

"I enjoyed this evening, but you take notice. I'll still have bad dreams."

After scraping the snow off his windshield, George drove home carefully. The snow was covering his windshield so thickly his wipers barely kept ahead of it. He had to admitt Heidi's fears weren't exaggerated. Dave was bound to strike out at somebody if his operation was shut down.

Chapter 24

T hrough wet roads and snow-covered roadsides, George drove over the Gap to Stanard's strip job. As they had agreed, all of Stanard's crew had left for the day. When Landsetter reached the site, Stanard was waiting by his truck.

As they shook hands, George asked, "It's been almost a month. You've been careful?"

"I tried to be. I have the goods. It was pure pleasure. If you have any more jobs like that, I'll be glad to help out." Grinning, he handed George a package. "Everything's in here." For emphasis, Standard turned and sent a stream of tobacco juice onto a pile of white snow. George detected an act of triumph.

George could smell the acrid odor of a recent mining blast, but his elation was mixed with worry. "Do you think you'll need any follow-up?"

Wayland shook his head. "The FBI gave me a list. I got information about every item down the line. She was paid to come down to Virginia from New York by Dave Blackmun to provide sex for special clients. He sent her the airfare from New York to Tri-Cities."

"Did you get evidence of that?'

"Photographed the ticket stub and recorded her account of how her meetings went down. Wanda had "dates," which included sex with me and eight other men, including Cameron MacCloud, at five hundred a shot after Dave's freebe. Dave took a hundred and fifty dollar fee for each "date" arranged through a woman named Arachne Smith, who took a fifty dollar cut. Dave doesn't know about our last four dates, so she didn't charge me but three hundred each time for these last two. It's all on the tapes. Do you want the four hundred I didn't use?"

George shook his head. "As far as I'm concerned, it's yours— payment for the pictures and the tapes. You've taken a big chance. I hope you warned her not to reveal any of this to Blackmun or the other women."

"I told her not to. At the least, he'd be mad as hell about her moonlighting with me, but it could be worse. I told Wanda that Cameron MacCloud's body had been found with a bullet in the skull, and that some people suspected Dave had him killed because he wasn't paying the blackmail."

George felt Stanard was trying to alert Wanda adequately to their danger. "Did she mention how many other women he brought down from New York?"

"She said she had seen six. She mentioned several, Janice Switzer, Betty Macomb, and Arachne Smith."

"Maybe you should caution her again not to mention her moonlighting to them. Arachne Smith has a close relationship with Dave Blackmun. She's probably getting more than a cut of the sex money."

Wayland smiled and nodded. "I'll make another date and warn Wanda again."

George phoned Heidi after he got back to Virginia. "Can you fix another dinner for Mike?"

"We could do it tomorrow night if that's okay with Mike."

"Great, I'll ask him if he can make it; our man said he got what we needed."

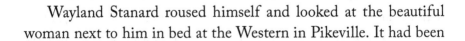

Wayland Stanard roused himself and looked at the beautiful woman next to him in bed at the Western in Pikeville. It had been worth the extra money to be with Wanda again. He had spent more time warning her of the danger they were in. She had said she was trying to be careful. He knew they shouldn't meet again anytime soon. She was too expensive for more than an occasional evening. That was the hell of it. He really liked her. She soothed the hurt he felt for what he considered the bad treatment he'd received from his wife. Wanda had helped him overcome his depression.

He got out of bed and showered and shaved. When he came out with a towel wrapped around him, Wanda was sitting up on the side of the bed. He walked over to her, enjoying her lavender scent.

Later, as Wanda and Wayland dressed and ate the breakfast he had ordered from room service, Stanard warned her again about the need to keep their latest "dates" a secret, being especially careful to keep the information from Dave and any of the other women from New York, especially Arachne Smith.

"I've told you that a man you had sex with, Cameron MacCloud, was killed because he fell behind in his blackmail payments. The person who told me thinks Arachne Smith is very close to Dave Blackmun and probably gets more than her cut of the money. So don't let her or any of Dave's other women know you've been moonlighting with me. It could be dangerous for both of us."

"I hope I haven't said anything to make them suspicious. I've told them I was out shopping when we were together. I'll try to be careful. Maybe we shouldn't meet for a while."

"Let's cool it for a month. I think we should use our same code when we talk in case they bug your phone. I like pretending to be a clerk at a store where you've shopped. I'll still say your order has come in."

"All right. I'll try to watch out. If you think it's dangerous for me to moonlight, I think we'd better slow down. I do enjoy our meetings. You're quite a guy. I almost wish you'd make an honest woman of me."

"I wouldn't mind doing that, but it would be dangerous right now. I sure would like to have you around permanently."

They finished their bacon, grits, biscuits and gravy and had another cup of coffee. Then they kissed goodbye. "I sure will miss you, Wanda."

"I'll miss you too. Our next meeting will be on me…. Except for the room."

—————————— ✦ ✦ ✦ ✦ ✦ ✦ ✦ ——————————

Two weeks later, Mike Barton heard from Jason Brackenridge. "That last package was what we needed. We're ready to move any time there's major activity. We're depending on you to give us a signal. If you think a big weekend's likely, call and tell me the fox is in the henhouse."

Mike called Heidi. "I want you to tell George to keep an eye out for activity at the place we've been watching and let me know if he sees something. Big Daddy is ready to act."

"Come by now for dinner and tell him yourself."

"There are parts of this undercover work I like. I'll be there."

Heidi called George at his office. "Don't be late. Mike's coming to dinner tonight. He has something to tell you. I'll fix pork chops again."

The days had been growing longer, spring was on the way, and it was only dusty dark when George arrived at Heidi's. He rang the bell a couple of times before Heidi opened the door.

"Come on in," she said. "Supper's going to be on the table soon." He leaned down and kissed her.

While he waited, he fixed drinks and helped Heidi with the salad.

He did what she asked, taking breaks now and then to kiss her, until Mike arrived. "I've heard from Jason, but let's eat first. I'm hungry."

Mike and George ate the pork chops, as well as several helpings of green beans and sweet potatoes. Pronouncing the food delicious, Mike said, "I'm glad you invited me tonight. I'd have hated to miss this great meal. It'd get Julia Child's seal of approval."

"I didn't have time for a pie, so I made some cherry cobbler. George, pour some wine while I get the dessert."

Dinner finished and the dishes cleared away, Heidi led George and Mike to her sitting area. "Okay, Mike, it's time for your news, "Heidi said.

'The FBI is ready to strike, George. They want you to let me know when you see there's something big going on at the Pit. The next morning you can signal me if there are any Kentucky license plates on trailers. I reckon you can detect that with the high power on your scope you use to watch birds. You'll be spending some time birding on Black Mountain for awhile."

Mike and George discussed plans for about twenty minutes before Mike said goodnight. "My watch starts in ten minutes. I'm sure glad you invited me to dinner, Heidi," Mike said as he stood to leave.

"You watch out tonight. The weather's bad," she said as she closed the door behind him.

"I reckon we're in for some excitement now," George said.

Heidi shook his arm. "Yes, it's exciting, but I want you to be careful."

"I promise not to take unnecessary chances. I'm glad you're worried about me. I hope you'll agree to marry me sometime soon, You could at least agree to become engaged," George said.

"Is this a proposal? Are you serious? What would Jennifer say?"

"Yes, I'm serious." Rather than say anything that might lead to an admission he was still wrestling with how to end his affair with Jennifer, George kissed Heidi.

Preparing to leave after much petting hours later, George again told Heidi he wanted to marry her, or at least become engaged to her. "I love you, and I think you love me."

"Yes, I do, but I want to be sure your family will accept me and Jennifer is ancient history. Then you can buy me an engagement ring."

Chapter 25

G azing out toward Black Mountain on a March morning, George could remember the splash of fall color that lured people to drive over this unpopulated road to see the gorgeous pinks, reds, and yellows of the hardwood forest. The drive was still pretty despite the surface mining that had denuded the northern side of the mountain and turned lush wooded slopes into a barren, scarred landscape. The change did make it easier for George to keep tabs on the traffic headed to the Pit. He was keeping a close watch for activity and always checked whenever his work permitted him to take the route over Fox Gap.

During the winter there had not been a great deal of activity. Cross-border fights came to a standstill, although the Pit staged a few bouts between local contestants. Now that spring was in the offing, George had to keep a closer surveillance to alert the FBI to cross-border activity.

George stared at the rusting machinery left to avoid reclamation. *At least they've provided habitat for blue grosbeaks, field sparrows, yellow-breasted chats, and prairie warblers. We don't have much habitat for those species in the mountains, but proper reclamation would save more soil.*

This morning the sun was shining, bringing the warmth of spring in early March. George's reverie was interrupted when a cloud of dust appeared on the road to the Pit. Three vehicles were racing down the road. Through his binoculars, he saw one vehicle with a Kentucky license plate. *They may be getting ready for a big match this weekend.*

I'd better tell Mike to get word to Brackenridge." He stayed watching for another hour as more traffic drove into the Pit. Several more cars sported Kentucky license plates.

That Thursday afternoon, George called Heidi. "It's short notice, but would you like to go to Possum Hunt for dinner tonight? I've got to get in touch with Mike."

"Why don't I see if he'll come over to my place for dinner?"

"It's such late notice."

"Nonsense, I'll just whip up some spaghetti again, if he can come over."

"Okay, either way we'll have a pleasant evening. I'll bring some beer."

George's phone rang as he was drying off from his shower. It was Heidi.

"Mike's coming by. Come over whenever you're ready."

"I'm just out of the shower. I'll be there in half an hour."

It took him only a quarter of an hour to dress and begin the drive to Heidi's.

He was looking forward to the evening, after he had passed on his information to Mike. He could hardly wait to be alone with Heidi. He noticed a few jonquils and forsythia in bloom, brightening the landscape in the dying sunlight of the early spring evening. If he and Heidi kept watch on the Pit from Black Mountain Saturday, there might be some migrant birds to see, or if not, they'd find other ways to pass the time.

George sipped a beer while he watched Heidi working in the kitchen as he savored the aroma of the spaghetti sauce on the stove.

Heidi was just finishing her dinner preparations when the doorbell rang.

"George, would you please let Mike in?"

"Sure. I'll open a couple of the beers I brought. Do you want one? I'll put the rest in your fridge"

"Okay, but I don't want beer; pour some wine for me."

He let Mike in and handed him a beer. Then he poured Heidi's wine.

"I have news for you. I saw activity at the Pit this morning."

"How many vehicles?"

Eleven—three together and the others later—it looks like this weekend will be busy. At least four Kentucky license plates. You need to let the FBI know to get ready. I think I'm right, but Heidi and I will go up to Black Mountain Saturday morning to look for spring migrants. You need to find a spot where you can signal Jason.

"Okay, I'll take some high-powered binoculars," Mike said.

"I have a couple of walkie-talkies. I brought them with me. You take one. If they don't work we'll use a white flag for go ahead, if action's taking place and there're animal rigs with Kentucky license plates. You can pass on the information."

"Sounds like a good plan. I'll give this news to Jason."

Heidi interrupted. "Dinner's on the table. Come on and help yourselves to spaghetti, salad, and garlic bread. I'll warm up some apple pie for dessert.

Mike chuckled as he pulled out a chair. "I'm convinced the best thing about our undercover work is eating the meals Heidi provides as cover for our meetings. I'm indebted to Dave for bugging my phone."

Heidi blew Mike a kiss. "Thank you, Sir."

Early Saturday morning, George joined Heidi for breakfast. After eating, they headed to Black Mountain. Heidi brought their lunches in a backpack. He was happy to have her along and hoped they would see some migrating hawks and other birds, even if his hunch about the Pit turned out to be wrong.

The ride up the mountain in the morning sun revealed spring beauty. The serviceberry was beginning to bloom and white patches of it dotted the forest on the mountainside like bunches of bouquets dropped from heaven here and there in the midst of dark branches beginning to show swelling buds. Odors from George's truck mixed with a faint odor of skunk and other forest smells.

"What are all of those white blooming trees? Are they dogwood?" Heidi asked.

"No, that's sarvis, serviceberry. It blooms earlier."

"They're like diamonds set in the dark forest."

Around nine o'clock, they reached the fire tower, standing like a sentinel looking down over the valley and across to Fox Gap. George took the lead as they clambered up the tower.

"Slow down," Heidi said. "I can't climb as fast as you, and I'm carrying a backpack."

George looked back and grinned. "Sorry, I'll slow down. Be careful."

Halfway up, he pointed out their first hawk, a red-tail, making circles in the sky.

"Probably a local bird rather than a migrant," George said. "We won't see any kettles of hawks today. Spring migration is more scattered than the fall."

Heidi let out a whoop. "It's great to be eye to eye with a hawk in flight. I guess he wonders what we're up to."

She watched the red-tail for a while, then gazed over to Flat Gap. "Look over to the Pit. I think I see dust on the road in, and there're already several vehicles around the building."

George lifted his binoculars with one hand as he grasped the ladder with the other. Heidi was correct. There were vehicles on the road, trucks and SUV's pulling trailers with cages on them. "Good spotting," George complimented.

"It's a great view, but I don't like looking down while I'm climbing. I'd rather wait and do my viewing after we get up the ladder."

"Okay, let's get to the top We can see four states from there: Virginia, Kentucky, North Carolina, and South Carolina."

When they reached the platform at the top of the tower, Heidi gave a sigh. "I'm glad to be up here, glad I made it." George set up his scope to get a close-up view. Through the 60-power lens he could spot both Kentucky and Virginia license plates on trailers containing chickens and dogs. "I was right. This is going to be a busy weekend at the Pit. We'd better signal Mike."

Heidi took out their two-way radio and sent a message to Mike. "Chicken coop filling, State lines busy—Notify hawks."

She smiled when the return message came. She relayed it to George. "Raptors are aloft, Mike says."

"Great, I hope they catch Blackmun."

She pulled George's arm. "We've done our main job. Now we can enjoy the morning watching the birds come by."

George nodded and pointed. "Look, there're a couple of broad-winged hawks soaring to our east."

"Look south. A kestrel is going to come right over us." She yelled. George thought she glowed, proud of her newly acquired bird identification skills.

George was pleased at her progress. "Hear that song? That's a blue-headed vireo singing. He's saying, 'See Heidi, I'm a vireo.' He's just to our left in the top of a hemlock tree. This is going to be a great morning. Look in the next tree left of the vireo, there's a small flock of yellow-rumped warblers. They're almost in full breeding plumage."

"I see them. They're gorgeous. Not like those drab things you showed me months ago."

"I told you then the butter-butts would be pretty soon."

Heidi looked below them. "What are these birds flying by so fast?"

"Swallows—purple martins and rough-winged swallows. They're strong flyers."

"Look, there's a swallow with a long, forked tail."

George followed her binoculars with his. "It's an early barn swallow. Listen, I hear cedar waxwings giving their high-pitched call. There're three in the tree above the warblers."

As she looked at the waxwings, Heidi trained her binoculars on the Pit. "The road in to the Pit is full of vehicles. The Pit clients don't know just how much excitement they're going to have today." She pulled George over to see. "I hate to think of all the blood that might have been spilled, yet I'm happy it won't be. I hope no people get hurt but a lot get arrested."

George laughed. "It's a big crowd. We'll get a bonus."

Heidi grinned. "How much does the FBI pay for a big bust?"

George wrinkled his brow. "On second thought, we need to remain incognito. We don't want Blackmun to know. We've got to remain undercover."

"Now we have all morning to watch birds and then eat the picnic lunch I fixed."

George licked his lips. "For dessert, we can have a little loving."

Heidi held up her hand. "I packed some cookies for dessert."

"It won't hurt to have a kiss or two to go with the cookies." To make his point, George pulled Heidi to him and gave her a long kiss, pushing his tongue into her mouth as he braced himself on a tower bar. She wrapped an arm around his neck and returned his kiss before she tweaked his ear. "Signal Mike again, and then show me some more birds. It's not time for lunch yet."

George laughed and took the walkie-talkie to signal Mike: "House Full." When he got a response, he turned his attention back to Heidi and pulled her to him, nibbling her ear as he fondled her.

Laughing, twisting from his grasp, Heidi asked, "What's that bird that's calling?"

George listened. "A yellow-bellied sapsucker's to our left. It's a woodpecker. Look for it climbing that big black gum tree. Look for its white wing stripe. Sapsuckers get their name from drilling holes in trees and sipping the oozing sap and eating insects caught in it."

"I see it. It's a pretty bird."

"It's a male. It has a lot of red on its head." George gave her a big hug and another long kiss.

Catching her breath, Heidi laughed. "Looking at that blue jacket you're wearing, I'll call you my blue-bellied sapsucker. I'm worried. You may take all of my sap if you keep kissing me like that. We'd better have an early lunch."

Heidi unpacked the pimento cheese and tuna sandwiches she had made and passed one to George along with an apple. She poured two lemonades and handed one to him. As they ate, George told Heidi to listen to the nuthatches.

They interrupted their lunch several times to listen to the nuthatches and watch passing hawks. George pointed out white-breasted nuthatches going up and then down headfirst on trees close by. "Nuthatches climb up trees and then go down head first. It makes them easy to identify."

"As nuthatches, maybe, but there're two different kinds," Heidi said.

George nodded. "The red-breasted has a higher-pitched call. There must be three or four of them at least. They're giving their *yank-yank* calls. Both species do that. Notice how much shriller the red-breasted calls are."

Heidi lifted her binoculars. "I'd love to see a red-breasted nuthatch. The picture in the book shows a pretty red breast and a black and white face mask."

George took her hand and pointed it. "Look on the trunk of that pine tree over to our left. There're two."

Heidi focused her binoculars. "They're prettier than my field guide's pictures."

"That's often the case. Painters usually work from skins or photos."

After finishing their lunch, they spent time watching new birds, petting, and keeping a lookout for activity at the Pit.

George stood and looked at his watch. "It's well after two o'clock." He scanned the road to the Pit with his binoculars. "The feds are making their way to the Pit. The show's beginning."

Heidi looked through George's scope. "There must be at least ten FBI vehicles, including that large bus. They must be planning to arrest lots of people."

"I hope Dave Blackmun is one of them," George said.

◆ ◆◆◆◆ ◆ ◆

Jason Brackenridge sat in the lead vehicle wondering whether they would catch Dave Blackmun at the Pit. He had high hopes of apprehending the headman and all of his main lieutenants actively engaged in crime. He radioed his instructions.

"As soon as we reach the Pit, I want four cars to circle the building and leave three men guarding every exit except the entrance. I want four agents there. Nobody should be allowed to exit the building until you have orders to stand down. The other agents will follow me into the building and begin making arrests. You all have pictures of Dave Blackmun, Arachne Smith, and Rod Mashburn. Make a special effort to arrest them and any dog and chicken owners you find."

As George watched, the FBI agents spread out around the Pit. Looking through his scope, he saw Jason Brackenridge directing agents into the building and stationing others at the exits.

Before long, other agents were conducting people out of the building and onto the large FBI bus. Among them, George saw Dave Blackmun and Arachne Smith being led to the bus in handcuffs.

He grabbed Heidi and hugged her. "They've arrested Blackmun and Arachne."

"Oh, let me see." Heidi looked through the scope in time to see Dave and Arachne being pushed into the bus. "Dave is struggling against getting on the bus. Dave knocked one agent to the ground. Two other agents have pinned the miscreant to the ground and recuffed his hands before pushing him onto the bus."

Many other culprits followed. George had mixed emotions when he spotted agents leading Rod Mashburn to the bus.

He sighed. "I reckon Cousin Rod will get off without too much trouble."

Heidi patted George on the back. "He's got to pay for his crime. Let's pack up and go back to my place," Heidi said as she began to fill her backpack. "I told Mike to drop by for drinks."

George and Heidi were eating pie and drinking beer when Heidi's doorbell rang. Heidi opened the door, greeted a smiling Mike Barton, and ushered him to the food and drink.

Mike and George shook hands. "It was a major bust. Jason was ecstatic about their success.," Mike said. "They caught Dave and Arachne at the Pit. Arachne was with a man, and they were caught on camera in the act. They arrested another of Dave's ladies too. The Pit is out of action."

"Yeah, Man. And the three of us got to watch from a distance," George said. "Heidi and I had a good look through the scope."

"I'm happy for our parts in this to go unrecognized; I don't want Blackmun to take revenge on us," Heidi said.

"I'm with you," Mike said, laughing as he accepted the beer, the bacon quiche, and cherry pie offered him. "I'm not rushing forward to claim any glory. Jason can have it all. He's promised to keep us unnamed and out of his report as much as possible."

Chapter 26

D ave Blackmun's anger induced a black mood after he, his women, his clients, and their fighting animals were apprehended by the FBI. Agents confiscated the dogs and roosters and all of the gambling machines. They locked up the Pit and took cameras discovered with film featuring Arachne Smith and Diane Switzer having sex with men.

After making bail for himself and Arachne, Blackmun sought to find out who had brought him this grief. The FBI had torn the Pit apart, taken everything that was portable including all the drugs, money, and gambling equipment. They had taken thousands of dollars in cash, not to mention all of the credit card receipts. Then they hauled him and Arachne and the others they arrested over to the FBI quarters in London, Kentucky. Getting back home hadn't been easy even after making bail. That required him to arrange for over three hundred thousand of dollars in bail money. Luckily, he didn't have a criminal record. He wasn't going to accept this reversal of fortune without seeking revenge. *Somebody had tipped off the Feds.*

Back at his house with Arachne, he questioned her repeatedly. As he reviewed the events, he lit an expensive Cuban cigar and filled the room with tobacco smoke. "They knew about the fucking blackmail. That means somebody involved blew the whistle on it. Do you think Diane could have done it?"

Arachne put her hand to her forehead. "No, Diane didn't, but

Wanda Goetel may have let something slip. She made an offhand remark to Diane about moonlighting."

Dave grabbed her arm. "Did she say who the john was?"

Arachne pulled away. "No, but Diane said Wanda has mentioned a Wayland in connection with some shopping."

"That's not a common name. It has to be Wayland Stanard. He stopped paying, and I sent his wife pictures of him with Wanda. His wife left him and took his kids. He went bonkers. I'll bet he squealed for revenge. I'll take care of him."

"You should be careful, Dave. You're already in big trouble. She opened a window. "I've got to get rid of that tobacco odor."

Dave laughed and blew some smoke her way. "Don't worry, I'm not going to do it myself." He didn't tell her what he planned to do. He couldn't be sure she hadn't had a hand in his troubles. He had more than his share of enemies, but he'd let them know not to fool with him.

Arachne didn't say anything more; she fled the tobacco smoke.

———————— ✦✦✦✦✦✦✦ ————————

Around six o'clock that night, Josie Roper answered her telephone "Roper here."

"Josie, I want you to meet me.," Blackman said.

He knew she'd recognize his voice. "I'm not eager to. I just got out of the shower," she said. "If I do, I want to avoid a crowd. You're a pretty hot item now from what I hear."

"Where can we meet?"

"I'm toweling. I don't want to be seen with you. What about out at one of your strip jobs? Aren't all of the workers gone?"

"Okay, come over to my Winding Fork job around seven this evening."

In the last sunlight a little before dusky dark, Josie parked her dark blue Explorer beside Blackmun's black Durango and got out. Dave lowered his window.

"Come over here and get in."

Josie's carrot-top was still visible in the fading light. Dave couldn't help admiring her five-foot six figure crammed into blue jeans and a tight blue blouse. What was she like in bed now? He was too clever to attempt her now. She might turn on him.

She opened the door and climbed in. "I hope you've written out what you want. I don't want this to be taped, and I know you're not above doing that."

Puffing on his cigar, Dave grinned. "I'm sorry you don't trust me."

"You haven't given me much reason to trust you. You've screwed me, literally and figuratively. Remember my terms. Half up front, half after the job's done. Double what you paid for the most recent job. By the way, that cigar stinks."

Blowing smoke in her face, Blackmun handed her a note, a photo, and two wads of bills. "Count. The name's on the paper. How you do it is up to you."

"That cigar may be expensive, but it's still repulsive. You're lucky I need the money."

She counted both wads. She was surprised that Dave had anticipated her demands. "Okay, just have the rest ready. I'll contact you. We can meet back here then."

Josie began to look at the note. Blackmun said, "It reads, 'Wayland Stanard, Coondog Mining, Kentucky.'"

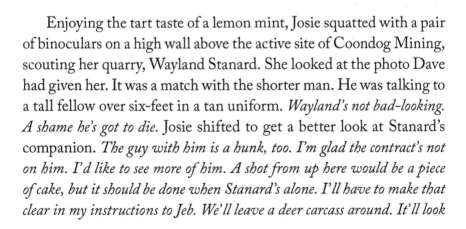

Enjoying the tart taste of a lemon mint, Josie squatted with a pair of binoculars on a high wall above the active site of Coondog Mining, scouting her quarry, Wayland Stanard. She looked at the photo Dave had given her. It was a match with the shorter man. He was talking to a tall fellow over six-feet in a tan uniform. *Wayland's not bad-looking. A shame he's got to die.* Josie shifted to get a better look at Stanard's companion. *The guy with him is a hunk, too. I'm glad the contract's not on him. I'd like to see more of him. A shot from up here would be a piece of cake, but it should be done when Stanard's alone. I'll have to make that clear in my instructions to Jeb. We'll leave a deer carcass around. It'll look*

like a careless poacher killed it and Stanard. Her decisions made, she headed to the Kwickee Shop at the Gap.

George pulled into the Kwikee Shop at the top of the gap on the Kentucky-Virginia line to get a soft drink, some chips, and a hot dog. He was surprised at the crowd inside. All of the tables were occupied. He noticed a good-looking carrot-haired woman sitting by herself at a table drinking coffee. Taking his order, he walked over to her table. "Mind if I sit down? My name's George Landsetter."

Josie Roper looked him over as if she'd seen him before. "Have a seat. I'd like some company. My name's Josie Roper."

"Are you from Kentucky?"

"No, I live over in Virginia. I'm just doing a little sightseeing. That cliff they made when they built this four-lane is a marvelous bit of engineering.

"Yeah, I hear geology classes from all over visit just to see it," George said as he bit into his hot dog.

"How about you? Where're you from?

"I'm a Virginian, too. I was just over in Kentucky to see a fellow about some work he's doing in Virginia. I'm with the mining reclamation bureau."

"So that's the reason for the uniform."

"Yeah, I'm on duty."

"I thought maybe you were a policeman," Josie said.

"I am, sort of. I do have some police powers, but they don't extend beyond supervising surface mines, unless there's an emergency. Want some chips."

"Thanks." Josie took several. "You aren't carrying a gun?"

"I left it in my vehicle. I wear it when I visit strip jobs."

"Did you hear about the big FBI operation over at Flat Gap? They really put some gamblers out of business."

George grinned. "Yeah, I heard about that. The papers gave a detailed account. I wonder how the FBI found out. Sheriff Mulberry claims he knew nothing about it."

Josie stopped drinking and laughed. "I've heard Sheriff Mulberry always claims that."

George and Josie talked for about half an hour. His chips and hot dog gone, George finished his drink and forced himself to stand up and say goodbye. "I'm happy to have met you, Josie, but I've got to get back to Virginia."

"I'm sorry you have to go. I hope I'll see you again sometime, Mr. Landsetter."

"I hope so, too. So long."

George thought about Josie as he drove down the mountain. She was a sexy babe, no doubt about it. She was more pleasant to think about than Dave Blackmun, whose strip job he was scheduled to inspect the next day.

Under a dark cloud covering half of the sky, George saw Dave's black Durango as he drove up to the mining site. He had hoped to avoid Dave, but now the mine owner had more time than before to devote to his mining work. *Damn, an example of unintended consequences.*

George smelled the lingering acrid odor of an explosion mixed with tobacco odor as he approached Blackmun. "I hope that blast was legal, Dave. You wouldn't want to ruin a great day."

Dave flicked the ash off his cigar. "Okay, Pollyanna, tell me what's so good about it."

"God's in his heaven and sunshine's beaming down," George said as he watched a kestrel kiting over the mined area, looking for a mouse.

Dave scowled. "Chicken shit, there's a cold front on its way. I can smell it, and I've got coal orders to fill."

"Okay, take me on a quick tour, and I'll get out of your hair," George said.

"Have you thought any more about stripping that five hundred acres?"

George shook his head. "I've told you I promised Papaw to keep it for hunting."

Blackmun took his cigar out of his mouth and spat. "That's black gold you're sitting on."

"You know Moon has part of the mineral rights. Maybe you should talk to him."

"A helluva lot of good that would do unless I could find a way to pressure you. You're passing up a fortune. You two and your damn hunting make me want to puke. You think you and Moon are reincarnations of Daniel Boone."

Dave was right about a cold front moving in. George completed his inspection as fast as possible and left Blackmun muttering about bureaucrats wasting his time. George worried Blackmun was trying to find a way to seek coal-stripping money to replace the illegal money he'd lost from the Pit's closure. *He'll be more demanding than ever about mining my five hundred acres. More unintended consequences. I should have expected that would happen. Heidi was right. I'll have to be careful.*

Looking up the valley, George gazed at his five hundred acres of woodland standing in stark contrast to Dave's rape of the land. *I hope my children and grandchildren have that woodland to enjoy and protect.*

Chapter 27

A wet spring snow was falling on George. He shook off the snowflakes as Heidi greeted him at the doorway and told him Mike would join them for supper. George turned to go back to his truck.

"I've brought some beer and the holly and pine and mistletoe you mentioned a few days ago. I thought you might like some now."

She eyed the greenery and smiled. George wondered where she would use it. Its scent was already permeating her apartment. "Your gift makes me think of Christmas. Mike says he has some news he must discuss with the two of us," Heidi said.

"That sounds ominous. I wonder. Is it something involving the raid on the Pit?" George asked.

"I'm afraid it might be. I told him to bring some beer. If it's bad news, we'll have enough beer to drown our sorrows."

Ten minutes before seven, Heidi's doorbell rang and George opened the door for Mike, who was standing there with a six-pack.

George took the beer. "Come on in. I'll open some of these. Heidi says you have news. Is it bad?"

Mike stamped his feet and wiped them on the doormat. "Serious, at the very least."

"Dinner's on the table. Sit down and have a beer."

"Does your news involve the raid on the Pit?" George asked after their plates were full and they'd begun eating.

Mike cleared his throat. "Yeah, I think so. Wayland Stanard was found shot at his mining site."

George stopped eating. His fork dropped to his plate. Heidi gasped.

George made a fist. "Damn, I talked with him there two weeks ago about one of his Virginia jobs. I told him to be careful and to warn Wanda to keep quiet."

"The police over there don't know quite what to think about it. There's evidence to suggest it was a careless shot from a deer poacher. But we know better. It's probably a revenge killing arranged by Dave Blackmun. I'll bet he hired Josie Roper to arrange the hit."

"Josie Roper? Come to think of it, I met her at the Kwikee Shop at the Gap the day I talked to Wayland. She said she was sight-seeing."

"Probably she was scouting the hit. I doubt that she did the actual shooting, but I'll bet she set it up," Mike said.

George recalled his last conversation with Wayland. "I reckon Wayland didn't convince Wanda Goetel to be careful enough. I warned him. Dave's clever. He must have figured Wayland was involved in the FBI sting. He had him killed to serve notice to others who've ceased paying blackmail and want revenge."

"Do you think Wayland might have mentioned you, George?" Mike asked.

George shook his head. "I don't think so. He seemed to take my advice seriously. Wanda must have dropped just a word or two that got back to Dave, and Blackmun reckoned Wayland had something to do with the FBI raid."

Heidi listened to their conversation with growing apprehension. She grabbed George's arm. "You two had better watch your backs."

George nodded. "Dave may not connect us with the raid, but he's putting more pressure on me already about stripping my five hundred acres. I think he's hatching a scheme to blackmail Moon and me."

"How would he put pressure on Moon?" Mike asked.

"I can't think of anything, but you know how resourceful Dave is when it comes to doing crap. Maybe he'd put a hit out on Moon or me.

"That's a dreadful idea," Heidi said.

George banged the table. "He'll try something."

"I think we have to be ready for anything,." Mike said. "I'm going to relay our suspicions to Jason Brackenridge." They finished dinner in a somber mood.

Heidi sighed. "I need another beer. I didn't think dating George was going to be quite this thrilling. You two don't lack for excitement."

George laughed as he put his hand on her shoulder and handed her a beer. "Let's go out birding this weekend. That'll take your mind off our troubles."

"You two nature lovers better be careful out in the woods," Mike said. I'm going to leave now. I'm off to Possum Hunt to see Mable. Thanks for a wonderful dinner, Heidi."

As they said their goodbyes, she said, "Drive slowly. Be careful."

Closing the door, Heidi turned to George. "That goes for you too. I don't want to be a widow before I'm a wife."

George took great hope from Heidi's comment. She obviously was thinking about marrying him. He had to end his affair with Jennifer right away in a way that would convince Heidi it was over.

A few days later George found a call from Jennifer on his answering machine: "My boss is sending me down to find out about Wayland Stanard's death and whether it has any connection to the FBI bust of Dave Blackmun,"

He returned the call. "So you want more background?"

"Yes, that and more."

George didn't intend to reveal much to her, but he wanted to tell her the sexual part of their relationship was over. "We have to be more circumspect in meeting. We can't go to Possum Hunt or the Western anymore."

"Why, what's the problem?"

"I don't want to discuss that, especially over the telephone. If you want to see me, you'll have to come to my apartment after dark. I'll fix a meal.

"This sounds like real cloak and dagger work."

"I don't want to be seen with you. It's too dangerous."

"Okay. What if I come by tonight at eight? It should be dark by then."

"All right. I hope you like pork chops."

George had dinner well underway when Jennifer knocked on his door. As he ushered her in to his apartment, he told her to have a chair at his small kitchen table.

George turned the pork chops. "We can talk while I finish fixing the meal."

Jennifer sat at the table and pulled out her notebook. "What do you know about Wayland Stanard?"

"He was a surface miner who owned Coondog Mining. He had strip mines in Kentucky and Virginia."

"So you knew him fairly well, didn't you?" Jennifer asked.

"Not really, other inspectors supervised his Virginia mines. I filled in for them in a pinch. I didn't deal with Stanard directly."

"Do you think his shooting was a hunting accident?"

"No."

"Why?"

George paused and then answered slowly. "Because ... he might have been on Dave Blackmun's black list."

Jennifer wrote. "On account of what?" she asked.

"Maybe he quit paying blackmail after his wife left him and took their kids."

"He was paying blackmail?"

"That's the rumor.

"So there's a connection between his death and the illegal gambling at the Pit."

George decided he had to close off this questioning. "I've already told you more than is healthy for me. I have personal problems with Blackmun."

George had another reason for wanting to avoid further discussion. He wasn't eager to tell Jennifer he was going to end their intimate relationship. He was having a difficult time deciding how best to accomplish his goal of winning Heidi.

"Okay, now I know I'm on the right track. So you think Blackmun killed Wayland?"

George started putting dinner on the table. "I don't want to talk about that any more."

"All right. You've given me a leg up. How about helping me with something else."

"What?" George asked, even though he knew what she was going to suggest.

"I have this overpowering desire to enjoy the sexual prowess of a surface-mining inspector."

"Did you bring your marked cards?"

"I did. Would you like to play a few hands of seven-card stud?"

"If you think that's necessary. Apparently it turns you on. I think you ought to know I'm ending these sex games."

"I admit it does excite me, and I don't believe you're quitting me."

"What if you lose a few hands? Then I'll end it."

"Either way, I win. I don't think you can give up our relationship. You find me too desirable. Why don't you fix us some gin and tonics."

George decided that playing a card game was better than further conversation about Dave Blackmun. He had to have more time to think about how to end his affair with Jennifer.

"Okay, deal a hand while I fix the drinks."

After Jennifer left, George considered how he would end the affair in a way that would convince Heidi it was over. He had told Jennifer he was ending it, but he hadn't lived up to an implicit commitment he'd made to Heidi to see only her. He couldn't deny he still found his desire for Jennifer strong. She was sexy enough to make a dying man rise to fulfill her wishes. She had exhausted him. At one o'clock in the morning, he had told her he could not rise to her demand again. He repeated he was ending the sexual part of their relationship. She had laughed and proceeded to prove him wrong about fulfilling her request.

He knew she looked upon him mainly as a desirable convenience, a man who could provide her with information and pleasant entertainment. She wanted to become an award-winning journalist and wasn't going to let any man, however desirable, stand in the way of her reaching her goal. He must summon the strength to end the affair in a manner that would convince Heidi. What method he could use would require more thought.

Chapter 28

T he morning sun shone in through George's window. Sleepy, but awake, he remembered his date with Heidi. George picked her up at seven-thirty, a little too late to hear the full dawn chorus of spring bird song. He thought that could wait for the early summer, when it would be at its most vociferous. He took her to the town reservoir, a man-made lake surrounded by woodland.

Dressed in the drab green outfit George had recommended, Heidi yawned as she exited his truck. "Do birders always get up early?" Heidi asked as they stood in the parking lot and listened for song.

"It all depends on the birds they're seeking and the time of year. We didn't get up early to see broad-winged hawk migration. We waited for the thermals to provide uplift for the soaring birds."

"What are we looking for this morning?"

"Early passerine migrants—warblers, vireos, thrushes, and tanagers."

"Sounds like pretty birds, then. I've been studying my guide."

"Many of them are beauties. They're more likely to sing early in the day, and they're much less active when it gets hot."

"I hear a song. What is it?"

"That's a robin. It's a thrush. Listen to that *tu-tu-tu-tu*. It's a cardinal. Now I hear a yellow-throated vireo repeating its *vireo-three-eight*."

"It's worth getting up early. It's like Beethoven's *Pastorale*—a whole new way of appreciating birds," Heidi said. "The combination of sounds reminds me of a symphony orchestra."

"It's called the dawn chorus. I really enjoy listening to these songs with somebody who appreciates them." Unable to restrain himself, George grabbed Heidi and hugged her and kissed her. Jennifer was a distant memory.

Heidi laughed and returned his kiss. "And I thought good cooking was the way to a man's heart. What's that sound almost like a flute?"

"A scarlet tanager."

"Now I hear a violin."

"It's a hermit thrush, a migrant. Some of them breed on the highest mountains here where there's spruce forest. Most migrate up north."

"Okay, I understand why we got up so early."

They spent the next two hours listening to bird song. George was delighted to identify the songs for Heidi, who was enthusiastic about learning the singers. If he couldn't locate the singer for a look, he showed her the bird's picture in her bird guide.

About ten-thirty, Heidi suggested that they go to her place for lunch. "I've had a wonderful time, but I'm getting hungry. We ate so early."

George took her hand in his. "Why don't you go with me to Winding Fork and meet my Mamaw and Papaw. My mother might be there for lunch too."

Heidi tilted her head. "George, I thought you'd never ask. Are you sure you want them to meet me?"

"I'm sure." He pulled her to him and kissed her. All his hesitation was behind him.

They stopped by Heidi's to let her freshen up while George telephoned Serafina to ask if he could bring a friend for lunch. They'd bring a pie.

When he was off the telephone, Heidi asked where he planned to get the pie.

"I was planning to stop by a grocery."

"Don't. We'll take one of my pies from the freezer."

170

"Great." George was jubilant. "The folks will see what a great cook you are."

As they drove up the lane toward his grandparents' house at Winding Fork, George saw Carrie's car. "My mother is here, so you'll get to meet her too."

Heidi squirmed "I'm a little nervous."

"I'm sure they'll think you're wonderful." George felt certain Heidi's pie would break down any reluctance to their accepting an outsider, "a furriner." A woman's cooking was still important in the southern mountains.

Archibald was sitting on the wide front porch, rocking. He rose to greet them as they climbed the steps.

"Hi, Papaw. This is Heidi Leaves. Heidi, this is Archibald MacCloud."

Heidi held out her hand. "I'm happy to meet you, Mr. MacCloud. You must know that George sings your praises. He says you're the last of the great hunters."

As he grasped her hand, he laughed. "Don't believe all my grandson tells you, Miss Leaves. Won't you take one of those other chairs and join me?"

"Why, thank you. I love rocking chairs," Heidi said as she sat in the rocker closest to Archibald's.

George grinned. "Papaw, I'm going to take this pie to Mamaw to warm up. Would you entertain Heidi?"

Archie waved him away. "My pleasure, I don't often get to talk to such a pretty young woman these days."

"Now I see where George got his gift of a sweet tongue, Mr. MacCloud. He's been tutoring me in birdwatching. He says he learned all of his outdoor lore from you."

"I taught him and his cousin Moon how to hunt and how to live in the woods. I reckon I taught him all the common birds you can tell without binoculars. He's way ahead of me now."

George came back to tell them that Serafina was serving dinner. As they filed in, George introduced Heidi to a still handsome gray-haired elderly woman and a woman who seemed a younger, taller red-blonde version of her mother.

"Mamaw, Ma, this is Heidi Leaves. Heidi this is my Mamaw, Serafina, and my Ma, Carrie."

The women shook hands. "I can't remember George bringing a woman to dinner," Serafina said. "You're certainly welcome, Heidi."

George grinned with pride. "Heidi's the first woman I've met whose cooking is in the same league with the two of you."

Even in her green field outfit, Heidi was quite a beauty. Archibald patted Heidi's shoulder. "As you'll find out Miss Leaves, that's about as high praise as any cook could receive."

Heidi blushed. "I hope I deserve it. I'm savoring the delicious aromas from Mrs. MacCloud's kitchen and the food here on the table."

Serafina chuckled and passed the pork chops. "Don't you let Archie get the better of you, Heidi. He can't resist a pretty young woman. When I complain, he swears it's because they remind him of me."

Carrie grinned and tapped Archie on the shoulder. "Ma, Sometimes I wonder at you and Pa. You never seem to grow old."

"It's all due to our clean living and cousin Isaiah's corn liquor," Archie said as he helped himself to a pork chop and passed the plate to Heidi. "It's springtime and I've been digging sassafras roots. Serafina's made some sassafras tea. It's good for you. It tastes good too."

"I'd like to try some," Heidi said. "I remember having some my grandfather made when I was a little girl."

Besides the pork chops and sassafras tea, Serafina served spring onions with some wild spring greens that Archie had collected. From her garden patch, she offered steaming young Irish potatoes sliced and baked in a cream sauce, and freshly cut asparagus in a wine vinagarette."

Heidi ate with what George judged obvious relish. "Mrs. MacCloud, I see why George praises your cooking so highly. This food is delicious," Heidi said.

"Thank you. A cook likes to have praise. I tell Archie he's a lucky man whenever he becomes too used to eating good food."

Looking around after he had sampled everything several times, George saw that everyone was almost finished with the main course. "Come on, Ma, help me serve Heidi's pie." He was sure it would impress his mother and grandparents.

When all of them had tasted a piece of Heidi's cherry pie, Archie pronounced it a great success. "Why, if I didn't know better, I'd say this is one of Serafina's."

"Thank you, Mr. MacCloud. I'm aware that's high praise. George has described Mrs. MacCloud's pies in glowing terms," Heidi said.

"Where do you hail from, Miss Leaves?" Archibald asked.

"I'm a Midwestern farm girl from Logansport, Indiana. That's flat country. My grandparents were from Virginia. They always talked about its beauty. Except for its southern section, Indiana boasts large, flat cornfields that seem to stretch forever. I've grown to love the beauty of these mountains."

George pointed to Heidi. "Heidi heads up LEAPS, Papaw," George said. "You and she see eye-to-eye about surface mining. She's trying hard to promote good reclamation. Remember, she brought Moon to speak? About how a person can make money while mining responsibly."

"Moon learned to do it right. It still didn't replace the beauty it destroyed," Archie said.

George nodded. "I think he did a lot of good. I doubt that he reached Dave Blackmun, though. I'm afraid he's eager to change our hunting woods into a desert."

"Speaking of Moon, he and Gladys are bringing our great-grandson Andy over next weekend," Serafina said, tiring of mining talk. "We're looking forward to their visit. I hear you and Moon are going to do some spring turkey hunting, George."

"That's right, Mamaw. Maybe we'll bring you in a big gobbler."

"I hope so," Archie said, "those tame turkeys you get at groceries and even the ones Serafina raises can't hold a candle to a wild turkey when it comes to taste."

As Heidi and George were leaving, Archibald told her to come back and visit them anytime. "I'd like you to come over to Saturday dinner to help sample one of the gobblers the hunters get. I may even go out to help them. You're welcome here. Keep that in mind."

Heidi smiled. "I'm so glad you feel that way. You've certainly made me feel welcome."

Serafina gave Heidi an appraising look. "I hope my grandson has enough gumption to make you part of this family."

"I'm working on that," Heidi said, eying George.

Winking at her, George added, "We're both a-working on that. It's a sweatier job than I'd expected."

Chapter 29

Friday night the following week, Moon brought his family to Winding Fork for a visit while he went turkey hunting with his grandfather Archibald and his cousin George, who brought Heidi along to meet Moon's wife Gladys and his son Andy.

That evening Heidi and Gladys sat in the kitchen and watched the men make preparations for the spring gobbler hunt, cleaning and oiling their shotguns and putting aside some food to take for breakfast in the woods.

"The way you men prepare, I'm wondering if those poor turkeys have a chance," Gladys said.

Heidi teased. "I feel like I'm in a war zone. Be careful not to shoot each other."

"I'm glad we've got good land to hunt on," George said, ignoring the women's levity. "Dave's been pressuring me again to let him strip it. He says I'm passing up riches."

"There're things more important than money," Archibald said. "You just tell Blackmun you don't worship at the feet of Mammon."

Before sunrise, George, Moon, and Archibald dressed and readied to go to George's woods. Using flashlights, they went to their stands before daylight. They were eager for a shot at a male turkey.

Archibald couldn't resist a bit of advice. "Now you boys need to get a clear shot. Take your time. Serafina wants some turkey meat."

"Papaw, you've been telling Moon and me that since we were able to shoot a shotgun. We know what to do," George said.

Moon laughed. "I reckon he's right, Papaw."

Archie shook his finger at them. "One of us had better get a gobbler. I've taught you both a good hen call, but use a bought call if you've a mind to."

Once at his stand, George ate some trail food and an apple for breakfast. He washed them down with some coffee from his thermos as his nose detected a faint smell of skunk. As the sun began to rise, a ruffed grouse drummed and a raven croaked as it flew over. It was a good day to be in the woods. A flock of small birds moved through, following the lead of a downy woodpecker's call. Chickadees and titmice hunted insects through the trees around him. A yellow-bellied sapsucker made its sharp call like a jay or a red-shouldered hawk. Yellow-rumped warbler migrants fluttered through underbrush, and an early blue-headed vireo broke into song. A gray fox slipped through the bushes, stopped and sniffed the air, and then disappeared. It was good to be alive and out in the woods.

George gave his hen turkey call: *ca-r-rrp, ca-r-rrp*. After about a quarter of an hour, a shot rang out. It came from Archibald's stand. George waited, still making his turkey hen call. After about ten minutes, a gobbler answered in the brush twenty yards beyond his stand. As it moved closer, George slowly lifted his shotgun to his shoulder, ready for a shot. A pileated woodpecker sounded an alarm of *kek-kek-kek-kek*, but the gobbler continued to respond to George's hen call. Minutes passed. The tom came into the opening in front of the brush. Slowly, carefully, George aimed and squeezed the trigger. The turkey crumpled. Not long after, another shot rang out, this time from the direction opposite Archibald's stand.

George collected his trophy and headed over in Archibald's direction. He found his grandfather sipping coffee from his thermos. A large dead turkey gobbler lay in front of him. Archie looked at George's kill. "Good shot, Son, right through the head. Let's go see if Moon got one."

Before Archie could stand up—Moon appeared, carrying a third turkey, larger than the other two.

Moon dropped his bird by Archie's. "I reckon Mamaw will be as pleased as a fox in a henhouse."

George nodded. "But not until we've cleaned them."

They were back at the MacClouds' ready to clean turkeys before ten o'clock. Gladys and Heidi were in awe their hunting skill as the men held up their birds for them to admire.

"Are there any male turkeys left in the woods?" Gladys asked

"You've certainly reduced your turkey population," Heidi said.

They watched as the men defeathered the birds and gutted them, saving the gizzard and heart as well as the necks for soup.

Heidi asked for some turkey feathers to decorate her apartment. "You three certainly know how to shoot."

"Are you killing so many turkeys that you won't have any more?" Gladys asked.

Archie laughed. "No, we have spring gobbler hunts to increase the turkey population."

"I don't see how that could be true," Heidi said.

Archie grinned. "According to the Fish & Wildlife people, it's a matter of fertility. The old gobblers amass a flock of hens for themselves. They chase away younger, more fertile males. Removing old gobblers opens the way for younger males to sire more young. At least that's what the game officials tell us. And it seems to work."

Moon offered a footnote. "Don't get any ideas from this, young ladies. George and I don't want to be served for somebody's dinner so that some young buck can take our place."

"That's right," George said, "We want to eat turkey, not be turkeys. Tame turkeys are so stupid they'll drown in the rain." He gobbled to make his point.

✦ ✦ ✦ ✦ ✦ ✦ ✦

George and Heidi drove back from Winding Fork a little before dark after a long day of food and family, "I reckon you'll have to admit I've met one of your requirements. There's no doubt your're accepted by my family. In fact, they're practically demanding you be part of our family."

Heidi smiled. "I feel very welcomed."

"Then let's at least get engaged."

"There's that other requirement. Have you ended your affair with Jennifer?"

George laughed. "I'm a-working on it. I've told her."

"You have to make a clean break."

"Would you agree to our engagement if you were present the next time Jennifer approaches me about background information?"

"I'll take your word you've ended it," Heidi said.

"You say that, but I want to be sure. I'm determined to marry you."

Just as George was waving his fist to emphasize his serious intent, a vehicle appeared coming in the opposite direction. As it came closer, it swerved over to their side of the road and headed directly at them.

Heidi yelled. "Watch out, George! That driver's crazy. There's a big drop over here. It must be over fifty feet deep."

George gripped the wheel with both hands. "Yeah, but I'm going to fool him." The other vehicle came so close a crash seemed inevitable. At the last moment, George jerked his wheels over to avoid the onrushing menace, hitting some brush, Then he jerked the wheel back to pass beside the aggressor, just missing the other vehicle and getting back on the road.

Heidi got a good look at the offenders and their vehicle. "It's a black Durango. There was a man driving. I turned to look back and see the Durango edge close to the drop before heading back onto the pavement."

"Yeah, I'll bet it was Dave Blackmun's."

"I think I saw his Black Dog Mining logo on the door."

"He's getting serious about wanting to strip my five hundred acres, I reckon."

"There was a woman with him. She looked scared. I think it was Arachne Smith," Heidi said.

"When we get to your place, I'll call Moon and warn him to

be careful when he drives back to Asheville. Dave sure must be missing the money he used to make from his criminal activities to try something as crazy as that."

"I worry about you and Moon. Blackmun was trying to kill you. What would he do if he knew you were involved in taking down the Pit?"

"I hope he doesn't find out. I have enough trouble just trying to keep my land and me fit for hunting. I hope we're still intact for a deer hunt this fall."

"I'm almost glad Jennifer's getting information from you. You won't be much use to me dead. Shouldn't you report this to the police?"

"Which police? I sure will tell Mike, but I don't think it would do much good to tell Sheriff Mulberry. He and Dave are too thick."

"Well, get me home so I can get out of my wet underwear. I was scared."

As soon as they were inside Heidi's apartment, George called Winding Fork and asked to speak with Moon while Heidi changed clothes.

"What's up, Cousin?"

"Moon, Dave Blackmun tried to run Heidi and me off the road at the cliff at Long's Hollow. I managed to get around him, but I think you ought to be careful driving home."

"Thanks for the warning. I think I'll stop by Dave's tomorrow morning and have a few words with him."

"Don't. You'll just rile him."

"I want to put him on notice. I'm not bound to have a working relationship with him. I'll remind him of our past encounters."

"If you're determined to do it, I think you ought to go armed. Are you going to tell Gladys?"

"A good suggestion, but I've already decided not to tell anyone but you. Don't worry. Blackmun and I tangled in the past when I was a member of ODSUM. Blackmun probably still smarts from my fists."

George couldn't resist seeing some dark humor in Moon's parting comment. "You've got to be kidding, telling me not to worry. It's obvious we didn't have a close encounter of the Blackmun kind by accident."

Chapter 30

The next day, Sunday morning, Adamo "Moon" Lunamin made his way to Dave Blackmun's house around ten o'clock. Moon had expected to find Blackmun at home. Dave wasn't much of a churchgoer. As far as Moon knew, his antagonist had not graced a church door since his wife had left him five years earlier, complaining to her friends that Dave was too kinky and cruel to live with.

Moon knocked several times and was thinking about leaving when a woman dressed in only a robe answered the door. George had told him Heidi saw a woman in the Durango with Blackmun when he tried to run them off the road, but Moon was still surprised. She looked familiar. "Good morning, I'm here to see Mr. Blackmun."

"Dave's eating breakfast, Mr. Lunamin. I'll tell him you're here. Have a seat in the room to our left. He'll be with you shortly," she said.

Moon had been startled to see a woman in a robe answer the door, but he was even more bemused that this woman knew his name. He was still trying to remember where he'd seen her before when Blackmun appeared, smoking a cigar.

Blackmun blew smoke in Moon's face. "Hello, Moon. What do you want this early on a Sunday morning?"

"I wanted to talk to you about something that happened to George Landsetter and Heidi Leaves last night."

Dave exhaled more smoke in Moon's direction. "What does it have to do with me?"

Instead of answering that question or reacting to the tobacco smoke, Moon changed the subject. "I didn't know you'd remarried."

Blackmun snickered. "You mean Arachne Smith. No, I haven't remarried. But that's not what you were asking about. What happened last night?"

"I think you know. George and Heidi recognized your Durango, when you tried to run them off the road and kill them." Hearing the woman's name brought back memory of where he'd seen her. She was one of the women he'd met in New York when he was dating Gladys. Dave must be paying her a high price to be his mistress.

"I think they must be mistaken. I was home all evening with Arachne."

"Have it your way. I just wanted to let you know messing with George is the same as messing with me. He's my first cousin, but we're like brothers. If he has a suspicious accident, I'll be looking for you."

Dave took his cigar and stubbed it on an ashtray. "Damn you, Lunamin, you s.o.b—coming here on a Sunday morning to threaten me. Get out of my house."

Moon headed for the front door. "So long, then, Dave. You've been warned."

"Go to hell, you motherfucker."

Looking back, Moon saw Arachne standing nearby as Blackmun muttered loud enough for Moon to hear, "I'd like sending *you* there."

Driving back to Winding Fork, Moon drank in the white sarvis and purplish redbud trees along the highway—remembering their nickname, Judas trees, he thought of Blackmun. When he reached his grandparents' house, he called George.

"I let Blackmun know messing with you is dangerous. I think I made that pretty clear."

"You shouldn't have put yourself in his line of fire."

"Forget it. Do you know a woman named Arachne Smith?"

"Yeah. She's one of the high-priced women Dave brought from New York. Why?" George asked.

181

"I think she knew Gladys there. I think she remembered me. She might tell Blackmun about Gladys's past."

"All the more reason to be careful. I'll try to get some other inspector to take over Dave's strip job for me," George said.

"You pay one, if that's what it takes. I'll put up the money."

◆◆◆◆◆◆

Cursing, Dave Blackmun went back to his coffee and Sunday newspaper in the kitchen. "Damn that s.o.b. I'll have to find some leverage over him."

Arachne asked if he meant Lunamin. "I know him from New York."

"How's that?"

"He's the one that married Gladys Stayskill. He hired her as an escort, but they fell in love. He married her. He caused her to give up the business. She caused him to quit the surface mining and move to Asheville after being found not guilty of killing his first wife."

Laughing, Blackmun rubbed his hands. "Arachne, you're a jewel. I think I know how to pressure Landsetter and Lunamin into letting me strip those five hundred acres."

"What do you have in mind? I hope it's not as dangerous as what you tried last night. That was crazy."

"Don't worry. I may need your help, though," Dave said as he lit another cigar.

"Be sure not to ask for more than your bank account can stand, Lover."

"Now that you mention it, let's get back to where we were before Lunamin interrupted." Dave pulled open Arachne's robe to look at her nakedness.

"Let's go to the bedroom and get the toys, then. Put out that damn cigar," Arachne said as she pressed her hand to his loins to check. "I think this naughty boy needs a whipping."

After his "punishment," Blackmun considered his scheme for the rest of the day. He called Josie Roper the next morning before heading out to one of his strip jobs. He had to leave a message on her answering machine.

"I have another job for you. Come by my Winding Fork mining site after six or call me this evening."

———————— ✦✦✦✦✦ ————————

Josie Roper found the message on her answering machine when she returned from Kentucky that evening. She had been over the state line talking with Jeb Basherman, the man she had hired to shoot Wayland Stanard. Two persons had seen Basherman in the vicinity of the mine on the day of the shooting. He had carelessly left shells where he had made his two shots. Josie congratulated herself for supplying the gun and having him return it to her to dispose of. She would also supply him with an alibi, although she hated to say he was with her. She consoled herself with the knowledge that decent help was hard to come by.

Josie called Dave Blackmun. "I got your message."

"Meet me tomorrow at the entrance to my strip job at Winding Fork. Come around eight-thirty. My men should all be at work by then."

"Okay. I'll be there. I'll be having some breakfast, if anybody asks."

Josie was eating doughnuts and drinking coffee at eight-thirty when Blackmun arrived, "You're looking pretty," he said.

"Don't get any fucking ideas. You have enough women without your screwing me again."

"Just trying to pay a compliment. The job I have for you requires a little finesse. I want you to kidnap a woman."

"I can plan a hit, but I'm not into kidnapping. Have you become dimwitted? Kidnapping is crazy."

"What if I asked you to kill George Landsetter?"

"I know George. I like him. I wouldn't want that job."

"Then I want you to kidnap Gladys Lunamin."

Coughing, Josie dropped her doughnut. "That's not my line. It's too dangerous. I like clean work where I plan a hit and don't get too involved with the execution."

"I'll pay you double what I paid for Stanard."

"It'll take a lot more than that."

"What about twenty thousand now and the same if you can deliver her at the appropriate time unhurt and not knowing who kidnapped her."

"That's a tall order. It'll take a lot of planning. Where is she to be kidnapped?"

"Asheville or here. It doesn't matter. Arachne Smith may be able to lure her to a place where you can snatch her without her seeing you."

"I'll do it for forty thousand now, and forty thousand when I deliver the package. I'll have a lot of expenses. And I want in writing this cancels all my debt."

"That's a lot of money."

Josie was adamant. "You want me to assume lots of danger. Take my offer, or forget about asking me."

Dave lit a cigar. After a long silence, he agreed. "Okay, if it works, I'll make a fucking bundle."

"Then I'll need to talk to Arachne Smith as soon as possible."

Believing Dave had become addled, Josie Roper left him as fast as she could. She detested her partner in crime. She hated the smell of his cigars. Afraid of the risk she was taking, she was not happy, even though she had driven a hard bargain. Had her fear of Blackmun not exceeded her fear of taking on a kidnapping, she would have refused the job. She recalled the first day Blackmun had approached her after her father's death—citing her father's large debt to him, showing her the papers confirming the truth of what he said. Blackmun demanded payment. "With what?" she had asked. "I just graduated from college and don't have a job. I'm not aware of any stash of cash lying about." That's when Blackmun had suggested other forms of payment. The first installment had been the unpleasant task of bedding with him. After a few more bouts of sex, he had required her to plan whatever acts of enforcement, including murder, he demanded. A clever young woman, she had become a very successful enforcer for his criminal activities, while keeping a distance from the actual commission of the acts. Displeased at Blackmun's insane proposal, but afraid of crossing him, with many misgivings, Josie began planning her strategy.

Chapter 31

J osie Roper visited Arachne Smith at Dave Blackmun's house the same day she made her bargain with Blackmun. Arachne led her to the clean but unlovely kitchen and fixed coffee for them.

"Have a seat. Make yourself comfortable, Josie," she said.

Smelling lingering cigar smoke, Josie felt the presence of Dave as she sipped. "This coffee's good. Dave tells me you know Lunamin's wife, Gladys."

"She was Gladys Stayskill back in New York. We worked for the same escort service."

"Dave wants me to kidnap her, hold her, and deliver her back unharmed when he's ready. She's not to know who kidnapped her. That's a tall order. I think he'll ask me to kill her after he has what he wants."

"I agree. Dave has lost his wits, or at least his mojo. He's a perverted bastard to boot—likes to be whipped before sex."

"He likes to whip too. I know. I doubt that he'll want her to live if his plan works," Josie said.

Arachne nodded and freshened their coffees. "I please his kinky tastes because he pays well. He thinks he can pressure Lunamin and Landsetter by holding Gladys. He wants them to agree to his stripping George's five hundred acres. He says there's a huge amount of high grade coal under that land."

"He must think it's worth a king's ransom. He's paying me forty thousand dollars before and that much more after a successful kidnapping, just to get leverage on George. I need your help to pull it off," Josie said.

"I don't want to get involved in a kidnapping, but I'm afraid to buck Dave. He has a bad temper. I know first hand. But he's not the worst trick I've encountered, and he's a really good meal ticket."

Josie looked up from admiring her fingernails. "He's not the sort of guy you should cross. He's lethal. He takes advantage to get what he wants. He's held my father's debt over me and got me in too deep to quit. He agreed this job wipes out my debt. He put it in writing. That's the only reason I agreed to do it. I think it's crazy, even for that much money."

Arachne nodded. "I know. He tried to run Landsetter and Heidi Leaves off the road Saturday night at a place where they would have been killed. He almost killed us in the effort. I think he's losing his mind."

"Well, I've got to go through with it. Can you come up with a way to get Gladys where I could grab her without her knowing me?"

Arachne's brow wrinkled. "I probably can. She and Adamo visit here often. I'll try to come up with an idea. I guess you want to lure her to a secluded spot."

"Yes, that's the idea. I don't want onlookers."

"I'll think about a way to catch her off guard."

◆◆◆◆◆◆

That same day, George found another message from Jennifer on his answering machine. She was back in town. "I'm still working on the Stanard death. My editor got word that it's been judged a murder and linked to the illegal activities at the Pit, so he thinks I should write another story uncovering the link. I'd like to talk to you about it again. Please call."

George was not pleased to have Jennifer to deal with while he was wrestling with how to break off with her. He didn't want to be harsh, yet he must find a way convincing to Heidi. Besides, revealing any more to her about the FBI operation might be dangerous to himself and others. He reluctantly returned her call.

Jennifer answered on the second ring.

"This is George. You said you wanted to talk."

"Yes, I need more background. I could use a little social interaction, too."

George felt nauseous. "I don't know what else I can tell you."

"Well, I don't want to discuss it over the telephone."

George considered how lucky (or unlucky) it was that this was not his night to be with Heidi. He didn't have a back-up plan yet for dealing with Jennifer. "Then come by here after dark. I'll fix some something. Come after nine."

"I'll be there. I'm bringing my cards."

George checked to see if he had something to go with the pork chops he knew were in the freezer. In his pantry he found some canned black-eyed peas and a can of green peas.

At a quarter past eight, the doorbell rang as George's chops were sizzling and adding to the aromas in his apartment. He turned down the stove and unlocked the door. Jennifer stood there, dressed in short shorts and a short tight blouse that revealed her figure to great advantage, and she exuded a lavender aroma. A large purse was slung over her shoulder.

George couldn't help admiring her outfit as he ushered her in. She certainly was sexy. "You're really taking advantage of the warm weather."

"I just slipped on something comfortable."

"Have a seat at the table. I still have to finish the chops."

"Can you tell me anything more about Wayland Stanard?"

"I've already told you more than I should have."

"They've ruled it a murder now. You told me he was on Dave Blackmun's black list because he stopped paying blackmail. What's the connection to the goings on at the Pit?"

"According to rumor, Blackmun set up blackmail victims with the expensive women he brought from New York."

"If Stanard stopped paying blackmail when his wife left, how long ago was that?"

"Over a year, I think."

"Why would Blackmun wait so long for revenge?"

George grunted as he turned the chops. "I'm not privy to Dave's inner thoughts."

"You have to admit, if Dave Blackmun is as bad as you say, he wouldn't wait so long for revenge. There must be some other reason he acted when he did, *if* he killed Stanard."

George nodded.

"Maybe Stanard did something else to anger Blackmun. What do you think?" Jennifer asked.

"Maybe, I've answered more questions than I intended to. I'm not answering any more about Dave Blackmun. He's an s. o. b. I wouldn't put anything past.

"If that's where we are, what about offering me a gin and tonic."

"Okay, okay, but no more background about crimes." George set about making a couple of gin and tonics while he steeled himself to end their amatory relationship that night. He had to do it, if he wanted to marry Heidi.

Jennifer tried to get more information while they ate dinner, but George for the most part avoided answering, although he did admit that Blackmun must have blamed Stanard for the raid on the Pit.

After she helped George clear the table, Jennifer moved over to George's sofa and slipped off her sandals. She smiled at George when he handed her a gin and tonic.

"Thanks. I hope you have plenty of gin."

"No problem. I may run out of tonic, but I've got plenty of gin."

"Do you have orange juice?"

"Yeah."

"Gin goes well with that." Jennifer pulled a pack of cards out of her purse. "Let's play some strip poker."

"Are you sure you want to do that tonight? You don't have much left to strip."

"I came dressed for strip poker. Is seven card stud still our game?" George pushed aside his feelings of guilt about betraying Heidi again.

A half hour and ten hands later, Jennifer was without any clothes on except her bra and George was down to his underpants. They were sipping their fourth gin.

"I have aces over kings," Jennifer said. "Can you beat that?"

"No, I have three queens."

"Well, off with those drawers."

After George did what she asked, Jennifer admired his physique. She ran her hands over his lower body, encouraging him to arousal. "You are an Adonis. Turn out your lights and plug in this nightlight I brought. Then you light me up."

Hours later, as Jennifer dressed to leave, she thanked George. "I've had a delightful evening. Perhaps we can do this again before I go back to Roanoke."

George had prepared for this moment. "No, Jennifer. I can't. I have other plans for tomorrow. I'm ending the sexual part of our relationship. You are almost irresistible, but you don't want a permanent relationship. I've fallen in love with someone else. I want to marry her, but she won't have me as long as I'm having an affair with you."

"Will you still give me background information?"

"Yes, but I'm not playing any more poker or other games with you."

"I'll miss our games, if you hold to your decision. I'll be back to see whether you can hold to that resolve. I doubt that you can. I'll bring my cards."

"It won't do you any good. I've made my decision."

"We'll see. I don't want to be a bitch. Maybe after a few weeks you'll change your mind."

"I don't think so. I wish you well. I hope you win a Pulitzer, but I need more than occasional sexual encounters, no matter how pleasant they are."

Jennifer slapped his still uncovered loins. "I'm not tying myself down to any man. I'm after a Pulitzer," she said as she stomped out.

Feeling relieved despite pangs of guilt, George now knew he had to arrange for Heidi to be with him the next time he hosted Jennifer. He had made the break, but now he had to have Heidi witness the break so that she could truly believe it.

Chapter 32

T he next morning, George found a message from Josie Roper on his answering machine. "Mr. Landsetter," the voice said, "I met you up at the Gap when I was in Kentucky sight-seeing. I'm thinking of having some land I inherited from my parents strip-mined. I'd like to have some advice from a neutral party. You seem like the kind of guy who knows what's what. If you're willing to give me advice, give me a ring."

George did not consider himself a neutral party as far as law enforcement was concerned, but he could give her advice about what she should look for. Giving advice on surface mining was part of his job. He took down the number she left and called her. Josie answered on the third ring.

"Hello, this is George Landsetter, returning your call."

"Thanks, could give me some advice about surface mining?"

George remembered her pleasant voice and entrancing eyes. "I'll do what I can. That's part of my job."

"Would you have lunch with me at JG's Pizza today?"

George couldn't see any danger in a pizza lunch. "Sure. Their pizzas are excellent. What time did you have in mind?"

"Would one o'clock be too late for you?"

"No, I can inspect several mines by then."

"Okay, I'll see you at JG's at one."

George wondered what was going on. He had liked Josie, but he'd been warned about how dangerous she could be. He thought he'd better run her request by Mike Barton. He couldn't rely on one of their usual cautious cover meetings at Heidi's. He'd take the chance of calling Mike at work.

"Deputy Barton here."

"Mike, it's George. I have something I need to discuss. Could you meet me somewhere right away?"

"Yeah. I'll be patrolling out near Philemon Mullins' strip job. Can you meet me at the pull-off near his entrance at nine o'clock?"

"Great, I'm heading that way to inspect a couple of jobs. I'll be there. Afterwards I'll inspect Philemon's job."

George pulled in to the gravel pull-off a little before nine, and mulled over what Josie's call might mean while he waited. He had to be skeptical that the meeting was only about surface mining. A little after nine, a Wisdom County police car appeared and pulled in behind him. Landsetter got out of his vehicle and walked back to Mike's car and got in the passenger side.

"How're you doing, Old Buddy?" Mike asked.

"Hoping to make progress with Heidi."

"I expect to be your best man soon."

"My hope, too. Right now, though, I need your advice on something else. I had a call from Josie Roper this morning. I'm supposed to have lunch with her at one o'clock."

"I'd be leery of her. Did she say what she wanted?"

"I'm supposed to give advice about legal surface mining. It's part of my job. She says she plans on strip-mining some coal and wants my advice. She wants the opinion of a neutral party. I reckon I'm more neutral than any stripper." George noted what appeared to be a look of concern on Mike's face.

"That's probably a ruse, although I do think her father left her some land that might have coal. Why did she choose you?" Mike asked.

"The last day I saw Wayland Stanard over in Kentucky, I met her at that restaurant at the Gap. It was crowded. She invited me to sit at her table, and I did. She's pretty, you have to admit."

"Yeah, and has a helluva figure too, but she's bad news. You've been warned; she's suspected of arranging murders for hire for Dave Blackmun."

"That's why I need your advice. Can you think of any reason, other than her desire for advice about strip-mining, why she would want to see me?"

"Well, it could be she thinks you're a hunk, but it's probably something to do with your five hundred acres and Dave Blackmun." George noticed a smile struggling on Mike's face. "You need to be on your guard."

"Do you suppose Dave has a contract on me?"

"If he does, I don't think she'd try to execute a contract at a restaurant, but be careful. I don't think she carries out Dave's hits herself. Is this your night with Heidi?"

"Yeah."

"Okay, have her invite me over, and we'll talk about what went on at your lunch date. I'll bring some beer."

"You just want one of Heidi's dinners, but I'll do it."

"Great, anything Heidi wants to cook is okay with me. Call to give me a time."

After going through possible choices, Josie Roper and George agreed to order a medium pepperoni and sausage pizza to share. George gave the order and took their number.

When they found a booth and sat down, he questioned her. "What sort of advice about strip-mining do you need?"

"What should I be careful to look for?'

"For one thing, don't just take what seems to be the best offer without looking at the miner's record with the law, both during mining and then for reclamation." George bent forward and banged his fist on the table for emphasis "You want the land left in good condition. You need a stripper like my cousin Lunamin. He learned to mine legally, make good money, and leave the land in great shape."

"He's the one who started Lunar Mining?"

"Yeah, but he's out of the business now. Philemon Mullins operates pretty much the way my cousin did. So does Fred MacCloud, who took over Lunar Mining from Lunamin. You should try to get one of them, or someone who works like them."

Josie's questions were interrupted by the arrival of their pizza. "Savor the aroma. I hope it tastes as good as it smells," she said.

As he helped himself to pizza, George agreed. After a couple of tastes, he judged. "It's a great pizza. Getting back to mining, Lunar Mining is still making money mining the way Moon—that's what we call Lunamin—did."

"I've heard your cousin married a gorgeous woman and moved to Asheville," Josie said. "Is that right?"

"Yeah, but they visit here often. They bring Moon's son Andy to see his great grandparents."

"So Lunamin's wife comes with him?"

"Yes. Why? Are you interested in her?"

"You mentioned Moon was such a good surface miner. Did she get him to quit mining?

"I think she had some influence."

"Are you married, George?"

"Not yet." George thought he saw Josie smile a little.

The pizza was disappearing. There were only two slices left. Josie offered one to George and took the last for herself as she pursued her quizzing of George.

"You think Philemon Mullins would be a good choice to mine for me?"

"Yeah, not like some miners I could mention who avoid reclamation." George watched Josie, trying to detect a reaction.

Josie moved forward and put her hand on his. "Can you tell me some good reclamation jobs I could look at?"

"Philemon has begun to reclaim a site in Winding Fork. He's still mining. You might have a look at that. You can see good mining practices combined with good reclamation. I'll give you directions."

"If you could find the time, I'd rather you show it to me and explain why it's so good."

George stopped eating. He wondered if it would be safe to agree to Josie's request. After a long pause, he said, "I have a couple of inspections to make this afternoon, but if you're willing to follow me, I'll take you out there now and show you what I mean. I can go on from there to do my inspections." He figured he'd be safe at Philemon's mine even if Josie planned to kill him.

"Great, show me the way. I'll follow," Josie said.

George pulled out his wallet, but Josie protested. "You must let me pay, since you 're being so helpful."

The drive to Philemon's surface mining operation took about twenty minutes. The bulldozers were mounding the coal. Front-end loaders were dumping it in haul trucks, filling them and sending them off to a coal tipple. Amidst the humming of machinery and the odors from their exhausts, George spied Philemon. Leading Josie to him, George introduced her and asked Philemon if it would be all right to show her around.

Philemon gave Josie an appraising look. "Okay, as long as you stay away from my active operation."

"I mainly want to show her what you've already reclaimed."

Philemon nodded. "Go right ahead, but you assume responsibility for her."

George pointed out the efficiency of Philemon's active mining operation before he took Josie over to the land already reclaimed. "Notice he doesn't overload his haul trucks, so there's no waste along the highways."

Josie could see the trucks were not being loaded beyond capacity. "Do you think that saves money?"

"You don't get paid for wasted coal."

Once they were over at the already reclaimed portion of the site, he pointed out other efficiencies.

"Mullins reclaims as he goes. That way he's able to use equipment for reclamation when it's not in use for mining. Note that he's not leaving any steep high walls but pushing land back against the wall to create a gradual slope, making it easily usable. He spreads a mix

195

of grasses and black locust seeds over the reclaimed area at the same time, stabilizing the land soon after germination takes place."

George liked Josie's apparent interest.

"The reclaimed land is pretty. Is this the way your cousin Lunamin mined?" she asked.

"It's the way he learned to mine. He made money by being efficient."

"I'm puzzled. Why did he quit if he was doing so well?"

"His second wife didn't want to stay here. She thought they could start a new life in Asheville."

"Was his first wife's murder why they moved to Asheville?"

George worried about Josie's interest in Moon. He wondered if she knew of Gladys Stayskill's past. "Maybe, but they come back here often for long weekends. Moon wants to see his grandparents and to hunt with me."

George remembered what he was supposed to be doing. "Getting back to surface mining, I recommend you pick somebody who mines like Philemon Mullins."

"Honey, it's too bad you're not a surface miner. I'd hire you in an instant to strip for me."

George's neck felt warm. "Thanks for the compliment. I reckon I'd better get back to inspecting. I hope I've been helpful."

"It's been a pleasure. I'd like to see more of you."

George walked Josie back to their vehicles. When he extended his hand to her, she pulled him to her and kissed him. She pushed her tongue into his mouth. Surprised, George didn't resist but stood dazed as Josie broke away and climbed in her vehicle.

"So long, Inspector. If I decide to strip, I'll want some more help." She blew him another kiss.

George stood transfixed. Relieved to climb into his truck, he stared at her red vehicle as she drove off. He thought about what he'd tell Mike within Heidi's hearing. He certainly wouldn't mention Josie's kisses. He was having a difficult time thinking of Josie as a murderer, but she could be dangerous. He doubted that he was the target, but she might be planning some mischief involving Moon.

Before completing his inspections for the day, George called Heidi. "Honey, I know it's late notice, but would it be too much trouble to include Mike for dinner tonight? Something's come up that we need to discuss. I think you would find it interesting too."

"Okay, I was going to have steaks, but I don't have three. I'll just do spaghetti. He really seems to like that."

"He always says anything you fix tastes good to him. He'll bring some beer. I'll bring some wine. Should I tell him seven?"

"That's fine. Can you come over around six or earlier? I'd like to have a little time alone with you before he comes, and you can help me with dinner."

"Okay, I'll shower and come right over after work."

George had plenty to think about while he finished work and prepared to go to Heidi's. He checked on the coal reserves owned by Josie and found she had an extensive amount of high-grade coal under her land. He wondered about Josie's interest in Moon, but he couldn't see how that fitted with her obvious interest in her coal and him. His expertise about mining wasn't all that impressive. She must be attracted to him, but he sensed danger there. Besides, he didn't relish the idea of another admirer replacing Jennifer. He wanted to prove his trustworthiness to Heidi.

Heidi greeted George at the door with a kiss, which he returned with interest as he lifted her off her feet and hugged her with one arm while holding beer in his other hand.

She protested, laughing. "Whoa, you'll squeeze the breath out of me."

"No way, I just want to show I've missed you. I brought some beer and wine to make sure we have enough."

"I'm glad you thought about me," she said, running her hand through his blond mane. "I want you to long for me, pant for me. Now help me get dinner ready." George began making the salad as directed. While Heidi put the finishing touches to her spaghetti sauce, he opened a beer for him and poured red wine for her.

"I had a strange request today. Josie Roper asked my advice about surface mining—claims she may strip some land she inherited."

Heidi shook her head. "Isn't she rumored to arrange murders for hire?"

"Yes, and she seemed very interested in Moon, although she said her interest stemmed from my citing his surface mining expertise."

"Do you think Blackmun has put a contract on Moon?" Heidi asked.

George nodded. "I wouldn't rule that out."

When the doorbell rang, Heidi had dinner on the table and an apple pie in the oven. George let Mike in, took the beer he'd brought, and ushered him to the table.

"How did your strip-mine tutorial with Josie Roper go?" Mike asked as George passed him the salad bowl.

"I'm alive. She seemed really interested in Moon. I think maybe she's planning something involving him, although she said her interest was on account of my saying he did an excellent job of surface mining."

Mike's sarcastic laugh greeted George's explanation. "I agree she must be planning something. It wasn't just idle curiosity. You should warn Moon to watch out."

"I will. They're supposed to visit again in a couple of weeks. Moon and Archie are going 'coon hunting with me. Why don't you come along?"

"Okay, Old Buddy, thanks for the invite."

Heidi broke into the conversation. "If you're worrying about Josie Roper, Mabel tells me she held a long meeting at Possum Hunt with a hard case named Jeb Basherman a few days ago. Do you suppose they were planning something?"

Chapter 33

Urged on by Dave Blackmun, Arachne Smith set out to find all she could about Adamo Lunamin's wife, Gladys Stayskill Lunamin. She tracked down her home decorating business in Asheville, North Carolina, and learned of Lunamin's son Andy, her step-son. Arachne found Gladys's cell phone number and called it, pretending to be a prospective client who wanted a house in Big Stone Head decorated.

"My name is Merith Taylor. I need some ideas about decorating a house right away," said Arachne.

"I'm quite busy right now. I can't drop everything here in Asheville, although I do have some good help. Given time to plan, I could handle a job in Southwest Virginia. Perhaps we could discuss it next weekend when my husband and I visit his grandparents in Virginia. Would that be soon enough?"

"Yes, that might work, if you could start soon after we talk."

"I'll be at Archibald MacCloud's in Winding Fork. Give me a call on Saturday morning and we'll arrange a meeting."

"How early would you be available?"

"Nine-thirty or ten should be all right." Gladys gave the supposed Merith the MacClouds' phone number.

Arachne Smith called Josie Roper after she finished talking to Gladys. "I have your quarry set up thinking I have a house to decorate, but we need a house where we can arrange the catch. Dave's house won't do. Lunamin knows it."

"I own a rental house in Big Stone Head under another name. That will do. It's empty now and could use redecorating. We'll use that." Josie gave Arachne the address.

"All right. I'm going to wear a wig and dark glasses so that Gladys won't recognize me. You'll have to pretend to be kidnapping me, too," Arachne said.

"That's easy enough. We'll just have to make sure she doesn't see us before we get a blindfold on her. She won't know what we've done with you. We'll tell her we have you in another room."

Archibald was on hand to greet Moon, Gladys, and Andy when they made the drive from Asheville to Winding Fork on Friday afternoon. "We left Asheville early enough to be in time for supper with you and Serafina," Moon said.

"She is excited about having our great-grandson visit us," Archie said.

"Andy was excited about seeing his Mamaw and Papaw too," Moon said. "He's hoping Serafina's been baking."

Andy rushed forward to hug them. "You smell like cookies," he told Serafina as she kissed him.

Archibald laughed as he lifted the boy and hugged him. "I'm glad to see you're sill a cookie hound, but you mustn't eat too many. Save one or two for the rest of us."

Gladys was helping Moon carry in the luggage. They had extra stuff this trip because of the proposed 'coon hunt and her expected business appointment. "Moon's looking forward to the hunt," Gladys said.

"I've invited George and Mike to eat with us so that everybody will be ready to hunt. I'm supplying the 'coon dogs and the liquor," Archie said.

"What dogs are we using tonight, Papaw?" Moon asked.

"Two grandkids of Sap and Sookie—names Sol and Sandy.

They're not quite as good as their grandparents, but they're pretty good. I believe Sol may have a better voice than either Sap or Sookie."

"We had some good hunts with Sap and Sookie," George said. Moon nodded agreement.

Serafina interrupted. "You men can talk later. Right now Heidi and I are putting supper on the table. Come and eat."

All of them heeded the call and were soon consuming a dinner of ham, grits, greens, baked potatoes, biscuits and gravy. "It's good to have all of you here," Serafina said when she brought out a carrot cake for dessert. "You'll will enjoy this cake, I know. Heidi made it."

Slices of cake disappeared as quickly as the main course. "My compliments to our cooks," Gladys said.

"I agree. It was a fine meal. Thanks for including me," Mike said

Archibald didn't waste time moving his 'coon hunters away from the table. "There's going to be a full moon tonight, boys. It should be good coon hunting anyway because there's some good cloud cover. Let's get started."

Archie, George, Moon, and Mike hiked to the head of the stream at the spring on the ridge, then down to the next hollow, where Archibald told them there was lots of 'coon sign. "It's a sure-fire place to give the dogs the scent," he said.

Nosing about, the dogs easily picked up scent and began trailing down through the hollow as they bayed.

Listening with pleasure, Archie led the men as they climbed to the ridge crest and built a fire in a good location for hearing the dogs. They sat down around it, listening to the baying of the hounds. Skunk odor mixed with the smell of burning wood.

George shared his elation. "A night like this listening to the hounds is better'n a bag full of gold."

"That Sol has a great voice." Archibald said as he pulled out a bottle of moonshine and passed it around. "This here is pretty good stuff."

"Where'd you get it Papaw? From cousin Isaiah?" Moon asked.

"You bet—It's not quite as good as his daddy's, but it's top notch."

The four of them enjoyed swigs from the bottle as they listened to the voices of the dogs.

George struck a sad note. "It's good to be out here on this March night. The season's closing this week, so we'd better enjoy this night. It's probably the last time we'll get to do a coon hunt until a little after deer season—that's a long time."

"Enjoy it then," Archibald said. "Listen to old Sol. I don't believe there's another hound around with a voice like that."

The dogs chased a raccoon for several hours before they finally treed it. When the baying changed to rapid barking, Archie knew the 'coon had gone to tree.

Archibald stood. "I promised Serafina some wild meat for some mince pies, so I reckon we better get down there and shoot that critter," he said. He took another pull from his bottle and passed it around. Then they put out their fire and headed downhill toward the dogs and 'coon. In less than ten minutes they were there. Archibald shone a light into the tree and onto the animal. "Who wants the first shot?" he asked.

"You take it, Mike. You're our guest," George said.

"Okay." Mike lifted his rifle and aimed where Archie pointed the light. The 'coon glared at them as Mike pulled the trigger. The shot rang out and the 'coon fell from the tree. "Good shot," Archie said. George and Moon ran over to rescue the carcass from the dogs.

As they trudged back to Archibald's house with their trophy, George told Moon about Josie Roper's interest in him. "I couldn't say much to Mike the other night at Heidi's, but Josie came on to me pretty strong, so it was hard to say whether her concern about surface mining was entirely about the mining or because of her interest in you, or just a way to have time alone with me."

Mike offered his opinion. "I think she showed too much interest in Moon and Gladys for it to be only a yen for you, George. Remember, she's probably the one who arranges hits for Dave Blackmun. She's sexy, and she's dangerous."

George agreed. "You and Gladys need to be alert, Moon."

Moon didn't disagree. "You're right. We'll try. I'll warn Gladys before she goes to meet with that client tomorrow. You've got to be careful too."

"So this was a business trip for Gladys?" Mike asked.

"No, we had this trip planned for this 'coon hunt. The other day Gladys had a call from a woman who wants a house decorated."

"Does this female have a name?" Archie asked.

"She called herself Merith Taylor. Ever heard of her, Papaw?"

"No, there're a passel of Taylors around here. But I ain't heard of a Merith."

"Neither have I," Mike said. "I think Gladys had better be careful."

"Maybe I should go with her," Moon said, "but I promised Andy I'd take him for a hike to try out his new binoculars."

"She'll probably be all right. I'd say that Dave Blackmun would be after you, or me, not Gladys," George said.

"Just to be on the safe side, give me the address of the house she's going to look at. I'll try to find time to drop by to check it out." Mike said.

"Well, boys, we had a successful 'coon hunt. I'm glad you came along, so let's not worry about tomorrow," Archie said. "Serafina will have her wild meat."

The next morning before breakfast, Moon warned Gladys to be careful as he sat waiting for her to fix bacon, scrambled eggs and toast on Mamaw's new electric stove. Moon told Gladys what George had told him about Josie Roper's interest in them. He emphasized his worry by pounding the table when he told her that Josie arranged hits for Dave Blackmun.

."What do you know about this client?" he asked.

"Not much, she has a house in Big Stone Head she wants redecorated."

"Do you have an address?"

"Yes, 2235 Maple Street in Big Stone Head."

"Josie Roper has been asking George about us. Josie arranges Dave Blackmun's murders. So we need to be careful."

"The woman seemed legitimate. It should be a lucrative job, and it would mean our spending more time here. I want to do it."

Moon hesitated before agreeing. "Okay, but be careful. Mike is going to check out that address."

"I think you should take your own advice. You're the one he's after about mining George's land."

Looking at her golden-auburn hair and gray eyes, he hated the thought of losing her. "You can't tell what Blackmun will do. Just be careful. Give me a call when you get there." He kissed her and hugged her tightly to make sure she understood his love and concern.

He waved to her as she drove off in their white Mercedes.

An overcast sky darkened Gladys' drive from Winding Fork to Big Stone Head despite the blooms of serviceberry and redbud along the highway winding through the deep, narrow valley. Across the stream running below the highway, she could see the railway on which the Clinchfield Railroad had carried out tons of coal to the outside world. As she drove into Big Stone Head, she welcomed the more open view that confronted her.

She followed the directions her client had given her and made her way to Maple Street without difficulty. The house at 2235 turned out to be an imposing three-story Victorian structure. It's white paint was not peeling but seemed less than fresh. Gladys pondered whether she should recommend repainting the exterior as she parked her car in the driveway. *Redecorating this house should be fun. It'll keep me busy for awhile.*

She called Moon to tell him she had found the house in Big Stone Head without difficulty, then collected her bags of samples and made her way to the front door and rang the doorbell. A woman with black hair, wearing dark glasses, opened the door.

"Hello, I'm Gladys Lunamin, here to see about decorating this house."

"I'm excited about doing this house over. I hope you can give me some good ideas."

There was something familiar about this woman that Gladys could not explain. "I'm going to try. First, I need to look at it."

"I'll give you a tour."

"Do you want the entire house redone, or do you want to redo just the first floor."

"I haven't decided. I want to hear your opinion before I make up my mind."

Gladys had an odd feeling about this woman. Something in Merith Taylor's voice seemed familiar. Or her walk perhaps, they reminded Gladys of somebody she'd known before but couldn't quite place. Merith certainly didn't speak a Southwest Virginia dialect.

As they moved from one large, high-ceilinged room to another, Gladys felt sure she had heard that voice before. "Have we met somewhere before, Merith?"

"Not that I know of. I've just recently moved to Big Stone Head. "She rubbed her hands together and changed the subject, waving her hand around the second room. "This is the room I'd like to use as my primary room to entertain guests."

"Offhand I'd say a conservative wall paper with a pastel paint on the woodwork combined with matching drapes would work if you want it to be a fairly formal room, but you'll have to look at some of my samples and give me an idea of what you like. Let me see some of your other rooms before we get to that."

"Let's go down the hall to the room I'd like to use as the dining room."

Once they reached the proposed dining room, Gladys asked what kind of furniture Merith planned to put in the room.

"Do you have a formal dining set you plan to put in here?"

"Yes, it's a very old set my grandparents left me."

Gladys saw a small table in a corner of the otherwise unfurnished room. "Let me show you some samples. I'll open my books on this table to show you."

"Wonderful. Let's look at them."

Gladys spread out sample books and opened a couple to show Merith. As she and Merith bent over the table, Gladys suddenly felt herself grasped from behind by powerful hands while others wrapped a large blindfold over her face and fastened it behind her head. One of her attackers smelled of a stable.

"Help! Let me go!" She tried to twist free. "Merith! What's going on? What's this all about?"

"Just be quiet. Do as you're told and you'll be okay," a male voice said. "Merith can't help you."

Gladys sensed the woman who called herself Merith was moving away. "Merith, what's going on?"

"Don't you worry about her. We're taking her to another room," an unfamiliar female voice said.

Someone tied Gladys' hands and shoved her through a door and up stairs. When they reached a landing, the person pushed her into what seemed a darkened room. Shoved to a chair, Gladys complained, "I want to know what's going on."

The man said, "Shut up. You'll be all right." Then he tied her to the chair and tied her legs. "If you know what's good for you, you'll behave yourself. We don't want to hurt you."

Gladys remembered what Moon had told her that morning. Too late, she realized what must be happening. Somebody had kidnapped her to put pressure on Moon for some purpose. Probably Dave Blackmun was involved, pressuring Moon and George to sell him the right to strip George's five hundred acres. She wracked her brain, trying to remember where she had heard the voice of the woman who called herself Merith Taylor. She was sure she had heard it before. Merith definitely wasn't from Southwest Virginia. She was sure of that. She'd spent years working to change Moon's dialect a little.

The more she thought about it, she concluded the voice reminded her of New York. Moon told her that George said Blackmun had brought some women down from New York to use in his blackmail scheme. Moon had warned her not to repeat what he'd told her. What if the pretended Merith was one of those women? Maybe I knew her back in New York. Were the dark hair and dark glasses a disguise?—a disguise used because the woman knew Gladys from her life in New York? That limited the possibilities. She decided to bide her time and do nothing to antagonize her captors.

Chapter 34

Pacing the floor at Winding Fork, Moon was worried. He'd expected Gladys to meet him for lunch, but she hadn't kept their date. He called George.

"I'm concerned about Gladys. She didn't show up for our lunch date at Enchiladas."

"I think we'd better get Mike to check. I'll have him see whether or not your car's at that address she went to. What was it?

"2235 Maple Street in Big Stone Head, He probably remembers our car. At any rate it's a white Mercedes with North Carolina plates."

"Let me hear from you if Gladys shows up."

That afternoon Moon spent most of his time worrying, and George had a difficult time keeping his mind on his mine inspections.

Supper time arrived at Winding Fork, but Gladys hadn't returned. Moon called George again. "No sign of Gladys. I'm really worried. Do you think Dave's done something with her?"

"I wouldn't put anything past him. I'm going to call Mike again and have him alert the FBI. She may have been kidnapped. I'll tell him that nobody has heard from her since this morning. I'll ask him to check out the house and put out an alert for the car. Let me know if Gladys shows up or you hear from her."

When George called Mike, he told him they suspected Gladys had been in an accident or had been kidnapped. "In view of what's been going on, I think you should alert your buddy at the FBI."

"I agree," Mike said. "I've already put out an alert for the white Mercedes."

Waiting at Winding Fork, unable to account for Gladys's whereabouts, Moon paced up and down. Finally he called George. "Please call Mike and ask him to check again on the Maple Street address where Gladys said she was to meet her client. She didn't show up for our lunch date and nobody here has heard from her yet.

"Okay, you're right to be worried. I'll have Mike check that house on Maple Street, and then I'll call you back.

An hour later, George returned Moon's call. "It doesn't look good. I'm worried. Mike couldn't find the car or anybody at the house, but the front door was unlocked. He went in and searched the house from top to bottom. The only thing he could find were three of Gladys's sample books. He's going to have the FBI check them for fingerprints."

Moon spent the night worrying. The next day an envelope addressed to Adamo Lunamin appeared in the mailbox at the end of the driveway at Winding Fork. In the envelope Moon found a ransom note cut from magazines and newspapers. "You have two weeks to get ready two million dollars in bills of no more than $100. Further instructions will follow."

As soon as he finished reading the message, Moon cursed Dave Blackmun and called George "That bastard Blackmun has gone too fucking far. Gladys isn't just missing. At least she hasn't smashed the Mercedes, She's been kidnapped. They're asking two million dollars for her safe return. Knowing Dave, I don't think he'll let Gladys live even if I do kick in the money. I'd like to have that son of a bitch where I could beat the shit out of him again."

"Pour yourself a shot of Isaiah's 'shine and settle down," George said. "Keep the note for the FBI to check for fingerprints. I was afraid of Dave's doing something bad, but not anything as crazy as this."

"I could kick myself for letting Gladys go alone," Moon said.

"Blaming yourself won't help," George said. "Mike says the State Police found your car in Kentucky just across the border. It was parked in a pull-off parking area at the Gap. They're holding it for the FBI to look for clues. They ought to question Josie Roper. She arranges Dave Blackmun's assassinations, and you know he must be behind this. He's putting on pressure to get my coal," George said. "We'll just have to show the son of a bitch he's messing with the wrong people."

"I reckon you're right," Moon said. "We have to keep our wits about us if we're going to beat that bastard Blackmun. Maybe we can find Gladys by tracking Josie and Dave. I don't think we can afford to wait for Mike and the FBI. I don't think Dave will give us those two weeks."

"Agreed."

"Okay. We'll track the scumbags. I've arranged for a good man to handle my landscaping service for as long as I need. I'll keep an eye on Dave. From what you've said, you're the one to keep an eye on Josie. Just be careful," Moon said.

"Josie likes me. I don't think she'd kill me."

"I wouldn't count on that. Don't forget you're planning to marry Heidi. You don't want her to be a widow before she's a wife," Moon said.

"Don't lecture me. You don't want to lose Gladys either. Just keep your lid on. My land is what got you into this. I'll do what I can to get Gladys back alive for you, even if it means giving up my mining rights."

"Well, if we don't turn up something soon, I just may beat it out of Blackmun. Don't you do something rash. We won't wait for the FBI. We'll have her back before two weeks is up," Moon said.

George couldn't help chuckling at Moon's telling him not to do anything rash when his cousin was threatening to beat Blackmun to a pulp.

Chapter 35

Gladys heard footsteps approaching her. Then large hands grasped her and loosened the ropes tying her to the chair and around her ankles. It was a man whose unshaven beard brushed her hands. He smelled of horses. Gladys heard a woman's voice." Take her to the van." She felt herself pushed down a flight of stairs, out of the house into cooler air, onto a porch. After more steps and a concrete walk, she was pushed into a vehicle. Gladys could not see her feet, so she thought it was night. Then she smelled stable odor again as the man strapped her in and retied her ankles. Scared, she strained to hold back tears. She heard voices and could make out some of what they were saying.

Gladys heard the man grunt "Okay, we'll take it from here."

"Just be careful nobody sees you leave," the woman's voice said said. "Keep your disguise on for a while. We'll move her to where we'll keep her. Now I have to get rid of her car."

"We'll leave it in Kentucky," the man said as he climbed into the van.

Gladys heard the van door slam shut. They moved for about twenty or thirty minutes, Gladys guessed, then stopped. The driver's door opened and slammed shut. Night birds were calling, telling Gladys they must be parked in some wooded area. Another ten minutes or so passed. After doors opened and slammed shut, the vehicle began to move again. It stopped after a drive of what Gladys judged to be over half an hour. Her feet were untied, and she felt the circulation returning as she was pulled from the vehicle and led across grass to a door and pushed into another building. Growing tired of being shoved from place to place, Gladys couldn't help protesting. "Why do you keep pushing me around?"

"Shut up and be happy you're still alive," The male voice ordered.

Gladys did not protest again but wondered when her abductors would stop shuttling her from place to place. Her stomach nausea grew and her mouth dried as her fear increased.

As nearly as Gladys could tell, she was pushed down a hall to a room at the back of a house. She thought it might be an old house when they chained her to a radiator. She could not remove her blindfold because they kept her hands tied. Soon the man replaced the blindfold with a black hood, which was tightened at the base with rope, which she could feel against her neck. She had a brief glimpse of a sofa. She felt hopeful. Since they were trying so hard to keep their identities secret, perhaps they didn't intend to kill her. But as she remembered Moon's tales of bloodshed, she grew more and more alarmed at her situation.

◆ ◆ ◆ ◆ ◆ ◆ ◆

George called Heidi. He had to warn her what he was planning to do. He figured he might as well tell her, since she could hear of it second hand, become angry, and break off their relationship.

"It's my night tonight. I want to talk to you about a problem. How about our spending the early evening birding on the Knob and then eat at my place."

"Okay. Sounds like fun."

"I'll pick you up at five."

The Canada warblers were still uttering their bubbling songs, the pewees were doing their mournful drawn out evening call, and the veeries were winding their ringing songs and sounding drawn out *vee-er* calls. Wood thrushes were tuning their throaty violins with *e-o-lay-tee*. As the sky darkened, the Barred Owls began hooting *who-cooks-for you* and whip-poor-wills began the complaint giving them their name.

As they breathed the cool air and inhaled the crisp odor of the hemlocks, the pair listened to the evening chorus for about twenty minutes. Finally, George said, "I have some bad news."

"It seems a shame to ruin this beautiful evening."

"I agree, but Gladys has been kidnapped. Moon received the ransom note today. I felt angry when he told me. I wanted to shoot somebody, preferably Blackmun."

Heidi's face twisted, "How terrible! What did they demand?"

"Two million dollars, but Moon and I think that Dave Blackmun's responsible, and his real goal is to pressure me into signing over mining rights for my five hundred acres to him."

Tears began to form around Heidi's eyes. "Do you think that would get Gladys back alive?"

"I don't think so. Dave will have his henchmen kill her once he gets the mining rights. He's already bought several murders."

Heidi squeezed George's arm. "What are you going to do?"

"The FBI is checking for fingerprints and other clues. Moon and I think we shouldn't wait for the FBI. They're good, but we can act faster. He's going to keep an eye on Dave while I trail Josie Roper."

"Is she involved?"

"Mike thinks she's the person Dave hires to plan his hits. He probably persuaded her to expand her repertoire. If we can find out where they're keeping Gladys, I think we may be able to rescue her."

"That sounds dangerous. I don't want to lose you."

Heidi's complaint was punctuated by the distant hooting of a great horned owl and another cry that sounded like a woman screaming as dark settled over the mountain ridge. George felt Heidi shivering and pushing closer to him.

"Did you hear that? Was it a woman?" Heidi asked.

"No, that was the wail of a bobcat, but it does sound like a woman's scream."

"Do what you must to save Gladys, but come back alive, you hear?"

"I'll do my best. Will you marry me then?" George pulled Heidi closer to him and kissed her. He was worried that they might never have a life together.

"We'll see. We still have Jennifer to deal with."

"I've broken off with Jennifer. The next time Jennifer asks to come by for information, I'm going to ask you to be present. I want you to witness for yourself I'm through with her except for providing background."

Chapter 36

George found a note slipped under his door when he returned to his apartment after work. It was typed: *Meet me at the Blackdog Mining's strip job at Winding Fork tomorrow night at nine o'clock. I can help you free Lunamin's wife. Come alone. Bring the attached sheet with your dated signature.* The attached paper was a contract conveying the mining rights for George's five hundred acres to Blackdog Mining. George felt his stomach churning. He detected a faint aroma of tobacco on the papers that reminded him of Dave's cigars. It was obviously a set up to lure him to a dangerous encounter, yet it might suggest a way to find out where Blackmun's henchmen were keeping Gladys.

George spent an uncomfortable night trying to decide what to do about Dave's gambit. Before going to work the next morning, he phoned Moon.

"Something's come up. I need your advice. Can you meet me this morning at Winding Fork at eight-thirty?"

"Sure, I'll be here. The FBI has my car, remember?"

When George gave Moon the papers, he looked them over carefully before making a suggestion. "I think you should meet him, but we'll park out of sight, and I'll come in secretly as back up. In the meantime, you should make a copy of this contract to take with you. Give the original and the cover note to Mike to pass on to the FBI to search for fingerprints. We might link Blackmun to the kidnapping that way."

"Good idea. I'm sure Dave will have somebody in hiding, waiting to shoot me when I hand over a signed contract. He won't need me then."

"You'll hand him one with a flawed signature, signed Landsetten, not Landsetter. We have to assume he'll try to kill you once he gets the contract. I'm planning a distraction. I'll keep an eye out for a shooter. You'd better go armed."

George nodded. "Okay. I'm going to ask Philemon if he knows where Josie's parents' place is. She inherited it. Maybe that's where they're holding Gladys."

As usual, George's inspection of Philemon Mullins' strip mine was perfunctory. Philemon never failed to do more and better work than the law required. As they made their way around the operation, George posed his question.

"Do you know where Josie Roper's parents lived?"

"Yeah, they owned a place down in Crabtree Hollow. That's not far from here."

"I know the place. I've birded there. There aren't but a couple of houses in there."

"That's right. The Ropers' is the far place."

"That's a long way in."

George was even surer then that the Roper home site would be where Josie was holding Gladys. Leaving Philemon's mine, he drove to Crabtree Hollow. A heavy fog was beginning to lift, but it was still thick enough to provide good cover. Passing the first house, he drove on a mile and stopped just below the top of a rise, pulled into a lane into the woods, and parked. Putting his binocular strap around his neck, he scanned birds as he moved back to the highway on foot. If anybody saw him, they'd write him off as a birdwatcher. At the top of the hill, where he could look down to the Roper place, he stopped to scan. As a hooded warbler's *weebee-weeteeoh* rang in his ear and a cardinal sang *tu,tu, tuu*h, he saw a woman and a man come out of the Roper house and climb into a familiar red vehicle. It was Josie's Toyota van.

The Toyota pulled away from the house and turned onto the

highway, coming toward him. *Are they leaving Gladys alone? This could be a chance to free her.* He ducked back in the woods and fog, hiding behind a tree. From his hiding place he could see Josie at the wheel and a large man with her.

After the vehicle passed, George got back in his truck and drove down past the house and turned into the woods on a logging road paralleling a stream lined with rhododendron. George could hear the songs of Swainson's warblers and Louisiana waterthrushes ringing along the stream edge through the fog. He parked, climbed out, and headed through the woods toward the Roper house. A faint odor of skunk mixed with the fog and smoke from the house.

Moving quietly but quickly through the woods toward the back of the house, he flushed a rabbit. Startled, he looked around to see if anyone else was about. The sounds of the stream were becoming faint. He saw and heard nothing other than the cawing of crows and the calls of blue jays, so he moved on.

Still concealed by the heavy fog, George reached the house without being detected or seeing anyone. Jumping up to look into a back window, he saw Gladys tied to a chair. Keeping low, he climbed onto the back porch and tried the door. It was locked. Going back to the window where he had spied Gladys, George tried raising it. It was unlocked. George searched a nearby shed and found a wheelbarrow. He moved it below the window. Standing on it, he raised the window and climbed in and crossed the room.

Hearing him, Gladys tried to move her chair. Quickly George stepped to her. Whispering to Gladys through her hood, he told her who he was and asked her to be quiet. Then he cut the rope tying the covering over her head and pulled it off.

She sighed in relief. Next, he untied her arms and legs. She stretched and struggled up. Helping her, he led her to the window, slowly, as she recovered from being immobilized and stood unsteadily. Climbing out the window, he stepped on the wheelbarrow and then the ground. Pushing the wheelbarrow firmly against the house, he helped Gladys out the window.

Once she was beside him in the yard, George motioned her to

follow him as he crouched low and ran to the woods. Once there, he could hear her sobbing and stopped a moment to hug her. "I know you're upset, but try not to make noise. I'm parked on a logging road. We need to hurry."

When they reached his vehicle, he opened the back door and took her hand. George whispered, "Get on the back seat and lie down. No one will know I'm not alone." He covered her with a tarp from behind the seat. As they headed out to the highway, Gladys, cheered by the sun breaking through the fog and creeping under the tarp, could not keep silent any longer.

"I'm so glad to see you, George. Where's Moon?"

George could hardly contain his elation. "He's okay. I didn't have time to call him. I took a chance that you were in the house when I saw two people leave. Was there anyone else in the house with you after they left?"

"I think there was an old woman, but she's deaf."

"I was quiet. She probably didn't hear a thing, but she might check and find you're gone. You stay hidden."

Gladys gave a quiet laugh. "Aye, aye, sir."

"When we get back to the main road, I'm taking you to Winding Fork, but you stay down. I don't want anybody to know you're with me. I'll leave you with Archie and Serafina, if Moon's not there. Then I'll go about my inspections as if nothing happened."

"Oh, George, you don't know how scared I was. They said they weren't going to hurt me, but I didn't believe them. Who are they?"

"Josie Roper and her assistant. We believe Dave Blackmun hired them."

They made it to the main road, and George drove several miles without encountering anybody as he headed toward Winding Fork. Then he saw what looked like Josie's red Toyota headed back to Crabtree Hollow.

"Stay down, Gladys! We're going to pass your kidnappers. I'm going to ignore them. I travel all of these roads every day doing my job, so they shouldn't be suspicious."

"I'll make myself as small as possible."

George kept his eyes on the road as the two vehicles passed. He didn't know whether Josie saw him, but he felt sure they couldn't catch him, even if they turned and followed. He stepped on the gas.

At Winding Fork, George delivered his booty to Serafina. He was sure the delightful fragrances in Serafina's kitchen would restore Gladys.

"Lord a'mercy, girl. I'm sure glad to see you." She said as she gave Gladys a hug.

"Not as glad as I am to see you, Serafina. I'm so happy to be back at Winding Fork. George is my hero. Where's Moon?"

"He's out back with Archie."

"I'll get him," George said as he headed to the back door.

Serafina patted George on the back. "You're a good man. Honey, Archie and Moon are preparing something for your meeting with Dave tonight. Maybe you should call that off now that we've got Gladys."

George scratched his head as he went outside. "I'll go out and talk to them. I'll bet Moon wants to go through with our shindig, but I'm not too eager to keep on. I need time to catch my breath."

George found Archie and Moon with Andy behind the house creating a weapon. They were loading a canvas bag with sticks of Dynamite. Moon was attaching a plastic shiner to the bag handle. A light breeze was blowing a faint odor of a mining blast from the direction of Dab Whacker's mining site on Isaiah's land.

"This will glow in the dark and make a shot easier," Moon said as he worked carefully with hands wearing plastic gloves.

"We may not need the explosives," George said.

"What do you mean?" Moon asked.

"I just brought Gladys back to you."

Moon grabbed George's arm. "Are you pulling my leg?"

"No, I took a chance on finding her at Josie's home place in Crabtree Hollow. When Josie and her helper left, I got Gladys out and brought her back here. She's inside with Serafina. She's asking for you."

"You son of a coon hunter. You took a big chance. You should have called me."

George shook his head. "I thought about it, but I was afraid there wasn't time. I figured Josie had gone out to get groceries or do some other errand. I found a window open. I didn't think I should waste a second. I was right about that. We passed Josie on her way back about three miles out on the main road."

Moon put down the bag of explosives and hurried into the house. About fifteen minutes later, he reappeared. "I'm sure obliged to you, Cousin. Gladys is still a little shaky and tired but as pretty and feisty as ever."

George grinned and slapped Moon on the back. "I'm happy I could help."

Moon went back to work on the explosives. "I think we should still go ahead with confronting Dave. We still can save your five hundred acres, and we have a chance to get rid of Blackmun for good. We need to keep our fingerprints off these explosives., so you'll wear plastic gloves."

George shook his head. "It's going to be dangerous, especially for me."

"That's why Papaw has come up with this rig. You just put down the bag with the fake contract attached and this shiner pointed our way, hand the paper to Dave, and back off. I figure that, when Dave gets the fake contract, he'll accept it as legitimate and signal his man to shoot."

George nodded. "That's what worries me. Won't Dave be suspicious of the bag?"

Moon shook his head. "It'll be dark. You can keep the shiner hidden and the bag behind you."

"I reckon that would work."

Moon zipped up the bag. "He won't notice you've signed George Landsetten instead of Landsetter. He'll start to signal. That's when you run, Archie shoots the bag to blow Dave up, and I shoot Dave's assassin. If Dave's still alive, we'll have him for kidnapping and attempted murder."

George grunted and slapped his thigh. "That's easy for you to say. You won't be the one shot at or blown up. What if Dave brings more than one shooter?"

"Well, I can deliver the bag and you can do the shootin'," Moon said.

"Now boys, let's not fight over who gets the glory," Archibald said. "The plan won't work unless George delivers the bag, so if'n he doesn't want to do it, the scheme's off. No denying it's dangerous. That's why I'll go along. It'll work better if we have two shooters to take care of Dave's assassin and the Dynamite at the same time."

George hesitated before speaking. "Okay, I'll go through with it, but I hope I can run fast enough and you're good enough shots. I'll feel better knowing Papaw's shooting too." He'd saved Gladys. He wasn't certain saving his five hundred acres tonight was worth going through the danger ahead.

"Then you call Mike and ask him to be there around nine-thirty," Moon said.

George spat before agreeing. "All right, it should all be over by then, one way or another," George said.

"It's settled. Let's go in and eat what Serafina's fixed for dinner," Archibald said. "Ham and biscuits covered with Serafina's gravy will take away our doubts."

George's misgivings did not ease as the aromas of the food hit his nostrils. but he did think about Heidi and the possibility he might never see her again. He was skeptical about his grandfather's faith in the gravy, but he was sure he would run fast. He hoped it would be fast enough.

Chapter 37

A t twenty-five to nine, three men climbed into George's truck and left the MacCloud house at Winding Fork. They drove in silence. When they neared the Blackdog mining site, George parked at a pull-off, and the men proceeded on foot. A nearly full moon lit their way. The man in the moon and the odor of honeysuckle blooming along the roadside ditch belied the danger George was to face. Soon the men split up. George headed down the road to the mine, carrying the bag of explosives, while Moon and Archie made their way with rifles through the shadows in the woods to the edge of a high wall from which they could survey the mining site.

George walked slowly into the Blackdog Mining operation, trying to scan it and gain a feel for where Dave's shooter might be hidden. He heard a screech owl calling as he made his way toward the office shack. *Somebody's going to die.* He pushed the old folklore out of mind and concentrated on staying alive. He looked ahead. There was a light on at a D-12 bulldozer fifty yards to the right of the office shack. A man was seated on the machine.

George assessed the situation. "The shooter's probably over by the office. He'd have a clear shot at the front of the dozer from there," George said to himself, "but he'll be exposed to my shooters."

He headed toward the dozer. When he was five yards from the machine, the man stood and called out:

"Let me see that contract. I reckon it's signed," Dave said.

"Yeah, it's signed."

"Then hand it up to me."

Out of Dave's sight, George put down his bag at the base of the dozer with the shiner toward his shooters and moved to where he could put the bulldozer a little between him and the office shack. Then he handed the fake contract up to Dave and began backing away, all the while watching to see whether Dave would signal his shooter.

"Okay, I see it's signed," Dave said after he had glanced at the contract. He started raising his hand.

George began running, bent low. Shots rang out, some from the office shack and some from the high point where Archie and Moon had set themselves. George felt a ricocheting bullet graze his arm. He jumped and rolled as a bullet hit the ground behind him. Then a loud yelp of pain came from near the office shack and, finally, the bag he'd left at the base of the bulldozer exploded, lifting the dozer with a spectacular burst of light and sound. After the *kaboom*, the acrid odor hit George's nostrils and he heard more gunshots as he scrambled on and kept running to the road into the site, leaving the smell of the explosion behind him.

He didn't stop until he reached the entrance. A little later he was sitting beside the road when Mike Barton's car appeared. He stood when Mike's lights hit him. Barton stopped and George climbed in. "I'm glad to see you're still alive," the deputy said.

"I'm lucky to be alive," George said. "I had doubts I'd make it, but I had back up."

"Well, I'm here to deal with what's left. I'm glad you were able to rescue Gladys before all of this came down."

"Me too, believe it."

When Mike and George stopped at the office shack, everything was quiet. The odors from the blast wafted through the night air. Moon and Archie had walked down to the building, They had Dave's shooter in hand. He was wounded in several places, but they had stopped the bleeding. They noticed George holding an arm bleeding where a bullet had grazed him.

"I'm glad that's just a scratch," Moon said after examining George's wound.

Mike treated himself to some jellybeans and told George and Moon to watch the assassin while he and Archie went over to the D-12 to see about Dave Blackmun. They found him alive, but with a broken arm, both legs broken, and a gash on his forehead. He had a gunshot wound in his unbroken arm and burns where hot metal had hit him. He was moaning. Mike called for an ambulance for the two culprits.

"It's hard to believe he survived the blast. I'll call the FBI and let them take care of this mess," Mike said. "Since we can link Dave to the kidnapping, and the kidnappers crossed state lines with Moon's car, there should be no doubt about FBI jurisdiction."

Looking at Dave, Mike laughed. "I don't think they'll have much trouble with Dave. It goes without saying they'll need to pick up Josie Roper and her accomplice."

The ambulance arrived twenty minutes later. Mike loaded the posse of three in his police car and followed the ambulance to the highway, where he let his three passengers out at George's vehicle. As Mike headed off, following the ambulance, George drove the three of them back to Archie's to tell the good news. Serafina and Gladys gave them a warm welcome.

While Gladys tended to George's wound, he basked in the glow of compliments to his bravery, but as soon as the bandages were in place, it occurred to him that he ought to call Heidi.

She answered so soon he knew she must have been sitting by the phone. "Heidi, I'm calling to give you good news. It's been a busy day. I rescued Gladys, and Moon, Archie, and I took care of Dave Blackmun tonight. If it's not too late, I'd like to come by and tell you in person."

"I'm relieved to hear you're all right. I'll be upset if you don't come here and regale me with your exploits."

"I'll be there as soon as I can."

George drove as fast as the winding roads would safely allow. At ten-thirty he rang Heidi's doorbell, happily humming the old ballad,

Greensleeves. When she opened the door, he embraced her in a bear hug and buried his face in her rose scent. "I'm glad to see you. There were times today when I had doubts that we'd ever be together again."

Heidi saw the bandage. "Let me see that arm."

George submitted it for inspection. "It's just a scratch. Gladys patched me up."

Heidi pushed him to her sofa. "Sit. Tell me all about your adventures."

An hour later, George's tale told, Heidi kissed him again and ran her fingers through his hair. "I'm sure Jennifer will be down to do a story on the kidnapping and the bulldozer blast. I should be present at the interview."

"Then you'll marry me?"

She tweaked his ear. "There's a good chance, if you behave with Jennifer. How could I turn down such a great hero?"

George kept silent, holding her close, reveling in the idea that Heidi would accept him as husband material at last. He was happier than he'd been for many weeks.

Chapter 38

The call was from Jennifer. "Hi, George. I'd like to have the lowdown on what's been going on down in coal country. Seems like you've been in the middle of the action. You've known more than you've been telling me."

George was not surprised Jennifer called. He wasn't going to succumb to her blandishments this time. He would have Heidi with them to observe. "I'll tell you what I can. You can come by my place tonight around seven."

"Great, see you then. I'm bringing my cards."

Immediately, George called Heidi. "I want you to come to my place tonight."

"But it's my turn to have you in."

"I know, but I need you to be my guest tonight. Jennifer's in town and wants an interview for her story. I want you there to witness that I'm through with the sexual part of our relationship. You said you ought to be present, remember?"

Heidi couldn't resist a little humorous sarcasm. "How can I resist such an eloquent invitation? What time?"

"Be here by six-thirty if you can. She's coming at seven, but we'll have dinner after she's left. I'm planning to cook pork chops with green beans and sweet potato fries."

"Sounds delightful. I'll be there by six-fifteen."

George was readying the sweet potatoes and green beans when Heidi rang his doorbell. "Come in. The door's open."

As Heidi walked in, George looked up and saw her remove the long raincoat she was wearing. Underneath, she had nothing on. For the first time, George saw her entire body without adornment. Startled, he almost dropped the can of beans he was emptying into a pan. He rushed over to greet her. "Damn, Heidi, you're prettier than even I could imagine. I've never seen you like this." He hugged her and started kissing her, savoring her rose scent.

"Whoa! I wanted you to see the whole package, since you're giving up Jennifer, but seeing is enough for the time being."Heidi had a bundle of clothes with her. "I'll slip into the outfit I've brought while you finish preparations for our late supper." She ducked into the bathroom with her clothes.

"I'll try to keep my mind on preparing the meal, though at present my thoughts are cannibalistic."

When Heidi returned in blouse and shorts, George was putting the beans and greens in pans on the stove. "Pull two chops out of the fridge, please, Honey." As Heidi handed him the pork chops, she gave him a kiss on the cheek. "I like these chops, too."

At ten minutes to seven, the doorbell rang again. "I reckon that's Jennifer," George said.

Heidi nodded as George headed to the door, opened it, and ushered Jennifer Coffee in. She was dressed in shorts and a very brief blouse. A scent of gardenias came in with her.

"How are you, George?" Jennifer eyed his still-bandaged arm. "It looks as if you've been in a scrape."

"Much better than a few days ago," George said as he waved her to the table. "I'd like you to meet my fiancée. This is Heidi Leaves. Heidi, this is Jennifer Coffee."

As the two women sized up each other with intense stares, Heidi found her tongue first. "I hear you want the facts about our recent crime wave."

"Yes, that's what my editor sent me down here for. I'm hoping this story will get me my Pulitzer."

George poured wine for each of them. "We'll have a little wine with our conversation."

"When are you two tying the knot?" Jennifer asked.

"We haven't set a date yet," Heidi said.

George sighed. "We've been pretty busy the last few weeks."

Jennifer laughed. "I've heard you're a hero. You freed your cousin's wife from kidnappers."

Heidi shot an admiring glance at George. "It's no joke. He did. He figured out who had Gladys and where. He didn't wait for backup. He saw his opportunity and took a big chance. The result was a daring rescue."

Jennifer waved a hand toward Heidi and laughed. "George, you have a great press agent here."

George took a sip of wine before speaking. "It's not finished. Dave Blackmun survived a blast that would have killed other men. So we have the trial of Blackmun to look forward to."

"Doesn't the FBI have him dead to rights on unlawful interstate gambling? On illegal dog and chicken fights as well as prostitution and blackmail?"

"Yeah, and we may be able to persuade some of his co-conspirators to testify against him about kidnapping, attempted murder, and even murder, "George sipped wine. "That depends on their willingness to cooperate. They may be too afraid of Blackmun to testify against him. But we have a lot of other evidence of his involvement with the kidnapping and attempted murder."

"What are the odds that you can persuade people to testify?" Jennifer asked.

"I'm working on it, but it's not going to be easy."

Jennifer's questions continued for another hour.

"I guess the FBI has jurisdiction in this kidnapping case against Blackmun, too," Jennifer said.

"Yes, they've been in charge ever since we knew we were dealing with a kidnapping."

"But you didn't call them before making your rescue. Did they reprimand you?"

"No, I think I'm supposed to get some sort of commendation.

They're busy debriefing Gladys, trying to glean information about her kidnappers to use against Blackmun."

The interview concluded, Jennifer put away her notebook and thanked George for the information. George was relieved Jennifer was taking her leave without recriminations.

Jennifer stood and extended a hand to her rival. "Heidi, it was good to meet you. You'll have a real hero for a husband. I hope you and George have a happy marriage and I win a Pulitzer."

Heidi put her arm around George. "Thanks, Jennifer. I hope you do win a Pulitzer some day. I suppose we'll see you again as you follow this story?"

"Sure thing, Southwest Virginia's doing its best to further my career," Jennifer said.

George went to the door with Jennifer. "I'm going to miss our card games," she said, whispering.

As George opened the door, he couldn't help feeling happy to be escaping without an unpleasant scene. "Good luck chasing your Pulitzer," he called after her.

Still feeling a little guilty, George turned to Heidi. "That concludes my relationship with Jennifer except as a news source. Thanks for being a biased observer. I'm sorry it took me so long to break off with her." He pulled Heidi to him and kissed her. "Now, when do we get married?"

"That requires some planning. How big a wedding do you want?" Heidi asked.

"I don't care. A justice of the peace would suit me, but I guess you and my family would like a church wedding. Why don't we talk this over during dinner."

George poured some more wine, and Heidi set the table while he finished the dinner preparations. Soon the room filled with the smell of cooking pork chops and vegetables. As they consumed the meat and vegetables, they talked about what Heidi would like for their wedding ceremony, and George used the time to plead with her not to wait for the wedding. "You *must* spend the night with me," he claimed.

"I think we should amend that statement. You should have said, 'If you're willing to spend the night, I'll try to convince you I'm no longer pining for Jennifer.'"

"I think I could convince you better in the bedroom."

"So that's what you planned for dessert?"

George grinned. "We could take our ice cream to the bedroom."

Heidi recognized the pun in George's mountain dialect and broke into laughter. "You're incorrigible, even if you are a hero."

* * * * * * *

Jason Brackenridge was having trouble keeping up with the fast-moving criminal activity in Southwest Virginia. He had been lucky to have such dedicated help, but now it was up to him to build a strong case against Dave Blackmun for kidnapping, attempted murder, and possibly, murder. He had already received commendations for his work on Blackmun's illegal activities with animal fights and his prostitution-blackmail scheme.

Jason had a source of information in Gladys Lunamin, if she could remember something that would tie Blackmun directly to the kidnapping to go along with the fingerprints they'd found on the note and the fingerprints on the contract Blackmun had sent George. The kidnappers had proven adept at concealing their identities from the victim, but she had heard them speak. Brackenridge was preparing a ploy to reawaken her memory.

"Mrs. Lunamin, we've prepared some tapes of the voices of people we suspect of being involved in your kidnapping mixed with other voices. I'm going to play them for you to identify."

"I'll do my best."

"All right, when you hear a voice on the tape that sounds familiar, write down the number preceding that voice."

Brackenridge played the tape, which had twenty voices on it, those of Josie Roper, Arachne Smith, and Jeb Basherman plus a number of people having nothing to do with Southwest Virginia.

Listening carefully as the tape played, Gladys jotted down the numbers of the voices that she thought she'd heard during her ordeal.

"Now I'll play the tape a second time. Again, if you think a voice is familiar, write down its number," Jason said.

After a third playing, Brackenridge asked to see the sheets where Gladys had written the numbers for familiar voices. Three numbers appeared on all three sheets. They were the numbers for Roper, Smith, and Basherman.

"Thank you, Mrs. Lunamin. You've confirmed our suspicions."

"I believe I know one of the female voices," Gladys said. "I believe it's the woman I know as Merith Taylor. She's the person who hired me to the house in Big Stone Head. I think I knew her in New York, but not by that name," Gladys said as she stood to stretch.

"Does the name Arachne Smith mean anything to you?"

"I knew an Arachne Smith in New York."

"She heads up the women Blackmun imported to provide expensive escorts to lure men for photographs to be used for blackmail. She's living with Blackmun. We'll pick her up and see whether we can get her to testify against Blackmun. We want to nail him for the kidnapping as well as attempted murder. The other two voices you recognized are those of Josie Roper and Jeb Basherman."

"I haven't met either one, although George told me about her."

"They're the people who held you until Landsetter rescued you. We may be able to persuade them to turn on Blackmun."

◆ ◆ ◆ ◆ ◆ ◆

The sun was beaming in his window when George woke late the Saturday morning after his goodbye to Jennifer Coffee. He and Heidi had made love until early morning. He looked at his clock. Nine o'clock. He could smell bacon frying.

"Wake up sleepy-head," Heidi called from the kitchen. "I have breakfast ready. You promised to take me birding today—and to buy me a ring. Remember?"

He roused himself and looked for his bathrobe. He peeped out the bedroom door and saw that Heidi was wearing it. He grabbed his pajamas off the door and put them on. Then he found slippers and emerged.

Heidi appraised his appearance. She laughed. "I don't recall your having pajamas on last night. I think I like you better without the pajamas."

"I don't recollect your wearing my bathrobe either. Why don't you take it off?"

Heidi rolled her eyes. "We have a lot to do. Eat your bacon, eggs, and toast and let's get started. You have promises to keep."

✦ ✦ ✦ ✦ ✦ ✦ ✦

After an hour of birding at Isaiah Timmon's land, George asked Heidi to get back in his vehicle. After a short drive, he turned his truck onto a side road. "This is Crabtree Hollow. That's where they were keeping Gladys."

"Are you sure it's safe for us to be here?"

"I don't think we'll have any trouble. Josie may not even know yet I'm the one who rescued Gladys. Even if she does, she'll think twice about causing trouble. I want you to hear the Swainson's warblers and Louisiana waterthrushes down along the stream below Josie's house. I'll bet we'll be gone before anybody notices us."

As they drove by the Roper house, George could see that Josie's red Toyota van was parked in the driveway. She must have made bail. He drove to the logging road and turned in, putting down the windows.

"We won't even need to get out. We'll just sit and wait for the birds to sing, listen to the stream, and smell the forest aroma." George said.

He stopped the vehicle, and they lowered the windows and listened, The sound of the stream and the scents of the woods rushed in. As if on cue, the birds sang, and he pointed out the differences in their similar songs. For a quarter of an hour, they listened tp the warblers and other birds. Then George turned his truck around and headed out to the highway as a pileated woodpecker flew across he road in front of them, giving its raucous *kek, kek, kek* call.

"There goes a woodhen," George said.

"What a gorgeous bird," Heidi said. "This was a beautiful way to spend a morning."

"It's hard to believe that a person growing up here in this wonderful place could orchestrate Dave Blackmun's murders. And she's beautiful, too."

"Dave must have some hold over her."

"I'm sure he pays a big price for her services, but there must be more to it than the money. I'm going to try to persuade her to testify against him."

"That's a tall order."

"She's asked for my advice about strip-mining some of her land. I'll suggest she could get immunity by testifying against Dave. Then she could mine her land and live on the proceeds. Her high-grade coal could make her a wealthy woman."

"I hear she's pretty —I've heard it from people other than you," she said as she saw him grinning. "I'm not sure I want you spending time with her. She might turn your head. We just settled the Jennifer problem. I don't want to lose you as soon as you've freed yourself from Jennifer."

"You know I love you. I'm not going to get involved with a killer just because she happens to look like a starlet. If I can convince Josie to testify against Dave, Rod Mashburn may decide to become a witness for the state too."

"Why don't you let the FBI handle Josie?"

"I want to make sure that Dave goes to jail for a long time or faces execution. I'm hoping he'll get over his obsession about mining my five hundred acres after a long time in jail. If he's executed, I'm sure my woodland's safe. If Josie testifies about the Stanard murder, he might receive a death sentence."

Heidi shook her head. "It's too bad Dave didn't die in that blast."

Just then George saw a hawk soaring above them. He pulled off the road and parked just before they reached the main road. When they had climbed out of the vehicle, he pointed to the soaring bird. "That's a broad-winged hawk. Look at the broad white bands in the tail,." The broadwing gave its high-pitched call. "Listen to its whistle."

"That's a good way to end our birding—a good omen," Heidi said.

"Let's go to Winding Fork and tell them that we're planning to marry. I'm so happy about it I'd like to share it with Mamaw and Papaw and Ma," George said.

"I was wondering whether you were afraid to tell them.

"No way, I just want us to tell them together."

What about the ring you promised to buy for me today?" Heidi asked

"Before we go, I do have something I want you to wear."

"Are you ashamed of my field clothes?"

George grinned as he reached in his pocket and pulled out a small jewelry case and opened it. "No, you look great in field clothes, but I want you to wear this on your left hand." He took out the diamond ring and slipped it on her ring finger. "I've been carrying this around for weeks now. So you and I are now engaged—unless you want me to take the ring back." He leaned over and kissed her.

"No way—it fits. I'm counting on you to be true to me. I have to warn you. I'm a pretty good shot with my twenty-two." She laughed and returned his kiss.

Chapter 39

Although she disliked the smell of hospitals, Arachne visited Dave as soon as she could get permission from the FBI. Jason Brackenridge stipulated that she must undergo a body search before entering Blackmun's room any time she visited. After she saw how serious Dave's condition was, Arachne laughed about the requirement. She was amazed when she saw his bandaged head and arm and examined his other arm and both legs in casts.

"You're lucky to be alive.," Arachne said as she looked at Dave. She waved her hand, trying to push away the hospital odors "I hate these hospital smells. The FBI must really think you're a bad actor," she jibed as she patted his casts. "Even in your weak condition, they're afraid you're up to something."

Fighting through a drug-induced fog, Blackmun spoke slowly. "I do have a plan." He paused, then continued. "We need to get married."

Standing by his bedside, Arachne chuckled. "You must be joking. You're not able to perform."

"I agree about that. But if we're married, we can't be forced to testify against each other. We have to keep this to ourselves, away from the FBI."

Arachne pulled a chair up beside his bed and sat down. She found his proposal quite interesting. "I'm hurt. I thought you couldn't live without me."

"I find you delightful company, but think about a trial. You have almost as much to gain as I do from tying the knot."

"You don't intend a church wedding?"

"No, we need to do it on the sly as soon as possible. I now have a $500, 000 bail bond on me. You get a llcense from the County Clerk and contact Minister Jeff White. He owes me. Bring him here the day I'm discharged. He'll perform the ceremony with just the two of us. Then I'll figure out how to even up things with George Landsetter."

Dismayed by his vengefulness, Arachne turned away to compose herself before answering. She wanted time to think about his proposal. "You should forget about him."

"Forget him? Never! Now I want more than his coal. I want revenge."

"That's a dangerous desire," Arachne said.

Blackmun couldn't move, but growled. "Let me worry about the danger."

"OK, Ok, I'll arrange for the minister.

"Arachne felt advantage coming her way. She had made a quick evaluation of the situation. Dave's desire for revenge might prove a boon to her. He must be too angry and hurting for clear planning. She began considering how she could turn this weakness to her profit. The hospital odors no longer bothered her.

Later that day, George found Arachne at Dave Blackmun's house. When she opened the door as far as the chain allowed and saw him standing there, she tried to shut it.

Grabbing the door handle to prevent its closing, George pushed hard. "I need to talk to you." The lingering odor of Dave's cigars fought his concentration.

Arachne resisted. "You fucking bastard, I'm busy. I wouldn't have time for you, even if I weren't." She struggled to close the door.

"You might profit from listening to me."

"I don't see how."

"You're going to stand trial for kidnapping. You could profit from making a deal with the FBI."

"What makes you think that?"

"You set up the kidnapping of my cousin's wife, Gladys. You knew her from New York, where you both worked for an escort service."

"Have you been smoking pot?"

"What if Gladys can identify you? The FBI thinks she can."

"Go away, Landsetter. I have a marriage to arrange."

Stunned, George stopped pushing on the door. "Marriage?"

In his bewilderment, George forgot to hold the door, and Arachne shut it in his face.

That evening, during dinner, Heidi told George she had some news that would interest him.

"Does it involve a marriage?"

"Yes. How did you know?"

"I tried to persuade Arachne Smith to testify against Dave, and she said she had a marriage to arrange."

"I have friend at the hospital who heard Arachne and Dave talking about a marriage. They already have a common law marriage. They're living together."

"You have eyes and ears everywhere. I wonder if I should mention this to the FBI. Dave may be trying to make sure Arachne won't testify against him. Neither could he be forced to testify against her. A good move, but he can't marry any more possible witnesses."

"I don't see how they can marry without the FBI knowing. My friend also told me Dave was muttering about getting even with somebody. I think we can guess who."

"You see, I was right. Dave's still dangerous."

"It's good evidence you need to be careful." Heidi snuggled against him and pulled him toward the bedroom. "He's a killer. He might try to kill you."

"It's proof I need to talk Josie into testifying against Dave

"There're things more important than convicting Dave—unless you're losing interest in me now I've agreed to marry you.

"No way, Babe," George said. He savored her rose scent as he nuzzled her breasts. He picked her up and headed to the bedroom.

The next day, as soon as he had inspected enough sites to be able to report a day's work, George called Josie Roper.

After a few rings, Josie answered. "This is George Landsetter. If you remember, we talked about your surface mining your land."

Josie laughed. "Oh, yes, the reclamation officer."

"I wondered if you'd considered any more about mining your land. I'd like to discuss a few things with you."

"I'd like that. I'm still thinking about doing the mining. Would today be too soon?"

"No, I've taken care of everything on my schedule for today."

"Do you know Crabtree Hollow?"

"Yes, I've done some bird watching there."

"My house is the second of two on the road into the Hollow. Why don't you drop by now?"

"All right. I'll be there in about twenty minutes."

George had more time to study Josie Roper's house than he had taken during his latest two trips into Crabtree Hollow. It was a two-story brick house that could have graced an antebellum plantation in the Tidewater or Piedmont.

Josie opened the door a minute or so after he knocked. "Hello, Officer Landsetter, come in. May I call you George?"

George smelled a faint violet scent. "Sure." She really was sexy. He had to remind himself that this woman had planned murders.

She led George into a room to the right of the hall past stairs. "Have a seat.' She waved toward the wing chair, "That chair's comfortable. Would you like something to drink? Whiskey? A gin and tonic? A soft drink?"

He realized he had to be careful. "A coke would be great."

George was impressed with the room. It was full of what were obviously eighteenth-century pieces or excellent replicas. The wing chair he was sitting in, the drop-leaf tables, an elegant sideboard, and an antique chest of drawers caught his eyes.

When Josie returned with his drink, she had a gin and tonic for herself on the tray. Putting the tray on the table, she handed him his coke before taking her drink. He couldn't help noticing how gracefuly she moved and what a good figure she had. She was a knock-out red head and as pretty as he remembered. It was difficult to imagine her planning a murder shot.

"This room shows someone in your family likes antiques."

"Yes, my mother adored them, and Daddy built this house for her to fill with the antiques she loved and bought."

George took a sip of his coke. "It's a handsome house. Filled with antiques like this, it must have been expensive."

"Yes, but Daddy didn't have much money left for me when I came home from Sweetbriar without a husband and with no means of support."

"Is that why you had dealings with Dave Blackmun?"

"You know about that? Yes, Daddy borrowed a lot of money from Dave, and he held Daddy's debt over me after Dad died. I've just cleared that up. I have Dave's release in writing. Daddy didn't finance my Sweetbriar education so I could be Dave's lackey."

"But you did business with Dave." George drained his glass.

"He paid well, and he threatened me when I tried to stop. I knew what he was capable of. I didn't have the guts to challenge him."

"I've looked into your mineral rights. You have a rich seam of high-grade metallurgical coal on your property. If you stripped your land, you would be set for life."

Josie grimaced and sipped her drink. "That may not be much of a help to me now, though I'm out from under Dave's debt." Josie sighed as she finished her drink. "How about another coke?"

George handed her his can. When she returned with new drinks, he decided it was time to propose a deal.

George leaned forward. "Look, you don't want to go to jail. If you would testify against Dave, I believe the FBI would grant you immunity for your crimes."

Josie looked at him intently. "Do you really think so?"

"You'd have to pledge to go straight. You could mine your land and have enough money to live comfortably the rest of your life."

George saw disbelief in her expression. "Impossible!" she said. She rose a little out of her chair. "You're kidding me," she said as she put down her drink and leaned forward.

238

George put down his coke. "If I could arrange the immunity, would you testify against Blackmun?"

Her answer was non-committal. "He's a real bastard—a mean son of a bitch."

"I know. He's tried to kill me."

Josie touched his arm. "I'm aware of that. He tried to arrange a hit on you."

George was surprised by her candor. "You didn't take the contract? Why?"

Josie purred. "I like you. I hoped you and I could get together. Maybe we can since I'm not in debt to Blackmun any more."

He had been right about her finding him attractive. "I'm glad you turned him down. You're beautiful enough to tempt any man."

"If I stripped, would you be willing to sweeten the deal?"

Aware of the ambiguity of her question, George replied with a cautious question. "In what way?"

"George, you're a hunk. I'd love to know you better."

George felt obliged to tell the truth. "Josie, you're gorgeous. I'd love to oblige, but I just ended an old relationship so that Heidi Leaves would agree to marry me. I swore I'd be faithful."

Josie shook her head, frowning. She pushed back her hair. "Well, you're missing a treat. We'd be good together. You could at least seal a deal with a kiss, or two, if I mined my land, couldn't you?"

"If I can work something out with the FBI and you testify, I'll make sure you get a good deal on stripping your land. Let's leave it at that for the time being."

"Okay. You see what you can work out. If you can persuade the Feds, I'll pay you a fee to arrange for surface mining my coal in a way that improves my land and makes me financially independent." She paused. "Let me know if you change your mind about other rewards," she said, stroking her neck and slightly parting her legs.

He rose and moved toward the hall. "I'll see what I can do." George didn't want to close any doors at this point, but he didn't want to lose Heidi. He'd have to turn down those other rewards.

Chapter 40

After leaving Josie, George didn't waste any time getting in touch with Mike Barton, who had a rare day patrol in the Winding Fork area. Taking a chance since he would reveal nothing, George put his call through the Sheriff's switchboard. "Could you meet me at Philemon's mine entrance this afternoon?"

"How about four?"

"See you there"

George enjoyed the drive. The sun beamed on the blues of roadside chicory and the white of Queen Anne's lace. Here and there a bank of black-eyed susans provided a splash of yellow.

Mike was waiting for him. George parked and walked over to Mike's car. "Josie says she'll testify against Dave if the FBI will grant her full immunity for the work she's done for him," he said as Mike got out.

"That isn't enough to convince the FBI."

"There's more. She claims Dave has been forcing her to work for him for years to pay off debts her father owed him. She's got a release from those debts in writing now. She'll give up criminal activities if she's granted immunity. She's sitting on some rich coal seams. I've promised to help her mine them to her best advantage, if the deal with the FBI goes through."

"I'll talk to Jason," Mike said as he popped some jellybeans in his mouth and offered some to George, "I think they really want to make a solid case against Dave. I believe they'd be willing to give Josie a break, if she's as ready to turn her back on crime as you say."

George took a few jellybeans, although he preferred gum as a substitute for the chewing tobacco he'd given up up for Heidi. "She's already turned down making a hit on me for Dave, she says."

Mike laughed and popped a few more jellybeans. "I reckon I was wrong. She must like you."

"I sure hope so. She sounds sincere. I really want that bastard Blackmun put away for a long time. Please tell Jason that I'm convinced Josie wants to get away from Dave's blackmail and murders—and to give up all criminal activity. She can testify about the kidnapping and Stanard's murder."

"I'll do my best to convince him. I want to put Dave away as much as you do. I'm pretty sure he's been holding something over Bo Mulberry. My mother doesn't think Bo's turning a blind eye to crime has been his own idea. She thinks he's scared shitless of Blackmun. If that's true, and we can put Blackmun away, my life would become a lot less complicated." Mike pulled out a few more jellybeans. "I might have less night duty,"

✦ ✦ ✦ ✦ ✦ ✦ ✦

Dave Blackmun recovered faster than his doctors expected. Though still in casts and on crutches and using a wheelchair, he went home with his future bride in a little over four weeks—after his marriage. He knew the FBI had him under surveillance awaiting trial, though they couldn't hold him because he had made that $500,000 bond.

Arachne was skeptical. "Don't you think you're rushing things?"

Dave lit a cigar. "I'm eager to begin our honeymoon. You make sure I have some painkiller around. I'm relying on your expertise."

Arachne scowled as the smoke reached her. "You're in no condition for sex. You can't wheel me across your threshold, much less carry me. You're a tough guy, but it's not easy to do much with all the casts you're wearing."

"I'm perfectly able to perform. I'm counting on your fucking skills in these matters." He patted her buttock for emphasis.

Grinning, Arachne felt between his leg casts. "So, you're just horny. I thought your desire to get George was luring you out of the hospital."

"The two aren't mutually exclusive. Drive me out to Dab Whacker's strip job."

Arachne walked out of the hospital following Blackmun's wheelchair and then helped the nurse get her soon-to-be new husband into his Durango. The Rev. White was waiting in the Durango. "It's a good thing Virginia doesn't require witnesses." White said. The marriage ceremony took place as they drove away. Arachne dropped the minister off at the County Clerk's to file their marriage license.

"I hope you lovebirds enjoy your honeymoon," Rev. White said.

"Thanks. We will. Just make sure that license gets filed right away."

Arachne drove as Dave directed, but she demanded he open his window to lessen the odor of cigar smoke.

Dave did as she asked. "Okay, but you have to admit we put one over on the FBI." They were soon at Dab's surface mine at Winding Fork. In spite of her objections, Dave insisted on getting out of the vehicle using his new crutches.

"Do you see this Dab Whacker anywhere? You've told me so much about him, I feel like I know him even though we've never met." When she had Dave settled in his wheelchair beside the Durango, she looked around at the front-end loaders piling their loads onto a huge mound while others transferred the coal to a fleet of haul trucks. An unpleasant acrid smell assaulted her.

"What is that horrible odor?" she asked as she felt a small pebble hit her leg.

"They've just set off an explosion to uncover some more coal," Dave explained. We just missed the blast. Let's get to business. Find Dab Whacker for me."

Arachne didn't jump with joy at being the facilitator of this meeting. "How would I find him?" she asked. "These machines make a lot of noise."

"He's probably on a bulldozer somewhere. Ask around. Bring him here."

"Okay, by the way, what does the Dab stand for?"

"It's short for Dabney. He hates Dabney. He thinks it's a sissy's name."

"Should I ask around for Dabney?"

"Not unless you want to make an enemy."

"I'll ask for Mr. Whacker, then."

"That should work. Get going."

Arachne had asked only two workers when one pointed to a large dozer with a man on it. She stepped carefully, avoiding muddy spots, in the direction of the D-12. She was over halfway to her goal when the man saw her and waved.

The machine coughed to a stop, and Whacker climbed down. As he strode to meet her, the closer he got, the more he picked up his pace. Arachne saw a handsome, broad-shouldered, muscular man around six feet tall. He had close-cut blond hair. She liked what she saw. She hadn't expected a friend of Dave's would be such a hunk.

"What's a pretty woman like you doing in this hubbub?" Dab asked.

"I'm looking for Mr. Whacker."

"You've found him."

"I'm Arachne Smith Blackmun. Dave wants to talk to you. He's at that black Durango over there." She pointed to where Dave was sitting.

"Are you his sister?"

"No, I'm his wife. We got married today, on our way here from the hospital."

"You're one of the women he brought in from New York?"

"Yes." Up close, Arachne gazed into blue eyes. The set of his jaw indicated a man who brooked little disagreement. "Aren't you two buddies?"

Avoiding a mud hole, and her question, Dab repeated his praise.

"I'd say a vulture like Dave doesn't deserve a beauty like you. You're too much woman to be tied down to a beast like him."

Arachne didn't want Dab to think the marriage was based on love. "People get married for lots of reasons."

As they neared Blackmun, Dab kept ogling Arachne. "It's a shame you're married to Dave. He shouldn't have anybody as pretty as you. I hope we see more of each other," he said, as he waved to Dave.

A few yards closer, he hailed Dave. "What's up, Blackmun?"

"I need your help with a project."

"Anything to do with a helpful mine blast?"

Dave nodded. "You must be psychic."

"You rarely come to see me just to pass the time of day. And you've brought your new bride. Have something important in mind?"

Dave followed Dab's eyes. "You've met Arachne. I can see you're drooling with envy."

"True, but I'm too late. You've hid her from me. So, what do you want?"

"Help to get rid of your favorite mine inspector."

Dab whistled. "Damn! You're planning a hit on Landsetter? That blast at your mine must have addled your brain. You'd be at the top of the suspect list, and I wouldn't be far behind." Dab shook his head. "I don't have that big a beef with George. I just ruffle his feathers for fun."

"All you'd have to do is prepare a big charge to be set off at the right time. I'd do the rest. Who knows what I might say once they get me on the stand for the kidnapping?"

Dab turned his head to spit a stream of tobacco juice. "You can't implicate me in your crooked dealings. I'm not worried about that, but you don't look like you're in any shape to do your own hit."

"I'll be fine in a few weeks, when I get rid of these casts."

Dab shook his head. "Okay, you get back with me then. Now I've got work."

After helping Dave back in the Durango, Dab walked around

the vehicle with Arachne. He slipped her his business card and whispered. "Call me when he's not around. He's gone bonkers."

As Arachne drove away, she questioned Dave. "Don't you think you're in enough trouble without trying to kill Landsetter again?"

"I can get his coal if he's not in the way. Besides, he's a main witness against me," Dave hit the seat with his fist. "I hate his guts."

"You'd better cut your losses. You could sell out, skip the country, and live like a king somewhere pleasant."

Dave curled his lip. "Yeah, I could. But I'm gonna get even with George and keep making money here."

Arachne remembered the card Dab had slipped her. She felt sure he'd fit into her plan. "I'd better call Dab," she mused. "He thinks like I do. Dave's gone crazy, and Dab obviously finds me attractive. Maybe we can get together and make me a wealthy widow. Dave's headed for disaster. No need for me to go down with him if I can live in luxury with an Apollo who could manage Dave's mines for me." She beamed as she imagined a future with Dab instead of Dave.

Chapter 41

A few weeks later, Mike told George something might be worked out for Josie if she testified against Blackmun. The possibility that this deal could come to fruition led George to approach Rod Mashburn again about testifying. Moon was in town for the weekend, so George enlisted his help.

Calls to Mashburn's apartment went unanswered, so they decided to look for him at BeeBo's Lounge, where he often ran a big-stakes poker game some weekends. They approached the lanky, moustached barman, Jay Schreider.

"Is Rod running a game this weekend?" George asked.

"Who's asking?"

"Damnit! You know Moon and me, Jay. We're Rod's cousins. We just want to talk," George said.

"Yeah, I know you. You ain't Rod's favorite people."

"Just tell him we're here and we'd like to talk to him when it's convenient. While we wait, how about a couple of draft beers?" George asked.

"What's your pleasure?"

"Have any bach on draft?" Moon asked.

"Yeah. Large or small."

"Two, large," Moon said

As they sat in their booth sipping their beer, George noticed a couple in a booth in a dark corner of the lounge.

"Don't be too obvious, but check out that couple in the corner over on our left," George said.

Moon followed his cousin's directions. "That's Arachne Smith and Dab Whacker. I wonder what brought them here together. I thought you told me she and Dave got married."

George nodded. "They married after he left the hospital."

Moon shook his head. "Do you think Dave would approve of his wife's meeting Dab here without him?"

"Not the Dave I know, even though he and Dab are buddies."

"No doubt Dave's marriage was a ploy to prevent Arachne from testifying against him, but he was living with her as a common-law wife anyway," Moon said.

"Dab's not a bad-looking man and younger than Dave. Maybe he and Arachne are cooking something up behind Dave's back. From a moral standpoint, their actions may be deplorable, but from my standpoint, they're giving Dave treatment he deserves."

"At this rate, you'll become a philosopher and claim that the deserts Dave creates are beautiful. You remind me of ODSUM and B. G. Hooper's defense of surface mining.at Heidi's symposium," Moon said.

"Scientists call it the principle of complementarity."

Rod Mashburn interrupted George and Moon's wonderment.

"What can I do for you, Cousins?"

George answered. "Have a seat. We think the FBI may work out a deal with Josie Roper to testify against Dave. You told me, if Josie Roper agreed to testify, you might be willing too."

Rod sat down and gave them a long look. "Yeah, I remember telling you that, George."

Moon joined in. "How do you feel about it now?"

Rod hesitated, then spoke cryptically. "Dave's a bad enemy to have, but he's not a good friend either."

George gave a soft chuckle as he leaned forward. "I'm sure he's out to get me. I doubt he has time for anybody else right now."

Rod nodded. "Yeah, Dave is going to have at least a handful of enemies to deal with. He's definitely got you on his short list. He's lost his marbles. There's safety in numbers. If the FBI might go for it, see what you can arrange for me."

"Okay, I'll work on that, Cousin. Let me buy you a beer."

Rod stood to leave. He laughed. "Thanks, but right now I've got to get back to my game and help some guys lose their money." He turned and walked away.

"He's going to testify," George said.

Moon made a fist and gently tapped George's shoulder. "Damn right! Good work."

As they watched Rod disappear into a back room, George noticed that Arachne and Dab had disappeared.

Moon admitted they'd sneaked out. "I didn't see our mystery couple leave. Did you?"

"No, but BeeBo's has rooms in the back besides the poker room. Some of them accommodate couples for secret meetings, I'm told." George took out a packet of gum and offered Moon a stick. "Heidi and Gladys have something in common. Heidi made me give up chewing tobacco too."

Moon grunted but took the gum. "I doubt that Blackmun approved this rendezvous. They're taking a chance. If Dave finds out, they're in trouble."

"The more trouble Dave gets into that doesn't involve me, the better I like it," George said.

"Be careful what you wish for, Cousin. He won't give up on you."

Arachne had noticed George and Moon as Mashburn walked over to them. "Look, Dab, there's George Landsetter and Adamo Lunamin. Let's slip out to that back room we arranged. Rod Mashburn's going to hold their attention for awhile."

"Don't worry. This rendevous has Dave's approval. We're supposed to be arranging George's murder, remember. Dave doesn't know we're planning his demise," Dab said, grinning.

"I revel in the irony," Arachne said.

They got up quietly and disappeared. Inside their room, Dab reached for Arachne. She pushed him away. "Let's finish our business first," Arachne said. "I'll get Dave off to your mine before dark. You call me when you've set off the blast. I'll call Heidi and get her away from home. Then I'll call George and make him think Dave has Heidi at your mine. Then I call you. The blast must occur before Landsetter gets there, but it must seem aimed at him."

"I understand. You have the number for my mining trailer. When Dave arrives. I lure him to a spot I've prepared with extra explosives, I call you with the word of the blast. You call Heidi first and get her out to her office so that George won't question she's in trouble. You call George and then me to tell me George is on the way. I'll wait a few minutes after you tell me. Then I'll call 911 and leave."

"I'll get Dave to send George a letter threatening Heidi. That should lead George to believe what comes later," Arachne said

Dab agreed that would help. "Why don't you send Heidi one, too, threatening her? Make sure not to leave any fingerprints."

Arachne nodded. "That should take care of Dave. Now what about us? We should celebrate our partnership."

Dab laughed. "You should soon be a rich widow, or close to being one." He put his arms around her and kissed her.

"I already have Dave trained. The first thing you do, get rid of that tobacco. I've got some gum you can have."

"Give up my chew? That's a lot to ask."

"And wash out your mouth. If we're going to be close friends, it's part of the bargain. I have to receive as much pleasure as I give you. Dave is all taking and not much giving, other than money, and he's not too free with that."

Dab walked into the john and came back with a clean mouth. "Show me what pleases you. I'm eager to satisfy."

"You start with my breasts," she said, unbuckling his pants and fondling him as he freed her breasts from her scarlet bra.

"You have a beautiful pair, "Dab said as he began to kiss them.

"And all mine, no additives." she said, as she enjoyed his tongue's caresses. Then, she pushed him to his knees in front of her, copying the method an ancient empress of China used to gain control of men.

Hours later, Arachne contemplated an exhausted Dab Whacker. "You're a hunk, but you need training. Not too bad, lover boy, for a first time. You have stamina, but you'll need to learn how to wait until I'm ready. Practice makes perfect, the adage says."

"I'm willing to learn. How soon do I get another lesson?"

"I'll tell Dave that you and I will need to get together in a few weeks—just before he's to get rid of those casts— to work out the final details."

Arachne and Dab left separately. She sent Dab out the back way to avoid prying eyes. Arachne left in high spirits. She foresaw a luxurious future ahead, whether she could get full control of Dave's assets or not. And she looked forward to training Dab to provide her pleasure. It seemed that Dave's desire for revenge on Landsetter might even help her weave a web to gain complete control of her husband's wealth. Only in her most optimistic dreams had Arachne imagined her plan would work so well.

◆◆◆◆◆◆

George wondered what Arachne was planning with Dab and thought maybe he should try to enlist her to testify against Dave despite her marriage to him, or at least find out something about what she was planning. He reckoned she wouldn't respond well to him, so he asked Gladys to arrange a meeting with Arachne at a public place.

"That's asking a lot. I'm not sure I want to have lunch with a woman who helped kidnap me."

"We need to build a good case against Blackmun. The more people we turn, the better.

Gladys looked at George intently and sighed. "You saved my life. I owe you. I'll do it."

Next day Gladys phoned Arachne and set up a lunch date to meet her at Enchiladas.

Gladys arrived ten minutes before the 11:45 a.m. time they had agreed upon. She ordered a glass of house wine. While she waited, sipping her wine, she looked over the other clients. It was a mixture of the young and the old, teenagers, twenties and thirties and fifty and sixty-year olds.

When a striking blonde with dark sunglasses appeared, Gladys waved her to the booth she occupied. "Hello, Arachne, or would you prefer for me to call you Merith?"

Arachne removed her glasses. "No, Arachne's okay. I apologize for my part in the kidnapping. I couldn't refuse Dave. Even though you and I were friends in New York, he's too scary."

"Would you be willing to testify in court that Dave forced you to help him?"

"No, I can't do that. Dave and I married so that we wouldn't have to testify against each other. I don't want to go to jail, but I have to be careful. It's dangerous to get on Dave's hate list. I have to keep him happy; I have great plans for Dave's money and the Pit."

Gladys could not conceal her skepticism. "You're not planning more dog and chicken fights, are you?"

"No way—I'm planning family fun, mainly music and dancing. Photography will be limited to recording family groups. I've discovered this county could rival Nashville. Every hollow and hill has a musical group. And clogging and flatfoot dancing are local traditions." Arachne sipped the wine Gladys had ordered for her. "It's hard to believe how many good gospel groups are around here. I won't lack performers who'll work for free. They'll compete for modest prize money."

"Sounds like a legitimate enterprise."

"I'm going straight."

"You and I both know human motives and morals change as our perspectives alter."

"Southwest Virginia's not New York, that's for sure."

"Let's order. The aromas are making me hungry. I'll promise you not to bring up the subject of testimony again until after we eat. By the way, I'd prefer not having anyone know about our life in New York. We're a world away from that town's standards."

"I understand. You don't have to worry. What happened in New York stays in New York as far as I'm concerned." Arachne leaned forward and spoke with enthusiasm. "I'm busy planning renovations of the Pit. It'll compete with the Carter Fold and Nashville as an outlet for country music. We'll provide a venue for all of the local musical groups. For the contests, audiences can place bets on their choice for the winning groups."

"You're really planning to be legal? How does Dave feel about that?"

"As long as I can keep him satisfied and make some money, he'll go along."

After a meal of chicken, refried beans, and rice, Gladys brought up the subject of testifying again,

Arachne shook her head. "I can't do it. I have too much to lose, but you tell George to watch his steps. Dave isn't finished. He's making plans for revenge."

◆ ◆ ◆◆◆ ◆ ◆

Whenever George was to make an inspection of surface mines near Winding Fork, he took his lunch break nearby at the section of Isaiah Timmons' land that Moon had mined and reclaimed. It had become such a birdy place, George always ate lunch there when his schedule allowed.

This day he decided to eat his lunch on the huge flat rock overlooking the large pond on the site. He had finished his ham sandwich and was drinking some fortified lemonade from his flask. He smelled the fragrance of pondweed flowers as he listened to male red-winged blackbirds singing *conk-a-lee* around the pond. As he watched them flash their red and yellow epaulettes, a strange bird flew past him and lit in a bush on the other side of the pond.

The bird was a beauty. It had long, deeply forked tail feathers and a rich salmon lower breast and flanks. George had never seen anything like it. As he watched, the bird sallied from its perch to catch a flying insect, then returned nearby.

George hurried to his truck and grabbed his bird guide. He turned quickly to the flycatchers. Flipping the pages of color plates, he saw a picture of what he had been watching. It *was* a male scissor-tailed flycatcher. According to the range map in his guide, this bird was way north of its usual range. It was supposed to be down in Texas or on the Gulf Coast.

He found his binoculars and went back for another look. He examined the bird feather by feather. It was definitely a male scissor-tailed flycatcher.

George had to share this bird. He called Heidi. "I don't usually bother you when you're at work, but this couldn't wait. I've just seen a male scissor-tailed flycatcher. It's a beauty. It's supposed to be down in Texas, not here in the mountains."

"That's a great find. Will you show it to me? I can leave work early today. I'm caught up on my paperwork."

"I still have to inspect Dab Whacker's mine today, but I can quit then. I'll pick you up at work around two-thirty or three and we'll come back here and look for the flycatcher."

"I'll be ready. I have my binoculars with me."

While George inspected Dab's mine, he had a difficult time keeping his mind on mining. He kept thinking of that flycatcher. He was in such a good mood, he complimented Dab on the restraint of his blasts the past few weeks.

"I haven't had a complaint about your work for three weeks now."

"I've been trying to be a law-abiding citizen. Arachne insists. I'm glad you appreciate it."

"I do. It makes my life a lot easier."

George completed his inspection in record time. Then he headed to Heidi's office. As he parked, she came out, binoculars around her neck.

"Hop in," George said, as he leaned over to open the door on the passenger's side. Heidi climbed in and off they left at a high speed.

Soon Heidi pleaded. "Slow down. I want to see the bird. I can't if I'm dead."

"Okay, calm down." George slowed to forty and made the curves at what Heidi considered a much more suitable speed. The redwings were still displaying and singing lustily at the pond. George and

Heidi did not see the flycatcher at first. "Let's just sit on the big flat rock and wait,' George said.

They sat and waited, After several minutes without the flycatcher's appearing, George leaned over and kissed Heidi, pushing his tongue deep into her mouth, tasting her sweetness. After the kiss, Heidi questioned him. "Was your tale of a rare flycatcher just a gambit to get me alone here?"

"No, but I didn't want to waste the time." Just then, as she tweaked his ear, the flycatcher appeared, flying over the pond, turning and revealing its long divided tail feathers and salmon breast as it snapped up a dragonfly.

Heidi saw it and whispered. "Oh, what a beautiful bird."

They watched in silence as the scissor-tail devoured a gray-and-blue dragonfly. Finally, it had swallowed every morsel except the transparent wings, which fell onto the surface of the pond and floated. The bird flew to a higher perch to look for more prey.

George grinned. "Aren't you ashamed you doubted me."

"Yes, the bird is every bit as beautiful as you said."

"And you're so delicious I can't resist you," George said as he kissed her deeply again and slipped his hand under her bra.

"George, we're out in the woods. What if somebody sees us?"

"Are you afraid of being seen by deer and a scissor-tailed flycatcher?"

"I guess not."

"I love you, Heidi. I want you. We're engaged, but I don't want to force myself on you."

"I want you, too. It's just that I'm not used to being *au naturel* in a sylvan setting."

"Okay. You take the lead." He lay back on the rock.

Later, Heidi lifted herself from him and turned around, putting her legs around his head. She giggled. "I'm *your* scissor-tail."

After half an hour, as they lay together watching the scissor-tailed flycatcher, she pulled him to her for another kiss. "You know, I'm glad I didn't realize how wonderful our sex would be. I don't believe I could have held out so long if I'd known. I want more now." George embraced her, and they spent half an hour making more conventional love.

As they gazed at each other, the scissor-tailed flycatcher made another foray over the pond and caught a dragonfly just above them. It lit on a perch near them and devoured it. The lovers watched it, savoring its beauty as they savored each other.

"It's our special bird," Heidi said.

George kissed her in agreement. "From now on, you're my scissor-tail and I'm your dragonfly eager to be caught."

Recognizing George's surrender, Heidi kissed him. "I'll treat my dragpmfly with tenderness."

Chapter 42

D ave Blackmun learned of Arachne's luncheon meeting with Gladys Lunamin from Rev. White, who was having lunch at Enchiladas when they met. Dave was still in his casts and unable to move around easily. He watched a lot of television. He mulled the news over in his mind a day before confronting Arachne. The next morning he woke up in a very foul mood. Finishing a breakfast of eggs and toast, he lit a cigar. As smoke filled the room, he finally posed the question.

"Why did you agree to have lunch with that woman? She'll be testifying against you." He blew smoke at Arachne, who coughed as she moved away.

Waving a handkerchief to brush the smoke away, she grimaced. "If you mean Gladys Lunamin, I thought I owed her that much. We go back a long way. We were friends in New York." She moved to the window and opened it.

Dave lifted up his arm without a cast to point a finger at her. "Are you planning to flush me out, testify against me even though we're married?"

"No, don't be so paranoid. She tried to persuade me to testify, but I refused."

He blew more smoke in her direction. "I'm not sure I can trust you."

"You don't need to be so suspicious. I know your problem. You're feeling neglected. Here, let me solve your problem." She took his cigar, carried it to the other end of the kitchen and dumped it in the disposal. "I don't work in cigar smoke," she said when she returned. She waited for the smoke to disperse and the odor to become less offensive, then sprayed with an air freshener before beginning to pacify Dave's libido.

Afterwards, her task completed, Arachne asked, "Do you want more?"

"Not now. I'm exhausted—let's wait until tonight."

"Whatever you say. I'm going out shopping. Do you want anything special?"

"No, whatever you think. Maybe you could get steaks."

"Okay." Arachne allowed herself a moment of triumph. She had Blackmun in her web of control. Her plan was working to perfection. She looked forward to dressing in stylish black, a grieving black widow.

A few days before Dave's casts were to come off, Arachne brought the morning newspaper to Dave, who was finishing his coffee. Arachne told him that she needed to see Dab.

"I'll meet Dab Whacker today to make the final arrangements about Landsetter," she said as she handed him the paper.

Dave nodded. "Okay, but be sure he understands that I'm doing the hit."

Arachne freshened his coffee. "Don't worry, I'll make that clear, if he's forgotten."

Dave opened the paper. "How late do you think you'll be?"

Arachne put up the window shade over the sink to let in sunlight. "I don't know. I should be back before ten."

As soon as she saw Dave engrossed in the newspaper, Arachne slipped to the next room and called Dab to arrange the meeting. "Can you meet me at BeeBo's around seven o'clock?"

"I'll be there unless something unexpected comes up."

"Call me there if you can't make it. We'll have until after nine."

Eagerly awaiting his rendezvous with Arachne, Dab sat in his office trailer eating a hard-boiled egg to complete his lunch. Dab conjured up an image of her beautiful body. Noting his arousal, he looked forward to her whetting his appetite. He had always prided himself on being in control. *Dave's lost his mind. He's a fool to pursue revenge! I'm looking forward to living with Arachne and pleasing her a lot.* He couldn't resist a bit of day-dreaming about their coming encounter. His lust for Arachne had begun to threaten his desire for more millions. He congratulated himself with the knowledge that fulfilling his desire for Arachne and amassing millions were not inseparable but could be achieved together.

Arachne arrived at BeeBo's at fifteen to seven. It was dimly lit except for the area around the bar. She enjoyed the rustic wooden beams left exposed running across the large room. Walking to the bar, she arranged with Jay Schreiber to have one of the back rooms at seven-twenty. Then she ordered a glass of red wine and took it to a booth in a secluded corner to wait for Dab.

He was prompt. A few minutes after seven he entered and checked with Jay, who pointed to Arachne's booth. Dab ordered a draft and walked over.

A faint scent of violets came to him as he reached her booth. "Do you want to get a short order before we go to the room?" he asked.

"Yes, I'll have a cheeseburger."

"I'll get one too. I'll put in the order."

When he returned, he sat down across from Arachne. "Are our original arrangements still okay?" he asked.

"Yes, Dave's sent George an anonymous message that Heidi will be in danger if George doesn't meet him at your mine on Thursday night before nine o'clock. I've sent Heidi a warning that she'd better watch her back. Dave's casts come off late Tuesday, so the hit's got to be for Thursday night."

Dab thought about their plan. "If we don't get George to go to my mine, our whole plan falls apart. It's important to convince him he needs to get out there. Maybe we need to give George a preliminary call, warning him again that Dave is planning to harm Heidi."

Interrupting his summary to kiss Arachne, Dab continued, "The key to our scheme is to make the blast seem aimed at George. The sooner it's done, the better—I'd like to be spending every night, all night, with you."

When their cheeseburgers and fries arrived and had been consumed, Dab ordered a bottle of wine and glasses. In their room, Dab filled the glasses and offered a toast. "Here's to new business partners and lovers."

Arachne lifted her wine in response. "To us."

Dab had brought a tape player and some tapes. He put on dance music.

"May I have this dance?"

"I'd be delighted."

To Arachne's surprise, Dab was an excellent dancer. She enjoyed pretending they were in a fancy ballroom. "You're a marvelous dancer. Where did you learn?"

"That learning was a part of my naïve, misspent youth."

Arachne lost herself in enjoyment of dancing to the strains of *The Tennessee Waltz*, thinking what a find this young stud had turned out to be. He was worth the effort she was putting into the alliance they were forming. A man as accomplished and agreeable as Dab was worth a long-time investment of energy.

"So you haven't been a miner all your life?" she asked as the music stopped.

"No, that's why I'm trying to make up for lost time. I want to be a millionaire several times over before I'm thirty."

Arachne feared she might have another Dave to deal with. "You sound as money-hungry as Dave." She took a sip of wine.

"No way I'm that hungry. It's a sickness with him. For me five million or so would suffice quite well. No amount of money will satisfy Dave."

"I think I could do well with less than five million dollars if I had the right partner. You're just a couple of years younger than me. I think we'll be good together, Are you ready for another lesson?"

"The student's ready, if the teacher is."

Dab followed instructions for over half an hour; then Arachne signaled her readiness, and they moved to a mutual climax.

Arachne glowed with satisfaction. "You're a fast learner, Dab."

"You're a great teacher."

"I guess I'd better shower before I go back to Dave's."

As he put on more dance music, Dab begged. "Don't go yet. I'm enjoying your company. We have at least a whole hour before you need to leave." He pulled her to him and sniffed the pleasant aroma she exuded.

Arachne petted him. "I like an eager student. I guess we do have time."

As he whirled her about to Montevanni's music, she felt exhilarated. Her web weaving was progressing splendidly. Following his lead, she thought how pleasant to have an ardent male like Dab to deal with instead of cranky, kinky Dave Blackmun. *He makes me feel like a whore. Dab makes me feel like a young girl again. Dab's full of desire and eagerness please me. He'll be an excellent partner for my scheme. And he dances divinely. Besides, he could run Blackdog Mining better and more profitably than Dave.*

Chapter 43

Dave's casts came off as scheduled, and he gradually became able to walk easily again with the help of crutches, He was happy to be in control of his life again, or at least to think he was, although he was still dependent on Arachne. He was pleased to be able to move around his house in Big Stone Head. "We need to make up for lost time," Dave said. He lit a cigar to celebrate.

Arachne laughed despite holding a handkerchief to her nose when the cigar smoke drifted her way. "You seem to be in good health—much more demanding. I thought your libido was pretty good—even with the casts on. You didn't have a cast around your sex machine."

"No, but I was always forced to be a passive recipient—dependent on your expertise. Now I can be active again and, besides, I can get even with Landsetter. "That anonymous note I sent him should get him out to Dab's mine. You've made final arrangements with Dab, haven't you?"

She nodded. "Dab has everything down pat. He'll be ready." She opened the curtains and looked at the sunny yard. "You have a yard with a lot of potential, but you need some flowers and shrubs," she said, apparently trying to change the subject.

Dave nodded but brushed her comment aside in an effort to emphasize his interest in revenge. "You should call him tomorrow to make sure."

"If you're worried, maybe you or I should meet with Dab—early on Thursday," Arachne said.

"I need to get back to my mining operations. I've been away from day-to-day operations too long. Want to run out to Whacker's mine and check things out? That's okay with me. Take my Durango. I'll be taking my truck out to my Blackdog sites."

"Okay, I'll set up a meeting," Arachne said.

After Arachne and Dave ate the breakfast of eggs, bacon, and muffins she fixed Thursday morning, he left for one of his sites away from Winding Fork. Happily watching Dave's truck disappear down the sun-kissed street, she no longer concealed her jubilation as she congratulated herself on the way her scheme was progressing. She just had to keep Dave happy and unsuspicious. She called Dab.

"Dave wants me to come out to your site to make a last-minute check for tomorrow night. Can you fit me in your schedule?"

"I'll be pleased to oblige. When will you be out?"

"In about an hour."

"I'll be here. Come to my office trailer."

Arachne took her time getting ready. She wanted to look her best. She lingered in the shower, dried and dabbed on her subtle violet perfume. She tied her long hair in a ponytail. Then she donned a pink dress over scarlet lingerie and slipped into pink pumps. In a little less than an hour she was at Dab's mine. She parked and walked over to his trailer and knocked.

She heard Dab's voice. "It's open. Come in."

She found him alone. "Can we go over the details for tomorrow night?" she asked.

"Why don't we step into my private office?"

She followed him into a room with a desk, a chair, and a bed. He closed the door behind them and put his arms around her.

"We won't be disturbed here," he said. He kissed her as he fondled her breasts.

"What's left to do for tonight?"

"I'll finish this afternoon after my crew prepares for tomorrow and leaves. At their request, I'm letting them off an hour early to attend a musical program. I'll have plenty of time."

"Great, Dave asked me to check on the arrangements. You're sure everything's ready?"

"Yep. We'll have a big blast tonight. Get Dave here on time and George out here after the blast."

Arachne rubbed against Dab. "It's all set, then. Dave's eager."

"Do you have time for a little fun now?"

"I do. And I see you have a bed we can use. Take off some of your clothes. I came prepared," she said as she raised her dress over her head and revealed scarlet lingerie covering her nakedness.

Dab eyed her. "Damn, you're sexy. We can't take a lot of time.

"I'm looking forward to a longer performance tonight.

Arachne was pleased with the result of her rendezvous with Dab. It had been a real romp. She was looking forward to a new life with him after Dave was history. She was expecting to become a wealthy widow with a skillful partner who could run the day-to-day operations of Blackdog Mining and then dance with her at night.

On her way home she stopped to buy some Willie Nelson recordings and food for her lunch and supper with Dave. Arachne was beginning to enjoy country music; she was having fun making plans for the Pit as a venue for local musicians, but she understood the need to keep Dave happy. She didn't want him to become suspicious of her plans for country music or him. She would do all in her power to placate him and avoid his paranoia—wine and dine him and whip him to bed afterwards. *That's what he likes, and that's what I'll provide. He won't be around much longer to enjoy the good life, so why not let him have a little pleasure before he goes.* Arachne smiled as she considered the beneficence of her actions. She hummed *So long, it's been good to know you* while she prepared lunch for Dave.

✦ ✦ ✦✦✦ ✦ ✦

George was busy with mine inspections, but he wanted to keep track of the scissor-tailed flycatcher. He had been checking on it during his lunch breaks, even when it wasn't convenient to his inspections. He had revealed his plan to Heidi, and she had suggested she would bring a picnic lunch for them to eat while they checked on the flycatcher.

"I think it's a magnificent bird. That bird and this pond will always bring back wonderful memories for me. And for you too, I hope," Heidi said, as she spread the lunch she had prepared for them.

George sat down on the cloth she'd spread and set his camera beside him. "No doubt about it. It's a special bird, and it's chosen a special place for us." He leaned over and kissed her. He'd grown fond of their ritual of mixing lunches with birding and heavy petting

She handed him a ham and cheese sandwich. So far the flycatcher had not failed to put in an appearance during their lunches. Today, George was planning to photograph the bird to have proof of its presence.

"Sweetheart, I'm worried about you," Heidi said. "I heard Blackmun got out of his casts yesterday. Gladys told me Arachne Smith warned her that Dave was planning to hurt you."

George knew she was right but was glad he hadn't told Heidi about the threatening note he'd received. He still thought it better not to mention any threats to her. They had to be from Dave, he figured, but he didn't want to worry her. Dave wouldn't try to hurt him during working hours. He'd stay alert, just in case.

"Don't you fret. Dave's back at work, but he won't try to attack me while I'm inspecting his mine. He's more devious than that." George took a bite of his sandwich.

Heidi pulled his ear to make her point, "But the man *is* evil. And he's angry about his current troubles. He's dangerous. It's hard to say what else he'll do."

Suddenly, the scissor-tailed flycatcher appeared close by, perched in a bush at the pond's edge. George raised his camera and took many shots of the bird. Then it flew out to catch an insect, and he added several flight pictures.

"I hope a few of these turn out, especially the flight shots. Some should. I 'm taking a whole roll. We're lucky it's come so close."

The flycatcher flew a loop as it captured another dragonfly.

Just then, thunder sounded in the distance and a dark cloud approached, covering the sky from horizon to horizon. "We'd better gather up this picnic stuff and get it to cover before the rain hits," Heidi said as she rushed to pack up their picnic.

George began carrying things to her car.

✦ ✦ ✦✦✦ ✦ ✦

Thursday night the rain clouds had disappeared and there was a full moon. Arachne saw Dave off a little after half past seven. He seemed content with a full stomach and a satisfied libido. She wanted him to get to Dab's surface mine well before dark, but she didn't rush him. She made sure he went full of steak, satisfied and unsuspicious.

"Be careful. You don't want to kill yourself driving too fast on those crooked roads." Arachne was aware of the irony of her comment, considering what she and Dab had in store for him, but she wanted to maintain an air of normalcy. She even stepped outside to wave goodbye.

Blackmun arrived at Dab's mine a little before eight. The sun would soon be disappearing. Dab Whacker was waiting in front of his trailer.

"You're right on time," Dab said. "Let's hide your Durango." He laughed to himself. Dave would be dead by the time anybody else saw it.

Having moved his vehicle, Dave was all business. "Show me what you've planned."

Dab led Blackmun to a spot he'd prepared. "My men have fixed a blast for tomorrow morning. Here's the place for you to hide. You'll wait here for Landsetter. I'll direct him closer to the blast area." Dab pointed to a white marker about fifty yards out. "When you see him reach that white post, push the red button on this." He handed Dave a control. "That will set off the blast. Be careful not to set it off too early. Wait until he reaches that white post. You understand?"

"Sure, I set off the charge when he reaches the white marker."

"That's it. Keep your place here." Dab began to move off. "I've got to go back to meet Landsetter and tell him Heidi's tied up out there. He should be here any time now."

When Dab was close to his trailer, he took out the real control for the blast and pressed the red button. Two horrific explosions, almost simultaneous, hit Dab's ears as a combination of fire and smoke rose above the mine at the white post and at the place he'd left Dave. He entered to his office and called Arachne. "The blast just went off. Call Heidi and George."

A few minutes later she called Heidi. Disguising her voice, she told Heidi to get to her office. "There's been a break-in at your office. There's smoke. I've called the police and the fire department."

After repeating her warning to Heidi, Arachne waited for five minutes, then hastened to make the call to George, disguising her voice as much as possible to sound like a man. "Blackmun's holding Heidi Leaves at Dab Whacker's mine. He says you'd better go out there or she'll be dead and you'll be sorry."

Then Arachne called Heidi again to make sure she had left. Receiving no answer, she returned Dab's call. "Landsetter should soon be on his way."

Whacker looked at his watch again. Six minutes had gone by. He picked up his office phone and called 911. "There's been a terrific explosion at Dab Whacker's surface mining site at Winding Fork." Closing his office, Dab got in his truck and left the site. He headed to Dave's house in Big Stone Head.

George was worried. He called Mike.

"Mike, I think Heidi may be in trouble. Blackmun may be holding her at Dab Whacker's mine. I just had another threat, Whoever it was said Dave's holding Heidi at Dab's mine, and Heidi doesn't answer her phone."

"Call Heidi again. If she doesn't answer, pick me up at my place." George rang Heidi's number for about five minutes. There was no answer. He raced to Mike;s. As Mike climbed in the truck, George said, "I can't help worrying since I received that anonymous note and the e-mail threatening Dave would harm Heidi. The two headed to Whacker's mine at a high speed. Entering the site, they saw smoke and fire from a large blast. As they were getting out, a police car followed them in. The two deputies recognized Mike. "How did you beat us here, Mike? We came as soon as we got the 911 call," one said.

Mike introduced George to the speaker, John Marks, and his partner, Hiram Mullinax. "George is a reclamation officer. He received an anonymous call around eight. He was warned Dave Blackmun was holding Heidi Leaves here and that George would be sorry if he didn't come out here. Lately George has received several other threats against his fiancée."

"Have you found anything?"

"We had just got out of George's truck when you arrived. We haven't had a chance. Let's look over at the smoke and fire."

"The call to 911 was anonymous," Officer Marks said. "It reported a huge explosion."

They found that the blast had exposed a huge seam of coal. "Looks like the miners prepared an explosion for Friday, and somebody set it off prematurely," Mike said.

Officer Mullinax called from thirty yards away. "Hey, there's a body over here."

George, Mike, and Officer Marks ran over to where Mullinax was kneeling, bent over a body. "Mike, take a look. I think this guy may still be alive."

Mike checked the body. "It's Dave Blackmun, and you're right. He's still alive, but he's not in very good shape. Call an ambulance, John."

Officer Marks ran to his patrol car and made the call. In less than half an hour, the emergency squad arrived, They soon had Blackmun loaded into their vehicle and on his way to the emergency department at the local hospital, followed by Marks and Mullinax.

"He may be dead before they get him to the hospital," George said.

Chapter 44

There were few lights on at Dave's place in Big Stone Head. Dab and Arachne were having an amicable but very active celebration of their new relationship on the living room couch when the telephone rang for several minutes.

Dab tried to ignore it but failed. 'Who the hell would that be?"

Reluctant but determined, Arachne pushed him away and walked over to answer. 'Let's hope it's a call to tell me my husband's dead. Time to play the grieving widow."

The voice on the phone did not deliver the message she had hoped for. "I'm a nurse at Wisdom General Hospital. I have some bad news, Mrs. Blackmun. An ambulance with police escort brought your husband in less than an hour ago. He's in intensive care. The doctors think they may be able to save him,"

Arachne did not speak for almost thirty seconds. She hoped her chagrin would translate as shock." Do you think I could see my husband tonight?"

"He's in a coma. You can, but I'd wait until tomorrow The police aren't letting many people in."

"I'll check tomorrow.... Thanks ....."

Arachne banged the phone down. "Damn, the bastard's still alive. How can one man survive so many blasts? He must have cat genes."

"Dave must have moved from where I put him. I gave him strict instructions not to move. If he'd stayed there, he couldn't have survived."

"Dave's barely alive. He's in intensive care."

"Shit-luck bastard," Dab said. "That will give the government something to punish."

"There's no point in worrying about it tonight. It will go down as another mining blast gone wrong—another black mark on Dave's record, if more comes of it. As long as we stick together and keep our stories straight, we'll be okay. If we're asked, we'll say that Dave was talking of getting even with George Landsetter, but we didn't think he meant murder," Arachne said.

Dab picked up where Arachne left off. "Right, and as far as any of my men know, they had prepared the blast for our mining Friday and Dave added to it. And for them or anybody else, your meetings with me were lovers' meetings that Dave knew about. He didn't care because your marriage was a marriage of convenience."

"Now that we've settled our stories, let's get back to sealing our partnership," Arachne said as she pulled Dab to her.

* * * * * * *

George and Mike listened to Elvis Presley singing *Always on My Mind, You Don't Have to Say You Love Me,* and other songs on the radio as they drove from the explosion back to town. They had more questions than answers.

George tried to figure out what had happened. "I had those warnings that Blackmun was planning something bad for me, then threats that he was going to hurt Heidi to get even with me, and finally that anonymous warning tonight. Dave got caught in his own plot against me, but something doesn't add up."

"It looks like Dave got his due, but you're right that something doesn't seem to fit. You've got to admit, though, he's a hard guy to kill,"

Mike said as he pulled out a half-full bag of jellybeans from his jacket pocket and offered some to George.

George popped a few jellybeans in his mouth. "I wonder if there'll be enough of him left for the government to prosecute. I hope so. I've worked hard to help get people to testify against him in return for immunity."

Mike chewed on jellybeans and put the bag back in his pocket.

"Yeah, people did things for Dave out of fear of what he'd do to them if they didn't cooperate, but if there's enough left to prosecute, I'd bet the FBI will be eager to nail him."

George nodded. "After I drop you off, I'm going by Heidi's to find out if she's okay and let her know I'm all right."

Heidi's lights were still on when George got there. He rang her bell and waited for her to answer. She opened the door to the length of its chain and peered out. Seeing him, she took off the chain.

"Thank God you're alive. Are you all right?" she whispered. "I got a strange call this evening telling me that there'd been a break-in at my office, that my building was on fire, but there wasn't anything wrong as far as I could see."

"Part of Dave's plot, evidently. I'm okay. Dave got caught in his own trap at Dab Whacker's mine. He was blown up in an explosion he meant for me."

"I heard on the radio. You could have been killed," she said as he wrapped his arms around her. "I've been terribly worried about you."

"I'm here, and no harm's been done except to Dave Blackmun. I reckon he's fighting for life."

Heidi sat on the sofa. "Sit down and tell me what happened."

George sat down and took her in his arms, and spent the next hour recounting the events of the night. Between kisses, he said, "I think we should get married as soon as possible."

"Maybe you should move in with me right away. It would save money and time and make life easier. Stay with me tonight. I need you. I want to go to sleep nestled beside you."

George hugged her closer. "I'll be happy to oblige."

Next morning, George awakened as Heidi bent over to kiss him. She gazed several minutes at his well-formed, naked body.

"You must be dreaming about last night. I'm having a delightful morning watching my sleepy lover, but I think it's time for you to wake up."

Though still half asleep, George became aware of Heidi's naked body above him. He embraced her, and they played for half an hour before collapsing in orgasmic delight.

"I love going to sleep and waking up with you," Heidi said.

Fully awake, George agreed the new order was delightful. "It's certainly uplifting. I'm enjoying our new arrangement."

During breakfast, they discussed their day's work.

George reminded her of their daily ritual. "Don't forget our lunch with the scissor-tail."

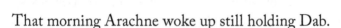

That morning Arachne woke up still holding Dab.

Contemplating him, she massaged. He muttered as if he were dreaming when she succeeded in her efforts. Pleased with her progress, she tried to wake him, "Sex is more fun with a conscious partner," she said as she straddled him.

Gradually Whacker began to move from his dream world into a dawn of fornication. "Am I dreaming, or am I being banged by a beautiful woman?"

"If this position was good enough for Roman emperors, it's good enough for you. Wake up."

"What time is it?"

"It's almost seven."

He began to withdraw. "I've got to get to work. There'll be a big mess to clean up."

Arachne tried to delay him. "You may not be able to work today. The police are probably looking through things."

"All the more reason I need to be there. It'll look bad if I'm not. I'll check Dave's mine just to make sure everything is going all right there too. You'll need to go out there yourself sometime soon."

Arachne had to admit the truth of what Dab said. "If you insist on going to work, I'll fix us some breakfast." She put aside her frustration and left the bed, putting on a housecoat.

As they ate bacon, eggs, and toast, Dab spoke about Dave. "The bastard can't have survived intact. You need to find out what damage he sustained." Dab waved his fork for emphasis.

"I'm going to the hospital this morning to play the grieving prospective widow. I'll find out what shape he's in. He deserved whatever he got. Maybe he won't survive."

At the hospital, the doctor in charge of Dave Blackmun's case told Arachne not to hope for her husband's complete recovery, if he lived. She ignored the hospital odors she found so unpleasant in order to get a full explanation of Dave's condition. Her hope for a less than satisfactory report overcame her nausea at smelling disinfectants.

"If he survives, his activities will be curtailed. Besides spinal damage, he has damage to the brain and internal organs. Frankly, we're amazed he's alive. I don't think he'll ever walk very far."

"You don't know that for sure, do you?"

"No, we'll have to wait and see. You've seen he's lost an arm He may not survive. We'll do our best."

"Surface mine explosions kill a lot of people, and Mr. Whacker has a reputation for setting large charges. "Arachne said. "Dave may have added some explosives."

"At any rate, he's lucky to be alive and he's breathing on his own. We'll let you know if there's any change in his condition. He'll be in ICU a long time."

Arachne was all grieving wife. She even managed some sobs. "Thank you. I'm sure you are doing the best you can." *I hope your best efforts fail.*

Watching the sun rising, George recalled his night with Heidi. *Yeah, it was worth the wait.* He recalled John Denver's song about the sun on his back making him happy. He hummed its tune all the way to Whacker's mine. The first person George saw there was Mike. "Morning," he said as he raised his hand in greeting.

Mike was amused. "You seem pretty chipper for a guy who barely escaped being blown up. You look like a bear who's robbed a honey hive."

George raised his right hand, fingers forming a V. "The evening ended well. I'm moving in with Heidi."

"Congratulations," Mike said. "I won't inquire further. We'll have to think about a party. Sheriff Bo has put me in charge of figuring out what went on here last night." Mike picked up a rock and hurled it toward the coal seam uncovered by last night's blast. "He wants an investigation that's on the up-and-up. He says if any one gives me trouble, to tell them that the FBI requested me."

George felt the sun warming his back. "That's progress. Do you think Sheriff Bo sees a chance to clean up his act with Dave out of the way?"

"That's how I read it. If Dave recovers like he did before, I'm not sure Bo's new leaf will stay turned. I'm tired of the night shifts Bo put me on to please Dave."

George nodded. "I don't blame you. I hope that page's turned for good."

"I'll enjoy the new one while it lasts." Mike pulled out a bag of jellybeans and offered some to George.

George took a handful. "I need to examine the area to check what environmental damage was done here and in the surrounding area."

"Go ahead. I'll tell my men to let you go wherever you want. Dab Whacker got here a few minutes before you" Mike pointed to two men having a conversation. "He's over with his foreman next to that D-12 'dozer."

"Okay, I'll start with them." George strode toward Dab.

Mike called after him. "I'll want to hear what you find out before you go."

When George approached Dab and his foreman, they were discussing how much explosive they had used.

"I put in a legal load, Dab. I'm telling you the truth. A maximum—but I was careful. I know Landsetter here has been on your case about big loads. It was in good order when we left it yesterday. The ammonium nitrate and fuel oil were ready to set off, just like you told us to fix it."

"I reckon Dave brought some extra stuff with him. Seems too much damage for a normal load. What do you think, George?"

"I agree; the damage seems excessive. Maybe Dave did add a little extra. You've uncovered a lot of good coal, though."

"I'm sure somebody added to the charge after I left," the foreman said as he picked up an object. "Look, here's a control unit."

"That could've set off the blast," George said.

"This is where Mike said ya'all found Dave last night."

Dab examined the unit. "Dave must have been too eager."

"I reckon he was keen to see the last of me," George said.

Dab chuckled. "You ain't his favorite person, for sure."

"I'll check with the neighbors to see if they have any damage. I'll get back to you, if they do. This blast was way over the limit," George said. "Still, it wasn't much bigger than some of yours that caused trouble. Maybe you'll get by without much damage, since it happened so late."

"Please note what Jake said. He set a lawful amount yesterday," Dab said.

George nodded. "You appear to be off the hook, Dab. I'll check with some neighbors. I'm going to inspect the Blackdog operation next. Want meet me there? You're running Dave's mines now, aren't you?"

"Sure, I've told the men to do things right and stay out of trouble. There shouldn't be a problem. I'll be over there in an hour if Mike finishes with me," Dab said.

"Then I'll talk to Mike, and meet you there."

Barton and another deputy were looking at something they had picked up some distance from where Blackmun had been found.

'Check this out, George." Mike handed over a piece of a box. What was left of the label indicated it had held Dynamite.

George examined the label. "Somebody added to the explosive charge Dab's foreman oversaw Thursday afternoon. They don't use Dynamite. By the way, you need to talk to Jake. He found a control unit near where we discovered Blackmun last night. Dave must've set off the charge prematurely."

"Fits what I've found," Mike said.

"Jake insists somebody added explosives to his charge. I think he's right."

The rest of George's morning inspections lacked any excitement from failures to observe mining regulations, but he saw several kestrels and a black-billed cuckoo. No neighbors had reported harm from the blast at Dab's mine. George was in a good mood when time for his lunch meeting with Heidi arrived.

She was spreading their picnic lunch on a cloth on the grass near the big rock at the pond. He hurried over. He could smell some fresh apple pie. Heidi smiled up at him and handed him a sandwich.

"Hi, I hope you like tuna. How did your morning go?"

"Everybody thinks that Dave or somebody else added to explosives Dab's men prepared for today."

Heidi gazed at him for several seconds and caught his hand. "That blast was meant for you. I'm worried. I've decided we've already waited too long to get married. I don't want a church wedding after all. Let's get married at your grandparents' place at Winding Fork—as soon as we can—just family and a few close friends. Then we'll honeymoon at the Smoky Mountains National Park or some other place nearby where we can enjoy the forest."

"Suits me. Sounds great—what brought this on?"

"If you're going to be in danger all of the time, I don't want to wait, but if I have to wait, I'd rather wait as your loving wife than as your lover."

"Hoorah! … All right, you make the arrangements with Mamaw and Papaw and make a list of no more than twenty people other than family to invite. I'll see about making reservations at some rustic place close by, maybe the Breaks Interstate Park."

As George was beginning his second sandwich, the scissor-tail flew into a bush across the pond, chattering. "Look, there's our bird."

Just as he spoke, another bird flew in. This bird had a shorter scissor-tail and a pale lemon breast and flanks instead of salmon feathers.

Heidi asked, "Is this another scissor-tail?"

"I think so. It looks like the picture of the female in the guide. I believe we may have a nesting pair. We'll have to wait to see if she sticks around."

"How exciting!" Heidi hugged George. "Maybe we should have our wedding here. Do you think Isaiah would mind our marrying at this pond?"

"I think Mamaw and Papaw would be happier having it at their place. We could have a groom's reception here for a small group."

"That's a good idea."

"I have another. I'll start moving in to your place this evening, if that's okay."

"You start this evening, I'll help after supper. I'm looking forward to another night with you."

"Before we go, help me look for some fossils for Andy. I promised him I'd have some for him the next time he visited Mamaw and Papaw."

Heidi began to search. "Okay, I love hunting for them."

That evening, after a dinner of spicy shrimp creole, garden salad, and carrot cake, Heidi and George spent four hours moving almost all of his possessions to her apartment. He and Mike would bring the sofa and his few other pieces of big furniture later. He'd give notice when he had time. Then the couple showered—together, for the first time—and donned bathrobes. Heidi sipped a red wine and George downed a beer while they sat on the sofa listening to John Denver's *Calypso*.

"If this is what married life is like, I think I'm cut out for it," George said.

Heidi nibbled his ear. "I'm glad you're so easily domesticated. You make me feel like a successful lion tamer, but I don't want my lion too tame."

George crouched on the floor. "Grrrrr.... he pawed aside her robe and pretended to bite her as he nibbled her ears, breasts, and stomach, tickling her as he moved down while she pretended to push him away."

Between gasps of pleasure, she managed to say, "I think we need to get to the bedroom."

◆ ◆ ◆ ◆ ◆

Arachne Smith Blackmun paid a visit to the Blackdog mining site at Winding Fork in the late afternoon. At the office shack, she found Dave's foreman, Hamilton Stafford. She found him talking on the telephone. When he finished, he rose and took the hand she offered him.

"Hamilton, how are things working out between you and Mr. Whacker?"

"Don't know of no problems, Mrs. Blackmun. How's the boss?"

"He's still in intensive care, and things don't look good. The doctors say he's not likely to walk much and his mental processes are liable to be impaired. He won't be able to have an active life, if he lives."

"They don't think he'll make it?"

"They're not sure. It's fifty-fifty. I'm sure I can count on you to keep things going here."

"Sure thing, if I need advice, I'll talk to Dab, but things are smooth right now. Our last blast brought out a nice seam. We have enough coal to meet our contracts for the foreseeable future."

"I'll let you know of any change in Dave's situation. Thanks for your help, Hamilton. Please tell the men I appreciate their hard work."

"You bet, Mrs. Blackmun. We'll keep digging the black gold."

Arachne drove back to Big Stone Head. She congratulated herself on the success of her scheme, even if the amount of her control was still in doubt.

Arachne did her best to excite Dab's interest. After a perfumed bath, she pulled her hair back in a ponytail and tied it. She put on her sexiest black lingerie and covered it with a skimpy red outfit that clung to her to reveal a curvaceous body. She appraised herself in the mirror with satisfaction. When Dab arrived, she greeted him with a kiss. "Shower while I finish fixing something to eat. Just throw on a robe and come on down.

The scene at the Blackmun house was less joyous than that at Heidi's, but quite amorous. Arachne could not wipe the uncertainty of their situation from her mind. She had twinges of regret—not for what they'd done—but for the lack of a more decisive outcome. Still, she was excited about their new relationship and celebrated the prospect they might be able to continue unabated, even unhampered by Dave's presence, if he lived.

When Dab returned, she had steaks and a garden salad on the table. Then she poured red wine. "How did things go?" she asked.

"Pretty well—everyone agreed somebody added more explosives to what my men had prepared. They assumed Dave added it. How is Dave?"

"Fighting for life—the doctors don't think he'll recover fully even if he lives. He's lost an arm, the left arm."

"That's lucky. He's right-handed." Dab said.

They settled to eating their steaks and salads doused with a rich syrupy wine vinaigrette.

"You did a great job with these steaks," Dab took his time, savoring the beef. "They're just right."

"Thanks. I tried to avoid too well done."

"No way, just a perfect pink." When Dave finished his steak and salad, he asked, "What's for dessert?"

Arachne opened her jacket. "I hoped you'd think I'm dessert. See if I'm tasty enough?"

"I think you are. Damn, you look sexy tonight." As Dab moved to Arachne's side, his robe fell away, revealing his arousal. He took off her blouse and bra and reached for the vinegarette. Dripping it on her breasts, he began to lick the liquid off of them, enjoying the aroma of the dressing mixed with Arachne's musky perfume.

She purred her approval.

Later, Dab played some dance music, and they enjoyed dancing, a romantic interlude before they continued their celebration in bed.

Chapter 46

George feared Dave's malevolence less, even though he was still alive. Defying the odds, Blackmun had survived the explosion he'd intended for George, but the blast had left him with permanent disabilities: missing one arm, unable to walk much more than a few feet at a time, and effectively confined to a wheel chair. Dave had little memory of the night of the blast. He was not his old vehement advocate for number one. He could attend to necessary body functions, but his short-term mental abilities were weakened—he was way more than an imbecile but unable to handle day-to-day business complexities on his own. The court had deemed him able to understand his place in the legal system, so he could not escape his past, if all those who had promised George and the FBI they'd testify against Blackmun kept their word.

Months later, a much diminished Dave Blackmun was awaiting trial in a Virginia court, held under house arrest, charged with attempted murder and murder. Convinced by the lawyers Arachne had hired, the Virginia State Police felt him unlikely to mount an escape. If he managed to escape punishment by the State, the FBI was waiting with a long list of lesser crimes. George hoped his five hundred acres of woodland would soon be safe, and those who knew Dave hoped for a guilty verdict, pleased Virginia still retained the death penalty.

The October air was cool and the leaves were turning gold and red. The sourwoods had turned deep scarlet when George invited

Mike Barton and Moon to go deer hunting with him on his five hundred acres of woodland. It would be doe day, and they would be able to shoot any deer that appeared, not just a buck. There were plenty of ravens flying around, croaking as they searched for the remains of deer kills.

As they readied for the hunt at Archibald's place in Winding Fork, Moon asked about Arachne Smith Blackmun.

George laughed. "She's ended up with control of Dave and Blackdog Mining. Dab tells me she has power of attorney and takes care of all of Dave's business affairs. Dab's running Blackdog."

"Gladys still thinks Arachne took part in the kidnapping because Dave forced her," Moon said.

George nodded. "Dab says so. He and Arachne seem to get along pretty well. He helps her care for Dave—even has a room of his own in Dave's house."

Mike laughed as he paused in working on his rifle. "All indications are she and Dab are lovers. She keeps Dave happy but takes her pleasure with Dab. At least that's the talk among the deputies."

"If Dave's convicted, she won't spend time nursing him. The prison system takes over. I'm happy she's the *de facto* head of Blackdog Mining and all of Dave's enterprises," George said. "She sees that Dab follows the mining laws."

As Mike finished cleaning his rifle, he added information. "Arachne's redone the Pit. It's now Flat Gap Casino. She provides family-oriented floor shows to complement bingo and other legal gambling. She's hired Rod to handle the gambling. He uses his legal work at the Casino to make contacts for his private gambling and pot business."

Moon shook his head, "So he's still in the pot business?"

"There's no hint of it at the Casino," Mike said. "The emphasis is on local music—including gospel— and dancing. Arachne's fallen in love with country music. It's rumored Johnny Cash and June Carter will perform at the Casino."

"You have to admit Arachne's smart," George said. "What about the other New York girls?"

Mike laughed. "Some have gone back to New York. Arachne's still including girls Dave brought down from the big city, but they're termed hostesses now. They earn their way by working as waitresses and entertainers."

Moon shook his head. "That's hard to believe. Do they do anything else?"

"They sing nights and compete when there're popular music contests." Mike said. "No secret cameras—they take pictures of patrons and their families for a fee. The girls can rent Arachne's private rooms while they're here. Arachne pays them to train local girls for additional hostesses.

"Are you sure they don't have cameras in those rooms now?" Moon asked.

"Nobody's found any." Mike said. "Arachne doesn't interfere. If they manage to snare a husband, I've heard she has them marry at the Casino. She waives the cost or gives a big discount if she thinks they've attracted enough money for her casino."

"I reckon Arachne's at least partway reformed," George said.

The three men were in the woods before daybreak. George took Mike and Moon to stands he'd picked out for them and then went to his own. Barred Owls were still sounding *Who cooks for you?* as he settled at his stand.

When dawn broke, George heard migrant thrushes giving night calls as they dropped from the sky into the woods. Soon there were call notes of serveral thrush species all around him. The *whit* calls of the migrating Swainson's thrushes led the dawn chorus. Local birds were already flocking. He listened for the *pik* note of the downy woodpeckers. He knew they would be leading the feeding flocks of titmice, chickadees, and nuthatches.

Searching for the woodpeckers, he saw a deer moving toward him. Slowly raising his binoculars, he counted antlers with at least eight points on this buck. Slowly he moved his rifle into position and aimed for a spot just behind the buck's shoulder. The buck stopped to sniff the air and George carefully squeezed the trigger.

The buck jumped at the loud report and ran about fifteen yards before collapsing.

As George moved from cover to inspect his kill, he heard another shot from the direction of Mike's stand. By the time he finished preparing his prize, he'd heard yet another shot, this one from Moon's stand. In half an hour, the three of them met at their rendezvous, each dragging a deer. Mike had a large doe. Moon had a two-point buck.

Moon congratulated George. "That's a trophy buck. Nine points. We'll get these back to Archie's to hang them up. Then we'll see if we can wrangle Mike an invitation to dinner." Moon turned to Mike, "You'll stay, won't you? Archie killed a young buck two days ago, so Serafina should have some venison steaks and maybe a mince pie."

As George and the other hunters sat on the porch with Archie, waiting for a call to eat, Moon mentioned that Gladys had run into Arachne in Big Stone Head a few days earlier. "She told Gladys Dab's doing a great job running Blackdog. She hasn't merged it with Dab's company. She wants to keep Dave happy. He likes to think of Blackdog as his, even though he can't run it. He has Arachne drive him to the sites once or twice a week."

"Did Arachne say anything else. How does Dave spend his time?" George asked.

Moon laughed and slapped his thigh. "Dave's occupying himself with Russian roulette."

George stood up and stretched. "Damn, that sounds dangerous,"

"She tries to keep him happy," Mike said. "That's the scuttlebutt at the sheriff's office; she lets him play with his Colt Trooper. Makes sure it's unloaded, she claims."

Moon laughed as he untied his boots. "Arachne told Gladys she's trained Dab to be a thoughtful lover."

"What's a thoughtful lover?" George asked as he sat down.

"Thoughtful lovers don't tear a woman's clothes off. Their women believe they're foolish to keep them on."

"Do you think Arachne might marry Dab, if Dave gets the death penalty?" George asked

"She told Gladys she plans to remain Mrs. Arachne Smith Blackmun whatever happens. She likes being in control. She expects Dave to go to prison despite the fancy New York lawyers she's hired. They think they can get Arachne a suspended sentence."

"She evidently likes being the equivalent of a rich widow," Mike said. "I still think she and Dab caused Dave's plan to kill George to backfire."

George nodded. "If they did, I'm grateful."

Heidi came out to the porch to summon them to dinner, After a meal of venison steak, green beans, and potatoes, Serafina served minced-meat pies. Everybody had praises for Serafina's cooking. As he lifted another of her cookies Andy praised, "Mamaw is the best cook I've ever known. Her cookies melt in your mouth."

"And she was a wonderful hostess for my marriage to George. She made it a truly splendid affair," Heidi said. "She brought us good luck, too. I'm two-months pregnant."

Amid clapping, Gladys patted Heidi on the shoulder. "How marvelous. I wish you a healthy pregnancy. I'm hoping for something like that before another deer season."

Heidi raised her hand with crossed fingers. "I guess the success of our scissor-tailed flycatchers rubbed off on us. They raised a brood of four."

Gladys nodded. "I read about the flycatchers in our Asheville paper—under Jennifer Coffee's by-line. It was really a big event in the birding world. Those birds aren't supposed to be this far north, much less breeding."

"They established George and me in Virginia birding circles," Heidi said. "He took a lot of pictures to document the event. I've become an ardent birder. I'm known by a lot of the men and lady bigwigs in the Virginia Society of Ornithology. That was a great story. Jennifer may just get that Pulitzer one of these days."

George beamed. "Heidi has ramrodded the Black Mt. Bird Club into existence." Then he remembered the fossils. He went to his truck and brought a bag in and gave it to Andy. "Here are the fossils I promised you. Heidi helped me find them."

"Thanks, George. You, too, Heidi. Are there any dinosaur fossils?"

"I'm afraid not. Our coal beds were put down long before there were any dinosaurs roaming around. Almost all of the fossils we find around here are of earlier animals from ancient seas or plants that formed our coal seams in shallow waters," George said.

"Will you help me identify these?"

"Sure thing."

"George is a geologist, Andy. That's a person who specializes in rocks and fossils," Heidi said.

"You might say George has rocks in his head," Moon said, grinning.

Everybody laughed. Heidi put her arm around George. "I'm so glad George introduced me to the out-of-doors in these mountains. It's so beautiful. And Moon's reclamation of Isaiah's land has produced a veritable Garden of Eden."

"If Dave's convicted, I think we can say we and the County have come a long way. Wisdom County will be a great place to live," George said. "But we aren't sure yet that he'll be convicted. Until then I won't feel my five hundred acres are safe."

George didn't add that he wouldn't feel his woodland would be safe until Dave Blackmun was sentenced to life imprisonment or death. He couldn't help himself. It wasn't so much a matter of seeking vengeance as it was an undefined uneasiness that Dave might still be able to find some way to ruin those five hundred acres. It was foolish fear, and George wasn't about to tell anyone else about his feelings, especially Heidi.

Chapter 47

As Blackmun's trial began and the people George had helped persuade to testify proved true to their word, it became more and more probable that Blackmun would be convicted in spite of Arachne's having hired hot-shot lawyers from New York. They had managed to arrange Dave's in-home arrest with a compliant judge, who had settled for an ankle monitor and twice-a-day police visits. Dave regarded it as a modest dividend on an investment. To his disgust, the New York attorneys had not performed as well as expected. Reading the Roanoke newspapers, George learned the jurors seemed to dislike them, according to Jennifer Coffee reported in her newspaper accounts of the trial.

"How did the trial go today?" Heidi asked, when George came home late from work on the day he was to testify.

"Pretty well."

"Did your testimony go okay?"

"I reckon. I gave it and then inspected five surface mines. Mike called me to say Josie Roper testified later. She didn't finish, but he said her testimony so far should convict Dave of murder."

"You worked hard to get her to testify."

"Yeah, and he's less fearsome now—almost completely dependent on Arachne. The trial shouldn't take long. There can't be many defense witnesses to testify. Who would the defense put on the stand?"

The people George had helped persuade to testify proved true to their word as Blackmun's trial began, and, it became more and more probable that Blackmun would be convicted in spite of Arachne's having hired hot-shot lawyers from New York. They had managed to arrange Dave's in-home arrest with a compliant judge, who had settled for an ankle monitor and twice-a-day police visits. One of his caretakers told George Dave regarded it as a modest dividend on an investment. To his disgust, the New York attorneys had not performed as well as expected at trial. The jurors seemed to dislike them, Jennifer Coffee reported in her newspaper accounts of the trial.

"How did the trial go today?" Heidi asked, when George came home late from work on the day he was to testify.

"Pretty well."

"Did your testimony go okay?"

"I reckon. I gave it and then inspected five surface mines. Mike called me to say Josie Roper testified later. She didn't finish, but he said her testimony so far should convict Dave of murder."

"You worked hard to get her to testify."

"Yeah, and he's less fearsome now—almost completely dependent on Arachne. The trial shouldn't take long. There can't be many defense witnesses to testify. Who would the defense put on the stand?"

Heidi made a droll face. "I don't know anyone respectable who'd testify to Dave's good character."

"Don't be too sure. Dave still has money."

"I don't think he has enough to get *him* off."

George nodded and changed the subject. "I think Mabel should be worried. Mike's spending so much time talking to Josie Roper and Jennifer Coffee. Mike and Josie seem to be Jennifer's sources nowadays."

Heidi laughed and pretended to be dealing cards. "I wonder if either of them plays poker with her?"

Grinning, George poked her arm. "Do you want me to ask Mike? Or Jennifer?"

Heidi wrinkled her nose. "No, and make sure you don't play poker with her."

"Don't worry. Jennifer's getting her news from Josie and Mike. By the way, I think Philemon's interested in mining Josie's land. I've seen him with Josie a number of times. I'd bet they're discussing more than mining."

"Good. I won't have to worry if Mike, Josie, and Philemon keep the news hound occupied. I had a craving for pork chops, so we're having chops, greens, and sweet potato fries tonight. There'll be peach pie for dessert. I've put some beer in the fridge for you. "She sighed, "I'm making do with ginger ale spliced with bitters."

George smelled the pleasant aromas coming from the kitchen. "You're a great cook, but I'd settle for a little loving for dessert."

"Pass up my pie? I can't believe that, but I've been longing for you all day, so I won't take offense," Heidi said as she hugged him.

After they had feasted, Heidi kissed him. "Help me clean off the table."

Later, settled down on the sofa with a second beer, George watched as Heidi put on a John Denver record. As *Annie's Song* filled the room, he pulled her to him and kissed her. "'You fill up *my* senses, no doubt about that. I can't get you out of my mind."

"I'm glad to hear that." Heidi said as she unbuckled his belt. "You fill up my senses like a bird walk on a spring morning."

"I can't believe how much I love you," he said as he undressed her and caressed her breasts. Then he bent his head down to listen to see if he could hear the baby."

Heidi giggled. "It's too soon to hear it or feel it kick."

"That's all right, I'll just stay down here."

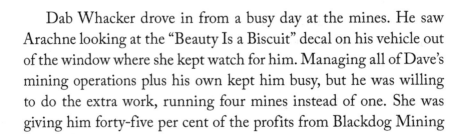

Dab Whacker drove in from a busy day at the mines. He saw Arachne looking at the "Beauty Is a Biscuit" decal on his vehicle out of the window where she kept watch for him. Managing all of Dave's mining operations plus his own kept him busy, but he was willing to do the extra work, running four mines instead of one. She was giving him forty-five per cent of the profits from Blackdog Mining as pay. Arachne's exciting variety was reward enough, even without the money, although he wasn't about to tell her. *She's worth the danger and extra work I'm taking on. Damn, she's hot.*

"How did the trial go?" he asked when he found her lying on the sofa in a pair of short shorts and a halter-top barely covering her breasts.

"I don't think Dave has a chance. His schemes to kill George have worked against him. The best news is the lawyers I hired say they'll get me off with probation. They think the jury believes Dave forced me to do bad deeds. At least that's what they're telling me."

Dab grinned. "We really did a good job putting Dave's own plan into operation—a rat caught in his own trap. Fuck Dave. The lawyers have earned their money if they get you off without jail time. Do you want to go out to eat?"

"No, we need to practice. I've planned to have steaks and potatoes and a garden salad. That's what Dave likes. We'll feed him well, and I'll slip some sleeping pills in his coffee. Check his pistol. He's like a child playing Russian roulette. Make sure his gun's unloaded. Go shower, and I'll get things ready. Then you can wheel Dave in."

When Dab returned in shorts and a tee shirt, Arachne had the table ready. "Go bring Dave."

Dinner went without a hitch. Dab told Dave about the activities at the Blackdog mines, and reviewed new coal contracts and possible new mining sites. Then they talked some about sports. Dave had been watching golf, the Master's tournament. He was disappointed Tom Weiskopf was doing so poorly. "I wish Weiskopf would beat Jack Nicklaus and win the damn U. S. Open just one time," Dave said. "I'm glad I didn't put money on that loser, Weiskopf."

The sleeping pills produced the desired effect. After eating, Blackmun dozed off.

"Wheel him to his room," Arachne said. "Be careful how you arrange things. Practice makes perfect."

She fixed a couple of gin and tonics and took them to Dab's room on a tray with fixings for more.

Sitting on the bed, clothed in scarlet lingerie, she was sipping her drink when Dab entered. "Is he still sleeping?"

"Like a baby."

She handed him his drink. "The pills seem to be working. I'll use one less sleeping pill next time." She lifted her drink. "Cheers."

Dab put on some dance music, and they whirled in dance for many minutes. As usual, the dancing provided an erotic stimulant for Arachne.

A week later, Dave's trial was put in the hands of the jury. They took only a day and a half to render a verdict. They found Dave Blackmun guilty of attempted murder and murder in the first degree. Sentencing would occur in a month or two, and everybody was betting he'd get life without parole, or execution. If less, the federal government would be waiting to charge him with kidnapping and other crimes, Those who knew him well were hoping for the death penalty, pleased that Virginia still meted out capital justice.

The night after the jury rendered its verdict, Arachne prepared her best steak-and-potatoes meal, and put two sleeping pills in Dave's coffee. Dave was depressed about the verdict, and it didn't take long for the pills to work. He didn't stay awake long enough for dessert. "Too bad," Arachne said, "He'll miss the banana custard. I made it just for this occasion."

Dab laughed, pulled her to him and gave her a pat of approval. "You're the soul of compassion," he said after he kissed her.

"Please wheel Dave to his room and arrange things," Arachne said. "I'll meet you in your room."

"Okay, I'm looking forward to an exciting night."

"Don't forget the gloves when you handle the bullets," Arachne said. She had made the banana custard for them, not Dave. She tasted the dessert, then put it on a tray with gin-and-tonic makings and carried the tray to Dab's room. After fixing drinks, she disrobed and sat down on the bed and applied custard to her body as she waited.

An hour later, as Dab was licking every morsel he could find from her breasts and elsewhere, a shot rang out upstairs. "I put in two bullets I put his fingers on the trigger using the gloves. I'll make sure he was playing Russian roulette," Dab said.

He started to stand up, but Arachne pulled him back. "Wait, let's finish our custard first. We have plenty of time. I want my share."

Dab pushed her away, stood and pulled on gloves." Not now, I've got to go up to make sure. I'll finish as soon as I can." He headed for the door. "Save the rest of the custard until I get back."

———— ✦✦✦✦✦ ————

Mike Barton answered the 911 call that came from Dave Blackmun's house. Dressed in a robe and slippers, Arachne appeared disheveled, when she met him at the door.

"He's upstairs in his room." She sobbed. She sounded sincere, but Mike doubted her. "Dab's with him," she said.

She led Mike up to Dave's bedroom. Through the open door, Mike could see Dab sitting in a chair beside the bed. Dave Blackmun was lying on the bed with his head on a bloody pillow—a pistol in his hand.

Dab rose to meet Mike. "We heard the shot downstairs. I had wheeled him up about an hour earlier. He was sound asleep, so I left him in the wheelchair next to the bed and went to my room. I heard the shot about forty-five minutes later."

"I guess he had bullets hidden. I didn't know he had any," Arachne said.

She sounded sincere, Mike thought, keeping his suspicion to himself. "Virginia executes. Dave expected the death penalty. I reckon he didn't want to spend a long time in prison waiting for execution."

Dab nodded. "He was depressed by the verdict. He was certain he'd be sentenced to death, but I think he was even more depressed by the idea of spending the rest of his life in a jail cell."

"A coroner's on the way. There doesn't seem to be much doubt about suicide." To himself, Mike said murder, but he didn't know how to prove it. Dave had never before taken the easy way out. Still, he was a shadow of his former self. If they had helped kill Dave, he didn't see how to prove it. "I'll wait and see what the coroner says after an autopsy and what the fingerprint tests give us." *If they killed Dave, they'll have to live with the guilt. They can always console themselves with the knowledge they did a public service.*

------------- ♦ ♦ ♦ ♦ ♦ ♦ ♦ -------------

After the coroner's preliminary verdict, George received a call from Mike, who asked if he could stop by George and Heidi's to discuss the apparent suicide. George told him to come on over. "Heidi's gone to bed, but I'll treat you to a beer.

"I doubt suicide. It's unlike Dave," Mike said as he took a sip of the bottle of Shiner Bock George offered him.

George nodded, "It's not Dave's style. What did the coroner say?"

Mike pulled out a bag of jellybeans and popped. a few in his mourh."He's ruled it a suicide. He said he had no reason to doubt Dave took his own life, but he'll do an autopsy. Dave's fingerprints appear to be on the gun. He was holding it in his hand when I first saw his body."

Mike offered his host some jellybeans.

"I agree with you," George said as he took a handful. "I'd never have imagined Dave a suicide."

Mike shook his head, "I think the two of them rigged it somehow. We'll see if the autopsy shows something, I'm having the bullets checked for fingerprints."

"Mike, if there're no prints other than Dave's, I'd just go along with the coroner. Let it be suicide, if that's what he says. He's bound to keep ruling suicide if the only fingerprints are Dave's. Maybe Dave couldn't stand facing a lifetime lacking control. or waiting for a death penalty. For me, it's worth a lot knowing Dave's not trying to kill me."

Mike shrugged. "Well, Arachne could still get some jail time for her part in the kidnapping,.

George nodded, "And Dab may get tired of taking orders from a woman once his lust has run its course."

"I talked to Josie Roper this morning. She says you tell her she's about to be a rich woman." Mike took another drink of beer,

"No doubt about it, unless the bottom drops out of the coal market. I've already talked to Philemon and Fred about a contract. I think Philemon's interested. You may have competition. He might be interested in Josie as well as her coal."

"I doubt it," Mike said as he pocketed his bag of jelly beans "He's such a God-fearing man, but I'm not angling for Josie. I eat jellybeans to make up for the chew I gave up for Mabel."

"Maybe he's trying to save Josie's soul. She swears she's given up criminal activities, and Philemon's a good Christian. He might forgive her sins and ask Lamb o'God's help to make sure she's born again."

Mike finished his beer. "I think you can believe her. She claims she acted under duress," Mike said, pullng the candy bag back out of his pocket.

"She won't need more money once her land is stripped."

"It's hard for me to believe how sweet she can be," Mike said. "I have a hard time remembering she planned murders, but fear can prompt peculiar acts."

George rubbed his neck. "You'd better be careful, even if she worked for Dave to pay off her father's debt. By the way, how does Mabel feel about Josie?"

Mike 'grimaced. "Josie's not a subject I bring up with Mabel. You and Heidi have influenced me. I've asked Mabel to marry me."

George slapped Mike on the back, "If she agrees, I hope to be your best man."

Mike gave George a playful jab on his midsection, "I wouldn't ask anybody else."

George finished his beer. "I'm glad I don't have to watch my back all of the time anymore. I'm looking forward to being a daddy and watching beautiful birds with Heidi and our child by my side or in the woods hunting turkey. You be ready for spring gobbler season."

"You bet, Buddy. Practice that hen call. The old Toms love it."

"I'll practice. Don't worry.

After seeing Mike out, George went to the bedroom to tell Heidi the news. "Dave's dead. Mike doubts he committed suicide. He thinks Arachne and Dab gave him help, but he can't prove it."

"They may have helped arrange Dave's finish, but you brought him down."

"I reckon I helped."

"You persuaded all those people to testify against him. He was going down whether those two killed him or not."

"I'm glad my five hundred acres of woodland are safe."

"And, for whatever reason, Dab Whacker has begun to reclaim his and Dave's surface mining jobs, instead of leaving them decorated with rusting machines."

"You're right. We've made progress."

Heidi pulled George toward the bedroom.

"You and I have less to worry about now. I think it's time for bed. I want your undivided attention." She kissed George as he picked her up and placed her on the bed like a fragile package, enjoying her scent of roses.

"Sweet Scissor-tail, I'm your dragonfly eager to be caught."

The End

Printed in the United States
By Bookmasters